No Neutral

Ground

For information contact;
Celebrate Lit
29078 Whitegate Lane
Highland, CA, 92346
www.celebratelitpublishing.com
Book and Cover design by Roseanna White
ISBN: 978-1541125285
Second Edition: December 2016
10 9 8 7 6 5 4 3 2

Praise for *No Neutral Ground*

No Neutral Ground gives a fascinating glimpse into a lesser-known aspect of the second world war–life inside a neutral nation. Wangard captures the thrill and fear of war when alliances blur and one can never be certain who is a friend or an enemy. From the cockpit of a B-17 bomber to the intricacies of espionage, this quick-paced story is well worth reading.

Christine Johnson, multi-published author of *Love's Rescue*

"Terri Wangard has created likable, engaging characters in an evocative story set against the backdrop of Europe during the Second World War. This novel's rich, authentic details will delight World War Two era history buffs. And readers will find themselves rooting for the hero and heroine's happily-ever-after in a world torn apart by war."

Lisa Carter, author of *Under A Turquoise Sky*

I thoroughly enjoyed reading this romantic historical novel, one of my favorite genres. The subject matter of No Neutral Ground ...World War II Sweden ... is a topic I have studied for several years. The author has researched extensively the activities of the American internees who force landed there in planes too damaged to get back to their airbases in England. There are many interesting details about everyday life in Stockholm during that period as well as some of what was happening at the American Legation which housed the Office of Strategic Services (OSS).

I haven't found another novel that focuses on our interned American airmen in Sweden. The story was entertaining, in particular the espionage escapades. I also respected the struggles that the American airman of German/Jewish heritage experienced.

Pat DiGeorge, author of *Liberty Lady*

Glossary

Abwehr = defense

Bitte = Please

Entschuldigen = Excuse me

Es tut mir lied = I'm sorry

Fliegerabwehrkanonen = Anti-aircraft guns

Frau = married woman

Führer = 'the leader'

Grossmutter = Grandmother

Grossvater = Grandfather

Guten abend = Good evening

Guten morgen = Good morning

Guten tag = Good day

Haus = house

Heilige Bibel = Holy Bible

Himmel hilf mir = Heaven help me

Jungvolk = young people

Kapitänleutnant = lieutenant commander; equivalent US rank is lieutenant

Kleines Mädchen = little girl

Kriegsmarine = navy

Leutnant zur See = midshipman; equivalent US rank is ensign

Luftwaffe = air force

Milchkühe = milk cows

Mischling = crossbreed, first degree: two Jewish grandparents

Mohrenkopf = small, chocolate-covered cream cake

Mutter = mother

Nicht wahr = Isn't it so?

Oma = grandma

Opa =   grandpa

Die Sahnefront = the cream front

Schnellboot, -e = Fast boat (similar to PT boat) singular, plural

Sieg Heil = 'Hail Victory'

U-Boot, -e = submarine, submarines

Vater = father

Verstehen = understand

Vetter = cousin

Waffen SS = armed SS

Wasser = water

Wehrmacht = armed forces

Wie geht es Ihnen (Wie gehts) = How are you?

Woher kommen Sie? = Where do you come from?

Part 1

This is my Father's world,
O let me ne'er forget
That though the wrong seems oft so strong,
God is the Ruler yet.
This is my Father's world:
The battle is not done;
Jesus who died shall be satisfied,
And earth and heav'n be one.

Maltbie D. Babcock

Prologue

Cologne, Germany
May, 1936

"Rolf, you may no longer remain in the Hitler Youth."

The nonsensical words sounded as though they came dredged from the depths of Herr Schultz's soul. A long moment passed. Rolf Schilling had done nothing wrong. "Why?"

"I'm sorry, Rolf." Sadness shone in the leader's eyes. "Jews are not allowed membership, and you are Jewish."

"What?" The word exploded out of him.

"Your mother is Jewish." Herr Schultz shifted in his chair. "That makes you a first-degree *Mischling*."

"No, that's not true." Rolf sucked in a lungful of air. He needed to stay calm. Raising both hands, he ruffled his blond hair. "Do I look Jewish? I'm German, the most Aryan-looking student in school." He pointed to his eyes. "Blue as the sky. Hitler should use me as his poster boy."

"Stop, Rolf." Sternness entered Herr Schultz's gaze as he held up a hand. He continued in a softer tone. "Don't speak such things. Be careful what you say." His hand dropped to the table. "There seems to be as wide a variation in the appearance of Jews as there is among Aryans. And the Gestapo reports," he sighed heavily, "the Svenson family is Jewish."

"Opa and Oma are Swedish. They came from Sweden."

Herr Schultz shook his head. "They were Jews living in Sweden."

"No, they're Christian. We're all Christian. I was baptized in the Cathedral." Desperation colored Rolf's voice, but Herr Schultz was attacking the core of his being.

"Your religion doesn't matter, Rolf. Your race does. Your blood is Jewish." Herr Schultz picked up a sheaf of papers and tapped them against the table into an orderly stack. Clearly he meant to bring this meeting to a close. "Personally, Rolf, I think well of you, but," he looked down, picking up a file for his papers, "you are no longer welcome here."

Heat flushed through Rolf, followed by an icy chill. He lurched to his feet and hurried from the room. A reviving breeze fanned his face as he stumbled out of the Rhine Haus. He stared at the spires of Cologne Cathedral rising above the treetops. Invisible birds twittered in the branches as though nothing had happened to jar the foundation of his life.

His cousin waited for him, sprawled on a bench. The other boys had scattered for home after their sailing excursion. Christoph jumped up.

"Rolf! What's wrong? You look like you're sick."

Spots danced before Rolf's eyes and he swayed. Christoph jerked him to the bench and thrust his head down. His vision cleared as he took deep breaths. He straightened slowly, cautiously.

"What happened?"

Rolf stared at Christoph. "I've been expelled."

"From what? The Naval Hitler Youth? Why?"

"Herr Schultz says the Gestapo says I'm Jewish. Mother's Jewish. Her parents are Jewish."

"Since when? They're Swedish."

"Herr Schultz says they were Jews living in Sweden."

"You look more Aryan than anyone. How can you be Jewish? Besides, you're Christian."

Rolf shook his head. "Doesn't matter. It's in my blood."

Christoph dropped down beside him and put his hands together, fingertip to fingertip. "Ridiculous. Your blood's the same as mine. I've seen it, remember? When our tree house fell out of the tree?" He tapped his fingers in an increasing tempo. "If it is true that your mother's Jewish, everything's going to change for you, and not for the better. Do you think Herr Schultz could be right?"

"I don't know. Maybe. Last year, Opa Svenson was so upset about the Nuremberg Laws. I didn't understand why. They didn't concern us. But maybe they do." He slapped his hands to his knees and rose. Anger heated his face. "This is 1936. We're a civilized country. How can they do this?"

Whatever reply Christoph may have offered died in his throat when Herr Schultz came outside. He hesitated, and then hurried to the car lot. Christoph took a step to follow him, but Rolf grabbed his arm.

"Let him go. He can't do anything. This wasn't his decision."

"What are you going to do?"

"What can I do? Go home. Talk to my parents, my grandparents. There's got to be a mistake." Rolf pivoted to face the Rhine. He caught his breath.

"What?" Christoph stepped up beside him. "Do you remember something? You've gone all pale again."

"Three years ago, when the National Socialists ordered the boycott of Jewish-owned stores, Mother insisted on pushing past the SA men standing watch in front of Bloch's Dry Goods. She bought some thread and needles which she didn't need. I remember Herr Bloch was so pathetically grateful for her little purchase, but her shopping spree upset Father." Rolf walked down to the pier. The Rhine gurgled on its way to the North Sea, as it had done all his life.

He spun back to Christoph. "He couldn't understand why she would deliberately attract attention from the SA. I thought it was more her nature to support the unfortunate than to defy the boycott."

"That took courage." Christoph blew out a breath. "I don't know if I would have done that."

Rolf's throat was as dry as the desert as he choked out, "She knows. She identified with the Jews because she is Jewish. She knew it could just as easily be us, and it will be us."

Chapter One

The wind sliced right through Jennie Lindquist's coat. So warm in Illinois, it now felt as thin as a pillowcase. Late winter was the wrong time of year to cross the North Atlantic. The temperature hovered around ten degrees, but with the wind and the ship's speed, it seemed far below zero.

Jennie perched on a stowage bin. Her gloved fingers had grown stiff from the cold. She had to keep sketching, though, or she would lose her model.

The soldier continued to stare at the spot where the Statue of Liberty had long since faded from view in their wake. The quivering of his chin was his only movement.

After adding several pencil strokes to shade the edge of his arm, Jennie held up her drawing and studied it through narrowed eyes. Had she captured his forlornness?

It would have to do. She shoved her sketch pad and pencil into her tote bag. Plenty of time remained aboard the ocean liner-turned-troopship to accomplish her goal of sketching a series capturing life aboard ship.

Overhead, the last escorting U.S. Navy patrol plane dipped its wings and turned back to New York. The *Queen Mary* was on her own to cross the North Atlantic and elude any skulking German submarines eager to hurtle a torpedo into her. Jennie scanned the horizon. Nothing but endless waves.

Ice crystals sprinkled down, luring her gaze upward. Lifeboats hung suspended overhead. A flexing chain caused more ice to break loose. Dismal gray camouflage paint hid the Cunard Line's signature colors of red, white, and black. Behind her, one of the ship's funnels belched smoke as the ocean liner charged full speed ahead at thirty knots. At least the frigid wind prevented soot from drifting down on the military personnel crowding the deck.

An officer standing ten feet away didn't seem to mind the arctic blast as he raised his face to it. Jennie avoided contact with the military men. Her father had warned her to be wary of their intentions.

This one, however, tempted her. His profile presented classic lines an artist would love to paint. Portraits weren't her specialty, but, my, oh my, his handsome features practically begged her to try her hand at capturing his likeness. Below the edge of his cap gleamed close-cropped blond hair; his eyes, when he turned his head, shone a startling blue. His heavy coat failed to hide broad shoulders tapering to a slim waist. To her eye, he presented the epitome of male perfection. Did the inner man match the gorgeous outer appearance?

Stray snowflakes swirled about him, and he brushed them away. She set aside Dad's advice and invaded the solitude surrounding him. "You must be a northerner to be enjoying this glacial wind."

He straightened to his full height, at least six feet tall, and settled his gaze on her. A quick grin lit his face, and her numb fingers itched to start sketching. "With a choice between enjoying the invigorating sea air or the warm, uh, unventilated air inside the ship, the cold air won."

"Unventilated air?" Jennie laughed. "How polite."

His smile came easily, as though he was used to wearing it.

"Someone on the last voyage must have been quite seasick in the room I'm assigned to. The smell was bad enough to drive me into this gale." Looking back out to sea, he hunched his shoulders and tilted his head to the right, then the left. Weak sunlight glinted off white-caps as the morning overcast broke up, but the restless waves continued to batter themselves against the ship's hull. He maintained his grip on the railing. "The way the ocean's churning, we may have a lot more gastronomic upheavals. And to think, I used to enjoy being in a sailing club."

"Did you sail on the ocean?"

"Sail, no, although I've been on a previous ocean voyage. Rivers or the North Sea was where I mostly sailed, but —" he glanced back at the milling crowd of servicemen "— we weren't packed in tight like this."

The North Sea? Wasn't that in Europe? Jennie grabbed the railing as the *Queen Mary* veered to port. Every eight minutes, the ship zigzagged to avoid a potential submarine's crosshairs. She'd timed the turns.

His voice held an unfamiliar accent. It wasn't English. He'd been on an ocean voyage, singular, and he'd sailed on the North Sea. He must be from Europe, maybe from a country overrun by Hitler's army. He should have some stories to tell.

The cold and the pressing crowd of soldiers faded into the background. "Where are you from?"

She leaned forward for his reply.

"Milwaukee."

"Milwaukee?" She stepped back. So much for hearing about foreign lands. "Really? I'm from Chicago."

His gaze roved over her. "You're not in uniform. What's a civilian doing on a troopship?"

Jennie straightened to her five-foot, six-inch height. "I'm joining my parents in Sweden. My dad's a military air attaché based at the American legation, where he works with interned American airmen. He came home on leave for the holidays and took my mom back with him in January. Now I'm going, too, to help out."

"My grandparents came from Sweden. Do you speak the language?"

"Enough to ask for help if I get lost." She laughed at his widened eyes. "Yes, I speak Swedish. Maybe not as fluently as a native, but I have Swedish grandparents, too. My mom's been pen pals all her life with a cousin whom we hope to meet." She tugged her hat down more securely and retied her scarf before the wind pulled it free. "Do you have relatives there?"

"Opa's brother, my grandfather's brother, lives on the west coast of Sweden."

"The west coast. Highly unlikely I'll be able to pay him a call and tell him I met you." As a group of rowdy soldiers brushed past them and eyed her, Jennie stepped closer to her new acquaintance and pulled her coat's collar tighter.

She turned back to face his puzzled perusal.

"There are twelve thousand troops onboard." He looked around the deck. "Are civilian quarters still available?"

"Well, I heard about the accommodations used by Prime Minister Churchill when he sails, but somebody already claimed those." She could get used to his grin. "Did you know there's a hospital unit onboard? I'm billeted with the nurses."

A soldier stumbled hard into the officer, who muttered something under his breath that didn't sound like English.

She stared at him. "You said something in neither English nor Swedish."

He looked at her for a long moment, and his relaxed posture stiffened. "I am Rafe Martell, second lieutenant and navigator in the United States Army Air Force. In a more peaceful time, I had another name and lived in Germany. But then Germany decided I wasn't good enough to be a German, and America offered me a new home."

A hint of challenge gleamed in his eyes.

Why would Germany not want him?

"I'm Jennie Lindquist."

"Jennie Lindquist? Good Swedish name. Do you sing?"

"Excuse me?"

"Sing. Have you not heard of Jenny Lind, the Swedish Nightingale? My great-grandparents heard her sing and my grandfather says they insisted they heard an angel."

The ship lurched to starboard, causing Rafe to stagger against the rail and inhale sharply.

Jennie grinned. So he wanted to know if she could sing? Now was the time to demonstrate her ability. "Rock a bye airman, on the ship's deck. When the ship rolls, the airman gets sick."

A startled laugh burst from Rafe. Tears welled in his eyes — from the wind? — and he used both hands to whisk them away. The childlike gesture was endearing.

"May I ask why Germany didn't want you?"

He stared out to sea as though he wouldn't answer. Why should he? His experiences were none of her business. Then his gaze probed her soul, and she resisted the urge to squirm.

"I'm half Jewish."

His clipped answer was totally unexpected. Jennie had read newspaper reports about the Night of Broken Glass a few years ago, when the German people destroyed Jewish property. The pictures in the newsreels had been stunning. Hard to imagine such crime could be committed by civilized people in this modern era. Editorials speculated the destruction was inflicted by members of the Nazi Party and most Germans hadn't approved. However it happened, Jewish lives and livelihoods had been ruined. That's what he'd faced? She hugged herself to stop a shiver.

His look dared her to say something. What could she say? He didn't resemble the people shown in the pictures.

"You don't look Jewish." She cringed at her rude reply, but a smile stretched across Rafe's face.

"I agree. I should have been pictured on Aryan propaganda posters instead of being forced to run for my life." He bounced his fist on the rail. "I had no idea my mother was Jewish until I was expelled from the Hitler Youth. That's a Nazi version of the Boy Scouts. To suddenly be lumped with a social group I had no relationship to or understanding of…" He paused for a moment as he searched the horizon. He shook his head. "It was a shock."

"How did you get away?" She might be probing an unhealed wound, but she might never have the chance to talk to someone from Germany again.

"My grandfather is a partner in a Dutch flower bulb business. I arrived in Amsterdam within two weeks of my disgrace, supposedly as an apprentice. The next week my grandparents, mother, sister, and brother arrived. The following summer, in 1937, we boarded the *Statendam* and never looked back." His grin returned. "And as of last summer, I am a citizen of a country where the nationalities are mixed up and melted together."

"What about your father?"

"He divorced us to keep his job."

Jennie opened her mouth to ask him to repeat that, but Rafe's flat tone hadn't invited questions. Bitterness, anger, and hurt glittered in his eyes. His jaw shifted as though he battled his emotions.

She looked out to sea to give him time to himself, and they stood in silence.

What was it like to have a father who would turn his back on his family? And what was life like for Jews in Europe? They were so far away. Jews in America had it better, didn't they? Did she know any? There may have been some among her colleagues at the art museum where she'd worked. How could she be so ignorant? She massaged her brow as her head began to ache.

"The Hitler Youth. Is that what we see in newsreels of the children marching in uniforms with swastika banners?"

"Yes, the regular groups. I was in the Naval Hitler Youth. Some of my best memories are of the sailing activities with my friends. We had fun."

"Didn't you have to learn how to be little Hitlers?" In conversations with her colleagues, they had speculated on how the German children were being brainwashed as Nazis.

"Our meetings weren't political. Some groups undoubtedly were. The leaders set the tone. Membership was expected. Some parents refused to allow their children to attend, and that could make life... difficult. If you didn't conform, you could expect a backlash. But my sister, brother, and I enjoyed our meetings. They were like scouting, from what I saw in Milwaukee."

"How old were you when you left?"

"Sixteen." Rafe grinned. "And that was eight years ago, if you'd like to do the arithmetic."

The wind should have already reddened her cheeks enough to hide the blush that warmed her face. All right, yes, she *had* wanted to know his age. Her subterfuge needed work. Lots of it.

"You're an airman headed for the war in Europe. Is that wise? What if you become a prisoner of the Germans, and they find out you have Jewish ancestry?"

A voice behind them answered her. "If we're shot down, all the Krauts will see is a blur. That'll be Lieutenant Martell, running like mad for the coast, and then swimming for England."

A group of six grinning young men, boys really, surrounded them. They didn't look old enough to be off to war, yet all wore air corps coats. One whipped off his cap and clutched it between his hands, gazing at Rafe with admiration, a big smile on his face.

Rafe folded his arms across his chest. "I understand the ship's crew is looking for help to swab the decks."

His comment sent the men scrambling, four in one direction and two in the other.

"This way. *This way.*"

The two skidded around and raced after their mates, bobbing and weaving through the crowd.

"Looks like they're doing fine." Rafe's shoulders shook in silent laughter. He jerked a thumb after them. "They're the enlisted men, the gunners, on my crew. We'll fly bombing missions in a B-17 Flying Fortress."

Passing men jostled them against the railing. Rafe fidgeted with his life preserver. "This thing is pointless."

Jennie's eyes widened. "Pointless? We're heading into a war zone. Sinking the *Queen Mary* would be a huge coup for the Germans. Precautions are necessary." His expression said she'd made another gaff. "What?"

He glanced around at the ebb and flow of soldiers and up at the lifeboats hanging over their heads. A spark of humor lit his eyes as he met her gaze. "You've heard the rule—women and children first. Should we be torpedoed, you'll be saved, if there's time to get to the boats." His eyes grew serious. "But we have twelve thousand passengers on board, besides a thousand crewmembers. That's ten thousand more than this ship carried in peacetime. The number of lifeboats, however, hasn't increased. Most of us would have to rely on rafts or these Mae West life preservers, and the North Atlantic isn't favorable for survival. No one would come to our rescue in time, so why bother?"

Just like the *Titanic* thirty-two years ago. Jennie stared at him. Her grandparents had known a couple who sailed on the ill-fated ship. The woman survived. Her husband's body had been pulled from the freezing water, strapped in a life preserver. The woman had been grateful for a body to bury. That was all the life jacket had been good for.

Jennie narrowed her eyes. "You don't seem bothered by those odds."

He flashed another heart-stopping smile. "I'm headed for combat in the air war. My chances of survival are better here than they'll be in the air. This crossing should be a piece of pie."

She blinked. "Cake. A piece of cake."

Rafe shrugged. "Besides, as my Oma says..." He adjusted pretend spectacles and spoke in a high-pitched voice. "The good Lord's already assigned you a number of days. Don't fight Him."

"Uh huh. Sure." Jennie brushed errant strands of hair off her face, and yawned. "'cuse me."

His brows rose. "Don't try to blame a sleepless night on rolling waves, because we were still in port last night."

She rolled her eyes at him. "The nurses and I didn't get on board until after seven and guess what? No supper service, and I was so hungry. Fortunately, a crewman escorted us to our cabins, or we'd still be climbing up and down those endless flights of stairs. My cabin's on the main deck, and it's this little bitty room meant for two. Instead, there are three bunks in tiers of four. I'm on the top. If I raise my head, I hit the ceiling." She spread out her hands, fingers splayed. "And there are no safety straps. If I get tossed out, it's going to hurt."

Rafe shook his head, amusement lighting his eyes. "Twelve occupants. How luxurious. Eighteen officers are stuffed into my stateroom. We've got hammocks three deep. And if that weren't enough, because the air is so foul in the bowels of the ship where the enlisted men are packed in, four of them came up to sleep on our floor."

Jennie wrinkled her nose. "If all those men are down in the bowels, why were so many marching past our door and tramping across the ceiling right over my head? All night long. And all the chatter in the bunks around me. The chatter finally died out, but then the snoring started. Oh my goodness. What a racket. I'm used to having a quiet, private bedroom."

His laughter could become addictive.

The jostling crowd shoved her toward him, and he caught her arm.

"Guess I've gotten used to noisy roommates during training. I slept well until the ship's engines vibrated me awake this morning as we left New York."

Jennie jumped at the blast of the Klaxon horn, and she searched the ocean for a periscope. Conversations around them ceased as others peered about.

Rafe slapped a hand on the railing. "Abandon ship drill. Time to report to our lifeboat stations, even if we don't have reservations."

Jennie returned his smile. A carefree attitude like his must make life less worrisome. His Oma was right. Trust God and don't worry over what couldn't be helped. She stepped back. Their time together had been too short. "My station is where passengers used to play tennis."

He nodded. "Stop by again. This is my self-appointed post for the voyage."

Jennie's smile grew as she turned to leave. So, he would welcome her company. She maneuvered around three soldiers who blocked the deck, oblivious to the flow of people trying to get past them. Another soldier winked at her, and her smile dimmed.

She hadn't told Rafe the real reason she was bound for Sweden. Going overseas during wartime to help her father, a member of the military, hardly seemed logical. Yet Rafe hadn't questioned her explanation.

They'd just met, of course. It's not like they had to immediately exchange life stories. He'd picked up on the fact she was heading for Sweden, a country with special meaning for him also. In the coming days, he might ask about her duties. And she couldn't tell him. Those were her orders.

A blast of icy wind swept over her, and she snuggled deeper into her coat. Those orders sounded so melodramatic. Her responsibilities wouldn't be life-threatening. Their country was at war, however. Far be it from her to give any aid or comfort to the enemy. Idle talk could result in serious repercussions. And Rafe came from Germany. He might not be welcome back, but he must still have friends and relatives, including his father, living there. His story was probably one hundred percent true. But she couldn't share hers.

Chapter Two

Rafe watched Jennie negotiate the crowded deck, a lock of her red-tinged blonde hair fluttering in the wind. Male heads turned to watch her pass, but she didn't seem to pay attention to any of them. He rocked back on his heels. This ocean crossing might not be so tedious with time spent in her company.

A spray of icy seawater slapped his face, stealing his breath away, as the *Queen Mary* plunged into a trough. He flinched at the salt on his lips. The bitter chill resonated all the way to his toes, but not until the last glimpse of her bright blue hat disappeared from his view did he push away from the rail and head for his station.

Why had he told her of his German background? At least he hadn't mentioned his old name. The Germans couldn't connect Rafe Martell with Rolf Schilling. If he wound up in their grasp as a known former German national, he could expect a torturous death.

An American airman who had escaped from a German prison camp reported how his captors knew all about his bomb group, all about his plane crew. But even if the Germans had acquired rosters of American airmen, they couldn't know Rafe's mother had remarried, or that he'd taken his step-father's name.

Unless they had agents in Milwaukee. No, they couldn't keep tabs on millions of Americans. As long as he didn't reveal his German name, he'd be safe.

Maybe he shouldn't have told her he was part of a B-17 crew, but he hadn't told her where he'd be based. He couldn't have if he'd wanted to, since he didn't know. And she knew he was in the military, so it didn't hurt to admit he was an airman. What would she think he was traveling to England for? Punting on the Thames?

He found his fellow officer crewmates among the gathered throng. Steve was engrossed in conversation with another man wearing matching pilot's wings. Alan yawned, his fingers twiddling with his bombardier's insignia. No wonder the clasp kept breaking.

Cal, the copilot, rocked back and forth, his hands shoved in his pockets. "I hope this drill doesn't make us late for our dinner shift. Getting only two meals a day is bad enough without missing one."

Rafe grinned. Cal was rail thin and always hungry.

A loudspeaker squealed and conversations ceased.

"Welcome aboard the *Queen Mary*. This is Captain Bisset speaking. My job is to bring this ship safely to port. You and I are expendable in this war. This ship is not. Do not betray her with carelessness."

Betrayal was an old friend of Rafe's. He hunched his shoulders up to his ears. Eight years had passed, yet his father's voice hadn't muted. Vile snippets ran like a scratched phonograph record that kept repeating. "Civil servants lose their jobs if they stay married to a Jew... I'm not leaving Germany, Hannelore... We'll get a divorce... Once Hitler leaves office, you can come back."

Sure they could. Only, Hitler planned on being in power for a thousand years.

Another officer of the ship's crew read off a list of orders. "The exits from the ship's interior have double tarpaulin over the passageways to keep any light from showing outside. Go through them cautiously to avoid exposing light. Portholes are covered and bolted shut. Do not try to open them no matter how much you desire a breath of fresh air."

All these things were common sense. Rafe studied the faces of those around him. Some men looked bored, others scared stiff. A few whispered among themselves.

Where was Jennie's station located? She was captivating with her ready smile, infectious laugh, and wide blue eyes. He exhaled hard. Time to pay attention. These announcements were important.

"Maintain complete blackout. Positively no smoking on deck after dark. Use of flashlights outside of enclosed areas is forbidden."

Jennie did have a nice singing voice. That was obvious from her impromptu "Rock a Bye Baby" verse.

What kind of music did she like? Current songs like "The White Cliffs of Dover"? Since she wasn't staying in England, she'd miss seeing the English cliffs. Hymns? He closed his eyes and the swelling strains of "O Sacred Head Sore Wounded" echoed in the Cologne Cathedral once again.

"Nothing is to be thrown overboard that can leave a trail back to the ship. Garbage will be disposed of at night so the current washes away our tracks by morning."

A hard elbow in his ribs popped his eyes open. Merciful saints, he'd been humming out loud. He slanted a weak smile to Cal and stiffened his spine.

"Should you fall overboard, the *Queen* will not stop to look for you."

Ha. As he'd told Jennie, why bother with the life preservers? Even if they weren't killed by the fall, no one would survive long in the North Atlantic. Maybe death by hypothermia was less painful than death by drowning. Hmm. Maybe the Mae West life preservers had a benefit after all.

The announcements concluded, and Cal grabbed his arm. "Come on. Time for dinner. Our shift starts in ten minutes, five decks down."

With Alan at his heels, Rafe followed in Cal's wake. They arrived in their assigned Tourist Dining Room and grabbed the first available table. Members of the ship's catering staff served their meals. The smell of the food assaulted Rafe like a physical force. He watched Cal bite into his corned beef with gusto, but he hesitated over the bright red slab of meat.

Eight years ago, he'd been miserably seasick the entire voyage. His siblings had scampered about the ship while he wasted away, losing ten pounds during the crossing. Now he tried a cautious bite of potatoes. Assured his stomach would keep an even keel, he continued eating.

Dozens of conversations buzzed around them, accompanied by the scrape of mismatched chairs on the floor. Little of the ship's former opulence remained. Cunard must have a very large warehouse to hold all the ship's fancy furnishings while the Royal Navy used the requisitioned *Queen* for transport duty.

Cal chewed and chewed before gulping down his bite. "I don't think they took the time to slaughter the cow first. It's way too tough and grainy." He drained his coffee cup and shoved the meat away. "When I saw corned beef on the menu, I had visions of deli cuts on rye, smothered with mustard. Only thing that's good for is to use as a door stop."

Warning noted. Rafe pushed aside his own portion.

"When we left New York this morning, we were flanked by destroyers, battleships and a whole mess of liberty ships." Cal sliced a roll into equal halves. "Blimps and planes flew over the whole convoy."

"And a couple hours later, they're way behind and we're on our own." Alan leaned back as a server poured his coffee. "I wonder if being on a merchant ship in that convoy wouldn't be better. There's safety in numbers. I don't like being out here all alone."

The ship lurched and a limp green bean fell off Rafe's fork. "The *Queen's* speed makes us safer than being in a slow convoy. This constant zigzagging will keep any U-boat from getting into firing position, although if one's ahead of us, I don't see why a good commander couldn't anticipate our turns." He speared the bean, and resumed eating. "Those convoys will take twice as long to reach England. I prefer the shorter trip."

Steve and his new friend pulled up chairs to join them. "Say, how'd you like that squall we went through a couple hours ago?"

"I didn't. The stench in our room is bad enough without adding fresh vomit."

Cal laughed and patted Rafe's shoulder. "Aw, Rafe. You look good in green."

Steve eyed his navigator with a quirked brow. "According to one of the ship's officers, that was nothing. This time of year, we can expect storms a lot worse."

Rafe stabbed his fork into his potatoes. That kind of news he could do without.

Rock a bye, baby. Watch me get sick.

Terri Wangard

Chapter Three

The North Atlantic Ocean
Thursday, March 2, 1944

Immediately after breakfast, Jennie headed for Rafe's spot at the railing on the Boat Deck. He wasn't there. She looked back and forth along the deck. Yes, this was the right place. Maybe he was at breakfast now, or waiting for the next shift. She'd wait right here. She had nothing else to do.

The brilliant blue of the sky and shimmering glitter of the ocean hurt her eyes. The wind generated by their movement tossed her hair about and stung her cheeks. With her face turned into the breeze, each breath caused her nose to prickle and tempted her to sneeze. Ordinarily she didn't consider herself claustrophobic, but the crush of people aboard the ship caused a yearning for wide open spaces. The endless ocean soothed that desire.

After yesterday's grayness, today was sharply in focus. Too bad she hadn't brought her sketch pad out with her. Once again, crowds of men cluttered the deck, but she ignored most of them. One young soldier stood ramrod stiff at the railing. His eyes stared straight ahead. He could easily be the subject of a Norman Rockwell painting. Young recruit scared witless. Jennie studied him carefully, memorizing every detail to create her own rendition.

"Maybe he stood her up."

"No, sirree. He wouldn't do that."

Jennie frowned. Who was talking about whom? She looked around. Standing pressed together in a semi-circle surrounding her were six young men who looked vaguely familiar.

"We're from the Coolidge crew." One of them raised his cap. "Where's Lieutenant Martell?"

Ah, yes. Rafe's crewmen. "Hello, boys. I don't know where your lieutenant is, but I expect he'll be along shortly."

The boy with the big smile nodded. "We'll be glad to chaperone you."

"Is that right?"

"Yeah," answered one with a hint of a swagger. "We know the dames are only interested in officers."

The boy two spaces over reached around to head-slap him.

"Uh, sorry, ma'am. The ladies don't look twice at us poor souls."

She could be amused or outraged at their audacity. Better yet, here was her chance to learn more about Rafe's world. "What about your other officers?"

"Aw, Lieutenant Coolidge is a stiff."

"Lieutenant Ellerbee's always disappearing."

"And Lieutenant Downing's always writing to his gem of a wife."

"Yeah, Ruuuby."

Jennie burst out laughing and the six young men tightened their circle, adoration in their eyes.

"Atten—hut!"

The six snapped to attention before wilting when they recognized the officer who stepped into their presence.

"We were just keeping your lady company until you came, Lieutenant Martell."

"Yeah, so nobody else would move in on her."

"How very thoughtful you are." Rafe eased next to Jennie. "Good morning." He pitched his voice low, but it was a sure bet all his crewmen heard.

A box tucked under his left arm rattled. When the crewmen didn't budge from their spots, he sighed. "Jennie, may I present Mickey, our engineer and top turret gunner."

The swaggerer. He grabbed her hand and shook it hard enough to rattle her teeth.

"Harold, our radio operator." With his big hands and big feet, he resembled a puppy before his growth spurt.

"George is our left waist gunner and Carlo is at right waist." One was blond and the other dark, but otherwise they could have been twins as they bobbed their heads in unison.

"Rusty is our ball turret gunner." The little guy had enough attitude to make up for his lack of stature.

"And Dan is our tail gunner." The eternal smile. He, too, reached for her hand, but not to shake it. He tried to kiss it. Rafe slapped his hand away. Even that failed to diminish his smile.

"Now, how about running along and finding something to do?"

"There's nothing to do on this tub," Rusty whined.

"Sure there is." Rafe shoved his box into Mickey's hands. "Here, this is from the Red Cross' recreation hall. You're responsible for seeing none of the pieces are lost."

"Why me?"

"I signed it out in your name."

"Chinese checkers?"

"Oh, swell. He gets the dame and we get marbles."

"Where's the rec hall?"

The crewmen moved off, arguing about who got what color marbles.

Rafe looked around at the horde surrounding them. He smiled. "Alone at last."

Jennie laughed as they turned their backs to the crowd and faced the ocean. "They remind me of a batch of puppies eager to play. Your boys idolize you."

"What makes you say that?"

"It's in their eyes. And you're accessible." No need to mention the suggestion of chaperoning. "They really are boys. They look like they should still be in high school."

"True. They're all eighteen or nineteen. Most of them have never been anywhere, were still living at home, and probably never expected to leave their home state. They make me feel ancient."

Jennie eyed him sidelong. "And you're their big brother who will be looking out for them."

Rafe groaned, and she laughed.

An alarm sounded. The Royal Navy gunners raced for the ship's six-inch gun and swiveled it. And fired.

Jennie clutched her chest where her heart threatened a coronary. She whirled seaward and grabbed the railing as the ship vibrated. "I don't see anything. Who are they firing at?"

"No one. They're just drilling. It's a test to make sure it's in working order and the crew stays sharp."

"Well, they ought to announce it's only a test."

Rafe grinned. "They did, in the Daily Orders."

"Oh. We're supposed to read those notices, aren't we?" She scanned the waves. Could a submarine be nearby, watching them from a periscope? She wrapped herself tightly in her arms. "So many ghastly ways of dying in a war. I'd like a painless death."

"Go to sleep one night and not wake up?"

"Yes. Is that too much to ask?" She ought to bite her tongue. Yesterday, the sleeping arrangements had prompted a complaint. Now she voiced another whiny complaint when he was the one headed for battle. She laughed too brightly. "The booming of the gun probably scared away any porpoises."

He too scanned the ocean's surface. "You're hoping to see some wildlife?" Passing soldiers bumped against him. "Other than what's on board with us?"

"Someone once told me about her voyage from England. About strolling along the decks and quiet conversation on lounge chairs. A dip in the pool, which had waves of its own. English tea time in the afternoon. But this voyage, what do we do for six days? I had to pack light, so I didn't bring any amusements other than my sketch pad."

"Welcome to the military life. Hurry up and wait." Rafe glanced across the deck. "The lounge chairs are gone and strolling would be akin to an obstacle course. The pool's been drained for the duration. However, they do serve tea at four o'clock in the lounge."

He snapped his fingers. "Say, do you like to read? Alan told me a big supply of books is onboard for distribution to servicemen. A lot of time in war is spent sitting around with nothing to do and these books have proven to be a popular diversion in Europe and the Pacific."

Jennie nearly clapped her hands. Rafe couldn't spend all his time with her, and a book or two would fill many hours. "I did see someone reading a book in the chow line yesterday. But I'm not military."

He shrugged and extended a hand. "You'll be working with a military staff. Let's go find them."

They met again later in the day and headed for afternoon tea. Many of the nurses were there, paired off with officers, and a few waved to Jennie. Rafe watched the waiters pour tea into dainty tea cups balanced on little saucers. Imagine his crewmates here, elegantly sipping tea. He nearly laughed out loud.

He'd never had tea in his life, but how different could it be from having coffee? He took a sip and nearly gagged. Must be an acquired taste.

Someone was watching him. He glanced up and his gaze collided with that of England's King George in a portrait. He sat up straighter.

"You said you have a brother and a sister?" Jennie offered him a reprieve from the monarch's censure.

"Yes, both younger."

"Ah, so you have practice at being an older brother. That explains your concern for your crew."

Her eyes sparkled with humor until she sipped her tea. Then they blinked rapidly. "Would it be rude to ask for sugar? Or do you suppose it's not available for tea due to rationing?"

Rafe chuckled. When a waiter brought by a cart of tea service paraphernalia, he joined her in adding a pinch of sugar to his cup. Easing back in his chair, he sampled the sweetened tea and eyed Jennie over his cup. She wore a navy dress with contrasting bands of bold lime green and turquoise around the bodice. The colors served as the perfect foil for her long blonde hair tinged with that hint of red. Curls framed her face. Truly, she was a vision of loveliness.

Her brows rose and a blush stained her cheeks. He'd been staring.

"What will you be doing in Sweden?"

Her cup rattled in the saucer as she placed them on the low table before them. "I am going to experience life in a foreign country." She sat back and laughed. "You look surprised. With the world at war, it's a strange time to go gallivanting across a war zone." She folded her hands and studied them. "I worked at the art museum in Chicago for a year until they made staff cuts. Last hired, first fired."

She looked up and pasted on a smile. "Dad never cared for the idea of me being alone while he and Mom are halfway around the world. I have a brother, Tom, but he's off in the Coast Guard. Besides, Dad's a firm believer in a quote from Augustine. 'The world is a book and those who do not travel read only one page.' This will widen my world." She reclaimed her tea and sipped. "When an office assistant became necessary, Dad signed me up."

Rafe managed to finish his tea. He set aside the cup and balanced the spoon across the top. The waiters should understand he wouldn't welcome a refill.

"You're close to your parents?"

"Oh, yes. Mom says I'm a Daddy's girl, and I suppose I am. He's always taken pride in my artistic ability and paid my way through art school. Mom and I get along well too, even if she's clueless about art. For every painting I've done, she says, "That's nice, dear.'"

Her bright laughter brought a smile to his lips but apparently not to his eyes. Her laughter died. "Are you not close to your parents?"

"Mom's great." He sighed and ran a hand down his pant leg before meeting her eyes. "But I think I hate my father."

Chapter Four

"Stupid, stupid, stupid." Jennie tapped the spine of the book against her hand as she inched toward the dining hall with some of the nurses.

"Goodness, Jennie, if that book is so bad, don't bother reading any more of it." Petite Lorraine didn't seem a likely candidate to endure the rough conditions an army nurse would surely face, but she was Jennie's favorite roommate.

Ann twisted a lock of blue-black hair around a finger. "I wish I could have brought some books, but my suitcase is stuffed tight. Add a sheet of paper and it wouldn't close."

Jennie held up her book. "I got this onboard yesterday from the Armed Services Edition collection. And I am enjoying it." She shrugged. "Just flaying myself for some thoughtless words."

Ellie tilted the book to read the title. "Oh, *The Robe*. I've wanted to read this. Where are the books located?"

"What else is available?"

"Who is that delectable officer I saw you with? Was he the recipient of your thoughtless words?"

Jennie laughed and tried to answer all their questions. "The books are available in the Red Cross lounge one deck down from the Boat Deck. They have lots of mysteries, westerns, popular bestsellers, nonfiction. I even saw copies of Walter Lippmann's *U.S. Foreign Policy* and Homer's *The Odyssey*. Rafe's a B-17 navigator. And yes, he must think I'm a real dreamer."

Not that he'd given any indication. But why, when he admitted to hating his father, did she have to insist he didn't mean that?

Because the very idea of hating her own father was outrageous, that's why. Their minister back in Chicago would have offered a beautifully worded response about the need for forgiveness and familial harmony. And if she'd been in Rafe's shoes, she would have walked away from the trite retort. The dynamics of Rafe's family situation were beyond her comprehension, and no bandage answer could cure it. He had mentioned when they met that his father divorced them.

She stroked the cover of her book. His selections had been a surprise. Oh, Mark Twain's *A Connecticut Yankee in King Arthur's Court* made sense. As he said, he'd be in King Arthur's land. But a book of Henry Wadsworth Longfellow's poems? *Biography of the Earth* suggested an interest in science, a more commendable choice than the western novels under debate by two soldiers too young to shave. She tuned back in to the nurses' remarks.

"Better be careful with him, Jennie. Those bomber crews don't have good life expectancy."

"Oh, Ann, that's a terrible thing to say." Lorraine turned to Jennie. "I've heard the increase in fighter planes is doing a fine job of protecting the bombers."

Jennie forced a smile. Lots of bombers were still being shot down, but two days of conversation with Rafe didn't exactly point to a long-term relationship. She wouldn't object though. If only she knew a cure for the pain in his heart.

Midway through their meal, the ship shuddered and the distant boom of an explosion sent shock waves through them. Ann froze with her coffee cup poised before her lips. Ellie's fork clattered onto her plate. Lorraine's face turned white. Jennie gulped down a mouthful of carrots before she choked on them.

Ellie jumped up and grabbed her Mae West hanging from the back of her chair. "We have to get to the lifeboats."

A passing server hesitated beside her. "Please stay calm and finish your meal, miss. The Klaxon alarm hasn't sounded, so we're fine. Enjoy your dinner."

The women looked around at each other. Jennie pushed her plate away. Enjoy her dinner? When it might be her last?

Rafe stared through his sextant.

"So, do you know where we are?" Alan's hand remained poised to jot down Rafe's findings.

"Yes. We're further north than you've ever been before." Rafe grinned as he reached for the notepad and slanted it up to catch the moonlight. "We're just south of the western edge of Greenland."

"How can you tell with that thing?"

Rafe turned to the frowning face of their waist gunner, George. In the press of humanity aboard ship, how did these guys always manage to find him, and in the dark? "This thing," he held up the sextant, "measures the angle between celestial bodies—you know, stars? — and the horizon. That angle relates to the distance between the star's geographic position and our position. Are you with me?" He had to bite his lip to avoid laughing at the blank expressions on the gunners' faces.

"I thought we won't be flying at night. What good is it if you can't see the stars?" Rusty could be counted on to grumble.

Dan smiled. "We'll take your word for it. Where's the boss?"

Alan waved a hand forward. "He and Ellerbee are visiting with friends in the Red Area."

"They're in the Red Area?" Mickey sounded incensed. "I thought we weren't allowed to leave the White Area. Or is that an officer privilege?"

This guy had a chip on his shoulder, but the cause remained a mystery. "We're all restricted to the White Area. Coolidge and Ellerbee are at the edge of the White Area, and the friends are at the edge of the Red."

The ship had been divided into three segregated accommodation sections and everyone had been given a colored identifying button when they boarded.

"All they have to do is find someone to switch buttons with and they can go into the other area." Rusty rubbed his hands together. "We should try that. Find someone with red or blue buttons. Then we can explore the rest of the ship."

"Forget it." Alan's tone left no room for argument.

"Yeah," Dan chimed in. "If they catch us, they might make us walk the plank."

"I'd like to see that."

Jennie's musical voice snapped Rafe's head around. The gunners immediately surrounded her. If he suggested to Jennie they walk up to the Sun Deck, the boys would invite themselves along. Dan beat him to it.

"Are you here for a moonlit stroll?"

Jennie turned her face to the crescent moon, the white light giving her an ethereal beauty. She shuddered. "Ordinarily I love to moon gaze, but now it seems deadly. Submarines for miles around must be able to see our silhouette." She inched closer to Rafe. "What was that commotion earlier?"

"A depth charge."

"The ship's sonar detected a submarine."

"Be a joke if it was really a whale."

"So they dropped a depth charge."

"Some guys said they saw oil on the ocean's surface, but I didn't see that."

Alan offered Rafe a sympathetic smile as the crewmen tripped over themselves, eager to tell Jennie of the day's excitement. "Come on, fellas, let's join the pilots and see what we can see of the Red Area."

He extended his arms and herded the gunners away like bleating sheep.

Their voices drifted back. Carlo's voice stood out. "I'm glad we're in the middle White Area. The forward Red Area has the most up and down motion and the Blue Area in the stern would have more engine noise."

"Yeah, and in the White Area, we're in the middle of everything." That had to be Rusty.

Rafe shook his head. "Like that's a good thing. Whether a sub or a whale instigated that excitement, it set off a flurry of activity among the ship's crew. They searched everyone's rooms for a radio that might have sent out electronic beams a sub could detect."

"Are you serious? Someone could carelessly get us sunk by listening to a radio?" Jennie turned to the rail and extended her hands in invitation. "'Come and get us, U-boats.'" She shivered and tucked her hands into her pockets. "We may as well turn on the deck lights."

"Someone's nerves are rattled." Rafe took her arm and tugged. "Come with me. I'll show you a different kind of light."

He led her upstairs to the Sun Deck and to the rear of the White Area. Here, they could look out over the Blue Area to the sea beyond.

"Ooh." Jennie clasped her hands under her chin. The ship's wake churned with phosphorescence. "It's beautiful. And look at all the stars sparkling in the sky. Lots more than at home."

Rafe smiled. Time ticked away. Jennie's company was much better than a movie in a crowded lounge. Then the wind had picked up, clouds moved in to hide the stars, and waves slapped the *Queen's* hull.

"We're in for another squall. I'll find out tonight how adequate our hammocks are."

Beside him, Jennie hummed *Rock-A-Bye Baby*. He laughed. "I suspect I'll like it better than a stationary bunk. I hear the old *Queen* is a notorious roller. You may find yourself tossed down to the floor."

Long after Rafe retired to his stateroom, the *Queen Mary* pitched through waves and plunged into troughs. Rolling from side to side to maintain a zigzag course, the ship creaked ominously. Swaying in his hammock, Rafe pictured the ship cracking in two. And to think, he'd once expected to serve in the German navy.

He grimaced at the sound of retching, and a malodorous stench saturated the cabin. Beneath him,

Cal groaned. Rafe tensed. A chain reaction of vomiting would likely commence. The *Queen* lurched into a mighty wave and their porthole blew open, slamming against the wall. Despite being forty feet above the normal water level, waves splashed into the cabin. Along with the water came bracing clean air. Howls of outrage erupted from the men nearest the porthole and those on the floor. Rafe clicked on his flashlight to guide those battling to secure the porthole. Others near the door went in search of mops. By the time the mess was cleaned up, the wind died down. The creaking abated. Very good thing he'd bypassed the navy and opted for the air force. Life at sea wasn't for him. Smiling into the dark, refreshed air, Rafe dozed.

Chapter Five

The North Atlantic Ocean
Tuesday, March 7, 1944

Jennie stood beside Rafe in their usual spot at the railing, watching for their first glimpse of Ireland. After the first two days of frigid temperatures, they'd enjoyed unseasonably balmy days above freezing and spent all their time outside at the railing. Tonight they would arrive in Scotland. Overhead, an RAF bomber circled.

"First part of our welcoming committee, it is." A *Queen* crewman nodded at the plane. "Soon we'll have an escort from the Royal Navy. We're coming up to the most hazardous part of the journey. We have to slow down to navigate the Firth of Clyde. Perfect chance for the Huns to sink us, right in sight of land." He tipped his cap to Jennie. "But don't you worry none. The king's own fleet won't let nothing happen."

Jennie stared after him. "He said, 'Won't let nothing happen.' That's a double negative, which cancels out his assurance."

Rafe patted her hand on the railing. "Look at it this way. If we're torpedoed now, the lack of lifeboats shouldn't matter. We'll have all those escort vessels to pick us up."

She hunched her shoulders up to her ears. "Is that your idea of reassuring me?"

He chuckled and squinted into the distance before raising a pair of binoculars. "There they are."

His quiet words made no sense. She stared forward. Only sea and sky filled the view from the *Queen*.

"There's smoke on the horizon. The plume from a ship." He shifted minutely. "And a second one. I'm guessing destroyers, still a couple miles away. Probably based in Northern Ireland." He offered her the binoculars.

Jennie gazed at the blobs of smoke. They were miles away? She looked up at the *Queen's* smokestacks. Smoke billowed away on the breeze. She swung back around. The oncoming plumes were now visible to the unaided eye. She gawked at Rafe. "We're leaving a smoke trail, too. We can be seen from miles away?"

Rafe demonstrated his unconcern with a single-shoulder shrug. "I suspect submarines can detect our presence from the sound of our machinery before they see any smoke." His hands planted on the railing, he offered a grin. "Though I could be wrong. Look at it this way. How many times has this ship gone back and forth across the ocean, and how many times has it been attacked?"

She drummed her fingers on the rail. "I guess our guardian angels have been kept busy watching over us."

A soft snort came from Rafe and he slanted a glance at her.

A hot flush swept through Jennie. "Don't you believe angels protect us?"

He straightened and covered her hand with his own. "Sure they do, sometimes. But..." he pursed his lips and looked out to sea. He waved his other hand toward the horizon. "How many ships have been sunk, and how many good men of strong faith have died?" Next he waved his hand through the air. "How many planes have been shot down, and many more good men died? I don't want to imply their guardian angels hid their heads under their wings, but they don't always keep us from harm."

Their gazes locked. Jennie blinked rapidly when her eyes filled with tears, and she had to look away. Of course bad things happened to Christians. They were not supposed to worry about the morrow, but that's what she'd been doing. What did that say about her faith? Shallow as a bathtub?

Rafe nudged his arm against hers. "We talked about this in catechism class at the cathedral. Someone questioned why the apostles suffered gruesome deaths. The priest said something like the temporal isn't God's main concern. The eternal is." His gaze swept the horizon before coming back to her. "And that's how we should view our brief and momentary troubles on earth. Our goal is our eternal home with God. This war just happens to be sending some of us there a little earlier than we might have expected."

A long-ago sermon Jennie had heard supported that viewpoint. Something from the list of heroes of the faith in the book of Hebrews. They longed for a better place — heaven. They had eternity in their hearts. A sigh escaped her. "I always figured I'd have to wait sixty years for my heavenly homecoming. More than once on this voyage, that childhood bedtime prayer has crossed my mind. 'Now I lay me down to sleep, I pray the Lord my soul to keep. If I should die before I wake, I pray the Lord my soul to take.'"

Rafe wrinkled his nose. "That's a frightening prayer for little children. They'll have nightmares thinking something scary might happen while they sleep."

A soldier squeezed up to the rail on her opposite side. "How do you like that?" He spoke over his shoulder to a buddy. "Our first sign of land in six days and it's just another stinkin' ship."

Rafe muttered something under his breath, and Jennie grinned. Probably something in German of which she didn't need to know the translation.

Rafe looked around her at the soldier. "You're looking in the wrong direction." He pointed to the right of the approaching destroyers. "There's land. Ireland."

A very young-looking soldier shoved forward with an eager gleam in his eyes. "Ireland? Boy, I wish we could stop. I'd like to catch me a leprechaun and find me a pot of gold."

Jennie's eyes popped open wide. Was the poor kid serious? He didn't seem bothered by the guffaws of the men who'd heard his exuberance.

Rafe grunted when an elbow jammed his ribs. The press of the crowd intensified as the throng of people eager to see Ireland grew. "Tea should be served soon. What do you say, should we get out of this mess? It'll be a while before we get to Scotland."

The lounge was a sanctuary of quiet after the clamor on the Sun Deck. Jennie sank into a chair. "Will we disembark right away when we arrive in Scotland, do you think? Or will we stay aboard overnight?"

"I'm sure we'll get off today. It should still be daylight when we arrive. Once the troops pass inspection, they'll be shown to the gangways, bid good-bye, and sent south into England." He kept his eyes on her while he sipped his tea. "How will you get to Stockholm? I assume you'll have to fly since Sweden is surrounded by German-occupied territory."

"Yes. Some sort of travelers' aid will make sure I get across Scotland to a Royal Air Force base on the eastern coast. The British operate clandestine flights." She licked her lips and set down her tea cup. Then she started twisting her hands, so she clenched them tight to still them.

"They only fly at night and when conditions are right. No moon, I guess, and with cloud cover. My dad described it like threading a needle to get through German radar." Now she was twisting her hair. She dropped her hand to her lap and grabbed it with the other.

"I'm getting nervous about what happens now, in Scotland. Not knowing how long I'll be there, not knowing anyone, being alone in a foreign country." She crossed her ankles. And uncrossed them. "And this is so ridiculous. You're sitting there, cool as a cucumber, and yet you're headed for combat. All I'm going to do is hang around Scotland for a while. I must be thinking too much. Once I get there I'll be fine, but the getting there has me on edge."

Rafe smiled. "Take advantage of your time in the land of bagpipes. Sightsee. I've heard they have lots of sheep here. You can count them."

A peal of laughter escaped her and heads turned throughout the lounge. Her face heated as she slouched down. "Rafe, you count sheep when you can't get to sleep. That would be terribly rude if I fall asleep on my host, or hostess. Whoever."

He took her hand. It was cold, another barometer of her nervousness. Rafe massaged it between his own hands.

"You'll do fine. You came aboard a troop ship with thirteen thousand men and conquered them. You'll conquer the Scots in the same way. They'll be begging you to stay."

He said the sweetest things.

"Can you write from Sweden? The plane must provide mail service along with passengers."

"I'm not sure. I mean, the plane does take mail, but I don't know if I can write to England." Jennie hesitated. "It's complicated. The legation in Stockholm collects all mail, censors it, sends it to the Pentagon in the diplomatic pouch where it's censored again, and then forwarded in a new envelope. My dad told me about an interned airman who wanted to write to his English girlfriend, but he wasn't permitted to. I don't know if I'll have the same restrictions since I won't be an internee."

"Tell you what." Rafe pulled an envelope out of a pocket and removed the letter. Crossing off the address, he wrote another. "This is my overseas address and the return address is my mother's. If you can't write to me, write to her. Tell her we met in our travels and you arrived safely. She'll pass on the news. Let's try to stay in touch."

Jennie accepted the envelope. "I'd like that."

She sat back and studied him. This could be the last day she'd ever see him. "Tell me about your family."

Chapter Six

By the way her brow wrinkled, her real question was, "Tell me about your father." A sigh escaped from deep within Rafe. He stared across the room. The *Queen Mary* vanished, pushed away by that day eight years ago.

"The day started out so well. I still can't believe the seismic shift that tore apart my world." He turned to Jennie and found her attention rapt upon him.

"We had gone sailing on the Rhine River, my Naval Hitler Youth group. We were in two sailboats, racing each other back to the Rhine Haus. My best friend, Bertil, was in the same boat as I. He didn't belong in a naval unit. He only joined because I did. But he wasn't a sailor."

Rafe laughed. "We talked about a visit to a destroyer planned for the next week. Ludwig said it was more to his liking than a submarine. He's claustrophobic and would go insane trapped in a tin can deep beneath the surface."

Jennie smiled at his wry aside.

"I wonder if the same might have been true of Johan. He planned to be a boss officer up on deck. None of that restriction to the bowels of the ship that an engineering officer could expect." Rafe took a deep breath and held it. "My cousin Christoph was in the other sailboat that day." He crossed his left ankle over his right knee, taking his time to brush at a speck of lint.

"You miss them."

He nodded once, clenching his jaw. His eyes smarted at the rush of emotion. He hadn't seen them in eight long years, but today they seemed close. Maybe because he was on his way to do battle against them. "Often I wonder where they are, if they're still alive. The *Kriegsmarine*, the German navy, hasn't been exceptional, except the submarines, and they're on the defensive now. My friends could all be dead." He pushed his foot off his leg and straightened. "But you didn't ask about my friends."

"They're a happier memory."

She quietly stated the facts without any meaningless embellishments like, "I'm sure they're all right." Folks meant well in uttering such false hope in impossible circumstances, but that always struck him as trying to evade daunting situations. Instead, Jennie's empathy made it easier to share his darkest pain.

"Christoph was ready to take on Herr Schultz, our Hitler Youth leader who informed me I was no longer welcome." Rafe shrugged and offered a lopsided grin. "Of course, he probably would have thought better of such an action had a Gestapo agent been the informant. At least he wanted to fight for me. My father didn't."

No, when Father learned the Gestapo knew their secret, he had retreated into silence. As the Aryan partner in his marriage, Father could've protected them. They might have been social outcasts, but they needn't have feared arrest and banishment to one of those concentration camps. But Father had only frowned and done nothing.

"When I got home that day, I immediately asked Mother if Herr Schultz's accusation was true. She stared at me, and this infinite sadness crossed her face. Then she took off her apron, got her coin purse, and asked me to watch the stove. She had to go next door to the apothecary and make a telephone call."

The memories grabbed him around the throat. Time to lighten the mood, or he'd be in tears. Or Jennie would. Her eyes already glistened. "Lot of good it did to tell me to watch the stove. Dinner could have burned or boiled over, for all I cared. My appetite was an early casualty."

Jennie smiled. Tears averted.

"She'd called Opa and Oma, and they came over that evening. Opa had been busy planning for the day we would likely have to escape from Germany. I still remember his words, about how life was going to get a lot worse. As each successive measure was accepted by the population without apparent objection, the Nazi Party was emboldened to twist the screws tighter. Our only hope was to get beyond their reach. That finally got a response out of Father." The ship made another zigzag turn, causing his tea cup to slide on the table. He pushed it back. "He was shocked Opa suggested we leave Germany. Yet what could he expect? Opa laid it out very clearly." He stared down at the carpet, fraying now under heavy use from thousands of soldiers.

Opa had seemed impatient with Father. His gravelly voice had boomed. "You've seen men who've come out of those work camps, Heinz, and heard of others who've died there. We can only imagine the horrors. Right now those camps may be populated mainly with political opponents and communists, but mark my words, the Jews can't be far behind. And I, for one, have no desire to experience them myself."

Father hadn't refuted Opa. He'd asked where Opa proposed to go. Rafe looked up from the carpet. "Opa had business dealings in Amsterdam. It was the logical place for us to go, since he frequently traveled there. His business partner was ready to extend any assistance we needed."

"The Nazis grabbed Holland early in the war." Jennie was quick to connect his situation to European events as they had unfolded.

"Opa foresaw that. Holland was too close to Germany, and we needed to get beyond the Nazis' reach. Sweden might fall to the Nazis too, so we had to go to America. He had friends willing to give us an affidavit to support us in Milwaukee, and we were already on the waiting list for the immigration quota through Holland. Father seemed more upset that Opa hadn't shared his plans than that he had made them."

A piano player started pounding out "Night and Day," a rollicking tune incongruous with his sad tale. "A week later, he informed Mother he had no intention of leaving with us, and they would divorce. We could come back when Hitler's out of office."

Jennie leaned forward. "Really? Will your mother return?"

"Nope. She's happily remarried to a man who treats her like a queen, and my sister and brother and I have fully embraced life as Americans."

A range of emotions flickered across Jennie's face. Pleased for his mother? Of course, she would be. Sorry for his father? Don't be.

She tilted her head. "Did you personally experience any anti-Semitism?"

"Indirectly. After I'd been expelled from the Hitler Youth, I'd headed for school Monday morning full of trepidation. If Herr Schultz knew I was Jewish, my teachers had likely been informed as well. But no one said anything. Frau Lessman may have looked at me strangely, but maybe I was looking for trouble that didn't exist. Then it happened a week later."

Rolf entered the apartment house lobby and headed for the stairs. Frau Heinrich had always seemed an amiable superintendent, if a little persnickety. Today she displayed her true nature.

A little girl stood at the foot of the stairs, clutching a small red purse. Probably the little Goldman girl from the apartment one floor above them. Her voice trembled with fear. "But we need milk. The milkman didn't come today."

"I told him not to bother. Jews don't need fresh milk. Now get out of my sight. You'll be leaving soon enough, and good riddance."

The little girl turned and scrambled up the stairs.

Rolf struggled to get air into his lungs. Frau Heinrich turned toward him, smugness oozing from her and galvanizing him into action. He strode to the stairs, giving her a brief nod. "Frau Heinrich."

He took the stairs two at a time before she could detain him and gloat.

The little girl's sniffles alerted him to her presence before he caught up with her on the third floor. What was her name? Maria? Magda? "Marta?"

She spun around and stared at him in fright.

He dropped to a knee in front of her. "You need milk?"

Her head jerked in a nod.

"I'll get it for you. Do you have the ration card?"

She offered the purse.

A quick glance showed the card and necessary coins. With a feather-light touch, he ran a finger down her cheek. "Go on home. I'll bring it to you."

Hands clasped tightly below her chin, her "Thank you" was barely audible before she scurried away.

"When I described what happened during supper, Mother's immediate response was, 'I'll stop by tomorrow and see if I can do some shopping for Eva.' Father frowned but said nothing." Rafe dropped his head back and bumped the wall. "I often wonder about Marta Goldman, what happened to her."

Jennie opened her mouth, closed it, then asked, "When the war's over, will you go to Cologne and look for your father?"

He drummed his fingers on the armrest. "The way Cologne has been repeatedly bombed, there's probably nothing left to go back to anyway. And Father, well, Father quite likely is dead."

Chapter Seven

Gourock, Scotland
Tuesday, March 7, 1944

The crew fought to stay together in the jostling throng as they were herded toward the A deck gangway. Rafe tightened his grip on his duffle and kept his eyes fixed on Alan just ahead of him. They spilled out onto the gangway and, as he descended to the pier, his gaze swept the area for one last glimpse of Jennie.

Bagpipes wailed a welcome, the kilt-clad pipers looking out of place among a shipload of young men arriving for the purpose of fighting a war. The scene was chaotic, but a system to the madness became clear. Officers directed the soldiers to their unit assembly areas, mustered them, and loaded them into army trucks. The air crews needed to head to the left.

Where was Jennie? Had she already been met? A group of nurses passed by, but he didn't know if they'd been her roommates.

"Rafe!"

He swung around at Jennie's call, and Dan tap-danced out of his way. All six enlisted men followed him as he hurried to her.

"No one's met you yet?"

"No, but I may need to wait until the crowd diminishes before we connect." Jennie's smile didn't reach her eyes, but she stood erect as she clutched her suitcase.

"Martell!" No mistaking Steve's displeasure.

"I have to go."

She nodded, tears filling her eyes.

He leaned toward her, but hesitated in the crowd.

"Go on and kiss her." Dan bumped him from behind.

They'd already said their goodbyes, but he shifted his duffle over his shoulder, leaned down, and touched his lips to hers. Hoots and whistles filled the air. Jennie's face flamed cherry red. He stepped back.

"Be safe." A tear broke free and slid down her cheek.

He nodded. His throat clogged and his "Bye" came out in a whisper.

Her head bobbed and another tear raced after the first.

His crewmen herded him back to the other officers. He glanced back. Her eyes stayed on him. He jerked his head to the left. A matronly lady hoisted a sign displaying her name. Jennie started forward. A squad of soldiers marched by, blocking his view of her. Steve urged them toward their mustering point. By the time Rafe got another glimpse, she was gone.

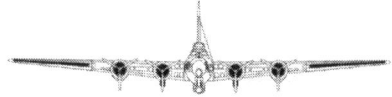

Jennie watched Rafe disappear into the crowd. They were unlikely to meet again and correspondence would be difficult. She fumbled in her pocket for a handkerchief. Tears kept slipping from her eyes and her nose needed attention. This would hardly do for meeting her contact. She approached the woman holding the sign with her name on it.

"Lass, might you be Jennie?" At her nod, the woman led Jennie to a group of ladies at a table near the bagpipers. "My name's Morag MacLaughlin. You'll be staying with my Lorcan and me tonight, and take a train for Leuchars in the morning. Come now. First we'll have a cup of tea before heading home."

A lady with wispy white hair smiled, her eyes disappearing in crinkles. She selected a clean cup and filled it with tea.

"Welcome to Scotland, lass." Her pronunciation sounded so musical as she pressed the steaming cup into Jennie's hands.

Jennie's first sip of tea warmed her as the ladies talked. When they all turned to her with expectant looks, her cheeks flamed.

"Oh, I'm sorry. I was so busy listening to your accents I didn't hear your words."

The ladies laughed. "We hear that frequently, but we don't understand it." One of them dimpled. "We speak the king's English as it ought to be spoken."

Jennie laughed, too. She'd crossed another hurdle. Tomorrow might present further challenges, but tonight, she could sleep well. She'd made it safely to a foreign country with a heart full of delectable memories. Surely her coming journey would present her with more.

Morag led Jennie away from the dock. "We'll have to walk to our house. Even if we had a car of our own, petrol isn't available to common folk like us. Fortunately, we don't live far off."

Outside the entrance to the harbor, a young boy waited with his wagon. "I'll carry your bag for you, lass."

"Isn't that sweet of you, Kiernan." Morag grabbed Jennie's suitcase and positioned it on the wagon. From her purse she withdrew something and tucked it in his hand. "There you go, lad. You may deliver it to my door."

Kiernan raised his cap. "Thank you, Mrs. MacLaughlin."

He set off down the street with a purposeful stride, his wagon trundling behind him.

"He knew I was coming to fetch you. Some folks object to the wee bairns making a profit off the war, as they say, but I see no problem in giving them a tuppence for their efforts. Even in peacetime we tipped them for their service. And it gives them a feeling of being involved."

Morag walked as briskly as she talked. Jennie was breathing hard by the time they scaled a slight incline. She glanced back over her shoulder and came to a stop.

"Beautiful." Across the firth, with its conglomeration of ships, snow graced the distant mountains. Fat clouds hinted at coming rain. A flock of birds wheeled up from the shoreline, and settled back down. She filled her lungs with air scented by the sea. "Chicago has nothing like this."

Morag came back to stand beside her. She surveyed the scene. "I guess I'm guilty of taking Gourock for granted." She smiled. "I've lived here my whole life, and I admit to being partial to it. Before the war, we'd sail in the estuary there and across the firth to Helensburg, where Lorcan has a cousin. Now, of course, you risk your life going out in a small boat with all those navy ships bustling about."

Jennie's brows rose. The warning on the *Queen Mary* was that the ship would not stop for anyone falling overboard. The naval ships probably wouldn't stop if they ran over a little pleasure boat either.

"Have the Germans come here? The harbor must be a very tempting target."

"We had frequent air raids in 1941. In May, it was. The target was the shipyards, but they were untouched.

Kiernan's mother and two sisters were killed when the Anderson Shelter in their garden took a direct hit. By September though, the planes stopped coming here. London became their choice. Submarines do still lurk about in the North Channel."

Jennie's gaze swept the panorama. That burned-out building there must have been bombed. She looked ahead toward Kiernan. Poor little fellow. War had come here and touched these people. She tried to imagine a bomb falling in her Chicago neighborhood, and couldn't.

Chapter Eight

The aircrews marched to a train alongside the harbor late in the day and jammed inside. The train consisted of small compartments with two facing seats for six or eight passengers, with a long corridor running the length of the train on one side. The Coolidge crew found two empty compartments side by side and piled in. Duffle bags, knapsacks, helmets, B-4 bags, and mess kits obscured the floor.

Rafe claimed a seat by the window and ignored the bedlam around him. He stared outside while his emotions played ping-pong. One week ago, he hadn't known Jennie existed. How could he already miss her? In another minute, he'd be bawling like a baby if he didn't snap out of this morose mood.

His crewmates jabbered around him.

"We're going to England. That's the best news I've heard all day."

"Come on, Mickey. We knew we were coming here when they issued us woolen underwear during processing. It was a sure bet we weren't going to the Pacific."

"Yeah, but we could have ended up in Italy."

"Ain't it hot there? We wouldn't need woolies."

"What's wrong with going to Italy? I like pasta."

"Can't trust 'em Italians, Carlo. They cozied up to the Krauts, remember? We don't have to worry about the Limeys."

"From what I heard, the Brits don't like having us all over here."

"Hey, turn off the light so we don't have to use the blackout curtain. This may be our only chance to see Scotland."

The quiet, smooth ride on British rails, so different from the clickety-clack rides on American trains, acted like a lullaby. Rafe shoved his knapsack against the window for a pillow and dozed.

Early Wednesday morning, the train deposited them at Stone Air Base, a Spartan cluster of ugly buildings, the home of a Combat Crew Replacement Center, near London. A captain welcomed the crews, informing the new arrivals they would be trained for combat, taught British procedure, and assigned to a Heavy Bombardment Group.

"Trained for combat?" an enlisted man from another crew repeated. "What have we been doing all this time?"

The captain hesitated. Was that pity in his eyes? "The training you've received is useless to you here. You'll need a lot more if you hope to survive a combat mission, particularly high-altitude formation flying. Half of new crews don't survive their first six missions.

We're getting better fighter escort now, but the Krauts are still shooting bombers down on every mission."

His voice droned on, but Rafe turned to a window. Here he stood in England. He'd seen the famous white cliffs of Dover seven years ago, when the *Statendam* sailed through the English Channel, but that was all. Now he would become familiar with the country that dared to stand up to Hitler.

His former countrymen wanted him and his new compatriots dead, and they were doing a bang-up job at making it happen. What were the chances of someone he knew being on the other side of the guns? Maybe he should have volunteered for intelligence, something as a noncombatant, like a translator.

The captain dismissed the crews to find their lodgings on the dingy base. The Coolidge gunners were directed to a tent for enlisted men. A recent rain had turned the dirt floor to mud. Rain-soaked blankets covered the cots.

George backed out and appealed to Steve. "Lieutenant, do we have to stay here?"

Steve shrugged. "We don't have any say in the matter. The army owns us now. We do what they say." When Rusty opened his mouth, Steve shook his head. "Sorry, fellas. They don't pay me enough to put you up at the Savoy."

The officers moved on to their quarters. Harold's voice drifted to them. "I liked the ship better."

You and me both. Rafe smiled. When a neighbor in Milwaukee heard the news that Rafe had joined the Army Air Force, he'd commented, "Oh, you're lucky. You'll get to sleep every night on a real bed with clean sheets instead of mucking around in the dirt."

Clean sheets? A real bed? Somebody, somewhere, was enjoying a good laugh at his expense. He dropped his duffle on a cot and the thing nearly collapsed. Three cushions made up a mattress. Further examination revealed two supporting slats had been removed from the frame. Someone must be using them for baseball bats. He just might be sleeping on the ground tonight after all.

The four officers left their gear and hastened back outside. Another officer strode past, whistling a merry tune.

"You're sure in a good mood." Cal looked puzzled that anyone should be happy.

The officer spun to a stop. "Why shouldn't I be? I'm headed for home. Sure is a swell feeling. Never thought I'd live this long, but I made it." His smile stretched across his face. "I got twenty-five missions under my belt. No sir, I sure didn't expect to see this day."

"Why not?"

Alan's question made perfect sense, but the other man shook his head. Did he also have pity in his eyes?

"We came in with three other crews and one more followed the next week. Five crews, okay? The other four didn't make it. On my crew, I'm the first to finish. Two guys are dead, and the other guys all have one or two or more missions to go."

Alan's face lost all color. "What happened to the other four crews?"

Yep, that was definitely pity in the guy's eyes. Rafe tensed, waiting for the response.

"They crashed, got shot down, blew up. Maybe they're prisoners of the Krauts, maybe not. They didn't make it back to tell us."

"Why haven't we been hearing about this?" Cal's voice was little more than a whisper.

"Are you kidding? Everybody'd go AWOL before you left the States." He turned to continue on his way. "I hope you make it." His tone contained sincerity and doubt.

Rafe and his companions watched him leave, their shoulders sagging. Going absent without leave sounded tempting. In the States, all thoughts about bombing Germany had been abstract, with the war being so far away. Recruitment films touted the great opportunities and experience they'd gain in defending their country, with not a hint of danger. Now, feelings of invincibility ebbed away as the prospects of violent death coalesced into concrete reality, which they would soon encounter.

Alan sighed. "I wonder if I'll get home to see Ruby again."

Steve stepped into his role as plane commander, responsible for maintaining his crew's morale. "Come on, guys. You heard him. He survived. Not all crews cash in their chips. Neither will we. We'll ace all the training and be the best crew in our group."

Maybe, but what good would being the best do if they were on the wrong end of a direct hit?

Cal adjusted his cap and looked around at the activity. "What exactly haven't we been taught yet, anyway?"

For Rafe, training meant learning to operate a British invention, the Ground Electronic Equipment Box. The GEE Box was a fast, accurate navigation system. This was one fun gadget. On their first practice flight, he fiddled with it incessantly. The box measured the difference between the arrival time of radio signals from a master station and a slave station. In half a minute, he had a position fix accurate within thirty feet. Back on the ground, he couldn't stop talking about it.

"Are your instructors pleased with your work?" Steve frowned at him. He'd been doing that a lot lately.

"Yeah, I guess so. They quit calling on me when they question us, saying the other navigators need a chance to respond."

"Looks like we got us a *wunderkind.*" Cal knocked off Rafe's cap and messed his hair.

Rafe swatted away his hand. "Maybe I should put in for a Squadron Navigator position."

Chapter Nine

Stone Air Base, England
Wednesday, March 22, 1944

They'd been at Stone for two weeks when their proposed several weeks of additional training were cancelled. Steve was summoned to the commandant's office. He returned with a dazed look and his voice pitched higher. "Grab your gear, men. We're moving out. We've been assigned to the 381st Bomb Group in Ridgewell. If we need any more training, we'll get it there."

Another train took the crew to their new base in Essex County, forty miles northeast of London. The afternoon ride gave them a good look at the passing English countryside. Rafe stared out the window. England — the land Hitler claimed should have united with Germany. Bicycles outnumbered automobiles. Signs advertised "My goodness, my Guinness!"

"Hey, look." Dan stabbed a finger at the window. "There's a red telephone booth. We really are in England now."

"Every village has its pub." Cal smiled over his shoulder. "Anyone in the mood for fish and chips?"

The train pulled into the Cambridge station. Narrow streets, ancient buildings, and thatched roof cottages gave an impression of a town forgotten by time. An army truck waited to transport them to their new home. Rafe was the last to board. First chance he got, he'd come back and explore.

The truck wheeled up to an unimpressive base gate, where a guard waved them through. Lots of prefabricated half-round metal buildings were scattered about in the mud. Hallelujah, no tents.

A major examined their papers. "I'm assigning you to the 534th Squadron. A driver will take you to your quarters. Good luck, men."

The runways lay to the northeast of most of the buildings. Their driver explained the layout as he sped along a dirt road, giving them a breezy ride with no canvas covering the truck bed. "We have three runways here. The two main ones are positioned like an X, and each of the four squadrons is based in one of the angles of the X."

"Whoa. Wait one minute." Cal dropped a heavy hand on the driver's shoulder as they approached the perimeter track around the runway. Parked on its hardstand sat a B-17 like they'd never seen before. The bomber that was supposed to be seventy-five feet long was several feet shorter. Its nose was missing. The chin gun turret remained, and what looked like the bombardier's chair perched on it. But everything else was gone, leaving only twisted, jagged metal below the cockpit.

The driver idled beside it. "Hmm, yes. This is one of the 535th's planes. The pilot managed to bring it home after taking a direct hit by flak."

Rafe's heart clenched. Hard to imagine the fierce wind that would have shrieked in through the holes in the fuselage. The crew must have been frozen by the time they landed. He fought to get air into his lungs. "What…" He licked his lips. "What happened to the bombardier and the navigator?"

The driver glanced over his shoulder, spotted Rafe's navigator's insignia, and winced. "The bombardier disappeared in the blast. The navigator was still in there when they got back." He hesitated before adding, "The chaplain took him to the American National Cemetery in Cambridge today."

"Lord God Almighty, have mercy on us." Alan's prayer lingered in the air.

Rafe would have uttered the prayer if Alan hadn't beaten him to it.

So what if the Stone instructors declared Steve's ability to fly in tight formation at high altitude the best they'd seen in a newly arrived pilot? The best pilot in the world couldn't avoid flak bursts. And so what if Rafe routinely pinpointed their locations with his brilliant navigating? What good would knowing where they were be if they were dead?

Numbness fogged his brain as the driver pulled up in front of a Quonset hut that looked like a gigantic tin can had been cut in half and planted in the dirt. "This here's home sweet home for the officers. Three crews per hut."

Rafe followed his crewmates inside. The other occupants present paid them little attention. Four cots had been stripped. He dropped his duffle bag onto one. Hooks hung from a shelf over the cot and he hung up his uniforms. Arranging his belongings on the shelf, he said to Alan, "After seeing that bomber, do we bother unpacking?"

Behind him, someone asked, *"Woher kommen Sie?"*

Rafe's heart nearly stalled again. Why would someone be speaking his native language to him here? He turned to a man who also wore a navigator's insignia. "Why do you ask?"

The man smiled. "My grandparents came from Pomerania. I know a hint of German when I hear it. I'm Paul Braedel. Where's home now?"

Rafe sank down onto the cot. "I'm Rafe Martell, from Milwaukee."

"Really? So am I." Paul's smile bloomed. "How long were you in Milwaukee?"

"Seven years."

Paul nodded slowly. "So you left before Hitler laid down the law. A high school friend returned to Germany about five years ago. She wrote to my wife that she couldn't find an elderly Jewish couple, and feared for them."

"If they didn't get out, they're dead." Rafe studied Paul's eyes. This man might be a good friend. First, he'd see if he could shock him. Find out how Paul felt about Jews.

"My blue-eyed, blonde, Christian mother is Jewish and my father divorced her a week after we learned the Gestapo was on to us. Without his protection, we would have been deported to a concentration camp. Getting out of Germany was still relatively easy and my grandparents got us all to Milwaukee."

Paul stared at Rafe. "That's unbelievable that things could be like that. I can't imagine living there. Or Heidi being there."

A knock sounded at their door, and a sergeant entered. He glanced around at the officers present. "Which is Lieutenant Kressle's bunk?"

Paul pointed at the cot by the door and the sergeant began stripping it.

"The lieutenant had an accident with a bicycle. His spine was injured and he might not walk again. At any rate, he won't be flying again." Gathering the unfortunate man's belongings, he turned and left.

An accident with a bicycle? Rafe looked down at what he held. Mother, Rita, Albert, Oma, and Opa smiled up at him from the photograph. He traced a finger over each family member. The chances of seeing them again seemed more unlikely than ever.

Chapter Ten

Leuchars, Scotland
Thursday, March 23, 1944

"Be at the air field by seven. No later."

Jennie returned the telephone to its cradle. Tonight. She'd leave for Sweden tonight aboard a secret courier flight. At least one flight had disappeared completely, likely shot down over water, everyone killed.

The warrant officer who had greeted her upon her arrival at Leuchars explained the clandestine route she'd take. "You'll be heading north a bit and fly over Norway before turning south to Stockholm. We don't stay with a regular schedule. That'd be too predictable for the Germans. The Krauts like to monitor our flights with their radar and interfere if they get the chance, but not to worry. You'll be fine."

Had anyone said that to the folks on the plane that vanished?

"Everyone boarding the flights must be dressed as civilians, so we don't violate Sweden's neutrality. 'Course, you're not military, so that's no problem. Lots of diplomats go in. On the return flights, we get lots of resistance people coming out, mostly from Norway."

Now, the time had come. At this hour tomorrow, she'd be in Sweden. Her belongings were ready to go, so Jennie left the hotel for a last walk along the winding roads of Leuchars. Maybe she could walk off the jitters coiling in her abdomen. Too bad Rafe wasn't here to help her deal with the nervous anticipation of the unknown.

Sweden. Think about Sweden.

Dad had told her a lot about the country. The Swedes supplied the Germans with iron ore which they used to make war on the Allies. Now that the war was turning against the Germans, the Swedes looked with greater favor on the Allies. Dad had cautioned against judging the Swedes with disfavor. They were hemmed in by the Nazis. If they hadn't cooperated with German demands, they would have faced invasion and occupation like all their neighbors.

Soon, she would live among them. Stockholm teemed with spies from the warring nations. How much wartime intrigue would she witness? What would Rafe say if he knew what she'd be doing in Sweden? She'd told him the truth when she said she'd be working at the legation, just not the full truth.

Instead of journeying with her parents in January, she'd spent time in the Washington DC area at secret schools. The Office of Strategic Services had her on their payroll. She'd trained in cryptography to code and decode messages. Classes in propaganda and rumor campaigns proved more interesting, but in a neutral nation, she may not have much opportunity in the Morale Operations branch of the Office of Special Services.

She walked past ancient buildings sprouting multi-flued chimneys that had so fascinated her earlier in the week. Today, they held no interest. Her jitters were doing jumping jacks. She hurried back to Ye Old Hotel for her luggage. It might be too early to show up at the air base, but that was better than being late.

A man lugging a suitcase and a portable typewriter took a paternal interest in Jennie as they dressed for their flight. "Quite a bother, all this. Blimey! To think, this is how the poor blokes have to dress every time they fly."

Jennie paused in pulling on the heavy jacket. "The poor blokes? You mean the air force fliers?"

This was how Rafe had to dress each time he flew? The flying clothes were like snow suits. Loaded down with fur-lined boots, gloves, and a helmet, she was ready for an arctic expedition. She eyed her parachute and life preserver. With no instruction in the art of parachuting, how would she manage should the need arise? In the dark, over water? Rafe's comments about the unlikelihood of surviving in the Atlantic rang like a death knell. She joined the other passengers waddling out to the plane.

A Liberator aircraft, painted black to blend into the moonless night sky, waited for them. Even the windows were blacked out. Jennie climbed the rickety stairs, gripping tightly to the railing. This flight probably wasn't the best introduction to flying. Daylight would be preferable, and with a view. Most especially, no one who would want to shoot them down. How in the world did the airmen do this day after day?

The airplane's bomb bay had been modified to carry people instead of bombs. Two benches lined the length of the bay on either side, with two more in the middle. Their heavy clothing wouldn't provide much cushioning on a flight lasting several hours.

An aircraft crewman presented brief instruction on how to use the oxygen mask when they reached ten thousand feet. "We'll let you know when these are needed."

The friendly Brit sat beside her, tucking his typewriter under the bench. "This will make quite a story, what?"

"Are you a reporter?"

"Oh, my, yes. With the *Daily Mail* for the past twenty-four years, I've been. Ever since the Great War. Most of the young blokes want to follow the army in

France but, at my age, I enjoy a few of the comforts of life. In Stockholm, telephone contact with Berlin still exists, you know. A bit limited, it is, but the Swedes also have their own reporters in Berlin. And I'll scrounge up the odd contact, and be able to file stories about what's happening in the enemy's own lair."

The plane roared down the runway and rose steeply into the air. Jennie's heart rate soared with it. Even with all the warm clothes, she shivered in the penetrating cold. Too soon, a crewman instructed them to don the oxygen masks. The mask pressed hard against the bridge of her nose. She pulled it off and fiddled with the straps, trying to loosen it.

The dour-faced crewman loomed over her. "Fasten your mask. We can't be watching for you to pass out from asphyxia."

The reporter helped her adjust the mask. "You probably have the straps too high up on your crown. If you get the straps around the back of your head even with your nose, the mask will sit proper-like."

The mask became more comfortable, although it probably wasn't much different than having her face clutched by a cold, clammy hand.

The cabin lights were turned off, plunging them into pitch blackness. Jennie gripped the edge of the bench. Deep breaths might help, but not with the face mask in place. Rough air bounced the aircraft and her stomach. She leaned back against the fuselage and prayed for sleep to obliterate her surroundings.

The lights came back on when the Liberator flew over Sweden, but they could see nothing through the blackened windows. After landing at Stockholm's Bromma Airport, Jennie rose stiffly. A crick in her neck throbbed. She queued for the exit, and turned to the reporter. "I wouldn't care to do that every day."

"No, indeed. Not without a pillow to sit on, and one behind the head."

Jennie paused while descending the stairs. Across the tarmac sat a plane with 'Lufthansa' painted on the fuselage and a bold swastika on the tail fin.

"Ah, yes." The reporter chuckled behind her. "I heard Lufthansa runs a daily flight from Berlin to Stockholm. Full of spies, no doubt, but also the odd contact we newsmen dearly love to cultivate. You can bet their flights are in warm, pressurized cabins with proper seats. Well, come along. We now have the tedious task of getting through customs. They treat us all like we're saboteurs instead of common folk interested in making an honest living. I say, have you a way to get into the city?"

Before she could answer, someone called, "Jennie."

She turned at the familiar voice. "Mom!"

Chapter Eleven

Activity in the officers' Quonset hut had finally quieted down, but then a knock sounded at the door. The officers all looked up. Normal procedure was to barge right in.

"How very quaint." A bombardier heaved himself off his cot and opened the door.

Dan, their tail gunner, stood in the doorway, and tightness gripped Rafe's chest when Dan's eyes settled on him.

"Begging your pardon, sirs." Dan nodded to the room at large and stepped toward Rafe. "We're flying tomorrow, sir. You and Lieutenant Ellerbee and me."

"What about the rest of us?" Alan looked both relieved and slighted not to be named.

"No, sir. The three of us are filling in with a crew where our counterparts got killed or wounded today. We'll be flying on *Jumping Jiminy*." Dan grimaced and cracked his knuckles. "The major says he wants the crew to get right back in the saddle. He says we're ready to join 'em till they get their permanent replacements."

Hot prickles swept Rafe, immediately followed by icy tingles in the pit of his stomach. This was it. He exchanged glances with Cal. After little time in flying practice missions, tomorrow they would go to war against Germany. He dragged in a deep breath. A phrase he'd heard often on the *Queen Mary* around the card games described the gamble they'd be taking: "Winner take all. Winner take all." Now, lives were at stake rather than a few dollars.

At the cot beside him, Alan scooped up their checkers and folded the board. "I guess you'll want to try and get some rest."

Try. That was the important word. How was he supposed to sleep, not knowing what tomorrow would bring? Long after lights out, he stared up at the ceiling. What was his father doing these days? Did Father ever think about him? About Mother? One thing he knew for sure: she was praying for her eldest child.

He shifted restlessly. Tomorrow he'd be replacing a guy who'd been wounded, maybe killed. Chances were good he might be killed, too. At least he wouldn't be going up against his old friends. They'd be in the navy, unless, like him, they switched to another branch of the military. What about Christoph? Did his cousin still live? What about Bertil, Johan, and Ludwig? Jennie was right. He missed them.

Around him rose snores from the slumbering men, their cots creaking as they shifted in sleep. Most of these fellows had no close ties with Germany. They harbored no hatred for Germans. They fought because

Germany had declared war on them. And the air war, fought miles above the ground, was impersonal. They didn't see the people on whom the bombs fell.

For a German, it was all personal.

Just before he'd left for basic training, Oma had shared some Bible verses with him. Something about God being the Father of the fatherless and, even though his parents might forsake him, God never would. Oma said whenever he wished he could talk to Dad, remember his Heavenly Father was always ready to listen to him. Rafe sighed. Angry as he was with Dad, he'd give anything to feel Dad's hand on his shoulder. He flipped over and bunched up his pillow. *God, I really need You now.*

"Think of God reaching down from heaven and laying His hand on your shoulder," Oma had said.

Rafe's tension drained away, and sleep claimed him.

Chapter Twelve

Ridgewell Air Base, England
Friday, March 24, 1944

A hand nudged his shoulder and a flashlight shone in his face. "Sir, it's time to get up."

"Wha time zit?" He couldn't have slept for more than a minute.

"It's one o'clock. The truck will be here to take you to chow in about fifteen minutes."

Rafe swung his legs off his cot in time to hear Cal's disgruntled mutter. "This means war."

A huff of silent laughter was all Rafe could manage. He pulled on his woolen underwear, necessary for a job at five miles above the earth where the temperature was typically thirty degrees below zero, before dressing in his uniform and heavy GI shoes. The rest of their combat gear could wait. He and Cal stumbled out to wait for the truck.

"What gives? It's the middle of the night." Cal pulled up his collar and tucked his head down like a turtle. "I thought the Brits did the nighttime bombing and we flew in daylight."

Someone behind them piped up. "The earlier the start, the farther we have to go. By the time we get there, it'll be daylight."

Germany. The target had to be in Germany. Rafe's shoulders rose and fell with his sigh.

His stomach wasn't awake yet, but he loaded his plate with fresh sunny-side-up eggs, fried potatoes, ham, and canned pears in red gelatin. They likely wouldn't see their next meal until late afternoon at the earliest. He'd like to wash the food down with coffee and juice, but didn't care to use the relief tubes aboard the aircraft any more than absolutely necessary.

Military policemen checked them at the door to the briefing hall. Only officers assigned to the mission were authorized to enter. On the platform at the far end of the room stood a curtain-draped map. Rafe stared at it. "What a nice theatrical touch. The rising of the curtain will tell us our destination."

Cal snorted. "I'd like to know who the pilot we're flying with is."

Colonel Leber, their commanding officer, strode to the platform. Someone yelled, "Ten-hut," and they all jumped to their feet.

"At ease."

At ease? As the airmen sat back down, Rafe raised his fingers to his mouth. He stopped with his mouth open. What was he planning to do, chew on his nails? He hadn't bitten his nails since he was a young child and Mother slapped his hands away. None of the other men assembled appeared to be so afflicted.

A staff member swept the curtain back. Loud groans filled the air.

"Schweinfurt." The colonel tapped the city.

Rafe wilted in his seat. Today marked his return to Germany. After an eight-year absence, he was going home. Not to Cologne, thank goodness. He wasn't ready for that. Schweinfurt held no special meaning for him. Still, he numbered himself among the enemy now. His former countrymen would do their level best to kill him, and he would aid in killing them. His insides were tying into knots.

The meteorologist stood up to report favorable weather conditions. "Clouds increasing over the North Sea, but with breaks. Good visibility at the target. Navigational winds are northwest, thirty miles an hour."

Around him, other men scribbled notes. Rafe tried to write too, but his shaky hand created chicken scratches.

After attending the navigators' briefing, he joined Cal for the trek to the equipment shop for their electrically heated flying suits, fur-lined boots, oxygen masks, Mae West life preservers, parachutes and harnesses, leather helmets with built-in intercom earphones, and steel helmets.

He nudged Cal and nodded to a sign posted over the parachute window. *If it doesn't work, we'll replace it.*

"Wise guys," Cal grumbled. "Their lives don't depend on the things."

In addition to the general gear, Rafe had his navigator's case. At least the thirty-pound flak suits of protective curved-steel segments waited for them at the crew chief's tent. Wearing some of their load, and carrying some of it, they rode in another truck out to the hardstand where their B-17 awaited them.

Dan stood outside the waist compartment door, looking anxious until he spotted them. Then his smile returned and he scrambled into the plane.

Rafe entered *Jumping Jiminy* through the forward escape hatch and crouched low to enter the bomber's nose. The plane stank of oil and, what was that? Blood? Rafe's nose wrinkled as he settled down at the navigator's table. He removed his log and instruments from his briefcase, arranged them on the table, and tucked the case out of the way on the floor. Folding his hands on the table, he breathed deeply. So far, everything resembled the training missions.

The bombardier slumped at his station, morosely staring out the Plexiglas bubble window that gave the nose its greenhouse atmosphere. He didn't appear to be the talkative sort, especially after the way he grunted when Rafe introduced himself.

Rafe plugged in his intercom link. Maybe he'd find a little distraction by eavesdropping on anyone who was talking.

The pilot's voice assaulted his ears through his headphones. "Don't touch anything unless I tell you to. Just sit there and stay out of trouble." Rafe's eyebrows shot up to his flying helmet. Poor Cal. Steve had given Cal plenty of flying time during their training flights. If Steve were disabled or killed, he wanted Cal ready to take over, but not this guy. Rafe smirked at Cal's "Yes, sir." The irony in his crewmate's voice told him Cal wasn't intimidated.

He stood and poked his head up in the overhead astrodome. In the cockpit windows, the pilot looked down, probably going through his checklist on his own. Cal spotted him and grinned, offering a thumbs up. Rafe snickered and sprawled in his chair, legs stretched out, arms crossed. The knots in his stomach started to loosen.

A white-white flare rose from the tower, signaling time to start engines. Through his headphones, the pilot was ready for the starting sequence. "Read through the checklist."

Really? He was going to let Cal read the list? That was proper procedure, of course, but he trusted Cal not to skip a line?

After a brief hesitation, Cal announced, "Master switch."

"On."

"Battery switches and inverters."

"On and checked."

Of course. The guy was allowing Cal to read the sequence while he flipped the switches.

"Parking brakes – hydraulic check."

"On, checked."

"Booster pumps – pressure."

"On and checked."

"Carburetor filters."

"Open."

"Fuel quantity."

Rafe hopped up to peer through the astrodome again. Cal's head was down. He was occupied with the checklist, but his head bobbed up and down. He was keeping an eye on the pilot's performance as per regulations. Rafe grinned. If anything went wrong, Cal wouldn't hesitate to take over.

A low whine announced engine one's start. Rafe watched the propeller spin faster and faster. The other engines started in sequence. So far, nothing differed from a practice flight.

When they trundled out to the runway, Rafe stood to watch the procession. More than a dozen bombers taxied ahead of them, looking like a bunch of prehistoric beasts. Hulking brutes performing a precisely-planned choreography.

They were really doing this. What would it be like to see Germany again? How would he react to being shot at? What if he was shot? Could this be the last day of his life?

Their flight to Schweinfurt proceeded smoothly. The carefully orchestrated ballet of forming up into box formations was impressive. None of the dreaded English fog obstructed the process today and he watched as each B-17 in turn slid into its designated slot. Too bad he didn't have a camera.

He noted their take-off time, form-up time, and time of crossing the English coast. He probably recorded more than necessary in his log, but the overbearing pilot wasn't going to have any cause to accuse him of carelessness.

An escorting flock of their Little Friends, identified by one of the gunners as P-38 fighters, intercepted the German Focke Wulf fighters that rose to meet them as they made landfall over The Netherlands. That year he'd spent in Amsterdam with his mother, grandparents, and siblings had been a year of upheaval and confusion. They'd been taken in, but it hadn't been home.

He noted the event in his log, and watched the small, occupied country recede below. With no need to fire the machine gun mounted alongside his desk, Rafe stared down at Germany, looking peaceful and inviting from twenty-five thousand feet. The sight of the Rhine River transported him back to that last happy day sailing with his Naval Hitler Youth friends.

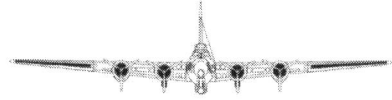

The Rhine's swift current that day in May, 1936, had brought their sailboat closer and closer to a collision with a river barge laden with cargo and incapable of quick maneuvering. "Traffic dead ahead," Herr Schultz yelled. "Come about!"

Bertil's frenzied effort to bring the boom in line failed when he stumbled on a coil of rope. Ludwig grabbed for the boom's line and missed. It swung wildly to starboard, sweeping up Bertil across his midsection and eliciting a startled "Oof." Rolf failed to hold back a chuckle as his friend clung to the boom, gasping for help as it wobbled over the Rhine River. He joined the other boys in hauling the boom back. Herr Schultz pushed them aside as he manned the tiller. The sailboat labored to port, missing the oncoming barge by a handbreadth.

"All right, boys, time to head back to Cologne. Think we can manage that without further mishap?"

"Have no fear, Herr Schultz." Johan knocked off Bertil's cap. "As long as everyone stays in the boat."

Rolf scooped up the now-wet cap from the sailboat's floor and handed it to Bertil. His friend had no natural sailing instinct. With his mechanical aptitude, he should have opted for the motorized units division, if not the regular Hitler Youth.

An explosion rocked the Flying Fortress. Rafe's reverie shattered as black smoke engulfed the Plexiglas nose.

Chapter Thirteen

The mission's apparent ease evaporated upon arrival over Schweinfurt. The German anti-aircraft defenders zeroed in on their altitude, and bursts from their *fliegerabwehrkanonen* exploded all around the formation. The resultant flak of the anti-aircraft shells blossomed in black clouds that looked harmless enough.

Rafe's jaw dropped as the lead plane in the element ahead of them took a direct hit in the gas tanks and burst into flames. The fire soared fifty feet above the wings and engulfed the entire plane.

The flames on the damaged plane streamed backward, enveloping the lead plane in his own element. The tail gunner of the second plane bailed out through the rear escape hatch. Why in the world did he do that? Did he think his plane was on fire?

Rafe looked ahead. The stricken plane continued flying in formation as a body tumbled out, flailing and on fire. It had to be an inferno in there. Then the plane banked down into a spin. After two rotations, it exploded into tiny, unidentifiable fragments, buffeting *Jumping Jiminy* with the blast. He swallowed hard.

Dan needed to be warned to always be sure any flames he saw really came from their own plane, and not from a nearby plane, before bailing out.

Seconds after the bombardier released their bomb load, a flak burst pummeled *Jumping Jiminy,* spraying it with shrapnel. The pilot yelled, "I'm hit!" and the plane lurched to the right before wrenching back into place. Rafe's head jerked up at the pilot's next words. "Fire! Everyone out!"

The bombardier grabbed his parachute and barreled past Rafe to disappear out the forward escape hatch. Rafe picked up his own parachute, but hesitated to snap it onto his harness. *Jumping Jiminy* maintained level flight.

Through the intercom, someone yelled, "Bring up that fire extinguisher."

Apparently not everyone was leaving. A burst of static filled his ears, then silence. His headphone was dead.

A moment of indecision passed. If there was a chance he didn't need to bail out over Germany, he didn't intend to. The Germans may have rejected him, but if he were captured, they'd consider him a traitor. Better a quick death in the crash of the bomber than a slow death at the hands of the Gestapo.

Rafe jumped up to the window. The left inboard engine propeller stood still, the blades edgewise to the wind. That engine had been properly feathered to avoid drag. If the pilot had jumped, Cal must still be here, flying the airplane like nobody's business. He craned his neck. No fuel leaks in sight. A parachute blossomed, followed by another. He banged his head against the window trying to get a closer look. More men had just jumped out. He scrambled through the narrow passageway up into the cockpit.

His crewmate wrestled with the controls. Adrenaline tingled Rafe's fingers and toes. He plugged in his communication wires to ask what was going on. Cal didn't give him a chance.

"Rafe! Get yourself in the pilot's seat!"

He wedged himself into the vacated left seat, banging his knee on the throttle handles between the seats. A hole by his leg let in a draft. That's how the pilot got hit. Rafe plugged in his heated suit cable and grabbed the pilot's abandoned oxygen line.

"Get your hands on the control wheel. This wounded bird is bucking like a bronco." Even with the frigid air whistling through flak holes, sweat glistened on Cal's face above his oxygen mask.

"What happened?" Rafe tightened his grip when the control column nearly yanked itself out of his grasp.

"Watching that flying crematory spooked everyone is my guess, especially after their experience yesterday. The engineer said their copilot was decapitated. That had to be a sickening sight."

Cal's gaze swept across the flight instruments. "Anyway, the pilot took a slug in the leg and jumped up. We nearly went into a spin before I got the controls properly positioned. Then he spots the fire in the radio room, yells to bail out, and takes off, with the engineer on his heels. The radio guy and one of the gunners put out the fire. I smelled gas and shut off a cross-feed and that seemed to take care of the leak."

He paused as he monitored their position with the plane on their right. "I needed help keeping the ship trim, so I waved for the guys to come up and assist, but I guess they misunderstood. They jumped out. I started thinking I'd have to bail too, when you popped up."

The engine rumble changed in pitch and Cal swore. "We're gonna lose number three." He adjusted the throttle controls. "Number two is already gone. If three quits, we won't be able to keep up. Where are we?"

"Still over Germany, last I checked."

With the loss of the flying coffin, other planes in their element had tightened up. The men in the plane now on their left gestured at them. Why? They had no fire. The instruments indicated no leaks. Did they question why they stayed after so many chutes came out? He waved back at them.

Peering down at the passing landscape, he spotted a large inland sea. "Good news. We're over The Netherlands."

He nearly jumped out of his seat when a hand landed on his shoulder.

"Where is everybody?"

"Dan! I wondered if you'd jumped, but couldn't spare Rafe to check on you. Keep an eye on the gauges, will you? Engine three is unhappy." Cal seemed invigorated now that he had both of his crewmates to help fly the ailing plane.

Rafe twisted around to face their tail gunner. "Did you see any problems on your way up from the tail?"

"Just an abandoned ship. I saw the waist door open and thought I'd better get out too, except the plane seemed to be flying okay, so I decided to wait. I'd rather go back to England to sleep tonight."

"Yeah, us too." Cal took a deep breath. "We've got an indicator of deployed landing gear. It's not or we'd feel the drag, but we may have lost hydraulics. Be ready to crank the wheels down."

"I can do that." Dan set aside his walk-around oxygen bottle and plugged into the engineer's station. He caught Rafe's eye and his eyes crinkled in humor. With the immediate danger past, and no enemy fighters harassing them, euphoria must be buoying them. They would survive their first mission.

Cheers filled the cockpit when England appeared on the horizon. After being airborne for seven hours in the frigid, unpressurized aircraft, Ridgewell's Quonset huts would seem palatial. True to Cal's prediction, the landing gear required hand cranking and Dan proved capable of getting them down in speedy fashion. They peeled out of formation in turn and queued up to land. Cal switched from the intercom to the Command radio frequency in time to hear a puzzling radio transmission.

"42-4013, identify who's flying the aircraft."

The three exchanged glances before Cal double-checked their plane's serial number and cued his mike. "The copilot is flying the aircraft with the able assistance of his navigator and tail gunner."

"State your aircraft's condition."

To Rafe, Cal said, "Coming in on two wings and a prayer," referring to a popular song. He switched back to Command. "Ah, one engine is out and another is on borrowed time."

No sooner had Cal transmitted his report than number three sputtered and shot sparks. He slapped at the controls to shut it down. "If they're worried about our status, I'm not giving them a chance to wave us off. We've got two good outboard engines."

Most likely, the squadron leader had tried to contact them after the other crew members jumped. Normally the pilot monitored the Command radio, and would have responded. Maybe that's why the other crews had been waving at them. They were trying to raise them on the radio. Rafe grimaced. He should have thought of that.

Cal landed short, giving them the full length of the runway. *Jumping Jiminy's* brakes squealed and groaned like a wounded thing, but by the time they reached the far end, Cal managed a graceful turn onto the perimeter track and proceeded around to the hardstands. They hadn't gone far when he cleared his throat. "Say, ah, do either of you know which hardstand we should aim for?"

Rafe snickered. He glanced back at Dan. "He flies through German air space with the greatest of ease, but can't find his own parking place back in England."

Dan guffawed and raised a hand as though to slap Cal on the back before thinking better of it.

Rafe slid open the side window and yelled to the nearest ground crew as they passed by. "Excuse me. Do you know where this plane belongs?"

The men stared at them open-mouthed, causing Dan to giggle like a schoolgirl. One mechanic waved for them to continue, holding up four fingers.

"I think we're on the right path. Try four spots ahead." Rafe pointed forward, adding, "That guy's yelling to someone in the next pit, and he's yelling on down the line. The news of our arrival is going through the grapevine." They trundled on.

All three laughed themselves silly when a couple of mechanics ran up to the taxi way, waving their arms. Rafe gasped, "They do a good imitation of wind milling propellers."

"Hey, Lieutenant," Dan wheezed, "I think they want you to hand over the airplane. They probably think the guys who bailed out picked up some hitchhikers. And lookee there. The rest of our crew."

Cal executed a sharp turn and eased the big plane into its proper resting position. The three tumbled out of the bomber, still laughing, and laughed harder at the dumbfounded looks on the faces of the ground crew and their own crewmates.

The crew chief stuck his head into the plane. "Where's Lieutenant Pike and his men?"

"They got the heebie jeebies and are now guests of *Der Führer*, dining on sauerkraut tonight if they're dining at all." Dan bowed. "And we're slap happy."

"You don't say." Steve Coolidge frowned at his men. "I'm thinking either oxygen deprivation or smuggled whiskey."

"Oh, no, sir." Dan stood ramrod straight and saluted. "We survived our first mission. We brought back the plane, and these guys," he waved a hand at the mechanics, "will have it flight-ready in no time. We're alive and free and over the moon. Isn't that what the Brits like to say? Say, do you have anything to drink? I sure am thirsty."

"You're wanted in interrogation and they'll have something for you. Pile into the jeep and we'll take you there."

Steve appeared unsure if he should be concerned or amused. He grabbed Rafe's arm when he swayed on his feet. Dan was right. They were alive and free. Free of the *Führer* and his goons. The adrenaline drained away and Rafe might have collapsed into a boneless heap if Steve wasn't marching him to the jeep. Given half a chance, he'd sleep around the clock.

The debriefing officer had trouble understanding why the veteran airmen bailed out and not the rookies.

"The Jumping Jitteries," Rafe mumbled.

"Yeah, and we're the Reckless Rookies." Dan planted his palms flat on the table, fingers splayed. "We didn't know any better. Except for one minute there when the tail jerked up and down like a yo-yo, everything seemed normal. I saw a couple parachutes but didn't think they should be from us."

Cal slouched in his seat, looking ready to fall asleep, mirroring Rafe's exhaustion. Cal looked at him as if to say, "Can you believe this guy?" Rafe grinned. Dan seemed to relish doing all the talking.

Finally, the debriefing officer stood but Rafe stayed seated. The man told Steve to take care of them. The words didn't register until someone grabbed his arms and pulled him to his feet. Next thing he knew, Alan steered him to his cot in their hut. His eyelids crashed down and refused to rise again. Before sleep descended, he needed to make one thing clear. "Nothing reckless about it. I will not set foot in

Germany until those Nazi goons are defeated. I'll die first."

"Sure you will. Want me to wake you for chow?"

Barely an hour had passed when Rafe woke. Cal still slept, but no one else was in the hut. He wandered outside. To find a bit of normalcy, he grabbed the bicycle he'd bought from an airman heading home and pedaled to the nearby village of Ridgewell.

He'd flown a combat mission against his homeland. Of course, he'd been little more than a passenger since they hadn't left the formation and the navigator in the lead plane had done all the work. But still, he had done it. He was at war with Germany. And he had no remorse, no guilt, no urge for revenge. He was only doing a job that needed to be done.

Cottages with thatched roofs nestled around an ancient church with blackened walls. He coasted past three young children playing in a yard with several kittens. When they spotted him, a boy called out an English child's standard greeting to Americans, "Got some gum, chum?"

Rafe shook his head and paused. "Sorry."

He hadn't acquired the American habit of chewing a wad of gum.

"Would you like to hold a kitten, mister?" A girl with unkempt dull brown hair, about seven years old, approached with two kittens clinging to her.

He pried loose one of them, holding it in the palm of his hand and stroking the soft calico fur. The tiny creature mewed.

"My name's Brenda Jane Prescott. What's yours?"

He had to swallow the lump in his throat. "I'm Rafe."

"Would you like that kitten? We have to find homes for them."

"I live on the air base. That isn't a safe place for this little furball."

Brenda nodded seriously. "You can come back and play with ours. We get to keep one."

Instead of seeing Brenda, Rafe saw Marta Goldman's frightened face. Was she able to enjoy carefree play with a litter of kittens? Had the Goldmans escaped? If she still lived, she must be twelve years old now. He handed back the kitten to Brenda Jane Prescott before tears welled in his eyes.

He rode back to base, concentrating on the seven men whose lives had suddenly lost all normalcy when they bailed out of *Jumping Jiminy*. Instead, they were experiencing their grim new world as prisoners of war, if they survived their jumps. And their bailing out had been a huge mistake. Such was the fickleness of war.

The war was no longer somewhere over there. He stood in the midst of it.

Chapter Fourteen

Stockholm, Sweden
Monday, March 27, 1944

The Lindquists resided in an apartment in Södermalm, an island comprising the southern part of Stockholm. Narrow brick walkways flanked narrow cobble-stone streets. Buildings in golden hues rose immediately on the opposite side of the street. No yards were in sight.

Leaving the apartment with Dad for her first day at the legation, Jennie walked in the street empty of motor vehicles but filled with bicyclists. Ground floor windows offered inquisitive passersby full disclosure of the inhabitants' lives. Thank goodness, their apartment occupied the third floor of their building. Only the neighbors twenty feet across the street could observe them.

"We'll take the train into the heart of the city, and walk the rest of the way. That way you can get a general feel for where things are. Stockholm consists of lots of islands and lots of bridges." Dad set a brisk pace and Jennie scurried to keep up. His words kept time with his stride.

"When you're out in public, be cautious. Sweden's neutrality makes it a magnet for all kinds of unscrupulous characters from all over. The Allies spy on the Germans and the Germans spy on us. In restaurants or department stores, someone may try to engage you in conversation or get close enough to eavesdrop if you're talking with someone else. He, or she, could be a German spy, even if you know the person to be Swedish. Swedish waitresses especially are suspect. When we get to the legation, you'll see the penetration reports you'll need to fill out on anyone with whom you come in contact."

Jennie's eyes widened and she glanced around. The tight-spaced buildings and narrow streets hemmed her in. A man walked toward them, hands in pockets, eyeing them. "Anyone?"

"If you exchange pleasantries with someone you pass in the park, no, you needn't report them. But if they get chatty and want to know what you do at the legation or who you know, then yes. They could be pumping you for useful information they can pass along."

Again, Jennie's eyes swept everyone in their vicinity. "How do you know who you can trust? Can we be friends with anyone?"

"You'll meet the folks at the legation. I think you'll like Phyllis, one of the secretaries. She's attending a get-together tomorrow evening, and she'll no doubt invite you to join her. You'll meet a few Swedes there. While they've been vetted, it's still a good idea to avoid political topics."

"So we should stick to recipes, hair-dos, and how to remove shoe polish stains from blouses."

Dad wrapped an arm around her shoulders and squeezed. "Try that with any young fellows and you'll scare them away." He continued in a quiet tone after they boarded the train. "Get them to talk about Sweden. Favorite places to go, recreation — the Swedes are big on outdoor activities. Ask if they have family who emigrated to the U.S. Maybe you'll find someone interested in art."

He pointed out places of interest as the train carried them into central Stockholm. They crossed one channel to skirt the western edge of the small island containing Staden, the old town, before crossing another channel to the modern city center. Nearby passengers eyed them curiously, drawn by their English conversation, no doubt. Still, someone could be following them, hoping for a juicy tidbit of American strategy. Maybe the lady with the new green hat. She was probably a secretary, but for whom? If she wasn't careful, Jennie would be seeing spies behind every door and tree. Could she lead a spy on a wild goose chase? She might end up practicing some Morale Operations tactics after all.

Dad disabused her of that idea as they exited the train and walked along the waterfront. "The Swedish Secret Police can be as much a problem as the German spies."

"The Swedish Secret police? Is that like the FBI or… or the Gestapo?"

"The FBI would be a better comparison. The British naval attaché's had quite a time with them. Last year he caught them in the attic of his apartment building with a microphone they'd lowered down his chimney to eavesdrop."

They passed the mammoth Royal Theater. Jennie's eyes lingered on the three arches in the front façade. Maybe she'd have the opportunity to attend a ballet. The view across the Norrbro Bridge of the Royal Palace in the Staden stroked Jennie's artistic soul. No wonder Stockholm had gained the moniker "Venice of the North." She'd come back to the small island to explore the old town at her first opportunity.

"How do the Swedes feel about Americans?"

"Since we joined the war effort and the tide turned our way, Sweden is more openly in favor of the Allies. In the early years of the war, when Britain didn't seem likely to hold out and fight alone, the threats of Germany's foreign minister were difficult to ignore. He isn't known for his subtlety. The Swedes even muzzled their press when Berlin complained about anti-Nazi articles. As long as Sweden granted the concessions they wanted, the Germans had no need to occupy the country." Dad kept his voice low.

The man in front of them leaned closer. To listen?

Apparently, Dad noticed as well. He held a hand in front of his mouth as he warmed to his topic. "The Germans demanded, and got, rail transport for their troops traveling between Norway and Germany, tankers to fuel their submarines, and shipments of Swedish iron ore and ball bearings, which the Allies also need. Now the Allies are taking a tougher stance, pressuring Sweden to stop benefitting Germany and prolonging the war."

They crossed a small peninsula, heading further north. Beyond the Nybroviken inlet resided an elegant row of buildings, mostly six or seven stories high, on Strandvägen. Beach Road. "This building on the left end here," Dad pointed, "houses the American legation. Some staff members live in apartments along the street, but they're a little too pricey for a lowly military attaché like myself."

Once inside, Jennie met more people than she'd remember names for. One, she would not forget.

"Oh, there you are. I've been waiting for you."

Jennie turned to the speaker. Curly red hair cascaded down a young woman's shoulders, clashing frightfully with the pink blouse she wore. Her tan skirt resembled a burlap sack. Despite her eyesore apparel, a merry twinkle lit up hazel green eyes. She advanced on Jennie. A quick glance around showed no one else likely to be the recipient of her greeting.

"Your dad promised me your help. Oh, we'll have a ball. Collating reports can be so boring for one, but two can have fun. You'll work with me this week, but next week you'll spend time with Ed." Her voice dropped to a whisper. "He's with our local OSS." Without missing a beat, she continued, "Have you seen much of Stockholm? Maybe we'll have time to go to Blanche's Café for lunch. It's not all that far from here, and you never know who you might find there. Oh, I'm Phyllis, by the way. Did your dad tell you you'd be working with me?" Linking arms with Jennie, she pulled her down a hallway.

Jennie snuck a backward glance. His shoulders shaking with silent laughter, Dad wiggled his fingers in a farewell wave before striding off in the opposite direction. She was on her own. No wonder Dad's eyes had gleamed when he said there'd be plenty of opportunities to help out at the legation. He knew she'd be collared by the garrulous Phyllis. Since he'd never steer her into an insufferable situation, he must anticipate that Jennie would enjoy her new colleague's friendship.

"I must tell you that speaking of our duties outside of the office is forbidden." Phyllis waited until they'd passed two men conversing in an open doorway. "Here, loose lips might not sink ships, but could still aid the enemy."

"Dad mentioned that. I understand we need to stick to recipes and fashion." Jennie cringed as soon as she uttered 'fashion.' If Phyllis' present outfit was any indication, fashion didn't concern her.

But her new friend laughed and clapped her hands. "Excellent. We'll come up with one hundred and one ways to prepare fish, which, as you'll soon discover, is the mainstay of the Swedish diet. Here we are."

Before they could enter the office ahead, an ingratiating voice behind them sent shivers up Jennie's spine. "Well, well, well, who do we have here?"

Phyllis stiffened. Without looking back, she replied in a bored tone. "Someone from a military attaché's family. No one you'll be working with, Stanley."

Before Phyllis could whisk her into the office and close the door, Jennie caught a glimpse of a man who must be at least forty and in dire need of a haircut. "Who is he?"

"He used to be a reporter in Berlin. That makes him think he's an expert on Germany. And speaking of fashion, your dress is beautiful, but you might want to dress down when you're here on Mondays. It's a surefire way to avoid his advances. He fancies himself highly attractive to women, if you can believe that. I'd rather be an old maid than take up with him."

Jennie sat at the table Phyllis indicated and accepted a bundle of forms. "Is that why you're dressed...?"

She waved a hand.

Phyllis responded with a burst of laughter. "This ugly outfit? You bet. Stanley quit bothering me after my first, uh, fashion show. Fortunately, he's not always in Stockholm and when he is, usually comes here only on Mondays. So I'm able to dress like a modern forties woman most of the time. And I'm wearing a respectable skirt underneath so I can whip off the burlap for a quick change if I need to meet with respectable people. How about you? Your dad said you used to work at a museum back home?"

"I did. I'm hoping to have time to paint lots of Swedish scenes. Have you heard of the Independent Order of Svithiod?" She smiled when Phyllis gave a wide-eyed shake of her head. She was as good at listening as she was at talking. "Its goal is to promote Swedish heritage and culture. I've been invited to provide an art exhibit when I return. I'd like to come up with a theme, something more than just pretty pictures."

Phyllis drummed her fingers on the desk. "We'll have to brainstorm. Maybe you'll be inspired as you familiarize yourself with Stockholm."

With another swerve in direction, Phyllis grabbed a stack of papers. "We need to sort and match these reports. Have you been told about Penetration Reports? You have? Good. We look for patterns. If a particular person asks the same questions of several people, it's a sure bet he's working for the Germans. And remember, don't say anything about this." She waved a handful of reports before dealing them out across the table. "If anyone asks, we've spent the morning playing cards. Oh, it will be so much fun having you here."

Chapter Fifteen

A flashlight shone in his face and a hand jiggled his shoulder. "Time to get up, sir."

Rafe groaned. Would they always have to rise so early? Hadn't he just gotten to sleep? "It's too early."

"Time to rise and shine." The flashlight moved on to Steve's cot.

Mouth wide open in a yawn, Rafe rolled into a sitting position and came face-to-face with Alan.

The bombardier stared at him through bleary eyes. "We gotta find us another line of work."

"Three o'clock." Cal swayed on his feet. "That's too early for a short hop to France, but not so early that we'll be going as far as Berlin, right? Must be Germany, though. Maybe Kiel or Hamburg."

Rafe required three efforts to get his top button matched with the correct buttonhole. He stifled another yawn, and stubbed his toe on his cot frame. That provided a jarring wake-up. He stumbled out of the hut after his crewmates.

A low overcast of cigarette smoke hung in the briefing room. The cheery yellow sunny-side up eggs at breakfast had started the day off right, but now Rafe couldn't relax. What was wrong with him today? Was this a premonition of disaster? Cal had guessed Kiel or Hamburg, but Cologne was in that general vicinity.

Not Cologne. Please, not Cologne. He wasn't ready. He'd never be ready. He slumped in his seat, only to leap to his feet at the call of "Ten-hut!"

The colonel mounted the stage. His aide pulled back the curtain. The red yarn dropped straight down, deep into southern France, to Montbartier. Rafe was spared from Cologne.

He glanced at Cal. They weren't going to Germany, but this was no short hop. Today's mission promised to be another all-day affair.

The crew found their assigned airplane, *Sweet Patootie*, and soon the B-17s thundered down the runway at thirty second intervals and began circling up through the fog. Colored flares fired from lead planes guided them as each plane found its slot in the group formation. Above the fog and cloud cover, the sun burst over the horizon, turning night into day. All too soon, they coasted out over the channel.

"Hey, are we going the wrong way?"

Rafe looked up from his log to check his compass.

Another gunner answered the first. "If we are, so's everybody else."

"But I see the white cliffs of Dover ahead of us. Did we turn back?"

Rafe squeezed in between Alan and a fifty caliber machine gun. "Sorry, George. Those are the white cliffs of France."

"They got them too?"

"Sure, the land went straight across until the water dug it out and left England by its lonesome."

Alan's shoulders shook in laughter at Harold's explanation as Rafe retreated to his desk.

"Haven't you ever heard of Darwin?" Mickey's voice dripped with condescension.

Alan turned around and mouthed, "Wise guy."

Rafe grinned.

Dan's cheerful voice chimed in. "Forget Darwin. Think Noah's ark."

"The ark dug the channel?"

Alan looked back again, his brows bunched together. Was there any hope for George?

"Not the ark. It wasn't big enough to scoop out such a wide channel. The flood did it."

"You believe that fairy tale?" Mickey was gathering steam to argue. "Are you religious or something?"

Steve put a stop to it. "Shelve the debate, boys. We're over France. Occupied France. Watch for fighters and keep the intercom free of chatter."

The bomb run proceeded in model fashion to please the brass back in England. Rafe joined Alan in the nose, surveying ahead with binoculars. The Spanish border was not too far away. Surely he was seeing Spain. It didn't look any different than France.

Pulling away his oxygen mask, Rafe yelled in Alan's ear. "Spain."

Alan looked up from the bombsight. "Ever been there?"

Rafe shook his head. He hadn't been anywhere in southern Europe.

When they arrived over the target, Rafe leaned over the edge of the Plexiglas nose to watch the bombs tumble down.

"Woo whee. Our employers ought to be pleased with the results. That's ninety percent or better of bombs on target." Alan's eyes gleamed above his oxygen mask.

Fighters and flak had been minimal. Rafe sat at his desk and recorded all the data on his log. He referred to the map where he'd traced their return flight. "Think the fog will have disappeared by the time we get back to England?"

"Put in an order for sunshine and clear skies." Cal yawned as he spoke.

"With France hogging all the sun, I'll bet England's still foggy." Count on Rusty to be negative.

Sure enough. As they flew over the English Channel, there it was. The first tendrils of wispy fog reached out to the planes. Then they were socked in, visibility dropping to nearly zero.

As they approached Ridgewell, a yell deafened Rafe. The airplane lurched to the side and the engines roared as more power was demanded of them. Looking out the window, Rafe spotted another B-17 right where they would have been if not for the evasive maneuver. They'd nearly had a midair collision. His pounding heart hadn't settled down by the time *Sweet Patootie* settled on the runway.

Parked on their hardstand, a weary crew tumbled out of *Sweet Patootie* after a long, ten-hour flight. Dan walked stiff-legged and stretched. "Apparently the Germans aren't putting enough fear of God into us."

Rafe frowned at him. "What are you talking about?"

"Fog is an act of God, right? He must be trying to get our attention, which means the Germans aren't doing a good enough job of it." Dan ambled to the jeep waiting to take them to interrogation, leaving Rafe to ponder his words.

Carlo stood beside him. When Rafe glanced his way, he asked, "Do you think God would do that to us?"

Rafe shrugged. How would he know?

His lackadaisical response didn't satisfy Carlo. "Maybe I'll go to chapel Sunday. The chaplain isn't Catholic, but it's supposed to be an economical service."

Not until that evening did Rafe ask about the chapel service in his hut. "Do you have to pay to go to chapel here?"

Paul Braedel looked up with wide eyes. "No. Why would you think so?"

"One of my crew said it's economical."

Paul grinned. "He probably meant ecumenical. Something for everyone."

Rafe stretched out on his cot and laced his fingers beneath his head. His eyes strayed back to Paul. An open Bible lay before him as he sat cross-legged, his chin propped on his folded hands. Mickey would call him religious.

"Do you think God caused that fog to get our attention?"

Paul's eyes rose from the Bible, but a slow moment passed before he turned to Rafe. "Nope. Fog is normal along the coast. If the fog drove home the realization that death is still a heartbeat away even when we're not in combat, and created a deeper longing for God, that's good. Faith flourishes when God is our only hope."

"So He does want our attention?"

"He always wants us to seek Him and spend time with Him." Conviction radiated from Paul's eyes.

Rafe studied the curved, corrugated roof arcing over him. Spend time with God. Exactly how did one go about doing that? Pray, of course. Prayer was supposed to be like talking to God, but unfortunately,

God never talked back to him. His gaze shifted back to Paul, who watched him patiently.

"It'd be nice if praying wasn't a one-sided conversation."

Paul had the gall to laugh. "If you listen right, you'll hear him." He pressed his lips together and dragged a hand through his hair. His gaze roamed around the hut before returning his attention to Rafe. "Not that I've been the best example since my wife died while I was in training."

Paul shrugged. "I suggest you read the Bible, starting with the gospels and the psalms. And not a swift scanning. Get familiar with it. I often find a verse comes to mind that is exactly what I need. It's like God's talking to me. The Bible is, after all, the word of God. The words may not be audible, but they still speak." He patted his Bible. "And if you need assurance of God's presence, go out some night and look at the stars. 'The heavens declare the glory of God; and the firmament shows his handiwork.' That's from Psalm Nineteen."

Rafe nodded. "My grandmother told me to think of God as my father after my dad rejected us. I wanted Dad's approval so badly, it hurt. But when I pictured God putting his hand on me in place of Dad, I felt assurance."

From his other side, Alan chimed in. "A father of the fatherless is God. That's in the Psalms, too. After my dad died, God became more real to me. Before that, God was someone we heard about at church, but no one I really related to."

Rafe tried not to let his surprise show. They'd been together for several months and this was the first Alan said anything about his dad. Whenever he'd spoken of family, it was Ruby this and Ruby that. Maybe, if he was married, he'd have only spoken of his wife and not his father or life in Germany.

He dug in his footlocker. Where was that Bible Oma had given him? He hadn't wanted to fill up space with it, but couldn't tell her that. Now it would be good to read the familiar, ancient words.

There, at the very bottom, under his spare slacks, with two books he'd never gotten around to reading. He pulled out the leather-bound book and blinked. *Heilige Bibel*. Why in the world had Oma given him a German Bible to read in the American air force?

Chapter Sixteen

Jennie tilted the magnifier for a closer look. This forgery had to be absolutely iron clad, air tight, and irrefutable to any German who demanded to see the spy's papers. The German stamp helped, but it was out of date. She touched her ink point to the identity card. The fours had to be exactly the same.

There. Perfect, if she could say so herself. She exhaled, and wilted. She cocked her head. For the third time, she'd been holding her breath. Asphyxiating herself didn't help the creating process. She pushed back from the desk and rubbed her eyes.

"You'll have a chance to do more exciting stuff once you meet with Ed. Being cooped up in here can get boring real fast." JB, the chief forger, leaned over her work. "Not bad. Not bad at all."

Jennie smiled. If Phyllis' story was true, this man had been arrested for forgery. Instead of jail time, here he was, putting his talent to use in a meaningful way. JB stood for jail bird and, in a way, the legation was his jail. Could the story be true? He seemed like a nice guy, but white-collar criminals must need to be charming to get away with their nefarious deeds. Asking him was out of the question. What if he said yes?

She fingered the space where the photo would go. "The photo with the genuine card is stapled with smaller than usual staples. Do we have that size?"

"But of course." JB retrieved a smaller than usual stapler from the desk drawer. "We got it from our embassy in Berlin before everyone pulled out when Hitler declared war on us. Most of our supplies came from German office suppliers. Helpful of them, wasn't it?"

Jennie laughed at his smug smile. "All of this stuff has lasted nearly three years?"

"Well, no." JB tapped a finger on his lips. Then he leaned down. "Some of it came from down the street."

The German legation stood down the street.

"What? Instead of going over and asking to borrow a cup of sugar, you ask for a pad of paper and some staples?"

"Nooo." JB sat on the corner of the desk and wiggled his eyebrows. "But if I told you, I'd have to kill you."

He winked and sauntered to the door. "Be right back. I need to go borrow a red marker."

Smiling at his behavior, Jennie practiced signing the German inspector's signature on scrap paper.

"Well, well, well. Look who's here." Stanley appeared beside her. He pulled up a chair, sat too close, and ran a finger along her arm. "How about coming to dinner with me, gorgeous, and you can tell me all about yourself."

JB's admonition rang in her ears. "Tell no one what you do in here. Not your dad, not Phyllis, no one. They may suspect what we do, but don't confirm anything."

Jennie scooted away from him and covered the ID cards with her scrap paper before rubbing his touch from her arm. "You don't belong in here."

"Come on, doll. How can we get acquainted if you don't warm up?"

"Extending your skirt patrol to Tuesdays, Lofton?" JB loomed over Stanley. "The ladies don't appreciate your harassment. And you can leave my colleague alone."

Balling his fists as he stood, Stanley snarled. "You think you're good enough for her?"

"Certainly not." JB's chin rose. "She's got herself a man in uniform."

Jennie covered her face with her hands as Stanley stalked off. She looked up at JB. "Did you get your marker?"

"I did indeed." He pulled it out of a pocket and twirled it. "I didn't have to visit the neighbors, after all. We have them here."

Jennie laughed half-heartedly. Finding Stanley beside her was akin to finding a spider in the room. "Why did you say I have a man in uniform?"

"My dear." JB pressed a hand to his chest. "We're in the spy business here. We must always sharpen our skills. And that includes ferreting out all the dope on our colleagues."

Picking up her pen, Jennie forged the inspector's signature. She examined her work and smiled. The inspector himself wouldn't realize he hadn't signed the card.

A man in uniform. Did JB really know something or was he fishing? Rafe probably wouldn't mind if she included him in a cover story to explain her reason for being in Sweden.

Would he?

Chapter Seventeen

Ridgewell Air Base, England
Wednesday, March 29, 1944

"Brunswick's getting a reprieve," Steve announced as the jeep that had stopped below his cockpit window continued on to the B-17 on the next hardstand. "There's cloud cover over Germany, though it's likely to clear up soon. We can get out of the plane, but stay close."

Rafe dropped through the nose hatch of *Sweet Patootie*, once again their plane for the mission. Maybe he could catch a few winks. He spread his flight jacket on the grass, and stretched out. Someone flopped down beside him. He opened one eye. Dan. So much for a nap.

Dan picked a long blade of grass. "Brunswick's reprieve might be to our disadvantage if we lose the clear sky we have now."

Rafe yawned. "Let's worry about that when, or if, the mission gets a go."

"Yeah, Quigley, why don't you put in a request for good weather with the Man upstairs?" Mickey stood over them, hands planted on his hips.

"Lay off, Mickey." Irritation stained Alan's voice.

Mickey might bully the other enlisted men of the crew, but showed the good sense not to argue with the officers. He stalked away.

An argument erupted among the crewmen. Mickey had started a squabble with Rusty. Rafe sat up and whistled. "That's it. Time out. Boxers to your respective corners."

The combatants drifted apart and silence reigned.

Steve frowned at Rafe. "Why do they mind you, but complain with me?"

"Lieutenant Martell's our den mother." Dan's grin filled his face. If he were a dog, his tail would be wagging.

"Den mother?" Like a bear in a cave? That's how they saw him? Rafe shook his head. *Jennie, you had it all wrong.*

"You know, like in Cub Scouts." Dan's smile slipped. He must have recognized Rafe's horror. "Don't they have Cub Scouts in Germany?"

Cub Scouts. Like the Boy Scouts? Well, he was right with the bear analogy. The question remained, how could being called a den mother be complimentary? "No, we had the *Jungvolk* and the Hitler Youth."

The jeep was making the rounds again. It paused by the *Sweet Patootie*. "Take off should begin in half an hour."

Rafe leapt to his feet and headed for the nose hatch. Good thing their work stations were separated. A bear. All this time he'd thought Dan liked him, and yet he compared him to a bear.

A swarm of fighters pounced on the bombers as they neared the Initial Point for starting the bomb run on an aircraft assembly factory. The escorting Mustangs dove on the FW-190s, driving most of them away, but one German was determined. He flew through the formation of B-17s, attracting fire from a dozen gunners.

Rafe stood behind Alan in the nose, alternately watching for landmarks and watching for fighters that came within range of his gun. They passed over the Ems River when the daredevil Focke Wulf turned straight toward them, and exploded.

Shrapnel raked the *Sweet Patootie*. The Plexiglas nose was no match for the missiles of steel. One chunk slammed into Rafe's chest like a hammer blow and threw him to the floor. He tried to breathe, and couldn't. Stars danced before his eyes. After skipping a few beats, his heart pounded. A trickle of air reached his lungs. Inhale, slowly. Exhale. Inhale. Exhale.

His peripheral vision cleared and he glimpsed something that shouldn't be there. His gaze trailed down. A five-inch piece of metal lay snagged in the overlapping plates of steel in his flak suit, the canvas covering torn.

All was not well with the plane either. Rusty's excited voice sounded in his earphones. "Flames are shooting out of engine three. Feather it."

"Not possible." Cal sounded annoyed, either with the engine trouble, Rusty's demand, or both. "Prop's gone."

"Shut down engine two."

Steve's words chilled Rafe as much as the wind blowing through the perforated nose. Two engines lost?

"We have to turn back. We'll never keep up. Harold, call for a fighter escort."

"Yeah, or we'll be a sitting duck." Mickey rushed his words. "I got the fuel pumped from number three to four and number two to one. The fire's out on three but, Rusty, watch if it starts up again."

"Rafe, what's the heading for base?" Steve grew angry. "Martell!"

Rafe tried to rise, but the chunk of shrapnel had to weigh at least fifty pounds.

Alan turned around. "Man, Rafe, what happened?" He tugged out the shrapnel with little effort, and pulled Rafe to a sitting position. "Are you all right?"

"Y, yeah... Must be... like getting kicked... by a horse."

"What's going on down there?" Patience wasn't one of Steve's virtues today.

"Our room with a view became a room to avoid. We've got hurricane winds blowing in all the holes, and Rafe took some flak in the chest." Alan pulled Rafe's log in front of him. "Do you know where we are?"

Breathing came easier in an upright position. Rafe checked the time and his last position fix. Only four minutes had passed. Amazing. Felt more like four hours. "Heading two—eight—one, for now."

Speaking was an effort, like he'd just run a mile.

He turned to his Gee Box to get a fix on their position when Harold made a strange announcement.

"That fighter off our right wing wants to know if we're happy."

"What channel's he on? Ask him to confirm our position." Steve still sounded irritated.

Steve didn't trust Rafe's navigating. So it took him a minute longer this time to get off the floor and calculate their position before giving a direction. That was hardly cause to lose faith in him.

They were on the far end of the Gee Box's reach, but it provided a solid fix. He pinpointed their location and figured a precise compass heading. "Navigator to pilot. Make our QDM two−seven−nine."

Harold chimed in. "The fighter agrees. Are we happy?"

"We're happy. Thank him, will you?" Cal answered, not Steve.

The fighter left when they were unlikely to encounter any more enemy planes, and they were on their own. With no lead plane to follow, Rafe had sole responsibility for getting them back to base. He spent the flight over the North Sea taking continuous Gee fixes.

By the time *Sweet Patootie* powered down on its hardstand, a nap sounded good. He watched Alan stand and stretch.

"Boy, it's been a long day, and it's not even noon." He paused when he noticed Rafe hadn't budged from his desk. "How ya doing?"

"Sore. Stiff. Tired."

"I'll tell the crew chief to bring a ladder so you don't have to swing down." Alan dropped to his knees and disappeared through the nose hatch. He directed the set-up of the ladder before Rafe managed to crawl the few feet to the hatch.

The gunners gathered around the ladder as he descended. Hands reached up to guide him. Their voices overlapped like buzzing mosquitoes as they queried his health.

Dan's assertion snagged his attention. "We should flag down a meat wagon."

"You go ahead. I'm not hungry." Just get the interrogation over and done with so he could hit the sack.

"Dan's talking about an ambulance, Rafe." Alan tried not to smile, and failed.

Carlo stuck two fingers in his mouth and emitted a whistle that made them all cringe.

"I don't need an ambulance." Rafe's protest went unheeded, and a passing ambulance was waved to a stop.

The pilots completed their post-flight procedures and dropped down through the nose hatch. Steve charged into their midst. "Martell, when I ask for a heading, I expect a prompt response. If you can't handle emergency situations, maybe you shouldn't be flying."

Silence reigned. Steve's face glowed red with anger. They'd lost the inboard engines over two hours ago. The plane had never been in dire straits once the fire was extinguished and they'd turned back. The emergency had passed. Rafe stared at him. Losing one minute in response time with their general direction didn't warrant this censure.

Alan apparently didn't think so either. "Chief? You mind taking a look at the nose? See all those holes? A lot of lead was flying around in the air today and each of those holes represents a chunk that flew into our compartment." He grabbed Rafe's briefcase and fished out the shrapnel. "When I pulled Rafe up off the floor, he was blue and this was wedged in his flak suit. But before he was even breathing easy again, he had our position."

Amid the gunners' expressions of awe at the size of Rafe's shrapnel, a medic pushed into the circle. "Where were you hit, sir?"

"I'm all right." Rafe raised a hand to his chest, and winced.

"Uh-huh." The medic opened the ambulance's rear door. "Would you sit right here, sir." He didn't ask. He ordered, and started unbuttoning Rafe's shirt.

Rafe loathed stripping down out in the open. "No, really. I'm fine. The vest stopped the metal. I'm just bruised."

"Sure you are. Right over your heart. Humor me." The medic stuck his hand in the neckline of Rafe's long underwear and pulled it down, exposing widespread vivid purple bruising that stopped Rafe's protest in his throat.

The gunners' excited chatter started up again.

Harold's eyes grew to saucer-size. "That would have killed you for sure if you hadn't been wearing the armor."

"Say, you could pose for advertisement photos." Herb saw dollar signs.

Rusty snorted. "Flak suit companies don't advertise."

"Yeah," Mickey chimed in, "no one's gonna come in off the street and buy a thirty-pound flak suit."

"Gangsters might." Dan sidled up to Rafe. "Maybe you'll get a Purple Heart."

"No, thanks. That one I don't want."

"Severe contusions like this call for a visit to the doc to ensure you have no fractures or internal bleeding." The medic prodded him to crawl into the ambulance.

If that meant getting out of this circus, fine. Rafe glimpsed Steve's face, and clamped his jaw before he laughed at the pilot's dumbfounded expression. Maybe he wouldn't hear any more about being unfit for flight.

As soon as he was ensconced in the base hospital, Major Blount poked and prodded, seeming determined to add further injury. Rafe held his breath and breathed deeply in turn.

"Lean back against the cushion and I'll let you rest with an ice pack." The doctor chuckled at Rafe's sigh of relief. "At least until the group returns from the mission, you're my only patient, so you get lots of undivided attention, Martell. Rest now. We'll check your vitals again in a few hours. You should be back in your own hut by evening."

He must have dozed. When he opened his eyes, Steve sat on the neighboring cot, watching him. He stared back. They might not be buddies, but until today, he thought they had a good working relationship. Now he waited for Steve to say he'd asked for a different navigator.

Steve cleared his throat. "I'm sorry I snapped at you in front of the men."

Rafe's eyes popped wide open. What about his transfer? "So, it would have been okay if they hadn't been there?"

"No." Steve twisted his cap in his hands. "No, I'm sorry I snapped at you. That was uncalled for." He tossed his cap to the cot. "I know you enjoy playing with your Gee Box, but I do *not* expect you to know exactly where we are every minute."

Rafe grinned. The pilot referred to Alan's announcement during one of their first missions. *Rafe's playing with his toy so you'll know exactly where we are every minute along the way.* Even the post-mission interrogators expressed surprise at his numerous log notations.

Steve sighed. "Maybe I'm the one who can't handle the stress. Today could have been a lot worse."

"Yeah, that burning engine could have exploded and torn off the wing. But it didn't. You handled it."

Steve's left shoulder jerked up in a shrug as he opened his mouth and closed it. He wiped his hands on the knees of his pants.

"I guess I'm jealous of your way with the crew." The words came out in a rush.

He could have said the infirmary was on fire and not been any more surprising.

Steve continued. "Sometimes I think you should be plane commander instead of me. I don't think they like me, especially after berating you today."

"They think you're stiff."

That brought Steve's head up from studying the floor. "Stiff? They told you that?"

"Not me. They told Jennie, my, uh, a friend on the *Queen Mary*." Steve's brow quirked at his stumble. "And she told me. They also described Cal as always disappearing and Alan as so in love with his gem of a wife Ruby. So they latched onto me. Jennie said I'm like their big brother, which is a lot nicer than comparing me with a bear."

Steve blinked. "A bear?"

Rafe pushed away his leaking ice pack. "You heard Dan. I'm like the mother bear in the bear scouts."

Steve laughed in a most unstiff manner. "You mean den mother in the Cub Scouts. The den mother is their leader. Dan's right about that. They look up to you." He stood. "Don't get too comfortable here."

Rafe laced his fingers behind his head as Steve left, but complaints from sore chest muscles brought his arms back down. Coming to apologize took courage. Steve was worthy of a lot of respect for that.

Given the chance, would his father apologize for turning them out? Or did he not even regret his conduct? A fresh stab of pain didn't come from his chest wound. It came from his heart, aching for his father's love.

Chapter Eighteen

Stockholm, Sweden
Saturday, April 1, 1944

Phyllis watched Jennie stroke blue paint onto her canvas. "This is a nice little studio you've got set up in your living room. Good lighting. What sort of work did you do in the museum?"

"Primarily special exhibits. Keeping track of what was where, how they were presented. I arranged special tours, mostly with school groups. We considered that as our war work, maintaining morale on the home front. We'd emphasize the beauty in the world and what we were fighting to save. Rather lame, but…" Jennie stopped talking as she worked on a precise curve.

"We can't all be Rosie the Riveters."

"Did you read Nancy Drew mysteries? I started borrowing them from my cousin when I was eleven, and loved them. Nancy could do anything, solve any mystery that came up in her father's legal cases. I wished I was brave and bold like her." Jennie waved her brush around the apartment. "This hardly equates, but here I am, helping out in my dad's place of work while a terrible war rages all around. In a way, I'm sort of living out a fantasy."

She dipped the brush in white paint and blended it with blue. "Doing something like creating fake German newspapers or falsifying coded messages has more appeal than an assembly line job, no matter how important that work may be."

Phyllis picked up a stack of sketches and thumbed through them. "I wish I was more than a clerk, but at least I'm on the periphery of the cloak and dagger stuff. To tell you the truth, though, I have no idea what you may be called on to do. The Penetration Reports are as deep in as I get." She sighed. "You are so talented. I wish I could draw like you."

Jennie blew a strand of hair out of her eyes. "Didn't you tell me you can crochet? That's your talent. I turn yarn into a knotted mess.

"Ooh la la." Phyllis' eyes widened. She held up one sketch, dropping the others back on the table. "He is gorgeous. Who is he?"

"Oh, uh." Jennie swallowed hard. How had Rafe's portrait ended up in that group? "One of the servicemen who came over on the *Queen Mary*. I sketched a lot of them."

"I should have had the luck to come over on a troopship." Phyllis sighed again. A dreamy look settled in her eyes.

Jennie pursed her lips. She needed to divert Phyllis, fast. "I also learned how to crack a safe and open sealed envelopes undetected." She grinned. "Just in case you have need of those talents."

Phyllis set down Rafe's sketch. "Oh, good. If we get bored, we can go on a crime spree."

The afternoon flew by as Phyllis entertained her with tales of life in Stockholm. "I hope we can get to Blanche's Café next week. It's too bad Emma, my friend from the British Legation whom I often meet there, wasn't available this week. We'll point out some Germans. It seems so peculiar. We're at war with them, but here we all wander about as we please. Anyway, you have to hear Emma's story of how she got to Stockholm three years ago. It'll blow you away."

Jennie spent Monday morning familiarizing herself with the embassy's cryptography room and decoded a message to her supervisor's satisfaction. A man entered the room in time to hear, "Well done." He was impeccably dressed in a dark blue suit with a handkerchief positioned just so in his breast pocket. Dark hair flowed in waves back from his forehead. Humor danced in his eyes. Ed, the OSS bureau chief.

"Coming along, are you?" He pulled up a chair and handed her an illustrated guide to Stockholm. "Spend the afternoon acquainting yourself with the Old Town. Memorize your surroundings. Should you ever need to elude someone, you must have a route instantly in mind. Determine hiding places—shops if they're open, churches, whatever. Don't go into a dead end. You must be as familiar with your surroundings as you are with your neighborhood back home."

Her pencil rolled away from her suddenly nerveless fingers. She opened her mouth, closed it, and tried again. "How dangerous is this job? I thought neutral territory didn't carry the risk..."

"We may not be operating behind enemy lines, but the enemy is here among us. You've trained in psychological warfare, so we'll utilize you with black propaganda. Any time you can do something to undermine the morale and unity of the Germans, do it. The OSS has been recruiting creative types like artists such as yourself with the idea you'll come up with creative ways to embarrass the enemy."

He stood and looked down at her from his lofty height. "Just remember, the Germans will try to turn the tables on you. They'd love to compromise you, embarrass the legation, get the Swedes angry with us. That's why you need escape routes." He slid a file across the table. "Here are lists of establishments that are favorable to Germany or are known hangouts for the Germans. Also those that support the Allies. Watch for them as you familiarize yourself with Stockholm so you know who to avoid or who may offer help. Get started this afternoon."

If he meant to be intimidating by towering over her, he succeeded. What had she gotten herself into? All the cases studies she'd learned in training had indicated she'd help produce subversive cartoons or posters, or create forged documents. But to need an escape route? She rested her forehead on her hand. Then she shot to her feet. Time to set aside such thoughts and find Phyllis to go to lunch.

It being Monday, Phyllis' burlap sack lay draped over a chair in case she needed it. Meanwhile, she wore a skirt in a subtle pattern of navy, orange and gold. She twisted her hair into a snood when Jennie arrived, and from her purse she pulled a scarf in colors matching her skirt. A few deft folds and twists, and the scarf draped her shoulders.

"Wow. Cinderella is ready for the ball." At some point, Jennie would ask for pointers in the fine art of scarf tying.

Phyllis' merry laugh rang out. "Just because I need to discourage Stanley doesn't mean I want to scare away everyone else." She held up the ugly skirt. "I don't wear this outside. The consul periodically sends around memos reminding us we are guests in a foreign country. How we act or dress will determine how the Swedes perceive Americans. When you think about it, that's a daunting responsibility. I don't want anyone thinking badly of us because of my revulsion to Stanley."

Whenever she said the name, she placed exaggerated emphasis on the first syllable. There might be a radio show she was imitating, but it escaped Jennie now. "Maybe all you need to do is let him know you have a man in uniform and aren't available."

They stepped outside into a cloud of suffocating fumes. Cut off by the Allied blockade, the Swedes had no gasoline. Ugly, three-foot high generators strapped on the backs of their vehicles burned wood or coke briquettes, the resultant gas providing power that couldn't have gotten more than ten miles per hour. In front of the legation, a car idled while its owner emptied a sack of cubed wood into his device. Jennie and Phyllis covered their noses and hurried away.

Her eyes streaming tears, Jennie coughed. "Back home, we have sufficient gasoline, but not tires. I never gave much thought to how Sweden is affected by war despite not being a belligerent."

"Bullets may not fly here, but it's no utopia."

They walked at a fast pace to avoid overextending their lunch period, and burst breathless into Blanche's Café. A petite, auburn-haired woman waved.

"There's Emma. And there's the server. Good. Emma's already ordered for us."

Emma greeted Jennie warmly, but she was not a chatterbox like Phyllis. Jennie valued Phyllis' friendship, but two such talkative companions could be wearying.

Jennie grabbed her chance to enter the conversation when Phyllis raised her soup spoon to her mouth. "Emma, I understand you had quite an adventure getting to Sweden."

The English woman raised her eyebrows. "How long did it take for you to arrive from, Scotland was it?"

"Under five hours."

Emma nodded. "So you flew across Norway rather than straight over the Skagerrak between Norway and Denmark. Considering Stockholm is nine hundred miles from London, that's not bad. It took me six months to get here."

Jennie frowned. She must have misunderstood. "Months?"

Her new friend laughed. "I left England in December of 1940. Two routes were available at that time. One was by way of the United States and the Trans-Siberian Railway. The foreign office opted for the other way around South Africa, the Middle East, and Russia. I traveled by ship the first month."

She interrupted herself, her eyes glittering with laughter. "Are you with me so far? A second ship traveling with us was torpedoed, and all aboard were lost. From Cape Town, South Africa, I traveled by train, then flying boat, eventually reaching Cairo, where I had passport difficulties."

Leaning back, she interlocked her fingers and stretched them forward, laughing again. "There's no such thing as an easy journey. I even crossed a canal in a rowboat. Getting a Russian visa was so time-consuming, I worked at our legation in Istanbul for a while. By the time my visa arrived, the Germans had broken through to the Black Sea. I had to cross Turkey to the Caspian Sea and eventually got to Russia through a barbed wire fence. I shan't bore you with the horrendous conditions and filth and bug bites."

She waved a hand through the air as if brushing away the memories.

Jennie glanced at Phyllis. Her colleague watched Emma with rapt attention, even though she must have heard all this before.

"I did finally reach Moscow, flew to Finland, and then on to Stockholm. And then the Germans attacked Russia. I have no plans for leaving Sweden until after the war." Emma smiled and picked up her spoon.

Jennie closed her mouth and looked at Phyllis before turning back to Emma. She laid a hand on the table between them. "I am so sorry I ever complained about that cold, scary, five-hour flight."

Phyllis nearly spit out her bite of ham roll, saving her dignity by slapping a napkin over her mouth.

Emma's grin disappeared behind her tea cup. Then she leaned forward, her tea cup rattling into the saucer, and she touched Jennie's hand. "That man at your one, no, two o'clock position. With the jowls and the ill-fitted suit? He's a German and loves to eavesdrop."

Jennie turned and looked right into the man's eyes. He stared openly at her. Her first enemy contact. She continued sweeping her gaze around the room. No one else seemed to pay them attention.

Phyllis fluttered her hands in front of her red face. She finally got the ham bite swallowed. "He must think we're chatterboxes with secrets to divulge."

"Too bad we don't have a story prepared. Something like a big meeting that's going to take place at such and such an address that turns out to be the residence of a German official." Jennie scooped up the last of her cabbage and cranberry salad.

"Oooh, I don't have any German addresses memorized."

"No matter." Emma raised a finger to gain their server's attention. "Plenty of opportunities will come up." She smiled at the server. "We'll have the baked apples with almond filling for dessert, please."

Jennie leaned back in her chair. She pulled a small notepad from her purse and quickly sketched the man's face. With the server's departure, she continued in a quiet tone, "Do you know who that German is?"

Emma replied in an equally low voice. "Thought to be in finance, often spotted at Enskilda Bank, owned by the Wallenberg family. He apparently fancies himself skilled at subterfuge, but makes no effort to blend into his surroundings." She leaned over to stare at Jennie's sketch. "That's amazing. I wish I had your ability."

"We likely have his picture posted on the rogues' board in the break room." Phyllis turned to Emma. "It's like Most Wanted posters of all the bad guys. Some of them are goofs though. We once posted a photo of an innocent Swedish mailman."

Lunch concluded and the three prepared to go their separate ways. "That'll confuse any watchers." Emma slipped into her coat and pulled on blue gloves that matched her hat. "They won't know who to follow."

"Sure they will." Phyllis wore a flamboyant, feathered hat that matched her personality. "Jennie's the new face. They'll want to work up a dossier on her." She grinned at Jennie. "Enjoy your sightseeing."

Jennie hesitated before heading for the Old Town, located on its own island just south of the legation. Might someone be following her? Quite likely. Phyllis was right. The Germans probably watched everyone who deplaned at the airport, and put as much zeal into identifying newcomers as the Allies did with them. She paused at a shop window, studying the reflection of the street and checking her periphery vision. Too bad she didn't have a colleague from Morale Operations to explore with. Somehow, she didn't seem as prepared as she'd thought to work in a neutral country.

Nancy Drew wouldn't quail from this opportunity to do some sleuthing. Jennie squared her shoulders. Neither would she. Pulling out her city guide, she got her bearings, and marched down the street.

Chapter Nineteen

Ridgewell Air Base, England
Saturday, April 8, 1944

Back to Germany today. Over a week of bad weather had kept the planes on the ground. Rafe shifted at his desk in the nose, waiting for takeoff. Only the mildest discomfort remained from the bruising he'd suffered.

A flash of color drew his attention to Alan. The bombardier nestled an orange in a towel and tucked it atop his control panel.

"An orange?" Rafe arched his brows. The fresh fruit would likely burst out of its skin when it froze at altitude. "Are you seriously considering peeling that with mitts on when the temperature is forty below zero?"

Alan looked up with a sheepish expression. "What can I say? Harold's jabbering about oranges made me crave 'em, and when I saw this in the mess, I couldn't resist." He hesitated at Rafe's frown. "Oh, that's right. You weren't at interrogation last week. Harold reported the conversation between that fighter pilot who helped us and his base. Something like, 'Orange Peel calling Orange Grove, requesting Orange Juice.' If the Germans monitored that call, they'd be none the wiser." He patted his orange. "I know it'll freeze, but it'll be like sucking orange ice like Ruby makes."

A westerly wind carried the bomber formation quickly across the North Sea. The planes' contrails formed vapors as deadly as natural clouds. Each succeeding squadron had to climb higher to rise above the contrail clouds. Rafe struggled to pinpoint their position. They were on the bomb run, their eyes glued to the lead plane, watching for its bombs to fall, when Carlo shouted a warning.

"Bombers at four o'clock level."

Rafe jumped up to the window. Another formation was flying right through their group. Two bombers collided nearby, exploding and falling to earth in large pieces.

Dee Marie strained to jump higher as Steve reacted. "Close those bomb doors. They're dragging us."

Alan slapped the switch and lunged for his rolling orange. It fell to the floor and shattered like glass into a hundred pieces.

The formation broke up as well. They were on their own, somewhere over western Germany. Only the drone of the engines told Rafe the aircraft remained intact and functioning in the sudden eeriness.

"We're the only plane in the sky when there should be hundreds around us. Where'd everybody go?" Carlo likely had his face plastered to his window.

Steve responded. "They're all below us in that cloudy murk. We'll stay at thirty thousand feet until we're sure we won't let down on top of someone. Keep your eyes peeled."

Steve's word choice prompted Rafe to look down at the legs of his flight suit. They sparkled with bits of frozen orange. He'd have a sticky mess when they melted.

He turned back to his desk and started calculating. "Navigator to pilot. What do you want to do? Head for the rally point in hopes of finding our formation? Or head back to England?"

"I think we'd better head for home. Our squadron was in the Tail-End Charlie position. By the time we get to the rally point, everyone will already be gone."

"All right then, new heading, two-six-four. We'll overfly the corner of Holland to the North Sea." Using a rule, Rafe traced their new route on his map. "After our wind sprints coming in, we're facing a marathon to get back with a headwind. Better start letting down as soon as possible or we'll need to stop at a filling station."

"Roger that. No stops for gas."

Alan swiveled and quirked a brow at him. Rafe shrugged. He hadn't expected Steve to respond to his joke.

"We still have our bombs." Harold's voice sounded like he asked a question.

"Should we salvo the bombs? Or should I stick the cotter pins back in?" As the flight engineer in possession of the only tools aboard the aircraft, Mickey often assisted Alan with the bombs.

"We'll hang on to them for now." Steve paused. "Rafe, watch for an alternate target. I don't care to drop indiscriminately, even if we are over Germany."

Cal started calling the routine oxygen check. Alan, Rafe, and Harold responded. Then there was silence. "Rusty? Come in, Rusty."

"Carlo, George, open up the ball." They'd probably already started for Rusty's turret, but Steve wasn't taking chances.

"His oxygen hose is disconnected," Carlo announced. "He's passed out."

"Rusty, wake up. Hey, Rusty." George was likely slapping his face, something he wouldn't dare try at any other time. "He's coming around."

"What are ya doing? What's going on?"

Rafe smiled. Nothing wrong with their pugnacious ball turret gunner.

They were down to ten thousand feet and off oxygen when the North Sea came into view. Not once had they glimpsed another bomber. With any chance of flak behind them, and no enemy fighters around, Rafe eased out of his flak suit and stretched. Shedding the weight was a relief. He turned to his Gee Box for a position fix. He had a ready answer when Harold called him.

"Radio to navigator. Do you have our exact position? Another Fort's going down and calling for Air Sea Rescue. They're at latitude 52.295042, longitude 3.581543."

"That's thirty to forty miles due west."

Steve put *Dee Marie* into a banking turn. "Might as well see how they're doing."

Again Alan twisted around and raised his brows. Rafe grinned. Maybe Steve thought the boys would enjoy a little side trip. He might never be buddy-buddy with the crew, but he seemed to be trying to ease up and earn their loyalty.

Using binoculars, Alan searched for signs of life rafts. "They're in for a rough ride. The wind doesn't look as strong down here as it was at twenty-five thousand feet, but those are still some mean waves."

"Air Sea Rescue thinks they'll get to them in thirty minutes. They ask if we have a visual."

"Not yet, Harold. Hold it. Yes, there's a raft. They released the dye marker. The plane's sunk. There's the second raft. Steve, come left a tad."

"They got company coming."

Rafe flinched at Rusty's yell. He took the binoculars from Alan and scanned the sea. "It's a *Schnellboot*, like our PT boats. It'll get to our men before Air Sea Rescue."

"Can we strafe 'em?" Rusty clearly wanted blood. His brush with anoxia hadn't affected him.

"Looks to me like the best chance I'll have to aim for a pickle barrel." Alan glanced back with a wolfish grin. "And we've still got our pickles. Steve, take us down to two hundred feet and give me control. I want to do a little target practice." He flipped a switch and the bomb bay doors rumbled open.

Dee Marie sank lower. Steve offered caution. "Remember, they've got guns too. I'd hate to be shot down by a little boat. Everyone be ready with your guns."

With a hand poised on the bomb release, Alan guided the plane on his improvised bomb run. "They're not sure what to make of us. They've slowed down and want to zigzag, but that will make it hard for their gunners to aim at us. One of them's trying to shoot. Here we go."

Twelve general purpose bombs fell away.

"Bull's eye," Rusty shouted. "But they didn't explode."

"No, they punched right through that boat though. At least three of 'em." In the tail, Dan now had the best view. "It's sinking fast."

"The bombs didn't have time to arm. We're too low for that. But five hundred pounders still pack a wallop when they fall on you." Alan sat back and laced his fingers behind his head.

Steve circled around to check on the downed airmen. They were cheering wildly. One man, trying to jump up and down in a rubber raft, toppled into the sea.

Rafe shook his head and searched for the Germans swimming amid their wreckage. He saw at least a dozen, and some likely hadn't survived the bombing. *S-boote* had large crews. As Steve continued to circle, he saw their faces look up.

Rusty proved unwilling to leave them alone. "I can get those two fellows crawling on that big piece."

"No!" The objection burst out of Rafe. "No strafing. The war's over for them. Air Sea Rescue will pick them up and they'll be prisoners. Leave them alone."

Why did he feel so strongly about those men? Germany started this war and all its horror. But many Kriegsmarine sailors came up through the Naval Hitler Youth. Maybe he knew someone down there. With a different heritage, he might have been serving aboard a vessel like that.

"The faces of war," Dan mused. "Now we've seen the enemy up close."

"Here comes Air Sea Rescue," George announced. "They'll be kind of crowded once they get everyone onboard."

They watched the launch pause by the first raft.

"They're coming in with air sea rescue and a prayer." Dan sang to the tune of "Coming in on a Wing and a Prayer."

"They didn't need a prayer. They had us." Count on Mickey for a tart comment.

"Sure they did. They prayed for deliverance and got it through us. We're an answer to prayer."

"Time to head for home before we run out of gas and join them. What's our heading, Rafe?" Steve swung *Dee Marie* toward England.

"Two-eight-three." Rafe responded, without need of a Gee fix.

The vibration of the engines rattled his soul. The faces of war, Dan had said. The *enemy* faces of the war. Had he known anyone on that S-boat? Would he ever know? He slumped in his seat. Weariness like a leaden flak suit weighed him down, and not because they'd been roused at four that morning.

Alan stared down at the sea. "How many planes litter the sea floor?"

"With how many men still in them?" Cal added.

Not a pleasant thought. Rafe rested his head on his arms and closed his eyes.

Dan's voice didn't let him doze. "If we're going to die in combat, I'd rather it happens fast, in an exploding plane. That's the way to go. No mangled bodies or food for fish or worms. Or on fire all the way down. We'd fly right up to heaven."

Mickey scorned such sentiment. "How do you know there's a heaven? Hell would be better. I bet it has more interesting people. No goody two-shoes, for one thing."

"You're nuts."

Rafe opened one eye to see Alan bolt upright. If the bombsight hadn't been in his way, he might have launched himself right out the window. "Even if all your friends and *interesting people* are there, you won't enjoy being with them. Hell is a place of torment to be avoided. Basic Sunday school stuff."

"Well, I ain't interested in sitting on a cloud and strumming no harp all day."

Rafe pushed his headphones down around his neck to avoid the full volume of Mickey's antagonism. Too bad he couldn't push away his thoughts as easily; they raced along another celestial avenue of musing, dragging him along for the ride.

How many German warriors entered heaven these days? Did they believe in God, or Hitler?

Someone in Milwaukee, or maybe Paul Braedel, had commented about Abe Lincoln saying during the Civil War that each side prays to the same God. The same held true for this war. Both Germans and the Allied nations prayed for safety and victory.

If only he could be sure his friends were safe.

Chapter Twenty

Stockholm, Sweden
Saturday, April 8, 1944

Jennie wandered from room to room of the National Museum to familiarize herself with the layout. Occasionally, she stopped to study an exhibit. Alternate display possibilities came to mind. That painting should be set apart with better lighting. This grouping looked too cluttered.

She paused by the display of Carl Larsson's watercolor paintings. *Her Royal Highness, Big Sister* brought a smile to her face. A young scamp saluted his sister. Good thing she had an older brother rather than a pesty younger one. Tom, though, probably considered her a pesty little sister. She moved on.

The painting titled *Grandfather* was perplexing. She stepped back to study it. Nearby was *Woman Reading*. Her gaze swung back and forth between the two. Both subjects were at the edge of the paintings. The setting worked for *Woman Reading* but *Grandfather* was nearly lost in his portrayal. How curious.

She was gazing at *Letter Writing*, once more off center but delightfully so, when a man also stopped. She moved on. So did he. This wasn't good. She turned down a passageway that looped back to the Larsson grouping. If he was here to look at the art, he wouldn't backtrack as she did. But he did. He was following her. She stopped at a display case. He paused, and then joined her. Her fingertips tingled.

"This is exquisite, is it not? The artistry is exceptional for the eighteenth century. The best Sweden offers." His Swedish sounded too formal. He had a trace of an accent. German? Had Rafe sounded like that? "By the way, my name is Lars."

If the Germans monitored every British plane that landed in Stockholm, they would have noted her arrival. Watchers would have seen her coming and going from the legation. Phyllis was right. They were compiling a dossier on her. This man must think she was so stupid she'd fall for his charm and spill all her secrets. Except his charm was akin to scratching fingernails on a blackboard.

Don't make eye contact with a predator. Excellent advice, but knowing who she was dealing with took precedence. Jennie risked a quick glance. A shock wave reverberated all the way down to her toes. The man wasn't looking at the display. He stared at her with a calculating gleam like a dog licking its chops over a T-bone steak unattended on the grill. Her gaze dropped immediately back to the case as she inched away.

Jennie pointed at the placard on the case and pitched her voice higher than normal. "Actually, these are Italian artifacts from the seventeenth century, acquired by Gustav III during his travels."

She tapped her fingernails on the glass twice. With a brisk "Good day," she turned and strode toward the exit.

Did he still follow her? She couldn't look back. He might interpret that as coy interest. She burst through the door into the cold, still winter air. Breathing deeply, she paused at the foot of the stairs, setting her reticule on the balustrade to button her coat. Through the veil of her hair, she watched a man exit. Same wide-brimmed fedora, same wingtips with a serious scuff on the left toe, same oversized coat that gaped open.

Her heartbeat quickened as she snatched up her reticule, leaving two buttons undone. She couldn't return to the legation with him on her tail. The Grand Hotel was practically next door, but she hadn't scouted it for exits.

She turned the other way and started walking. Across the inevitable bridge was Skeppsholmen. That island lacked the urbanization of the rest of Stockholm. Was that good or bad? Were there trails to hike? Wait a minute. Hike? Dressed like this? She ran a hand over the plaid skirt she'd purchased in Leuchars. She'd have to stroll, and be overtaken by Lars.

Before crossing the bridge, she glanced down the side street that curved around this little peninsula. And then it curved around the Nybroviken inlet and she'd be at the legation. No, head for the island.

She was nearly across when footsteps gained on her. *God in Heaven, hear my prayer. Keep me in thy loving care.*

He drew abreast. "We meet again."

"Hardly surprising since you're following me." She quickened her pace and looked everywhere except at him. Where could she lose him? The small island contained several military buildings and little else. Coming this way had been a mistake. Stupid, stupid, stupid of her.

"How do you know so much about the Italian artifacts?" The guy stuck like glue.

He must also be a moron. "I read the placards describing the displays, as anyone who wanted to know more about them would do."

"You're not Swedish, are you?"

What gave her away? Her accent? "Are you?"

He hmphed. She fought a smile. Score one for her. She could keep secrets.

"What did you like best at the art museum?"

Little information of value could be obtained from such a question, unless he wanted to put her at ease. Jennie mustn't tell him of her art background. That would score one for him. She cast him a sidelong glance. A wicked scar cut across his left cheek. What had someone said just last week in the legation about upper class Germans and their pride in dueling scars?

If this were one, it meant he didn't mind danger and pain, a bad combination.

"Actually, I prefer Chinese Ming vases, Peruvian Inca gold jewelry, and Russian Fabergé eggs and nesting dolls."

That shut him up for the moment. And hallelujah, deliverance came into sight. A tram trundled toward them. She raised her hand out of Lars' view and lifted one finger. The tram operator shifted his gaze from her to the man beside her and back, and slowed. She jumped aboard. Collapsing on a bench seat, she dug in her reticule for the fare with shaky fingers.

The tram brought her to the canal across from the legation. It had never looked so good. She quick-stepped to the front door, rushed down the hallway, and burst into Phyllis' office.

"Goodness, girl. I thought you planned on sightseeing."

Jennie pulled a chair up to the desk. "Don't mind me while I finish this sketch I started on the tram."

She shoved aside Phyllis' pencil holder and continued her drawing with quick strokes.

Phyllis leaned over and watched. "Emma's right. I can't believe how good you are. Who is he?"

"I don't know. He said his name is Lars. I don't think he's Swedish. He tried to engage me in conversation at the art museum, and then he followed me and started asking questions." She picked up her drawing and studied it before turning it to Phyllis. "Have you ever seen him? He's maybe a shade under six feet tall."

"I can't believe you whipped this out so fast and it's so good. I'd recognize him if I saw him on the street." Phyllis held the sketch out at arm's length, then closer up. "I am so jealous. I can't draw a straight line and you draw portraits."

Jennie blew a lock of hair from her face before raking it back with her hand. "So you haven't seen him?"

"Can't say that I have." Phyllis dropped the sketch on the desk, still staring at it. "His eyes look devious. He looks like he could be a spy in *Casablanca*."

"I doubt he's a spy. Too sloppy. Maybe another desk worker who wants to be."

Phyllis adjusted her cardigan, once more the dedicated office worker, and picked up a pen. "He claimed his name was Lars? And he's about six feet? How was he dressed?" With the notations jotted down, she rose. "I'll post this in the break room where we have our rogues' board. Maybe someone else will recognize him." She sailed out of the office with Jennie in her wake. "Don't forget to be here no later than two o'clock tomorrow so we can go to the ladies' tea." Her smile slipped. "Or did you want to meet me there?"

Jennie rushed to reassure her. "I'll come here first. I'd rather go in with someone I know. The Grand Hotel looks a bit intimidating, although I'm eager to see inside."

"We'll have a grand time at the Grand. You wait and see." Phyllis waved good-bye as they parted.

Before exiting the building, Jennie peered out for signs of Lars. If he suspected she was American, he might be lurking about. Cautiously slipping outside, she nearly stumbled out of her shoes at the voice behind her.

"You'll attract more attention acting furtive like that."

She whirled to face Ed. "I'd rather not meet up with the man who followed me earlier."

A frown puckered his forehead. He pushed back his sleeve to check his watch. "Do you have time to stop in here and have a cup of coffee?" He propelled her into an adjacent building to a lunch counter. They perched on stools at the far end of the counter and a waitress set coffee before them, nodded at her companion and returned to her other customers. "Tell me about him."

Jennie wrapped her hands around the steaming cup and related everything she could remember about Lars. "Phyllis posted his sketch on the rogues' board."

Ed nodded. "So you think he might be trying to impress his superiors. You may be able to use him by passing misinformation. If he approaches you again, toy with him."

Too bad she hadn't taken any drama classes in school. She licked her lips as the steam curled up from her coffee. "How do you suggest I do that?"

"Ask questions of your own. Art is your forte. Ruffle his feathers by commenting on Germany's propensity of stealing occupied countries' treasures. Observe his reaction. Don't be afraid to play dumb. He may feel the need to enlighten you and reveal more than he should."

Jennie swallowed hard. She'd trained for behind the scenes activities. Not face to face engagements. Especially with creepy guys like Lars. Talking to him held as much appeal as a dentist visit.

"Be ready with misleading statements in case you meet him again. If he asks what you're doing here, meaning your purpose for being in Sweden, answer in the moment. For instance, you're at the museum to look at art."

Jennie's smile bloomed. She'd done that at the display case. Her smile faded at his next words.

"Suppose he's watching us right now. No," he held up a warning hand. "Don't look for him. He may ask who I am. You can't stop and think. What would you say?"

"A Swedish councilman I'm trying to influence."

Ed chuckled softly. "Always remember he's the adversary. We'll assume he's German. I'll admit I'm generalizing, but Sweden's Secret Policemen are not as engaging, although with a pretty girl, they may try." He rushed on, as though his backhanded compliment was a faux pas. "Have you heard about the experience of the British naval attaché?"

Jennie returned home with her head spinning. She entered the apartment and looked around. Muslin sheets served as curtains, creating diffuse light. They would filter the glaring sun of Sweden's endless summer days in a few months. Their living room featured a monochrome of beige, cream, and white, a counterpoint for the dark of winter.

A Swedish tall case clock graced the corner. Farmers in need of additional income during the winter months had begun crafting the curvy clocks in the mid-eighteenth century. Jennie needed to include one in a painting for her art exhibition.

The fireplace drew her now. She cautiously poked her head in to examine the uptake. According to Ed, each flat's chimney had an individual uptake leading to the attic, with an access panel for cleaning. The attic contained storage lockers for the occupants. In the case of the British naval attaché, the Swedish Secret Police had entered his locker, opened the panel in the duct, and lowered a microphone down the chimney. Months

180

passed before the British discovered it. Might they not do that with all foreign diplomatic staff?

"Gracious, Jennie, whatever are you doing in the fireplace?"

Jennie jumped up and caught herself as her hair brushed the rim. "Mom! Don't sneak up on a body in such a precarious situation."

She backed away from the fireplace and brushed at her hair.

"Well, what was I to think? My daughter comes home and sticks her head in the fireplace. Not an everyday occurrence, if you ask me. Were you checking to see if we require the services of a chimney sweep?"

"My boss told me about the British attaché's experience with the eavesdropping police. I wondered if they might try to bug us."

Mom waved away the suggestion. "Highly unlikely. Captain Denham is prominent in Britain's efforts to learn secrets. Your father is not. His concern is seeing to the welfare of the interned American fliers. The Swedes would be bored to tears if they spied or eavesdropped on us."

Mom's heels tapped across the pine flooring. She settled herself on the settee centered between the two windows overlooking the street and clasped her hands together. "I'm afraid I have bad news. I had hoped we could travel to Norrkoping to visit my cousin Sigrid. I finally heard from her. She says we are not welcome."

Chapter Twenty-One

Ridgewell Air Base, England
Same Day

They were the last Fort to return to Ridgewell. Word of their North Sea adventure spread quickly. The interrogator hadn't been interested in their experience near the target in Oldenburg as much as he was in the part they played in preventing the capture of the downed crew and sinking the S-boat. Why those events warranted so much attention, they weren't told. Even Dan was subdued as they left the interrogation hall. Had they violated some rule by using their Flying Fortress against the German boat?

After seven hours aloft, they hurried to the combat mess hall. Hopefully the other crews hadn't eaten everything. The server spooned the last of the sausage-and-potato casserole onto their plates. The canned peas and corn were gone, but plenty of fresh Brussels sprouts remained. Dessert was a thin white cake with maple fudge frosting.

Rafe glared at his Brussels sprouts. They seemed to be the only fresh vegetable available in England. He shoved a sprout in his mouth, held his breath during a perfunctory chew, and gulped the thing down.

The bright afternoon sun illuminated the countryside and lured him off base. He bicycled around the fields surrounding Ridgewell until he spotted a lone oak tree near the lane. Under its shade, he propped his bike and sat gazing at nothing in particular. Dan's phrase kept echoing. The faces of war. The faces of war.

The upturned faces of the German sailors continued to stare at him. What went through their minds as they watched the huge bomber come their way, bomb doors open, a dozen bombs tumbling down toward them? And why should the image disturb him? What the sailors experienced lasted no more than a minute. The bomber crews, on the other hand, experienced far worse from the German anti-aircraft gunners who hurled their canisters of flak at them for hours.

Nagging thoughts circled like sheepdogs nipping at the heels of a flock. Somehow, the Germans being sailors made today's incident worse than dropping bombs on an airfield. What had become of his friends? Bertil, Johan, and Ludwig? What about Christoph, the best cousin a boy could hope for? Did any of them still live? If only he could find out. With his elbows on his knees, he dropped his head into his hands and raked his fingers through his hair. He had no way of gaining answers to his questions.

At length, he pulled a sheaf of paper from his pocket and located his pen. *Dear Mother.* His letter stalled. What could he tell her? Having a lovely time, wish you were here? With a groan he dropped his pen to the ground and let his head drop back against the tree. A bird soared high overhead. The sun, in its western decline, shone in his face. He closed his eyes. The breeze whispered in the branches. Nearby, a bird called and, further away, another answered.

He awoke with a start. Someone was with him. He opened his eyes. The kitten girl sat cross-legged in front of him. Brenda, her name was. Brenda Jane Prescott. She looked like an urchin with oily, mousy brown hair that might be pretty if it were washed. Her oft-mended dress could use a washing too. Ragged fingernails boasted crescents of dirt. Despite the cool spring day, her feet were bare.

She regarded him through serious eyes. "Don't you got a bed to sleep in?"

Rafe straightened and shook away the vestiges of drowsiness. "'Course I do." His voice croaked. He swallowed and tried again. "I wanted to get away from the base for a while."

"Because it's crowded and noisy?"

A smile jerked at the corner of his mouth. "Something like that." He nodded toward the paper in his lap. "And I wanted to write to my mother."

Brenda leaned forward and peered at the paper. "You don't have much to say to her."

"I have a lot on my mind."

"And you don't want to put it on her mind?"

His hands smoothing the pages stilled, and he sharpened his focus on the young girl. He could tell Mother about his dilemma. How they strafed a boat, and how he wondered about Chris, John, Ludie, and Bert. She would understand his deeper meaning hidden from any censor.

"She opens her mouth and speaks wisdom."

Brenda perked up, her eyes brightening. "Who, me?"

"Yes, you. My mother would want me to share my concerns. I don't need to hide my worries from her."

She watched him for a long moment before looking again at his papers. "You're only writing to your mother. What about your dad? Did he get killed in the war?"

"I don't know if he's alive or dead. I haven't heard from him in a very long time."

"My daddy got killed in the blitz."

"Oh, Brenda, I'm sorry. Where's your mother?"

"She has to stay in London 'cause she has a job for the war. Me and my brother Dickey had to come here because they don't have bombs here."

No wonder she wore such a forlorn air. "You miss her, don't you? I miss my mother."

Brenda cocked her head. "Are you a flying soldier?"

"Yes, I am."

"Are you going to be killed then?"

Rafe sucked in a quick breath. "I hope not."

Lips pursed, Brenda's head tilted over the other way. "Me and Dickey count the airplanes when they take off. And then we count them when they come back. They don't all come back."

"No, they don't all come back all the time."

A call drifted to them on the cooling air, "Bren-da."

"That's Mrs. Claridge. We live with her. I have to go. It's bath day." Reluctance slowed her effort to rise. She stepped back and raised a hand in what must be a wave. Turning, she shuffled four steps away. She looked back. "I'll see you again?"

Rafe offered a grim smile and a nod. In his profession, it was not wise to promise she would. He watched until she reached a hedge, turned and waved wildly, and disappeared.

An unfamiliar B-17 was parked near the control tower when he returned to base. This one lacked Ridgewell's large identifying L superimposed on a triangle high on the planes' tails. Other groups' planes landed here for fuel or mechanical or medical assistance that couldn't wait until they reached their own bases. No need to investigate.

A crowd gathered around the control tower, but that held no interest either, until a figure broke away and ran toward him.

"Lieutenant! Lieutenant!" It was one of the *Sweet Patootie's* ground crew mechanics.

"What's going on?"

"You'll never believe it, sir. Some general's here to see your crew. You gotta get over there." The sergeant was nearly bursting his buttons.

Rafe turned his bike toward the tower, and the sergeant trotted alongside, gasping out the news that couldn't wait. "That general was on the Fort that ditched and you fellas kept the Krauts from capturing."

Rafe whirled to face the sergeant, jerking the bicycle wheel and nearly falling. "There was a general in those rafts?"

"Yes, sir. And he's real glad not to be in Germany right now."

"I'll bet." The crowd opened up a pathway for him and he handed his bike to the sergeant. His colleagues smiled, some punching his arms, on his long, short walk to the front. There stood his crewmates, Steve looking shell-shocked, Dan's grin stretching from ear to ear. Rafe slipped into his place between Cal and Alan. This was unreal.

The general wasn't recognizable and no one mentioned his name. Only a one-star, but that didn't matter. The Germans would have been preening like peacocks to capture a general. What a propaganda coup for them to exploit.

The general described the trouble that led to their ditching. "We became aware of the German boat about the same time we heard the approach of your B-17. Coming from the south, we knew the boat had to be an enemy. Air Sea Rescue wasn't anywhere in sight. As much as we wanted to get out of those blasted rafts, transferring to a German vessel held no appeal. I had images of being taken to Berlin to pose for photos with Hermann Göring. Not a pleasant prospect."

He studied the crew standing at ease and shook his head. "We're used to Little Friends coming to the rescue, but today we had a big friend rescue us. Darndest thing I've seen in a very long time. A heavy bomber comes swooping in and drops a load of bombs on a boat roughly the same size. The crewmen dove off that boat like an old Keystone Kops silent comedy film. And a coquettish nymph swinging in a big D adorned the nose of the Fort overhead."

Rafe snuck a glance at Steve, and suppressed a smile at the color that rose in the pilot's face. He hadn't cared for the artwork on *Dee Marie* ever since Cal had pronounced the nymph cross-eyed.

"We don't have them with us, but you men will all be receiving Air Medals for your service today."

Cheers filled the air, from the gathered throng and from the Coolidge gunners.

The crowd was dispersing when Captain Hawkins, head of Ridgewell's photo lab, approached the general. "Sir, we have your photos ready, from both your strike camera and those with the British rescue team and the German crew."

Rafe's stomach clenched. "You have photos of the Germans, sir? May I see them?"

The German faces of war. That he might recognize anyone was highly unlikely, but still.

The whole crew followed Rafe into the hut where the photos were laid out. Clear and sharp, the Germans' expressions conveyed dismay, hostility, anger, resignation. One by one, Rafe discarded them. Until the second to last one. A wave of dizziness crashed over him. He struggled to catch his breath.

"Do you know their names, sir?"

"Not of all the crewmen. Only the officers." The general looked at the one that had captured Rafe's attention. "Ah, that's Cap-i-tan Lute-nant Beeker."

His attempt at a German accent was atrocious.

Rafe continued to examine the picture as he corrected the pronunciation, "*Kapitänleutnant Buecker.*"

Everyone stared at him, but the photo demanded his attention.

"Do you know him?" The general's voice was abrupt, incredulous.

Rafe nodded. His voice was barely above a whisper. "Yes, sir. Christoph, my cousin."

Chapter Twenty-Two

Stockholm, Sweden
Monday, April 10, 1944

The view of Strandvägen couldn't be better anywhere than from this spot across the Nybroviken inlet. Sunrise had been at four forty-eight and was now at the perfect height to give added dimension to the scene. A sigh escaped Jennie as she flipped to a clean page in her sketchbook. No bombs fell to destroy Sweden's capital. The stately buildings offered a sense of well-being in a world gone mad.

She selected a pencil to start a rough sketch. Setting up an easel with a canvas and her paints would have been her first choice, but not in the busy city. From her perch on the opposite bank, she used colored pencils for a rendering that would serve as a model for the real masterpiece. Borrowing Dad's camera to capture all the finer details was a stroke of brilliance. Color film would be perfect, but she was getting ahead of herself. Her pencils would document the colors for later reference.

The American Legation's home occupied the forefront on the left side, with the vanishing point on the right. She frowned. That ferry blocked her view. Of course, all the trees between the wharf and the buildings didn't help either. What she needed was an elevated viewpoint. That building behind her offered a choice prospect. *Excuse me, sir, could I borrow your window for the day?* Ha! Be grateful for what you have.

Now, what exactly was the shade of that roof? Something between muddy tan and reddish brown. Her pencil collection didn't offer that color. She grabbed her notebook and jotted down a description. This painting would be beautiful. The folks at Svithiod would be pleased to include it in a Swedish exhibit.

Once the sketch was complete, she picked up the camera and twirled the dials. The foreground came into focus. Another twirl and it blurred while the background sharpened. She'd shoot both options. Too bad the clouds rolled in. Oh, here comes the sun. Click.

"What are you photographing?"

The sudden demand nearly caused her to drop the camera. Swedish security police? Did they prohibit picture taking? No, she'd spotted someone photographing the royal palace just the other day. And that voice reminded her of, she pivoted slowly, Lars. His eyes devoured her.

"Scenery."

"What is so special about those buildings?" He spared them a glance. "They are just buildings."

She frowned. His accent pegged him as a foreigner and his behavior reeked of Gestapo, so he had no right to interrogate her. Still, he was quite capable of causing an embarrassing scene.

191

"Good architecture." She tucked the camera back into its case and snatched up her sketchpad. Time to leave.

He didn't take the hint. Instead, he reached for her sketchpad. "You are an artist."

She stuffed it into her tote bag along with her pencil case. *Take a deep breath and count to ten.* This guy was no art connoisseur. "It's a drawing."

His hand remained outstretched. "May I look at your drawings?"

Phrased like a polite question, but spoken like a demand. Easy for Ed to suggest turning the tables on him. Since he wasn't going to leave, she would. "Oh, look at the time. I'll be late for the Active Housekeeping meeting."

His sour expression suggested he'd puckered up with a lemon. Tsk. If he wanted to succeed in the spy business, he really needed to control his expressions. Still, he'd recognized the government title and hadn't objected to her statement. Maybe they really did have meetings. Mom had only mentioned that its objective, that of educating Swedes in using limited, rationed resources, was aimed at women. She'd guessed right that Lars wouldn't care to join her. She hurried away and refused to glance back.

Half an hour passed as she wandered about before doubling back to the legation. She burst in on Phyllis. "Any word on Lars' allegiance?"

Phyllis' head snapped up. "Jennie! Here, help me finish this and let's go for lunch." She shoved a file into Jennie's hands. "Lars must be a recent arrival. Sightings are reported, but last I heard, his specific task hasn't been identified."

"Yes, it has. His task is to bother me." Jennie described their latest encounter.

"Oh, that gives me an idea." Phyllis clapped her hands. "Let's see if Emma can join us for lunch at Regnbågen. Gestapo agents often go there. You can get a good look at the bad guys."

Phyllis' idea of an interesting lunch made Jennie's hands clammy as they entered the restaurant an hour later. Her gaze swept across the diners as they joined Emma at a corner table by the window. If these were Lars' pals, the girls should stay far away. Emma folded a newspaper in fourths and pointed to the movie reviews as a waitress brought bowls of soup.

"Why don't we plan on seeing *For Whom the Bell Tolls*? Fabulous story, that is. The righteous vanquish evil." She closed her eyes with a blissful sigh, missing the glare from the man at the next table. Her eyes popped up and she looked at Jennie. "Have you seen *Mrs. Miniver*?"

Jennie lowered her soup spoon. "That was beautiful." Discussing films couldn't be too bad. "Too bad *It Happened One Night* isn't showing here.

Claudette Colbert is my favorite actress. I believe I've seen all of her films."

"Clark Gable was her costar. Ooh la la." Phyllis sighed, her eyes dreamy before she straightened. "What's really too bad is the State Cinema Office hasn't approved *The Great Dictator*. Charlie Chaplin is hysterical."

Jenny smiled. "I saw it at home and laughed so hard. But it really isn't funny when you consider it's based on real events that aren't humorous at all."

Now the man glowered at her. These guys really did eavesdrop. And they were speaking quietly.

Her friends nodded.

Emma ran a finger around the rim of her tea cup. "How about *Casablanca*?"

Phyllis raised her coffee cup. "Here's looking at you, kid."

"Ah, Bogart and Bergman." Now Emma sighed with a smitten look. "The Swedes have every right to be proud of Ingrid. Not like Zarah Leander. *She* won't be welcome back home."

The Swedish actress working in Germany was said to be a favorite of Hitler's.

Emma held up the paper. "Look at this." Whispering behind the pages, she said, "Our listener is tasked with monitoring German activity, making sure everyone stays loyal. And the balding man over there? He's with the German Tourist Office. Who wants to tour Germany now? Any travel he arranges can't be legitimate."

Two more diners entered the room, a man and a woman. Jennie ducked to the side so Phyllis hid her from their view.

"Lars just came in," she hissed.

Her frantic whisper prompted Emma to open her paper and extend it to Jennie. She pointed to an article while her eyes sought the newcomers. "Ah, yes. His name isn't Lars. A report just came in on him from the Danish office. He's Werner Kratz, a recruiter who tries to entice Swedes into the *Waffen SS*."

Jennie held up the paper as though reading. Nothing good could happen if Lars—or Werner—whoever—spotted her. "So why is he after me? Surely he doesn't expect to get me to join the SS."

"No, but he could hope to learn something from you. Steal papers maybe. Or plant false information with you. Maybe embroil you in a scandal to embarrass the Americans. Who knows?" Emma pulled the paper from Jennie's grasp. "He sat with his back to us. You're safe for now."

Jennie dipped her bread in her spinach soup. Suddenly, lunch held no appeal. She wasn't cut out for this cloak and dagger stuff.

Phyllis took a quick look at the couple. "Who's the woman?"

"A Swedish secretary employed at the French Legation." A frown momentarily marred Emma's brow. "The French need to be warned they may have a security leak."

In the afternoon, Jennie strolled around Staden, the old town. It possessed an Old World charm unlike anything in the Chicago area. Her feet slowed as she matched locations to her map. The Royal Palace was easy, and the cathedral next door. The narrow cobblestone alleys, while quaint, hampered visibility of what was ahead.

A chilly breeze nearly snatched the map from her hands. It also brought a mouth-watering fragrance. Jennie took a deep breath. *Mmm.* A bakery must be nearby. Too bad she just had lunch.

Lunch at Regnbågen had been interesting. Emma certainly was daring. Phyllis had described her as a file clerk, but that was a euphemism for any intelligence job. Deliberately annoying Germans seemed a good way to land themselves on an enemy watch list. Ed better not expect her to initiate such encounters.

The church spire marking the highest point in Staden belonged to Tyska Kyrkan, the German church established over a century ago. It had been described as lavishly decorated, and she headed in its direction. German words adorned a mantle. *Fürchtet Gott! Ehret den König!* Something about God and the king.

The door was unlocked and she slipped inside. And smiled. Entering a quiet German church constituted the high mark of her own derring-do.

The vaulted ceiling soared high, creating an atmosphere of light and airiness. Colorful stained glass windows, gold filigree, and carved wood offered a visual feast. Reverent silence whispered peace. She eased into a pew and drank in the calm. *Let all mortal flesh keep silent.*

Someone sat beside her. Lars? Before she could jump up, a quiet voice murmured, "*Wie geht es Ihnen?*"

She gulped. German words in a German church. "Fine, um, *danke.*"

The clergyman had a gentle smile.

"You are English?" His accent resembled Lars', without grating.

"American." She jerked her eyes away and waved a hand. "I'd heard this church is beautiful. It's so peaceful."

He joined her in looking around. "Yes, touched by God, unlike most of the world."

Sadness shone in his eyes. His shoulders slumped as though burdened by a heavy weight.

"That saying above the gate, about God and the king, what does it say?"

"'Fear God. Honor the king.' Fortunately, those in the Fatherland are not aware of it, or they may insist on changing it a bit." His mouth smiled, but not his eyes. A sigh from the depths of his soul escaped him. "So much good has come from the church in Germany. The Gutenberg Bible, the Reformation." Organ music began softly, and he nodded toward it. "So much music."

The tune sounded familiar.

The reverend didn't hesitate. "'*O Haupt voll Blut und Wunden.*' How God's heart is wounded now."

"O Sacred Head, Now Wounded." Of course. Tears pricked her eyes. Jennie blurted, "I met a man on the ship crossing the Atlantic." She had his attention. "He's fighting for America now, but he used to be German. The Nazis found out he has some Jewish ancestry, and he and his family had to flee. Except his father. His father divorced his mother rather than protect his family. My friend is angry. At Germany, at his father."

She stopped to catch her breath. "I realize I've led a sheltered life, growing up in a single-culture neighborhood with classmates like me. I know the Negroes don't have the same opportunities, but it never touched me. I don't know any." She swallowed hard. "But Rafe is… he's wonderful. Why can't the Nazis see that? I'm glad he's American now, but why'd they run him off? Why did the Germans let that happen?"

The reverend glanced around. He kept his tone low. "Hitler seized power so quickly. At first, folks were enthusiastic because he brought great reforms. Employment, stable currency, no more of those foul reparations from the Great War. You have to understand the wretched conditions that existed in Germany. By the time people saw the danger, it was too late. He has the nation in a stranglehold." His chest rose and fell. "Those who know better are afraid to speak out. If they help the Jews or other unfortunates, they end up sharing their fate. Some try, but it is not healthy to be a dissident."

Someone entered the sanctuary, looking for the reverend. He patted Jennie's hand as he rose. "'Let him that thinks he stands take heed lest he fall.'"

That had to be a Bible verse, but what an odd choice. Was he warning her to be careful, or describing what happened in Germany?

If she lived in Germany, she wouldn't have spoken out. She would have been afraid. Maybe the reverend thought she felt superior to the Germans. No, spineless as she was, she identified with them. What about Rafe's father? How much of his choice had been prompted by fear? Just look at what his fear had cost him.

The music soared. It spoke of being caught up to heaven, sending a chill through Jennie. The beauty of the stained glass blurred as her eyes welled. A tear trickled down her cheek, followed by a twin. She murmured a prayer. "Father in heaven, keep Rafe safe in Thy loving care. And grant me courage. I don't want to disappoint those who love me."

Ed called her into his office as soon as she returned to the legation. "I have a job for you. A file needs to be delivered into the hands of a contact in Uppsala. You can do it."

In Uppsala? "Can't it be mailed?"

"It's too sensitive. We can't take the risk. And make sure no one knows what you're doing."

Jennie's breath whooshed out. "I'm not a field agent."

Ed waved a hand, cutting off her protest. "This is a simple courier job. Your mother can go with you. Since her family is from Uppsala, a trip to see the old town will be natural. Hand over the pouch to the contact, visit a few sites, and come back. It's an easy task that will get you out of the city for a change. You'll leave on Friday."

Jennie swallowed. Mom wouldn't go along with this. Would she?

Chapter Twenty-Three

"Today's target is," the major swept back the curtain, "Cologne."

Rafe's heart dropped down to the seat of his pants before bouncing up to lodge in his throat. *Cologne!* His family's apartment, the yacht club, the cathedral, all the places he'd known. Did they still exist? The Brits had staged their thousand-bomber raid on Cologne two years previously and were supposed to have destroyed nearly the entire city. Numerous missions had targeted the city since. What could be left to bomb now?

If he were paying attention, he'd know. His stomach churning, he focused his attention on the major. "The train marshalling yards are important to the Krauts because Cologne is strategically placed in the industrial Ruhr Valley, which follows the Rhine River, and also its proximity to the occupied countries."

The marshalling yards. His father's place of employment. Right next to the cathedral. Not far from their apartment.

He rose on shaky legs to head for the navigators meeting, and slumped into a back row seat. Classmates, neighbors, relatives. How many were still alive? How many had died? What about his father?

Nausea grew. Maybe he should beg off. He definitely did not feel well. But he was a navigator in the United States Army Air Force. He'd sworn his allegiance to America. Directing his crew to bomb his hometown was now his duty.

Aboard the *Pella Tulip*, he hunched over his desk, hands clenched, knuckles whitening.

"Hey, are you all right?"

He looked up into Alan's concerned face. "*Ja, es geht mir gut.*" Alan's brow furled. Oh, great. Now he was speaking German. "Yeah, I'm fine."

Alan picked up the briefcase that had fallen to the floor and pushed it against Rafe's arm. Rafe unclenched his hands to accept the case but didn't open it. Time enough later to pull out the maps and directions for bombing Cologne. He shuddered, tossed his garrison hat on the table, and raked a hand through his hair. Why couldn't their squadron have been on stand down today?

Their flight over the North Sea passed without incident. Belgium slid by beneath them and they crossed into the Third Reich. As they passed the Initial Point to start the bomb run, Rafe assumed his usual spot, standing behind Alan to watch for the target.

There, in the distance, it lay. He'd recognize the Cologne Cathedral anywhere. Amazingly, the Hohenzollern Bridge still spanned the river. But something was wrong. Why did the rest of the city look so, so blotchy? His eyes followed the Rhine. Chills that had nothing to do with being at twenty-five thousand feet swept through him.

Cologne was no more. The reports on the devastation of the British raid were accurate. Rafe grabbed his binoculars and zeroed in on the neighborhood near the cathedral. Skeletal remains stood amid stretches of nothing. Walls without roofs. Black windows that didn't reflect the sun because they had no glass.

He aimed at the cathedral and sucked in his breath. Holes speckled the cathedral's roof. The cathedral had been bombed. Roaring filled his ears that had nothing to do with the engines. The *Kölner Dom* was the pride of the city, of Germany.

Orders may have been given to avoid bombing the cathedral, but it had been hit. It still stood, but how bad was the damage? Had the beautiful stained glass windows been removed before the bombing started? The bells? Or had the Nazis melted them down? He'd had his first communion there. His mother had been so happy, his father so proud.

He staggered back and collapsed on his chair. His oxygen mask hampered his effort to breathe and he pulled it off.

Pella Tulip jumped as the bombs fell away. Alan turned away from his bombsight, his eyes crinkled in a smile that disappeared. He jumped up and put Rafe's oxygen mask back in place. "Rafe, are you all right?"

Alan's voice came from a distance. Other voices buzzed in his ear phones like annoying insects.

"What's going on down there?" Steve. Would he get mad again?

"I think he's in shock. His eyes are open but unresponsive."

"What'd you expect? Cologne's his hometown. His mom's in America, but his dad's down there." How did Cal remember that?

"We bombed his dad?" Dan's incredulity rang through the intercom.

"His dad worked for the railroad."

Blessed silence reigned. Everyone must understand the implication. They'd just dropped their bombs on that huge rail yard next to the cathedral.

"We bombed his dad." Dan's voice held quiet amazement.

But they didn't bomb his dad. No mistake about that. Father wouldn't risk his precious job to save his family, but he wouldn't sacrifice his life for that job either. He'd probably been the first one into the shelters. Anger straightened Rafe's spine.

Air. He needed air. He left the oxygen mask in place this time, but he needed to get out of here. How much longer until they landed? He pivoted to his desk, grabbed his maps, scanned the instruments, and tested the Gee Box for range. As his rapid breathing eased, he caught Alan's eye and pointed to the bombardier's drift meter. Alan's eyes brightened at their familiar sign language and he swiveled around to take a reading through his bombsight's superior optics.

Upon hearing Alan's drift reading through the intercom, Dan piped up. "Are you okay, lieutenant?"

Four lieutenants were in the crew, but everyone would know which lieutenant Dan questioned.

"Yeah." Rafe's mouth may as well be stuffed with cotton. He probably sounded like a frog, but no one remarked on it. The crew members exchanged light chatter while Rafe feverishly pinpointed their location and traced their homeward flight. If he kept busy enough, he wouldn't think of the devastation of Cologne. How did anyone survive down there, bombing after bombing?

By the time *Pella Tulip* was parked on its hardstand, Rafe had the forward escape hatch open, and jumped down. He was expected at interrogation, but he had no answers for their academic questions. He had to get out of here, away from any reminders of war and why they were here. Only the English fields, surrounded by the breeze and the sun, filled with birdsong and growing things, would do.

Steve dropped out of the plane and studied him. "Give me your briefcase. You don't need to go to debriefing."

Rafe didn't wait for a second opinion. He divested himself of his flight clothes, piling them into Dan's arms, and strode off before the waiting jeep took away the rest of the crew. He started jogging.

At his tree, he collapsed in the same spot he'd sat before. Leaning over on his propped-up knees, he grasped handfuls of grass, pulling it up by the roots. If only he could pull out his anger, which had boiled to the surface and would surely scorch anything or anyone he came in contact with. Anger at the British for their wholesale destruction of his city. Anger at the Americans, who did a lot of collateral damage in their vaunted precision bombings, even if they tried for military targets. Anger with his father for casting away his family like so many liabilities. Anger with the Nazis for starting this whole miserable war in the first place.

He ought to pray, but pray for what? The damage was done.

Tears stung his eyes. When he'd fallen down the stairs as a youngster, Father had whispered, "It's all right to cry. Tears release the pain." Was Father alive? He had to know. He might be mad at the man, but that didn't mean he wanted him buried in rubble.

Did Father ever think about him? About Mother and Rita and Albert? Did Father wonder what had become of them?

Time passed and a headache throbbed in his temple when arms came around him and a hand patted his back. Brenda, whose father had died in the blitz. What a pair they made. Two wounded souls. He reached up a hand and covered hers. Huddled together, no words were necessary.

The sun had slipped around to the western sky when a jeep ground to a halt on the nearby lane. Brenda moved away when two sets of footsteps approached.

Alan knelt beside him. "Come on, Rafe. Let's get you back to base."

With Cal on his other side, they pulled him to his feet.

"Bye, Rafe." Those were the only words Brenda spoke to him that day. He waved in her direction.

They took him to the mess hall and sat him down at a table. His gaze roved up to the Quonset hut's ceiling. A small parachute hung suspended like a giant white upside-down flower. He should send a picture of it to Opa Svenson. They could make nice decorations like that for the bulb business if it survived the war.

A mess steward brought a bowl of steaming soup. Rafe's mouth quirked. A bowl of chicken soup to cure whatever ails you. A plate containing a thick slice of crusty bread joined the bowl. He glanced up to give the steward a nod of acknowledgement. Determination to please gleamed in the man's eyes. Ridgewell's ground personnel did their best to pamper the combat crews. He picked up the spoon.

Fellow navigator Paul Braedel slipped into the seat across from him, and Cal and Alan disappeared. Paul didn't waste time with small talk.

"Our war is peculiar. All we're aware of is the damage inflicted on us by fighters and flak. We don't see any of the damage we do at ground level in Germany. Only what they've done to London."

Coming from someone else, Paul's words might be patronizing, but he could identify with Rafe's confliction. A good friend of his late wife lived in Germany, and Paul didn't know how she fared. With each other, they had the freedom to talk about their mixed emotions that the others might not understand. Paul had admitted he dreaded the day they might be called to bomb the friend's hometown.

Rafe lowered his spoon. "Cologne was a beautiful city. Buildings hundreds of years old. The cathedral has holes in its roof. Did you know it was started in the thirteenth century? Work stopped after a hundred years, but resumed just one hundred years ago, finally finishing in 1880, so it's practically brand new. And now it's been bombed."

Talking about the buildings was easier than thinking about the people and their fate.

The steward exchanged a dish of canned pears for the empty soup bowl and added a slice of white sheet cake with chocolate icing. After the man retreated, Rafe slid the dessert across the table and watched his friend consume it.

"Did you know the cathedral was built to be the repository of the bones of the Three Wise Men?" A grin jerked his lips when Paul choked on the cake, and he shrugged. "That's the legend. Of course, someone may have swindled the archbishop with three derelicts off the street."

Someone came up beside him and Paul's eyes widen as he prepared to stand up.

"As you were, gentlemen."

Rafe looked up into the face of the base commanding officer. Colonel Leber unclamped his pipe from his teeth and snagged a chair from the opposite table. He casually straddled the chair. Maybe he didn't plan on cashiering Rafe.

"Today wasn't quite how you envisioned your homecoming, was it, Martell?"

"No, sir. I knew it could happen, and at twenty-four thousand feet, it's hard to make out a lot of detail. But it's obviously not the same place I left in 1936." The colonel's mild expression prompted him to add, "A lot of familiar faces passed through my mind. The only one whose fate I know is my cousin."

"He's not too far from here. Are you interested in visiting him?"

Rafe gaped at him. "Is that possible?" To see Christoph again, to talk to him. Would they still be friends? "I'd like that. He probably knows if my father's still alive."

"We can make it happen. He's here in Essex County, at Camp Hill Hall." The colonel turned to Paul. "You speak German, Braedel, is that right?" At Paul's nod, he said, "You'll go with him. Watch his back."

Rafe swiveled around to watch the colonel leave. He turned back to a big smile on Paul's face.

"This ought to be interesting."

Rafe nodded slowly. "But I don't want Christoph knowing I was in the plane that bombed him."

Chapter Twenty-Four

"Mom, tell me about the relatives we're not going to visit." Jennie sat across from her mother in their compartment, both in a window seat as the train rolled north. "You corresponded with your cousin since childhood, but now you're not going to meet her. That's so wrong."

The mysterious pouch tucked into her valise issued a siren call for her to explore its contents. She clenched her fingers. What could possibly be so important to warrant this trip to hand-deliver it?

"My mother's family immigrated to Minnesota from Uppsala when she was nine, as you know. Her sister, my Aunt Frieda, married Claes Oleson, a visiting Swede, and returned with him in 1889. They settled in Norrkoping and never came back to visit. My cousin Sigrid and I were pen pals for years, but our letters were sporadic."

"And she has three children, Lily being nearest to my age." A second cousin Jennie had never met. They wouldn't have a chance to be close like she was with her first cousins in the States. Selma was two years older than she, but they'd always been close, giggling together at family gatherings and sharing dolls, later books, discussing clothes and boys, followed by debating whether they wanted careers. When Dad had informed her and Mom they would all be going to Sweden, she had anticipated a similar closeness with Lily.

"So why aren't we going to meet them?"

Mom stared out the window for nearly a minute before sighing. "Right after I arrived in Sweden, I wrote to Sigrid and suggested we get together, either in Stockholm or Norrkoping. She took a long time to respond, and then her note said only that her husband doesn't want us to associate with them. He's a member of the Swedish Nazi Party."

Jennie sucked in her breath. A Nazi in the family, like a skeleton in the closet. Despite the warmth in the train, she shivered. "Did Dad tell anyone in the military? We're still here, so it doesn't matter?"

"He informed the ranking air attaché and the legation head. Since Sigrid's husband is someone he's never met and whom we'll have no contact with, they felt we don't have a compromising situation. Sigrid ended her note saying she wished things could be different. Exactly what things she referred to is open to speculation, but I prefer to think she's not in favor of her husband's politics."

The train slowed and the conductor came down the aisle, stopping at each compartment and announcing "Uppsala." Jennie watched the city fill the window. A long building with silo-like corners caught her attention. A monastery? The train station blotted out her view and she reached for her valise.

"There's a guesthouse nearby." Mom pulled on her gloves and adjusted her hat. "Why don't we leave our bags there before you go off on your errand? I want to visit the cathedral. A museum in the tower contains treasures that your grandma still talks about. I want to see the display."

"The ball gown sewn with silver thread that weighs a ton? Yes, that's a must-see." Jenny maintained a tight grip on her case as they filed off the train.

They arrived at the cathedral at the same time as several other women. An elderly lady with a crown of snow white hair smiled at them. "Have you come to help out with the Ladies Alliance? We're sorting donations today for families who are suffering from the shortages caused by the war and whose men are away in the military."

Jennie hid a grin. Interesting way to greet sightseers. Put them to work. She didn't need to hear Mom's affirmative answer to know Mom appreciated the opportunity to mingle with local residents. This provided a chance to experience what her life might have been like if her family had never left Sweden.

She checked her watch. An hour remained before her rendezvous. Her nerves tap dancing over the coming meeting, she welcomed the chance to go inside.

She wasn't delaying the inevitable. Knowing exactly where Mom would be made sense.

Most of the ladies assembled in the meeting hall were Mom's age and older. Dad had told her that thousands of Swedish men had been conscripted, especially when the threat from Germany had been greatest. Just as in America, many Swedish women now worked outside the home. She fingered a paisley patterned skirt in one of the stacks piled on a table. Taking a deep breath, she said, "Mom, I'll be off now. I'll see you later."

Her voice quavered, and Mom looked at her sharply before her face relaxed in a smile. "Run along, dear. I know you're keen to do some sketching while the lighting is good."

Jennie swallowed a laugh. Dear Mom. She wasn't informed of the scope of Jennie's work with the OSS, but never hesitated to support her, even to the extent of offering excuses for her absence.

The park where she was to wait offered a splendid view of the monastery. Choosing the most advantageous bench, she pulled out her sketchpad and colored pencils and set to work. The scene took shape with quick bold strokes and subtle shading. Time slipped away. At length she held up her pad to judge the proportions.

"That's an excellent rendition."

Jennie shot to her feet, dropping her sketchpad to the ground. How could she have forgotten her reason for being there? She spun around. Behind her bench stood a short man. Check. He wore a fedora with a feather stuck in the band. Check. His tie sported red and black diagonal stripes. Not quite a check. Jennie had been coached to expect her contact's tie to be solid red. Maybe this was the best he could do.

"I'm terribly sorry. I didn't mean to startle you." His voice was much lower than she expected from a man of diminutive stature.

She waved away his apology. "I tend to get lost in my own world when I'm drawing." Now what? Did she invite him to sit? Push his packet across the bench so he'd unobtrusively pick it up? Ed's instructions at this point were sorely lacking. She scooped her pad off the ground and held it up. "Did I get the dimensions of the monastery right?"

The man's eyebrows shot up. "Monastery? That's Uppsala Castle, where kings were enthroned in years past."

Jennie dropped down on the bench. "Oh, I'm sorry. A castle? I assumed..." If she kept her mouth shut, she wouldn't reveal her ignorance. She peered up at him through her lashes, and spotted the man behind him. A short man, wearing a feathered fedora and a solid red tie, waved both hands at her. Merciful heavens above, *he* was her contact. If she hadn't been so distracted, maybe she would have noticed this man hadn't offered the identifying phrase. "Well, now I'll know how to title it. Thank you."

She gave him a nod of dismissal and turned her back.

The man didn't take the hint and lingered. The real contact approached. "Pardon me, have you noticed a poodle? My daughter's dog slipped its leash."

The identifier. She offered a smile that trembled. "No, and I would have noticed a lost dog. What color is it?"

"Brown. The small variety." He dropped the newspaper tucked under his arm to the bench and held up his hands, indicating the size of a basketball. The paper landed squarely atop the pouch. He pointed to her sketch. "Perhaps add a touch more shadow alongside the far parapet."

Surprised, Jennie looked at her sketch and then up at the monas-, er, castle. "Why, I do believe you're right. Good suggestion."

The man nodded and picked up his paper, leaving the bench empty in that spot. He took his leave. Jennie promptly shifted her bag and dug inside, hoping the interloper failed to notice the suddenly missing pouch. Finding her charcoal, she smudged in the shadow. Her mission was concluded, but her heart continued to race. However did field agents, especially those behind enemy lines, maintain their composure?

The false contact continued to loiter. Was he an undercover Swedish policeman wondering about the stranger in his fair town? Time to get out of here. Time to join Mom. Carefully closing her sketchpad, she shoved everything into her tote and stood. Aiming for a look of surprise to see him still there, she offered a nod, a cheery "Good Day," and headed off, expecting to hear "Hold it right there," any moment. The only sounds came from birds singing in the trees.

At the church, she hurried into a washroom and splashed cold water onto her face. Looking into the mirror, she muttered, "You'd never make it as a spy, you know that? How could you have been so stupid to nearly give away that pouch to the wrong man?"

Her reflection had no response.

Back out in the hallway, she blinked. She could be looking into a mirror again. Dark blonde hair lacked her tint of red, but the wide-set blue eyes, straight nose and full smile matched her own.

The smile widened. "We could be twins, so we must be friends just waiting to meet. I am Astrid Marklund."

Jennie's own smile bloomed more slowly. "And I am Jennie Lindquist. My great-grandparents emigrated from Uppsala, so maybe we're cousins. Their names were Björn and Ulla Setterdahl."

"Setterdahl? We must be related. That's my grandmother's name." Astrid led Jennie into the meeting hall and up to a woman whose face was wrinkled with smile lines. "*Mormor*, Jennie's great-grandfather was Björn Setterdahl. Did you know him?"

The woman clapped her hands together. "Björn? He was my uncle." She extended a hand to Jennie. "Oh, child. You are descended from Björn?"

Mom joined them with a puzzled expression as her gaze traveled from one girl to the other and back. Jennie introduced her.

Excited chatter rose among the ladies as they quizzed Mom about Björn and life in America. Astrid hugged Jennie. "So, we are cousins. What fun. I did not know I have American cousins."

Astrid's peal of laughter sent shivers down Jennie's spine. Even their voices matched.

Jennie noted the wedding band on Astrid's finger. "Is your husband in the military?"

"Yes, he's in the air force, based in Malmö. That's all the way down in southern Sweden, across the Öresund Strait from Copenhagen, Denmark. He flies patrols along the coast where many damaged warplanes enter Swedish airspace. I haven't seen Gustav in four months. Seems more like a year."

With the sorting work completed, Astrid and her grandmother joined Jennie and Mom in trekking up the north tower to view the treasury. The tower held a large collection of medieval clothing. Jennie went straight to Queen Margaret's golden gown from the early 1400s. Astrid pointed out the front of the gown was so long that the Queen had to lift it to walk. "Think how often she must have tripped on the hem."

Mom sighed. "I can picture in my mind my mother standing here as a young girl, gazing enthralled at this same gown."

"Birgit did love to come here." Mormor smiled, a faraway look in her eyes. "She always wanted to play dress-up, and Queen Margaret was her favorite character."

While the older ladies exchanged memories of her grandmother, Jennie broached the subject of their relatives in Norrkoping with Astrid. "I'm glad for Mom that we found relatives here. She's so disappointed not to meet Sigrid. This was a chance in a lifetime, but the war is keeping them divided."

Astrid nodded slowly and took her time in responding. "It may seem unthinkable to you that any Swedes would join the Nazis, but you need to understand, Sweden has traditionally been pro-German and against Russia. At first, my husband's family thought Hitler was good for Germany. Even the king initially favored Germany when the war started. Still, we heard Hitler vented his rage over the poor turnout from Sweden to join his struggle against communism. He'd thought we'd flock to his cause."

They strolled downstairs and outside to a vantage point to look out over the city. Jennie leaned on a balustrade. "What's it like, living in Sweden? And how did you meet your husband?"

They talked until Mom and Astrid's grandmother emerged from the tower. The ladies hugged before Mormor waved to them and headed in the opposite direction. Mom joined them.

Mom's eyes sparkled with her smile. "Astrid, I would have pegged you for our relative even if we didn't have roots in Uppsala. Your grandmother invited us for dinner tomorrow. Can you recommend a good place to eat for now? And please do us the honor of joining us."

Astrid led them to a cozy café down the street. The day's specials were chalked on a board at the door. Jennie's stomach rumbled as she studied the list.

"Mmm. *Köttfärs.* That's a meatloaf frosted with mashed potatoes, isn't it?"

A teasing smile tilted Astrid's lips as they sat at a table. "Are you aware that a meat dish not requiring a ration coupon is likely badger, or seagull, or squirrel, or rabbit?"

"Um." Jennie's stomach stopped it's growling. Meat was meat. She shouldn't care if she ate cow or badger, but she did. She looked back at the list. "I think I'll have the perch."

Mom sipped the coffee placed before her. "I suspect some substitution has been made here as well."

Astrid nodded. "I read in the paper over one hundred fifty types of coffee substitutes have been approved by the Food Commission." She sipped her own coffee and wrinkled her nose. "This is not one of the better ones."

Jennie sat back when the waitress delivered her perch and *rotmos*. "At least we know the fish and mashed turnips and potatoes are natural."

"Actually, the war has made us healthier." Astrid raised her fork like a teacher making a point. "The dietary restrictions have been beneficial, with greater consumption of fruits and vegetables and less of fat and sugar. And most people are bicycling with the lack of gasoline. That was in the paper, too."

Mom had ordered the köttkärs. Her face looked a bit strained. Some odd meat must have been used. "It's good that you can look at the bright side."

Astrid shrugged. "Mormor's always said, 'Be grateful for your blessings. Not everyone is so blessed.'"

Two days were hardly adequate to get acquainted. By the time Jennie and Mom returned to Stockholm, she and Astrid had plans to get together when Astrid visited Stockholm in the summer. Jennie would never meet Lily, but her newfound look-alike cousin more than made up for that. And the only reason they met was because she worked for the Office of Special Services. Bless Ed for sending her to meet the contact.

Chapter Twenty-Five

"Why'd the general give us Air Medals? We get Air Medals after five missions. There's nothing special about 'em." Rusty groused up a storm as the crew assembled at *Claptrap* for a mission to Oranienburg, near Berlin.

"The general didn't have to give us any medals, Rusty." Rafe slid him a glance before resuming his watch of the distant horizon for the first glow of sunrise. "He could have given us a simple pat on the back for our so-called heroics."

"I looked up the criteria for the Air Medal." Harold pulled a sheet of paper from his pocket, cleared his throat, and recited the conditions. "The Air Medal recipient distinguishes himself by meritorious achievement while participating in aerial flight. The medals are primarily to recognize those personnel on flying status which requires them to participate in aerial flight on a regular and frequent basis in the performance of their primary duties. That's the fifth mission award, with oak clusters for every subsequent fifth mission." He nodded to Rusty. "But this one's for our discernible contribution in keeping a general out of Nazi hands."

"Hear, hear." Dan's cheer garnered everyone's laughter.

Everyone's except Rusty's. "Yeah, yeah, nothing special. Throw the dog a bone. The Air Medal's the lowest award possible."

Rafe smiled as he tossed his briefcase up into the front hatch. "They save the big medals for the brass."

"Is that so, Martell?"

Colonel Leber's voice. Rafe could have cheerfully kicked himself in the backside. Turning, he spotted the twinkle in the colonel's eyes and saluted briskly. "Yes, sir, like the general we heard about at High Wycombe who got a paper cut and awarded himself the Purple Heart."

"You're digging yourself in deep, Martell. Maybe you'd like a shovel."

"Yes, sir. That'd make it easier." Open mouth, insert foot. Had he just talked himself out of a trip to see Christoph?

Leber put him at ease about that. "Tomorrow this squadron's on stand down. You and Braedel plan on going to Camp Hill Hall."

"Yes, sir. Thank you, sir." Tomorrow couldn't come fast enough.

Tomorrow almost didn't come.

Intense flak over the target riddled the airplanes. One plane lost two engines and went down.

"No one's bailing out." Dan watched it from the tail. "Of course, you can't expect to bail out in all this flak and reach the ground alive."

The flight for home provided excess excitement for the men in *Claptrap*.

"Two FW-190s coming in at twelve o'clock level for a game of chicken." Mickey sounded pleased with the chance to fight back.

The enemy fighters belched fire from their wing guns. Rafe flinched. Surely the bullets would slam through the Plexiglas nose again. How could they miss? Only Mickey and Alan had forward facing guns. They poured a hail of lead into the fighters' path, but still they came.

The lead fighter rolled left and barely avoided sideswiping them. Rafe could make out a line of rivets stitched across the fighter's belly.

The wingman waited too long to roll away. Or maybe he was dead. His fighter slashed into the bomber's fuselage between the waist gunner's window and the dorsal fin. The jarring impact flung Rafe and Alan to the floor. Rafe's parachute landed nearby, and he grabbed it.

Above the roar of the engines could be heard the banshee screech of metal tearing through metal as the fighter ripped free of *Claptrap* and tumbled to earth. The bomber shuddered and groaned. The machine guns swung from the ceiling. Any moment, the Fortress would drop into a fatal spiral.

But it didn't. *Claptrap* continued to fly as the engines' pitch changed at the pilots' request for maximum power. Rafe and Alan stared at each other, not moving lest they upset the *Claptrap's* equilibrium. The plane wobbled and lurched as it fought to stay airborne.

Carlo's voice trembled in their earphones. "Lord, have mercy."

"What's the situation back there?" Steve sounded stressed, like he was straining to keep their nose up.

"The whole tail section's nearly severed. It's cut through from top almost to the bottom."

A severed tail? Rafe pushed himself up. "Where's Dan?"

"He's still in there. His intercom must be cut, and his oxygen. He's using the walk-around bottle."

"Can he come forward?" As the engineer, Mickey could correct a lot of in-flight problems, but this would be beyond his ability to fix.

As long as Dan was still with them, it made no difference where he was. If the tail broke off, they were all in trouble no matter which section they were in. Still, better to all be together.

"The ball turret's not working. I can't get outa here."

"Harold, crank open the ball. Carlo, can you help Dan come forward? If we manage to get back to England, his bottled oxygen won't last that long. Rafe, what's our ETA?" Steve issued orders like a drill sergeant.

"We could use one of the cut cables as a rope if Dan can tie it around his waist." Carlo assessed their situation. "If George were still here, we could reel him in."

With the decision to eliminate one waist gunner from each crew, George had been transferred to a pickup crew.

"Harold and Rusty, hurry up and help Carlo."

The gap between the *Claptrap* and the rest of the formation widened as they fell behind, dropping down five hundred feet per minute to maintain their flying speed. They had a long way to go, and now they were alone over Germany.

"We've still got hours to go and more as we lose speed. Harold, can you raise any Little Friends to escort us? We're just south of Bremen and likely to encounter enemy fighters eager for an easy kill." Despite the frigid temperature aboard the B-17, sweat trickled down Rafe's face. "And Mickey, be ready with the red flares to get some friendly attention."

Dan sprawled into the nose compartment, bumping into Rafe's chair.

Rafe pulled away his oxygen mask and leaned close to Dan. "Glad to see you're out of the tail. Are you all right?"

"Yeah, I thought I'd see what life's like up in the front of the bus." Dan curled up against the plywood box holding the belts of ammunition. "Kind of crowded in here."

Alan swiveled his seat around. "Why don't you head back to the radio room, lie down and take a nap, Dan. We'll be back to base before you know it."

With a flick of his hand, Dan crawled back into the passageway, his movement shaky.

Claptrap held together all the way back to England. As they crossed the coast, the enlisted men sang a rousing rendition of "Coming in on a Wing and a Prayer." Rafe leaned back in his chair. The Dover cliffs never looked so beautiful.

Steve punctured their relief. "We've been ordered not to attempt to land. We'll fly over the base, you'll all bail out through the forward hatch, and Lieutenant Ellerbee and I will head back to the North Sea, bail out at the coast, and let the *Claptrap* ditch. Be ready to go when I ring the bailout bell."

Rafe dumped his instruments into his briefcase and hooked it to his belt along with his GI shoes. He snapped his parachute to his harness.

Ridgewell came into view. Word must have spread around the base. It looked like everyone was out to watch the show. As senior officer to jump over the base, Rafe waited to count heads before jumping from the forward escape hatch.

Steve banked to circle the base, and the bell rang.

"Go, go, go." Rafe slapped each man on the shoulder in turn. Dan sat on the edge of the hatch and peered out. Rafe put his boot against Dan's backside and pushed.

"Yooowwww."

Rafe watched until Dan's chute popped open, hiding him from view. He keyed his mike. "Six are away and here I go. Good luck."

He didn't wait for a reply from Steve or Cal before unplugging his communication cable. He swung through the hatch and let go.

Arms extended, back arched, toes together and pointed. Perfect swan dive form. Skydiving was fun. Rafe tucked and rotated to heads up. And fell past Dan.

"Open your chute, lieutenant." Dan's call faded away as Rafe plummeted past.

Chuckling, he tugged his ripcord.

Whomp!

That hurt. They'd been told the sudden deceleration could cause quite a jolt, but that was ridiculous. Why didn't they practice parachute jumps from planes instead of towers? A trainee had suffered a compound fracture from a tower jump in basic training. As long as there would be training accidents, they may as well have jumped from planes. A little experience in the heat of a dangerous emergency would be good. Some guys managed to land like they were stepping off a train. Now what had their instructor said?

Keep his legs tightly together. No, that was before pulling the ripcord, to reduce the opening shock. Too late for that. Now, keep his feet together and slightly bend his knees to land on the balls of his feet, and keep his hands on the risers. At the moment of impact, fall forward or to the side in a tumbling roll to absorb the shock. Stay relaxed, not rigid or limp. Rafe flexed his knees, ready to spring. Relax, flex, roll. Relax, flex, roll.

His descent brought him close to the barracks. No obstacles to hinder his landing. Good. He wouldn't need to hike through a maze of wheat fields trying to find the base. Lots of guys watched him, pointing. Why point at him? He looked around for his crewmates, floating down beyond the base. They were the ones everyone should be concentrating on. Shrugging off the mystery, he continued practicing his landing technique. Relax, flex, roll.

Paul Braedel lounged against a jeep, his arms folded, one ankle crossed over the other, watching him. Rafe would land right by him. Except he wasn't facing the direction of his drift. He needed to turn to his right.

To turn his body to his right, let's see, right hand behind his head, grasp the left risers. Left hand in front of his head, grasp the right risers. Pull simultaneously and, it worked. He turned right. Just in time.

He landed upright but before he could roll, the billowing parachute threatened to drag him off his feet until it snagged on a light post and collapsed. A few running paces secured his balance.

Paul inclined his head. "Afternoon, Rafe." Like tumbling out of the sky under a silk sheet was an everyday occurrence. "I understand we're going visiting tomorrow."

"It'll be something out of the routine." He tried to match his friend's nonchalant attitude.

"No kidding." Paul straightened up. "Interested in a bike ride to the local village?"

"That sounds good. I could use a little physical activity after being cramped in the nose all morning."

Paul grinned. "That was quite the physical activity you had going on the way down."

He brought up one knee, then scissored his foot back and forth.

Rafe groaned. So that's why everyone had pointed at him. He must have looked like a fool. He tugged his jacket collar with a show of dignity. "Having never jumped before, I tried a few practice maneuvers."

"Yeah, we ought to practice parachute jumps. Having a good jump under our belts would be beneficial." Paul took a big jump and flexed his knees low on landing. "Like shock absorbers, right?"

Together they jumped and flexed.

Two ground personnel arrived in a jeep to take Rafe to interrogation. Watching the officers practice their jumps, they shook their heads. One of them muttered, "Crazy flyboys."

Chapter Twenty-Six

Essex, England
Wednesday, April 19, 1944

Rafe wiped sweaty palms on his trouser legs. "I can't believe how nervous I am."

"What's the worst that can happen? He'll spit in your face?" Paul snapped his fingers. "He'll *punch* you in the face. Then the MPs will grab him and throw him in the brig."

"You're not helping, Paul." The jeep slowed and turned in at a gate. Rafe blew out his breath through pursed lips. "This is it."

Their driver stopped in front of a nondescript building. "Here's the office."

The explanation was hardly necessary with 'Headquarters' stenciled above the door.

Paul stretched as he looked around. "Not a whole lot different from base."

"No, except for lots of barbed wire and guards with guns," Rafe agreed. "And not a plane in sight."

The sergeant on duty studied Rafe's papers. "Christoph Bu-cker."

"Buecker, rhymes with seeker." Why did he bother to correct the pronunciation?

The sergeant shrugged. Whatever. "He's assigned to barracks four." He jerked his thumb behind and to the right. He eyed Rafe curiously. "We don't get many Yanks come to see the Krauts."

Rafe shrugged. Whatever.

Back outside, he and Paul negotiated the muddy pathways. Nissen huts stood in cramped rows. Prisoners stood or sat, singly or in groups. Some read, others talked. Several tossed a ball in a disinterested game of catch. Rafe stopped abruptly. There. The one sitting slumped against the barracks wall, one knee bent up, the other leg straight out.

Ignoring everyone else, Rafe approached. His cousin didn't look up when he stopped in front of him. "Chr…" He had to clear his throat. "Christoph."

Blue eyes slowly rose. A look of boredom or apathy or weariness changed suddenly into wide-eyed disbelief. "Rolf?" Christoph sprang to his feet. "Rolf?"

"Wie gehts, Vetter?" Rafe's voice strangled as his throat tightened.

Christoph swallowed hard. "Rolf!" He grabbed Rafe in a bear hug that threatened to squeeze the life out of him. "Where have you been? You disappeared, what's it been, eight years now? And never a word." He stepped back and eyed Paul in an American uniform. His gaze swung back to Rafe, and Rafe's American uniform. His shoulders slumped. "You're fighting against us. We figured as much."

"Germany didn't want me. America took me in." Rafe studied his cousin, waiting for disgust or revulsion. But Christoph nodded.

"Are you stationed in England? How'd you know I was here?"

"Did you know there was a general in the lifeboat you were heading for last week?"

Christoph's eyes bulged. "You weren't there, were you?"

Rafe chose his words carefully. "That general came to our base shortly afterwards. He had photographs taken on the Air-Sea Rescue boat, and I recognized you."

Christoph shoved his hands in his pockets and sighed. "One of those four motors dropped a load of bombs on us. We were just going to pick up the men in the water."

Paul swung around, his lips pressed together. Rafe hid a smile, divining his friend's thoughts. Like everyone else on base, he'd heard the general's description of the Keystone Kops act.

"Yeah, well, the general had visions of being hauled before Goering, or maybe even Hitler, for propaganda photos."

Christoph snorted. With a nod of his head, he indicated they should walk. "I don't doubt that."

A vacant playing field offered privacy. Time for some answers.

"Is my father alive?" Rafe held his breath.

His cousin nodded. "I saw him five months ago, and *Mutter* didn't mention anything happening in her last letter."

Rafe's breath whooshed out of him. He stared up at the clouds, defying the tears that begged for release.

"Uncle Heinz misses you."

"Sure he does. He couldn't get us away from him fast enough." Bitterness tinged his voice and swept away the moisture in his eyes.

Christoph quirked a brow and his shoulders hunched. They walked in silence for a minute. "Did you ever consider what life was like for your father growing up? Three older sisters, the first boy born into *Grossmutter's* family in three generations. They spoiled him. Petted and pampered. Whatever he wanted, Uncle Heinz got. Until the war came along. Suddenly everything's out of control. He can't have his way. He's told to get rid of his Jewish wife and he lacks the backbone to defy." Christoph offered a humorless smile. "I heard Mutter and her sisters discussing him. He's in a state of bewilderment and wants nothing more than life as it was with his family beside him."

"Never going to happen. Mother remarried."

Rafe grinned when Christoph's jaw dropped. "Why are you so surprised? Mother's a beautiful, desirable woman. Plays the piano like a prodigy and knits us sweaters for winter."

Christoph hadn't raised his jaw.

Rafe pulled an envelope of pictures from his pocket. "Here's Mother and her husband in front of their house. Mother is her father's daughter for sure. She has a huge victory garden of vegetables in the backyard and her flower gardens in front are the envy of the neighborhood." He flipped to another photo and chuckled. "Here's Albert. No doubting he's Opa's grandson. He'll study horticulture at university this fall, if he's not drafted. We hope to resurrect the business in Holland after the war and be the U.S. distributor. And here's Rita. She has another year of university, and then plans on law school."

"Wow." Christoph stared at the photos. "A huge house for one family? Not a noisy apartment?" He shook his head. "No need to mention that to Uncle Heinz." He sighed as he looked at his cousins' images. "Albert and Rita? What happened to Gottlieb and Brigitte?"

"We Americanized. Brigitte shortened to Rita, and Mother from Hannelore to Laura. Couldn't do anything with Gottlieb, but what are second names for?" When Christoph raised his eyes and waited, he added, "I'm Rafe. Ralph might have been the logical choice, but I borrowed a helpful neighbor's name."

Paul had drifted away to give them privacy, but now rejoined them. "Should we know anything about the guy glowering at us by the latrines?"

A casual glance back brought a scowl to Christoph's face. *"Leutnant zur See* Pruhst, my second-in-command on the S-boat. I don't know why he's here." He touched a white patch on his uniform. "We're supposed to be only whites and grays here, I thought. Those with no loyalty to National Socialism or with no strong feelings either way. Pruhst is hardcore. He should've gotten a black patch and been put in a different camp. I won't be surprised if he causes trouble and lands me in it."

Paul pulled a pen from his pocket. "Ensign Pruhst. We'll see about a transfer."

They circled around the camp, away from Pruhst's view.

"How's your family doing? You were back in Cologne at Christmastime?" The image Rafe had of the last family gathering was over eight years old. He could pass most of his cousins on the street and not recognize them.

"My parents live in the little cottage on their garden plot outside the city." Christoph's gaze strayed to the pocket where Rafe put his pictures. "One room, meant to facilitate their gardening in summer, is now their home. The apartment building disappeared when Tommy tried to wipe Cologne off the map."

Rafe cast a sidelong glance at his cousin for his reference to the British. For the first time, resentment tinged Christoph's voice.

"We heard about the Brits' thousand bomber raid. They left Cologne in bad shape."

Christoph nodded his acknowledgement. "My sister evacuated to Bavaria with her two sons, but she's not happy there. They aren't treated well at the house they're assigned to. The Bavarians resent having to share with them. Erich has difficulty understanding the local dialect and the children make fun of him at school. They have no choice, however. Her husband was killed in Russia, and Mutter and Vater have no room for them."

Christoph released a massive sigh. "*Grossvater* died after that big raid. Rescuers got him out of the shelter with no injuries, but then he suffered a heart attack. Grossmutter lives with Uncle Heinz in a basement portioned out for three or four family groups. Pretty dismal."

'Pretty dismal' accurately described Rafe's reaction. Once, he might have felt satisfaction over his father's misfortune. Now? A hollow place inside him wanted to cry. "How has your experience been in the Kriegsmarine?"

"Better in the navy than in the army, for me at least." A frown puckered Christoph's brow before smoothing away as he gained animation. "I enjoyed being at *die Sahnefront*, guarding *Milchkühe*. I didn't command my own boat yet, but that made my time more relaxed."

Rafe and Paul exchanged baffled looks.

"You were," Paul hesitated, "based on a farm?"

Christoph swung his head around, eyes wide. A smile started. *"Es tut mir lied."* He apologized, but that didn't stop him from snickering. "The cream front is Denmark, where there's lots of food and little fighting. The resupply U-boats are called milk cows. When I got my own S-boat, I transferred to Holland. Not as nice there."

Rafe smiled. "We thought it was beautiful during our stay before leaving for America."

"You went to Holland first?" Wistfulness swept across Christoph's face. "What was your escape like?"

Escape seemed an odd word choice, at least from his cousin, but Rafe didn't belabor the detail. "I was sent out first as an apprentice for the flower bulb business. That enabled me to take a bit of luggage. Oma sewed a lining into the trousers I wore to hide extra money. Opa's partner came to Cologne, ostensibly to consult with him and bring samples, and I accompanied him back to Amsterdam."

The day was eight years ago, but still as vivid as yesterday. Mother's tears. Opa's rigid posture. Gottlieb's eagerness to go with him. "Opa brought the whole family to the train station to stage a tearful farewell. He announced he'd bring the family to visit when he traveled to Holland in a few weeks, and maybe we could expect Gottlieb to take a turn as

240

apprentice someday. He intended that any Party spies would take note. Then just a week later, they followed. They carried only a bit of hand luggage, but Opa had been transferring money to Holland for some time under the guise of building up the business. We still had to pay the Reich Flight Tax."

Rafe turned to Paul. "The previous government implemented the tax to prevent capital from leaving the country, but the Nazis used it to steal from the Jews. They wanted us to leave, but with only the clothes on our backs." Anger infiltrated his voice and he clenched his fists at the memory. "But since Opa got away with most of his money, we were in good shape to start over in America. We stayed in Holland nearly a year before sailing for the States."

"Boggles the mind to think you had to do that." Paul had listened with slack-jawed interest. "And then you came to Milwaukee." To Christoph, he added, "I live in the same city, but we didn't meet until we were here in England."

Rafe pivoted to Christoph. "What about Bertil, Ludwig, or Johan?"

His heart sank when his cousin shook his head.

"I don't know anything about Bertil. He was more your friend than mine and, after you left, he transferred out of the Naval Hitler Youth. I think he joined a motorized unit."

Rafe sighed. Good. That's where Bertil should have gone to begin with. Would have, if not for the desire to stick together.

"Ludwig's dead. His U-boat disappeared a year ago."

"Ludwig? In a submarine? He's claustrophobic."

Christoph shrugged and continued in a lifeless tone. "And Johan went down with the *Bismarck*."

Rafe blew out his breath. "He couldn't have gotten to be the boss officer on a battleship."

Christoph's eyes suddenly flashed and his voice took on new life as he growled, "And there's no glory in dying for *Gröfaz*." Paul looked puzzled, and Christoph elaborated as he paced back and forth. "*Größter Feldherr aller Zeiten.* The greatest field commander of all time. Herr Hitler." He spat the words out in a barely audible tone and tilted forward in a mocking bow.

After a quick glance around, Christoph added, "I'm glad to be out of the fight. I have no idea what we're even fighting for, other than to fulfill that madman's illusions. You would not believe the stories I've heard coming out of the Eastern Front." He pointed to scrawling on the side of a barracks. *Aus der Traum.* The dream is over. Hands planted on his hips, he looked Rafe straight in the eye. "Ever since you left, I knew something was wrong with the dream, whatever it was. Uncle Heinz did you a favor, Rolf. You were lucky to leave Germany."

Chapter Twenty-Seven

Stockholm, Sweden
Thursday, April 20, 1944

The Best of Sweden. Sweden on Display. Spotlight on Sweden. Sweden Exhibit.

Jennie crossed the last one off. Too obvious. Spotlight on Sweden had a nice ring. She circled that one.

Her collection of paintings stayed frightfully small. Phyllis thought she sketched quickly. Well, sketching, yes, but paintings took longer. Maybe she'd have to take lots of photos to give American audiences a good look at Sweden. Maybe she could add small souvenirs, like a miniature tall case clock, a Dala horse. What else was quintessentially Swedish? Had there been a gift shop at the Uppsala cathedral? A doll dressed in a tiny replica of Queen Margaret's medieval ball gown would be great. She jotted down a note: *Contact Astrid.*

Her pencil tapping on her father's desk, she glanced at the papers lying there. The latest list of air crews to arrive in Sweden. She picked it up. No Rafe Martell. She picked up another list and winced. Airmen buried in Sweden. Again, no Rafe.

She snapped her fingers. Lots of American airmen were here now. She could focus an exhibit on Sweden through the internees' eyes. That's it. *Sweden, Shelter from the Storm.* What she needed was an internee from the Chicago area to help promote the exhibit back home. She began digging through the file drawers.

"May I help you find something?"

Dad caught her red-handed. She refused to squirm. "Do you have a list of the internees' hometowns? I need to talk to several airmen." She explained her idea for the exhibit. "How they fill their days, their impressions of Sweden, that sort of thing. And pictures. Lots of pictures to go with my paintings."

Dad heard her out in silence. He motioned for her to vacate his chair. Sitting down, he said, "I don't have a list of hometowns. Only their bases in England." Folding his hands, he added, "Your idea has merit."

Jennie's eyes widened. "But?" She perched on a visitor's chair. "I hear a great big 'but' coming."

Dad chuckled and swiveled to look out the window. He turned back. "Maybe not. Your exhibit won't take place until after the war. Then it will be okay." He nodded. "Yes, you have a good idea. Some people, including those high up in the Army Air Force, believe our air crews come to Sweden to avoid further combat." He slapped his hand down on the desk. "That could not be further from the truth. Drawing attention to the internees could help refute that claim." He pulled his calendar forward. "I'll be going to Malmö in a few weeks. It's just across the channel from

Copenhagen, Denmark, and that's where most of our planes land. Plan on coming with me."

Jennie started another list. She'd want pictures of the damaged planes. Maybe the local newspapers took photos at the funerals. Maybe a hospital visit. A picture of a wounded airman would help debunk the idea that flights to Sweden were to escape combat.

Her list continued to grow. Maybe she could even meet Astrid's husband.

Chapter Twenty-Eight

Ridgewell Air Base, England
Monday, April 24, 1944

"Ugh. The weather is stinko today." Cal hesitated at the Quonset hut door as if debating whether to go back to bed. Rafe pushed him out.

"Where you think we're going today? Another mission to France?"

"Does it matter? You'd think they'd be easier, but we're losing crews over France as readily as Germany." Just the day after their trip to Camp Hill Hall, Paul had been wounded over France. Now he was still in the sack while a replacement flew with his crew. Rafe pursed his lips. Being killed or wounded was a likely possibility in this business, but it was always supposed to happen to someone else. Paul was lucky to have dodged the bullet. He shook his head. What was he thinking? Paul *hadn't* dodged that bullet. Thank goodness his wound wasn't serious.

"Good morning, gentlemen. Today we're going to Erding, about thirty miles northeast of Munich. Your target is an airfield."

A groan rose in the Briefing Room. They could anticipate nine hours of flying time, much of it over Germany. Just great. And Bavaria—that's where

Christoph's sister was. *Please, not in Erding.* He didn't want to bomb another cousin.

"Your route will take you over France as much as possible. Keep your eyes peeled for convoys, in both France and Germany."

Rafe jotted notes. Weather must be good over the continent if they'd be able to watch the roads. Of course, that also meant the antiaircraft gunners would see them. He headed out for their ride, *Sweet Patootie.* Of all the planes they'd been assigned to fly, *Sweet Patootie* was his favorite. Each bomber had its own peculiarities, but *Sweet Patootie's* only peculiarity, in Rafe's opinion, was that she didn't have one.

The planes took off and got into formation without mishap. First hazard behind them. Rafe yawned and rubbed his eyes. Ahead of him, Alan's head bobbed over the bombsight. How many accidents happened because they were roused from bed in the middle of the night and couldn't keep their eyes open?

They were still climbing for altitude when a shout jerked him to full alert. Alan jumped up and grabbed the controls for his twin .50 caliber guns. Rafe gripped his desk as the whole squadron leveled off to avoid colliding with a stream of British Halifax bombers.

"Those guys don't fly a very tight formation, do they?" Standing behind the pilots in the cockpit, Mickey had a good view.

"They don't fly in formations for night missions. Too hard to keep track of each other's wingtips to avoid collisions." Cal didn't sound any more awake than Rafe felt.

Rafe took a Gee fix for the activity more than a need to know their position. Then he stood up and stretched left, right, up, down. If he stood directly under the astrodome, he gained a little space. Up to the dome, down to his toes, up to the dome. Alan turned around to watch. He began to direct Rafe's stretches, pointing up and down in a faster cadence to increase Rafe's pace.

"What's going on in the nose?" Steve's voice in his headset startled Rafe. "Why do we keep seeing hands appear in the astrodome?"

Rafe sat down in a hurry.

Alan nearly fell off his seat laughing. "It's time for morning calisthenics."

Curled up in the ball turret, Rusty said, "Never thought I'd say it, but I wish I could do some calisthenics."

Rafe ignored the exchange and took another Gee fix.

The intercom had been quiet for some time as they neared the Third Reich. Mickey shattered the silence. "What the…"

Something fell past the Plexiglas nose. A scrape beneath Rafe's feet indicated *Sweet Patootie* had hit it. It had been shaped like…

"Bandits at twelve o'clock high. They're dropping bombs on us. I just saw one go by." Harold sounded like he was coming unglued.

Rafe peered up through the astrodome. "Those aren't bombs. They're dropping their auxiliary fuel tanks."

Clank! Another one banged off the fuselage, followed by the staccato belch of a machine gun.

"Who's firing?" Steve yelled. "Don't waste your ammo on gas tanks."

"N… no one fired, sir," Carlo sounded indignant. "That gas tank caromed into the left waist gun and put it out of commission. It fired on its own."

"Clever of those Krauts. They don't waste anything."

Alan's wry comment curled Rafe's lips in a reluctant smile. "Maybe they want us to know how they feel when we bomb them."

Flak greeted them at the target. Lots of it, and the Germans had zeroed in on their altitude. *Sweet Patootie* rattled and shook in the hail of shrapnel.

Rafe took his usual position behind Alan to watch for landmarks. To their left, *Valiant Lady's* right wing jerked upward as a shell exploded beneath it, nearly flipping the bomber over before the pilots wrestled it back under control. Beyond them flew *Sly Buccaneer* with Paul's crew. Rafe watched the bomb doors open.

Suddenly, *Sly Buccaneer* disappeared. Rafe was staring at an expanding fireball. He couldn't turn away from the sight. If his friend hadn't been wounded the other day, he'd have been in there. Paul would be dead, along with his crew. Instead, someone else from their hut just died in his place. Marvin, a new father. Bile rose in Rafe's throat, and he swallowed hard.

"Thirty percent cloud cover, I'd say." Alan provided needed distraction and Rafe snapped back to attention. Unaware of the tragedy nearby, Alan pointed forward. "Or is that smoke to obscure the target? Doesn't resemble any other clouds."

"It's smoke. The only smoke in the area. They may as well have painted a big red X on the roof for all the good it does." Mundane little details to add to his log, and keep his mind busy.

He checked his watch and recorded the minute for bombs away. He noted their groundspeed and took a compass reading. He heard himself ask, "Dan, any chutes from *Sly Buccaneer?*"

"Are you kidding me?"

That would be a no. Just what he expected. Hopefully someone else would give Paul the bad news. How do you tell a guy his close friends are all dead?

His notes stared up at him. Watch for convoys. He grabbed his binoculars and scrutinized the ground.

"Take it."

Rafe yawned and looked around. He'd stopped searching for ground activity when clouds hid everything from sight. *Take it.* Alan's head was bobbing again. He hadn't said anything. Steve must have handed over the controls to Cal. They should be passing Brussels now. Soon they'd be over the coast and could start letting down.

Right into fog.

Steve put everyone on alert. "We're breaking formation to avoid collisions. Everyone keep your eyes peeled for Forts or fighters, and call them out."

They popped out of the fog over the North Sea.

"We're too far east," said Mickey, the know-it-all. "Everybody else is over there."

"We're fine." Rafe loved his Gee Box. "Heading two-eight-four."

Cal's acknowledgement overlapped Dan's yell.

"Bogie, six o'clock high."

Cal didn't give Dan a chance to use his guns. *Sweet Patootie* dropped into a violent left turn. No sooner had they banked than they wrenched into a tight right turn. *Sweet Patootie* shuddered and groaned. Rafe and Alan landed on the floor. Yells filled their ears. Halfway through the right turn, they pulled up, back to the left. Rafe slid into Alan.

"Cal," Steve protested, "this isn't a fighter plane."

They dropped six thousand feet in Cal's unorthodox maneuver. Rafe pulled himself up to his desk. His instruments had gone haywire.

"Dan," Cal called, "is the bogie still on our tail?"

"Holy Toledo!"

"Dan, is the Kraut still back there?"

"Holy Toledo!"

"Whatsa matter, Quigley? Ya got a bee up your drawers?" Snug in the ball, Rusty had missed being tossed around.

"*Dan.*"

"No, there's no one back here. I'm not sure I'm still back here. My mask is busted and I got a bloody nose."

Rafe's jaw was sore, come to think of it. He ran his tongue around his teeth. All present and accounted for.

"Boy howdy, my heart's pounding like a jack hammer. That was like playing Crack the Whip." Harold's voice sounded like a girl's.

Alan remained sprawled on the floor like he'd been smacked with a giant flyswatter. Rafe reached out a hand. "You're bleeding too, do you know that?"

Alan touched his split lip and grimaced. "Congratulations, Cal. What were you trying to do, qualify us all for Purple Hearts?"

"You only get Purple Hearts for being wounded by the enemy."

"Keep that up and you will be the enemy."

Rafe took a Gee fix, but decided to give Harold a task. "Can you get me a QDM?"

"The radio's jammed. Everybody's either lost or low on fuel." Less than a minute later, Harold called Rafe with the radio fix on their position.

"How'd you get that if the airwaves are jammed?"

"Easy. I screwed down my key and blocked everyone else. When I unscrewed, everybody had given up and I was first in line to get through."

No need to worry about Harold.

Ridgewell hove into sight at long last. Rafe made a final log note and packed everything into his briefcase. He paused at Steve's order.

"Fire a flare."

Rafe watched the flare arc red through the sky. A bloody nose and split lip didn't warrant an ambulance standing by. Come to think of it, Mickey had been strangely quiet.

An ambulance waited at their hardstand and loaded Mickey with a probable sprained wrist, Carlo, who held an arm tight against painful ribs, Dan, who sported a blackening eye in addition to his bloody nose, and Alan, who protested vigorously.

Steve wouldn't listen. He waved at the ambulance driver. "Take them away."

"Boy." Rusty slid his gaze past Cal. "You really did hurt half the crew. And all because Dan said he saw a fighter. I didn't see a fighter." He turned to Harold. "Did you see it?"

"No, I didn't see it." Harold looked at Rafe. "Did you see it?"

Shaking his head, Rafe grabbed the two enlisted men by their arms and spun them in the direction of a waiting jeep. "At six o'clock high, neither of you could spot a swarm of fighters."

Behind him, he heard Steve question Cal. "Where'd you learn a stunt like that?"

"An RAF pilot I met at a pub described it to me. If you get a fighter on your tail, he'll follow you in a turn, but you'll lose him when you skid out of your turn."

"An RAF pilot. Who flies at night. Of course you'd lose a tail in the dark. And what did this pilot fly?"

Rafe looked back to see Cal twist his mouth to one side. "Spitfires."

Steve shook his head and strode to the jeep. He spun back. "No more fighter jockey stunts."

Chapter Twenty-Nine

Stockholm, Sweden
Same Day

Ed summoned Jennie to his office. She stopped short at the door. Dad conferred with Ed over his desk. Both men looked up. "Come on in, Jennie." Dad smiled, but his eyes held a hint of apprehension. "We're planning a little trip to Rättvik for you. I'll give you paperwork to pass on to the internees housed there, but Ed has another purpose in mind for you."

He rested a hand on her shoulder briefly before leaving them alone.

From beneath his desk blotter, Ed pulled out a map of Rättvik. "Study this. Memorize it. You won't be able to take it along. The town is on the eastern point of Lake Siljan. Head for the wooded hills overlooking the town and lake from the south." His finger stabbed the location. "Take your art stuff and draw a picture of the view. That'll be your reason for being there. You'll also have this."

He hefted a backpack onto his desk.

Ed freed a rough sketch pinned to the pack and handed it to her. It looked like a treasure map, complete with an X to mark the spot. "This shows the path up the hill with various places for you to draw. Make sure no one is observing you, and leave the pack here." He tapped the X. "You should find a pile of evergreen branches. Toss them on the pack to cover it from view."

Jennie's heart rate sped up. She reached for the pack and tested its weight. Nearly ten pounds. "What's in here?"

"You don't need to be concerned about the contents. You need only to deliver it."

"I'm supposed to unobtrusively carry a heavy pack one way along with my art stuff, and hope no one notices I've left it behind?" She bit back the question of where she'd find a pack mule.

"Drape your coat over it. Hiking is a common pursuit. No one should pay you any attention. You'll leave on the train tomorrow."

The temperature hovered below fifty degrees and she was supposed to offer her coat to the backpack? She'd have to hike uphill burdened with the pack and her art stuff. That would make her sweat up a storm. Take your art stuff, he said, to draw a picture. The man had no artistic appreciation beyond how he could use her talent to further his own ends. Draw a picture indeed.

She shook the pack. It didn't rattle. Nothing shifted. Likely it held a box wrapped in a blanket. She'd be lucky if she wasn't arrested for supplying sabotage gear.

Chapter Thirty

Rättvik, Sweden
Tuesday, April 25, 1944

Ed had failed to reckon with one very important aspect of sending Jennie to an internee camp. She'd barely stepped off the train when she was surrounded by dozens of young American men starved for the company of American women. How in the world was she to slip away from the gang without raising questions?

Finding the senior officer in charge proved easy with so many eager guides. Dispensing with the paperwork took only minutes. The internees waited outside for her. Jennie smiled. She had found her pack mules.

"Someone at the legation told me to head up those hills for a great vantage spot to paint the view. I'm working on a Chicago exhibit for the Order of Svithiod, which promotes Swedish heritage and culture. Anyone care to help carry my gear and tell me your stories about being in Sweden?"

It didn't take long to find the drop site. She'd worry later how she'd leave the pack without her seven companions noticing. "Tell me how you spend your days."

"We eat and sleep," replied a young man who stared at her instead of the view.

An earnest airman in need of a haircut elaborated. "Summer comes late this far north. Then we'll be able to bike and play baseball..."

"If we had a bat and ball," interrupted the man giving her the willies with his staring.

"...or tennis, go canoeing or sailing. There's not much to do in winter when it's dark most of the day."

"We did try cross-country skiing. That's big here." A short fellow pawed through Jennie's art supplies. Without asking, he opened her smaller sketchpad, selected a piece of chalk, and tried to imitate her strokes.

Watching him, she frowned. They were bored. They needed to keep busy. There must be something they could do. "Would you be interested in woodworking or art classes, or Swedish classes?"

A hungry look entered the staring eyes. "Are you going to teach art?"

Jennie resisted gritting her teeth. Like refusing to show fear to a snarling dog, she couldn't show her exasperation. "No, I'm based in Stockholm." Jennie reigned in her smile so it didn't betray her relief. "But there must be Swedish teachers here in Rättvik who'd be interested in getting involved. You could carve Dala horses. You've seen those little wooden horses, haven't you?"

The budding artist chose another color of chalk. "We have a small band."

"What about a choir? We could probably arrange for you to sing at different churches." At their looks of interest, she said, "I'll talk to my dad about it. Most Swedes don't have personal contact with Americans. More involvement would promote good will."

"Hands across the water." The earnest internee shoved his hair out of his eyes. "It'd be nice to have something more to do than build model airplanes all day."

"Okay, brainstorm with me. Think of any activities you'd like to do or what you did back home that you could do here."

"I helped my pa on our farm."

"Here." Jennie shoved a scratchpad and pencil into the hands of the starer. This would get his eyes off her. "Take notes of all the possibilities. When I get back to Stockholm, I'll see what we can do."

Chapter Thirty-One

Ridgewell Air Base, England
Monday, May 8, 1944

The wake-up call came at three. Rafe squinted open one eye and watched the operations officer nudge Paul Braedel. With a grin, Rafe stretched and turned over. The Coolidge crew was on stand-down, a delicious day off. He planned to sleep in.

The roused crews may have tried to be quiet, but they made a racket anyway.

"Where's my other shoe? Come on, give me a light. I need to find my shoe." One of the new guys, who replaced Paul's old crew.

The overhead bulb blinked on. Rafe sighed, rolled back over, and propped his head on a hand. The new bombardier was on his hands and knees, head under his cot, rear end in the air.

"Found it." Bonk. "Oow."

Rafe caught Paul's eye and raised a brow at the cursing coming from the bombardier who rose up, rubbing his head. Rookies.

Paul managed a sleepy shrug. He looked like he needed a day off.

Rafe waved good-bye and snuggled into his pillow. Whop! Paul's pillow landed on his head. Silent laughter shook him as the hut darkened and the door closed behind the departing airmen. He aimed the pillow back at Paul's cot. Now if he could just get back to sleep.

Midmorning found him under his tree. This time, he'd brought a tarp borrowed from the *Sweet Patootie's* crew chief to avoid soaking his trousers on the damp, weedy grass. Brenda joined him in a lopsided skip and presented him with a fistful of wildflowers. Her solemn eyes studied him.

She plopped down beside him. "Where ya been?"

"Yesterday we flew to Berlin."

"Where's that?"

"Germany."

Her brows bunched together and her lips twisted to the side. "Germans are bad. Why'd ya go there?"

What would her mother want him to tell her? Brenda already knew about the destruction of war. People like her daddy died, and she and her brother had to live far away from their mother.

"We stop the factories where the Germans build things to hurt us. If they can't make their weapons, they won't be able to fight anymore."

She stared unblinkingly at him for the longest time before nodding. "You won't be killt doing that, will ya?"

That promise he couldn't make, again. "I hope not."

Long after Brenda scampered home, Rafe tried to read. The book failed to rouse his interest, and he tossed it aside. The promise of summer whispered in the breeze fanning his face. A bee buzzed around Brenda's wilting bouquet.

Mother must be spending lots of time in her gardens. Rita might complain about all the necessary weeding, but Albert ought to be taking a professional interest, not that a horticulturist would have to do his own weeding. What about Father? Living in a corner of a dingy basement, how safe was that with all the rubble of people's shattered lives waiting to tumble in?

Christoph hadn't said if Father lived in the basement of their apartment building. Maybe he'd had to claim some other place to bed down. As nice as their apartment had been, the cellar had been a fearsome place. One wall had been rough brick. Old Frau Schneer kept her dummy figures down there after retiring as a seamstress. The single weak bulb swayed on its cord, and cast shadows on the brick wall that looked like they were moving. Rafe's ears still ached from Brigitte's shrieks when she thought the shadowy people were about to grab her.

Those dummies must be gone now. Thrown out to make room for the living. A heavy odor of smoke and rubble dust must torment Grossmutter's sinuses. The cement floor would be hard to sweep clean of splintered glass and broken masonry. How did they cook or refrigerate food? Their apartment had boasted its own toilet. Now what? An improvised chamber pot?

Christoph hadn't mentioned the rail yard, but he wouldn't have been back since Rafe's bomb group had targeted it. That had to be a priority for the Germans to keep operating. Father's job would be secure. He wouldn't be drafted into the army.

The bee buzzed around his head and he waved it away.

"Ahoy there." The chaplain stood in the lane, perched on his bicycle. He pointed forward. "Is this the way back to base?"

Rafe chuckled. He'd ruminated enough for one day. "It is, although I can't tell you where to turn." He pointed to his left. "I cut through the field today."

Chaplain Hogan gazed across the field and shook his head. "If you say so." He parked his bike and ambled over. "You're a navigator. Suppose you fly in over the Dover cliffs. Would you be able to find your way back to Ridgewell without using your instruments?"

The question gave Rafe pause. He smiled. "Now that you mention it, maybe not. Everything looks the same."

"Exactly. No rhyme, no reason, anywhere. Like a patchwork quilt with hedges for seams. I've seen medieval walled cities with streets that meander every which way to confound invaders. I've wondered if the English laid out their fields and lanes to confuse an enemy."

Rafe chuckled. "They've done a good job of confusing their friends. Each village looks alike. From the air, their churches look alike. Their thatched roof cottages have little variance. Nothing stands out as a landmark."

The tarp had bunched up in the breeze. Rafe spread it back out in invitation, and the chaplain sat down. He turned his face into the breeze. "What do you hear?"

Rafe listened. "Birds, insects, the wind in the trees."

The chaplain smiled. "What don't you hear?"

A moment passed, and Rafe's smile matched the chaplain's. "I don't hear a single engine revving up."

"Precisely. The war is far away. Somewhere, people are dying violent deaths. They don't have the opportunity to step away from the horror. I wonder, how would I cope? I'm a man of peace, and enough of a coward to admit I'm glad I needn't experience the fighting."

Rafe stared at the chaplain. He was a man of conviction. Just days ago, Paul had told Rafe how the chaplain had gone against the rules and flown on a mission. "A coward's not going to finagle his way onto a Flying Fortress headed for Germany."

The chaplain's head dropped back as he laughed. "No, but a lunatic might." He sat up, suddenly intent. "How can I counsel you men of the combat crews when I have no idea what you're up against? Some men come back so shocked and traumatized," he wiped a hand over his mouth, "I can't say, 'Oh, it couldn't have been so bad.' In order to empathize, I had to go out on a mission." He leaned back on his hands. "And, you know? I thought those first bursts of flak looked downright pretty."

A snicker escaped Rafe. "Oh right. Pretty dangerous."

Black puffs suddenly transforming into orange flashes had been mesmerizing the first time Rafe had seen them. Sometimes the flash appeared red or yellow. No matter the color, the fascination evaporated quickly when their rain of shrapnel punched through paper-thin skin of the bombers.

Chaplain Hogan picked up the book Rafe had discarded. "*Fallen Bastions.*" He thumbed through it.

"This is about the Anschluss, isn't it? When Germany annexed Austria?"

Rafe nodded. The book was an odd choice for relaxation. He needed it, though, as a reminder why he was fighting Germany. The eyewitness report strengthened his resolve. *The Viennese laughed as an ashen-faced Jewish surgeon on hands and knees before young hooligans wearing swastika armbands and brandishing dog whips forced him to scrub the sidewalk, pouring acid over the brush and his surgeon's fingers.* That could have been him. Had his ancestry become known, how would the residents of Cologne have reacted to his "deceit" of living like an Aryan?

Chaplain Hogan set aside the book. "Paul Braedel told me about your visit to your cousin."

A simple observation. An invitation to talk. Rafe's throat tightened. "My father is a coward. Christoph said he misses us, wishes life could be as it was. Father lives in a cellar now, in the ruins of Cologne. All because he refused to go to America with us. His job at the railroad was more important than we were. The way we keep bombing the marshalling yards, it must be quite challenging work now. Maybe he wouldn't have been able to find employment in Milwaukee. Maybe he would have been dependent on Opa, his father-in-law. Would that have been so bad, considering how he's living now? Fact is, he didn't care enough about us."

His fingers clenched. Taking a deep breath, he forcibly relaxed. Even after eight years, even after learning of Father's situation, the hurt still festered.

"Don't hold it against him for being a fallible human being. 'All we like sheep have gone astray; we have turned every one to his own way; and the Lord hath laid on him the iniquity of us all.' Isaiah, chapter fifty-three, verse six. We have all sinned, Rafe. You, me, your father."

A bird landed overhead in the tree and began to sing. Many times Rafe had walked in the park near their apartment with Father. Not a bird flew near them that Father couldn't identify. He'd recognize this bird by its song without looking up.

Why couldn't you love me enough, Father?

A hand touched his shoulder.

"Let go of your hurt and anger. Put them in God's hands. He invites you to do so. And forgive your father. As Christ said, when he taught the disciples how to pray, 'If ye forgive not men their trespasses, neither will your Father forgive your trespasses.' That's in the sixth chapter of Matthew. Don't let your father's failing lead to failings of your own."

A pat on the shoulder, and the chaplain was gone. How many times had his father placed his hand on his shoulder?

He must have sat mourning the lost relationship all day. Distant rumbling became louder. The planes were returning from the day's mission. Time to head back. He picked up the tarp and Brenda's bouquet, and trudged through the field.

Alan and Cal looked up at his entrance to their Quonset hut. A uniform tunic lay on Rafe's cot. His own still hung from the peg where he'd left it. He turned to his crewmates.

Alan answered his unasked question. "*Judgment Day* went down. Chutes came out of it, but they're not coming back. They were deep in Germany."

Rafe swung around to Paul's cot. It had been stripped.

"Soon as we heard, we put all his gear together, ready to ship home. His, and Floyd's, and Tony's, and Roger's." Cal heaved a sigh. "We set aside Paul's tunic since the 381st doesn't issue replacement clothes and yours has a tear."

Paul was gone. Rafe stared at his new tunic. He'd rather have his friend.

Chapter Thirty-Two

Southern Sweden
Saturday, May 13, 1944

Fifty-nine large sandstone boulders stood in the outline of a ship. Jennie circled the boulder at the bow. Such settings usually served as burial monuments, but one theory held that Ale's Stones honored the crew of a ship lost at sea. That one sounded appropriate. Among the stones on the top of a bluff, she had a sweeping panorama of the Baltic Sea. Countless ships, maybe in sight of land, had sunk in that placid-looking water.

Today the sea was more likely to swallow airplanes. How many American planes, damaged in battle with the Germans, sought safety here in neutral Sweden but hadn't made it? How many men had disappeared beneath the waves without a trace? Their loved ones back home waited with hope that couldn't be fulfilled.

She heaved a sigh, and pressed a hand against the nearest boulder. This rock had stood here for centuries. Her exhibit would be a brief showing. And not to the dead airmen, but to those who survived. She sketched a quick drawing of the stones with plans to add a smoking bomber low on the horizon, desperate to reach a safe haven.

"Ready to go, Jennie?" Dad straightened from the boulder he'd been leaning against. "We should be on our way."

This southernmost county of Sweden featured more gently rolling farmland and less forest than the rest of the country. As they continued on to Malmö, Jennie watched the passing landscape. They could have been in the Illinois countryside. What were the flight crews' first impressions of their haven? Or maybe they didn't even notice, too preoccupied with keeping their damaged planes in the air or keeping wounded crewmembers alive.

Malmö looked a lot like Stockholm. Not only did the city occupy the waterfront along the Öresund strait, but a canal encircled the old city center. The restored remnants of a centuries-old castle graced a spacious park. Too bad they didn't have time to explore.

She and Dad arrived at Bulltofta Airfield, the home of a Swedish Air Force Fighter Wing in Malmö, in the early afternoon. The fighters spent their time in patrol duty, flying coastal reconnaissance flights to guard their neutrality, and guiding damaged aircraft of the belligerents to the airfield.

Jennie's heart skipped a beat at the sight of three parked heavy bombers, a Flying Fortress and two Liberators, and then sank. The planes looked ready to fly. "Oh, Dad, they don't look like they're in bad shape."

Dad chuckled. "Those ships have been repaired. They're waiting to be ferried to the storage field in Västerås, near Stockholm, to keep the airfield here from being congested." He pointed to three more Flying Fortresses in a beehive of activity. "Those planes arrived last weekend. The crewmembers won't be here, but the mechanics are internees from earlier arrivals. I'm sure you'll find someone glad to talk to you."

Scaffolding had been rolled up to the wing of one Fortress, and the nose cowl removed from the inboard engine. Perched on the platform with his sleeves rolled up and an arm deep in the back of the engine, a mechanic didn't look around at their arrival.

"How's it coming, Sergeant?"

The man glanced down, and his eyes widened to see an unknown officer addressing him. "The push rod tube and ignition lines were sliced up. We're replacing them with cannibalized parts, and this engine will be top notch in an hour, sir, and ready to go to Västerås."

"Very good." Dad turned to Jennie. "I'll be in the office."

With his departure, Jennie looked up at the sergeant. "Can you work and talk at the same time?" Stupid thing to say. Insult him right off the bat. "I mean, I don't want to distract you into hooking up your tubes into the carburetor or something."

Engines had carburetors. Her brother always had trouble with the carburetor in his car during high school.

The mechanic leaned away from the engine to study her. "That'd be a neat trick." He wiped his hands on a filthy rag hanging out of his back pocket. "You're American. What are you doing here?"

"I came with my dad." She nodded in the direction of the office. "I do office work for the interned aircrews, but right now I'm working on putting together a Swedish art exhibit from the internees' prospective, for after the war."

"Is the major your father?" At her nod, he added, "Of course he is." He gave an exaggerated sigh and a wink. "So what do you want to know?"

"Oh, your name, where you're from, what base you were at, how long you've been here, why you ended up here. That sort of thing. I'm Jennie, by the way. Do you mind if I take your picture?"

Selecting a wrench from the tools at his feet, he laughed. "You sound like a reporter. I'm Hal Neuser from Bismarck, North Dakota. I'm from the 388th Bomb Group based at Knettishall. I've been here since February after a mission to Rostock. One engine got knocked out and we were leaking fuel like a sieve. Never would have made it back to England. Thought we'd have to ditch in the North Sea. In winter, that would have been a death sentence, unless the Germans picked us up. They're nearby, you know. Denmark's only about twenty miles from here, across the Öresund Strait. Copenhagen's within spitting distance."

His hands disappeared back behind the engine. Jennie set down her notepad and snapped a photo.

"And you've been working on the planes ever since you arrived here?"

"Pretty much. They quizzed us about what service schools we attended to find out if we had technical skills. We work five days a week maintaining all the American planes. The pilots get to take them up to test the repairs and keep their skills sharp."

Another airman crawled up on the repair stand, paying more attention to Jennie than to what he was doing. He nearly dropped the gizmo he carried.

"Hey, careful with that tube, Stu. They don't stock 'em at the corner store, you know." Hal tugged something free from the engine and examined it. "Here you go, miss. A piece of German flak."

Jennie gingerly accepted the tangled shard of metal. Had it been flat, it would measure two inches by three inches. The bomber sported several holes in its fuselage. She waved a hand toward them. "Pieces like this made those holes?"

"Yep," Stu answered. "They tear right through the planes and the soft bodies inside the planes."

"This is Stu Luellwitz, by the way. He arrived in March in a B-24 Liberator bomber." Hal raised a hand to hide his mouth from Stu. "And he actually thinks the Libs are better than the Forts, if you can imagine that."

Jennie turned the shard around. Little pieces of flak like this were capable of inflicting so much damage. Unbelievable. She looked up at Stu's retort.

"May I point out that the B-24s provide our rides out of here?"

"That's because they can't spare the B-17s from combat."

Jennie interrupted before the friendly argument could escalate. "Do you know when you'll leave?"

"Since we're gainfully employed, we may have to stay for the duration. Those who don't work go back to England after a few months."

"Lucky devils," Stu interjected.

"Lucky nothing. They're probably headed for the Pacific now. I'll stay here. We even get our flight pay, for crying out loud." Hal gave the replacement valve a final twist. "The Swedes used to repatriate the Brits and the Krauts one for one. But they can't do that with us because there are so many of us. So they sneak us out during the darkest nights in a B-24 painted black and stripped of all guns. Non-military, supposedly. The Krauts would love to shoot 'em down if they catch 'em."

Before Jennie could tell him she'd arrived on one, sudden activity near the office interrupted them.

Several men, including Dad, came outside. All eyes turned skyward.

"Another bomber must be coming in." Stu shaded his eyes as he searched the sky.

Jennie began adjusting her camera for distance. Here was her chance to get a real action shot. Signs of damage would be good. Maybe a little smoke trailing from an engine.

What was she thinking? Damage meant danger to the crew. How awful of her.

"There!" Hal spotted the plane first. "It's a Fort with three Swedish fighters escorting it. No! One's a Kraut and he's still firing on the Fort. The Swedes are firing at him. That Fort's in big trouble."

The B-17 wasn't flying straight. It wanted to roll to the left. And there was smoke. Lots of smoke coming from both wings. If it couldn't straighten out, it wouldn't land on the airfield.

The German fighter turned away, chased by the two Swedes.

The Fort was out of control. It was going to crash in the farmland adjacent to the airfield. The sound of its struggling engines rolled across the land, ragged and popping. One wing dipped low. It scraped the ground and tore free with a screech. Fire burst from an engine.

The rest of the plane slapped down, throwing up waves of dirt. The remaining wing dug in and snapped off, tearing away a large section of the fuselage.

Various other parts broke off as the main body jerked sideways to a stop against an embankment.

Men ran toward cars and trucks. Hal and Stu jumped down and headed for a nearby truck. Jennie ran with them. She might not be welcome at the crash site, but she was going along. Hal assisted her into the cab before leaping onto the bed. Stu gunned the motor and they bounced across the field.

"Spare parts is all that bird's good for now."

Stu's assessment had to be correct. The devastation was astonishing. Debris littered the field for hundreds of yards. Fires burned at the wings, but not the fuselage. Still, could anyone have survived?

A Swedish rescue team rushed to the fuselage. From the hole torn open by the missing wing, they reached into the plane and guided the airmen out. Two men dressed in heavy leather jackets staggered out with dazed expressions. Three more carried one of their crewmates, his clothes stained with blood. Two more supported another man.

Jennie photographed the rescue. She framed them gently laying down the wounded man and snapped away. She focused on the walking wounded man who collapsed beside him, reaching for him. How could they have survived this wreck?

Chapter Thirty-Three

Over Germany
Saturday, May 13, 1944

"Bombs away!"

With the loss of four thousand pounds of bombs over Stettin, the plane should have bounced upward. Instead, it threatened to roll over. From his position standing behind Alan, Rafe stumbled back and his head hit the cheek gun suspended overhead. He grabbed the bombing control panel and staggered back to his desk.

Rusty's voice yelled through the intercom. "We just lost three or four feet off the left wingtip."

Harold added to the confusion. "One of the bomb doors didn't close. It's loose on one end."

"Engine one is starting to smoke." Rusty amended his report with another yell. "Fire in engine one."

Cal could be heard in the cockpit. "Fuel shut-off on one, and feathered."

A B-17 could fly nicely on three engines, but they were deep in Germany and they wouldn't be able to keep up with the formation. Tension coiled in the pit of Rafe's stomach. He noted the time and recorded their position and problems in his log.

Whump! Another shell burst right in front of them. Rafe and Alan were showered by fragments of

Plexiglas. Rafe brushed away the bits on his log. Engine three began to cough and spit. The vibrations rattled the nose.

"Reduce the manifold pressure and increase the RPM." Steve fired the orders. "Enrich the fuel mixture to cool it down."

Rafe glanced around the nose for further damage. His heart skipped a beat and he broke out in a sweat. "Ah, Steve? Red fluid is dripping down from the cockpit area."

Silence reigned for ten seconds. "Hydraulic brake fluid. We've got a broken line here."

The formation headed north-northwest to get over the Baltic Sea, cross Denmark, and fly southwest over the North Sea. In theory, the longer route would keep them away from flak. For damaged planes, however, the longer air time allowed problems to multiply. And their next problem didn't take long to materialize.

Hanging below the plane in the ball turret, Rusty watched for trouble no one else could see. "Fuel's gushing out the right wing tank."

"Fuel transfer?" As flight engineer, that was Mickey's job. This was his first mission back with the crew after recovering from Cal's bucking bronco exhibition. Carlo remained grounded with broken ribs, and George had rejoined the crew in his place.

"As soon as you're able, I need to know how much fuel we still have." The crew didn't need interruptions now, but Rafe needed an answer to plan their route.

"Maybe eight hundred gallons."

Rafe dropped his pencil. "We're not going back to England."

Cal couldn't accept that. "Are you sure?"

"Even if we turned due west right now, we could maybe make it to Holland, but that's no help." Rafe sucked in a lungful of cold oxygen. "We'll either be guests of *der Führer* tonight, or we can try to make for Sweden."

"I vote for Sweden."

"Me too."

Alan interrupted the gunners' vote. "Bogies, one o'clock low. Harold, call the fighter escorts for help."

Rafe straightened out the cartridge belt for the right cheek gun. At least they still had plenty of ammo.

The two German FW-190s spotted them and rose. Rusty had the best shot. His gun started firing when the enemy reached within a thousand yards of them. The fighters spread out. Rusty couldn't shoot at them both. They closed to six hundred yards and the fighter not in Rusty's aim raked them with his twenty millimeter cannon.

"We got more trouble," Harold squawked. "Fire in the radio room."

"Put it out," Steve ordered. "Mickey, help him."

The damage to the electrical system rendered the gun turrets inoperable.

"Get me out of here," Rusty wailed. "My electric suit's not working and I'm freezing."

"Hold your horses." Mickey's voice sounded strained. He probably could have used more ground time before returning to flight status. "Harold, give me some help here. We gotta crank it manually."

"Here's a bit of good news for you." Even in an emergency, Dan sounded cheerful. "Those fighters are skedaddling instead of finishing us off."

"Maybe they need to refuel. They may be back. Any more immediate problems?" When no one replied, Steve continued. "We're on our own. Harold, call group leader and tell him England's out of our reach. We'll try for Sweden."

A minute later, Cal laughed. He explained. "When Harold reported our plans, he added, 'Long live the 381st. Triumphant we fly.'"

Triumphant we fly. The group motto. Too bad it didn't apply to them right now. Rafe studied his map. They'd be passing Anklam and Peenemunde to the east. Both were guaranteed to have fighter protection. He scanned the driftmeter and altimeter, and fiddled with his G-1 True Airspeed Computer. With their reduced speed, they could expect to reach Sweden in an hour.

Half an hour dragged by. Steve and Cal discussed what type of airfields Sweden might have and how they'd manage without hydraulics. Rafe strained his eyes watching for the coast. They just might make it after all.

George delivered the final blow. "Bogies, eight o'clock level. You can bet they're not our fighters."

The ball turret was inoperative. The top turret could only be slowly positioned by hand cranks. That left George with the waist gun, unless the Germans strayed far enough forward into the range of Rafe's cheek gun. He swung it into position. Alan hurried up to the cockpit to help crank the top turret. He sent Rusty back to the waist, ready to man the opposite gun.

The whine of the engines altered as Steve coaxed a little more speed out of them. They couldn't outrun a fighter though.

The rattle of a waist gun vibrated through the bomber. Answering bullets smashed into the bomber. The fighters roared by and flipped around for another pass.

They were over the Baltic Sea now. Land shimmered in the distance. Sweden. Just a little closer and the fighters would have to break off and go back to Germany.

Guns fired again.

"They got me."

Dan!

"Rusty, get back to the tail."

Rafe dropped down to the passageway to go help Dan, but stopped. Steve's order made sense. He had to stay at his gun.

Rusty swore. "Dan's bleeding like a stuck pig. He got it bad in the shoulder."

The fighters weren't coming around to the front. Rafe started for the passageway again, but checked outside the windows first, and groaned. More bad news. "Engine three is smoking."

Cal answered. "Fighters at twelve o'clock level."

Rafe spun around. How could they have slipped in front? Those were strange airplanes. "Those are Swedish planes."

"Two of the Krauts turned back, but one of 'ems still after us." Rusty was manning the tail gun, not helping Dan.

Rafe yanked off his oxygen mask, no longer needed at their lower altitude, and scrambled up to the cockpit, squeezed past Alan in the top turret, dashed down the catwalk over the bomb bay and the open mangled door below, and ran through the radio room and waist compartment. Dan slumped in the passageway by the door, one hand pressed against the opposite shoulder, his face chalky white. Rafe fumbled in the escape kit attached to Dan's parachute harness for the morphine and administered a shot. He disconnected Dan's cables.

"We need to get you to the radio room. Can you walk?"

They shuffled forward, passing George, still firing the waist gun. "That guy just won't quit. Is he going all the way to Sweden with us?"

In the radio room, Rafe busied himself with the medical kit, removing Dan's cold weather gear, and pressing a pad to the wound. Blood continued to seep out. Too much blood.

Harold had plugged in Rafe's communications cable, so he heard Steve's announcement. "Alan, throw out the bomb site. Everyone to the radio room. Brace for a crash landing."

Rafe had to take care of his own equipment. "Harold, keep pressure on Dan's shoulder."

Without waiting for Harold's compliance, he dashed back across the catwalk and swung down into the nose. With a sweep of his arm he dumped his instruments and log into his briefcase. The maps went into a sack he weighted with empty .50 caliber casings. The rice-paper flimsie containing the secret codes for the day could be eaten to avoid falling into enemy hands. He hesitated. It would quickly decompose in the seawater. He shoved it into the sack. Alan added the top secret Norden bombsight. They tied the neck and hurried back to the radio room, dropping the sack through the open bomb bay door on the way. From the bottom of the Baltic, it would reveal no secrets.

Rafe relieved Harold to keep pressure on Dan's wound. Mickey, George, and Rusty piled into the room.

A loud bang, and the plane lurched to the left.

"There goes engine two. Fuel is shut off." Strain filled Cal's voice. "It won't feather."

"No matter now. This isn't going to be pretty. Brace!" Steve yelled.

They weren't in level flight. Their left wing gouged the ground. With a screech, the plane swerved and plowed into the ground. The men were tossed about. Rafe hung on to Dan, pressing his wound. His head smacked something hard and lights exploded in his eyes. A large section of the fuselage peeled away, leaving the radio room exposed. The plane jerked sideways to a stop.

Other than the thundering of his heart, only silence filled Rafe's ears. Boy, did he have a headache. Someone tugged at his shoulder.

"Rafe? Can you hear me? You're bleeding, Rafe. Let go of Dan. We've got him."

Hands pulled him upright. His vision swirled. Did that groan come from him? *"Wasser, bitte?"*

"Speak English, buddy. We're in Sweden at your request." Was Cal amused?

From their new opening, they saw a man run toward them, calling something in a foreign language.

"What's he yelling about?" Mickey looked uneasy. "We are in Sweden, aren't we?"

"He probably wants to know why we plowed up his field." Trust Rusty to wisecrack at a time like this.

Rafe gritted his teeth. He would not embarrass himself by throwing up. He shouldn't. Breakfast was twelve hours ago and his stomach ought to be empty. Why was it churning?

A truck pulled up. An officer greeted them in stilted English. "Welcome to Sweden, gentlemen. The war is over for you." He nodded to Dan and Rafe. "You have wounded. We have medical personnel here."

Alan directed Harold and George to help him lift Dan. Cal and Steve helped Rafe to his feet. Carefully avoiding ragged edges, they stepped down to Swedish soil. The wing was missing. Rafe turned his head to see where it had gone, but dizziness canceled that movement. He slumped to the ground beside Dan.

Dan opened his eyes. "Hey, lieutenant, d'ya mind? You're dripping blood on me."

Lots of people crowded around them. Medics set to work on Dan. One tried to assess Rafe. He leaned away. To lie down and sleep was all he needed. A gentle hand settled on his shoulder. "Rafe?"

His vision blurred as darkness threatened. He tried to focus. "My Jennie Lind?"

The darkness won.

Part 2

Mine eyes have seen the glory
of the coming of the Lord,
He is trampling out the vintage
where the grapes of wrath are stored;
He hath loosed the fateful lightning
of His terrible swift sword—
His truth is marching on.

Julia Ward Howe

Chapter Thirty-Four

Southern Sweden
Saturday, May 13, 1944

Jennie's heart thundered in her chest. Never in her wildest dreams would she have imagined recognizing the men stumbling out of the plane. So often she'd wondered how Rafe fared in the war, and now here he was. And he remembered her, even in his wounded condition.

His Jennie Lind. Her face heated as his crewmates stared and Dad's eyes popped.

"Who have we here?" Dad's voice sounded congenial, but a thread of steel girded it.

The enlisted men babbled answers.

"The peach from the ship."

"Hey, you're the lieutenant's girl."

Dad's brows slammed down at that tidbit.

"Ah, no, boys, you misunderstand. My father's asking who the lieutenant is."

"Your father?"

Suddenly, they were all stricken dumb.

"The lieutenant's girl, hmm?"

Their lips unsealed.

"They're good friends."

"The lieutenant's a swell guy."

"Even if he is German."

A medic waved smelling salts under Rafe's nose. He groaned and raised a shaky hand to his forehead. His left eye crept open, and slammed down.

If they weren't surrounded by his crew, Dad, and a bunch of Swedes, Jennie would have held his hand.

His eye opened again and settled on her. Its mate wrenched open. One blink threatened to keep them both closed. "Did I die?"

"What are you talking about?" The copilot, the one who liked to gamble, crouched beside him. "We're in Sweden. You know that."

After loading Dan into a truck, the medics returned with the backboard.

Rafe pointed a wavering finger. "I see an angel. She looks just like my Jennie."

Her face had to be glowing like a torch. What were the chances Dad hadn't heard his mumbling?

"Man, when you hit your head, you knocked out all your sense." Cal stepped away so the medics could move Rafe. "I'm telling you, we're in Sweden and that *is* Jennie."

Jennie walked alongside Rafe as he was taken to the ambulance. Asking to go with him would bring a firm no from Dad and probably the medics as well. She stood aside and watched the ambulance drive away, bumping over the field.

One of the crewmen sidled up to her. "Miss, here's your case."

The married bombardier so in love with his gem of a wife, Ruby. Alan. Why did he press a briefcase into her hands?

He whispered, "It's Rafe's, filled with his log and navigation tools. The Swedes don't need it."

Rafe's case! She hugged it to her chest. None of the Swedes looked at her as Alan stepped away. How sweet that they remembered her. They shouldn't mind being photographed. Two Swedes questioned the stiff pilot. Stu. No, Steve. He assured them the plane held no bombs, but ammunition remained in the guns.

Dad instructed the crew to find places in the trucks for the ride to the office. Jennie ran for her camera and snapped pictures of the crew with the plane in the background. She added her notepad to Rafe's briefcase. It tangled with something. She fished out some strange circular slide things. One was labeled PRESSURE ALTITUDE AT GROUND IN FEET. That made no sense, nor the spiraling line of numbers. She turned the dial. This is how navigators determined their positions? Rafe must be a genius.

Not until the next morning could Jennie visit Rafe at the hospital. He sat in an upholstered waiting room chair, clad in a faded yellow bathrobe. His color looked more natural. A bandage on his forehead hid the damage from the crash landing.

His eyes widened when he saw her and he came to his feet. "I really did see you yesterday? I thought I must have been hallucinating."

"You do say the sweetest things when you hallucinate." Jennie smoothed a hand across her skirt. She'd worn the prettiest dress she'd brought along. A rich maroon showered with polka dots, the V neckline was edged in lace and featured a fabric flower at the point.

He groaned and pressed a hand alongside his head, now bandaged. "All I remember is a wild ride down to a very rough landing."

He reached for her hand, then pulled her close for a hug. "You really are here."

Jennie laughed. "I've been here. It's you who is unexpected."

She laid a hand on the side of his face.

He turned his head to kiss her hand. "I've thought about you."

Jennie rested her head on his shoulder as she stood in his embrace. Who cared if anyone saw?

Rafe sighed. "Dan was shot in the shoulder. He had surgery and now he's wrapped up like a mummy. Do you know where the rest of the crew is?"

"They're staying in the barracks at Bulltofta Airfield for now. As belligerents in a neutral nation, you'll be interned. They'll take you to a town in northern Sweden in a day or two."

Rafe eased back down in the chair. "No more war." He stared at the linoleum floor. "No more bombing missions over Germany. No more flak. No one trying to kill us." He looked up at her. "Like a switch has been flipped."

Jennie sat in the chair beside him. "Has it been difficult for you? Being at war with your old homeland?"

"We bombed Cologne. Or what was left of Cologne." He reached for her hand and interlaced their fingers. His were cold and she rubbed them.

"My father's still alive. I saw my cousin Christoph in an English prison camp. He's glad to be out of the war. And you know?" He glanced around. "I am too. Germany's going to end up being one huge heap of rubble. I don't want to be part of that anymore. I should have been in intelligence or a translator or something else. I understand the need to smash Germany's ability to continue the war, but…" His head drooped, and he raised shaky fingers to massage his temple. "Last Monday, one of my friends didn't come back. Jennie, I'm so tired of it."

Jennie raised a hand to his shoulder. "You may be an American now, but Germany will always be your homeland."

He pressed his lips together and nodded slightly. Then a determined smile grew. "So, how have the last two months been for you? You obviously survived Scotland alone."

She laughed. "I stayed with a wonderful couple in Gourock, and as I traveled across to Leuchars, I did count sheep. You were right. They have a lot of them."

Rafe's eyes brightened, glistening with humor as they had on board the *Queen Mary*. "And you have magnificent paintings prepared for your exhibit?"

"Well, not exactly, not yet. But I've got direction now. It'll showcase the airmen's internment experience. That's why I came to Malmö with Dad." He looked interested, so she kept going. "I'll have a series of photographs interspersed with paintings and maybe small Swedish objects. The photos will show planes arriving, like yours yesterday. A local newspaper photographer promised me copies of his shots to go along with my own."

She jumped up and paced in front of him. "I also took photos of men working on the planes, and I'll take more at the camps, so it'll be a photographic record." She clapped her hands. "And since you don't live far from Chicago, you can come to the exhibit."

He was laughing at her. She laughed, too. He must think she was camp happy. Isn't that what the men called someone off his rocker? The war may still rage, but here she had a good friend at the legation, a wonderful new cousin, and now Rafe. She couldn't ask for more.

"Do you think Dan would mind if I take his picture? I don't want to hide the ugly side of war."

"He won't mind because I'll tell him he won't." He rose and took her arm. "This way. I'll probably be able to leave the hospital today, but they took away my clothes."

"You'll need to buy civilian clothes anyway. You aren't allowed to wear your uniforms in a neutral country."

Jennie accompanied the crew to a men's clothing store. Her jaw dropped as George tried on a grass green and black plaid suit. The garish outfit made him look like a clown, but he admired himself in a mirror with satisfaction.

She sidled up to Rafe. "Is he seriously thinking of buying that?"

Rafe pulled a cocoa brown, doubled-breasted suit from the rack. "At least he looks better than Rusty."

Jennie turned around, and slapped a hand over her mouth. Rusty wore a mustard-colored suit coat, loud plaid slacks a Scotsman wouldn't be caught dead in, a blue striped shirt, and a red tie. "He can't be allowed to dress like that. He'll be a laughingstock, and you represent America here."

"You tell him, honey." Rafe held up the brown suit with a pinstripe shirt. "Would I be presentable in this?"

"Very nice." She snatched a brown felt fedora from a hat rack. "And this will complete your look perfectly."

She marched over and tugged burnt orange trousers from Harold's grasp.

"Definitely not. Too gaudy." She assessed Harold's choices. "Nice charcoal suit. The matching trousers go with it. If you want to add some color to go with it, try this forest green shirt." She pulled out a suit he hadn't selected. "I recommend these black and white pinstripes for a dignified appearance."

She had the crewmen's attention. "Gentlemen, the suit coats and the trousers go together as a set. No more than two colors per outfit unless you have a plaid, but then," she eyed Rusty, "don't mix patterns. Pair a plaid with a solid. If you want bright colors, keep them in your ties."

Rafe stepped up beside her, clad in a navy suit with a crisp white shirt. His navy tie featured thin diagonal stripes of gold and red. She slipped her hand around his arm.

"Here is the look you want. The lieutenant won't be embarrassed by his attire." She swung her gaze back to Rusty and bit her lip. He was the guy with the attitude. Best to be frank. "Unless you're applying for a position as a clown, I strongly suggest you start over. And lose the mustard suit. Please."

"Do we have to wear suits all the time?" George tugged at his collar like it was a noose. "All I ever wear at home is overalls."

"You'll have plenty of opportunity for casual wear." Jennie pointed to a display of knitted apparel. "Those sweaters and vests are popular. You'll want sportswear, too."

After Rafe admonished the men to listen to Jennie, she was the artist, their choices improved. If she raised a brow, the selection was discarded. A smile meant they kept it. The shopping trip continued smoothly until they were handed their bills.

"Two hundred fifty?" Alan blanched. "I can't afford this."

Jennie held up a hand. "Remember, these amounts are in kronor. That's what the S-k-r means. One dollar is about equal to four kronor, so to figure your dollar amount, divide your total by four. Alan, yours is about sixty dollars."

He still looked ready to bolt. Jennie edged over to him. "As a second lieutenant, what is your monthly salary?"

"One sixty, plus fifty dollars for flying status."

"You'll still be receiving that, plus a per diem of seven dollars while you're away from your base. The average Swede doesn't make seven dollars in a day. So you can afford this." She patted his new light brown suit. "And I think Ruby will be pleased with your new wardrobe."

His eyes brightened at that, and he added a wallet to his purchases.

She returned to Rafe. He looked a bit peaked and could use some rest. "You should have waited to get to the internment camp to do your shopping."

"I'm fine. Headache's almost gone. Besides, you don't expect me to travel there in my underwear, do you?"

If he could be blasé about a mild concussion, so could she. "We would have found you a bathrobe."

He smiled. "What would we do without you to shepherd us through all this?"

His appreciation warmed her.

She led them out to Gustav Adolfs Torg, a large open square where they waited for a tram ride to the train station. The enlisted men ogled the foreign cityscape in silence. George especially seemed intrigued with the stairstep-like façade of steeply-pitched gabled buildings, rather than having flush roof lines. Mickey appeared uneasy with the indecipherable language of the people around them.

Steve joined Rafe and Jennie. "What will the camp be like, where we're going?"

"Oh, it's actually not a camp. You'll stay in resort hotels or spas or guest houses, maybe even private homes. You'll have Swedish supervision, but the camps, for lack of a better word, are handled by airmen appointed by the air attaché in Stockholm, my dad's boss. You'll have a roll call and calisthenics every morning, but then you're free within a twelve-mile radius. And you get a three-day pass each month if you want to visit Stockholm or some other place."

After boarding the tram, Cal asked, "What do we do all day?"

"Lots of sports. We're forming teams for soccer, basketball, tennis, and baseball. Lots of bicycling. During the winter, many of the men learned to ski or skate, but now you can sail, and we're discussing regattas. American magazines are brought in. Conversational Swedish classes are available in most camps, and other classes are in the works." They didn't brighten at the news of the classes she'd helped organize. Of course not. They weren't bored yet. They had to decompress from combat first.

"Those with mechanical skills will be sent to the airfields to restore and maintain your planes, and you pilots get to test fly them." She laughed when Cal scowled. "Don't worry. I haven't heard of any of those test flights ending in disaster."

As the tram trundled through town to the train station, the men watched the passing scenery. Except for Rafe, who sat with eyes closed, they looked apprehensive. Jennie might have felt the same way if she'd suddenly been plunked down in, say, Spain. She smiled. Her ideas for activities for the men were being acted on. Her work with the OSS was minor, her art exhibit nonessential, but she could help the airmen cope with their strange new lives.

Chapter Thirty-Five

Rättvik, Sweden
Wednesday, May 31, 1944

Rafe peered around the corner. That obnoxious girl wasn't in sight. A sigh escaped him. No sooner had he relaxed than a hand clamped down on his shoulder. He started, and spun around.

"Who are you spying on?" Cal leaned around him to look down the street.

"Just making sure Maj-Britt isn't anywhere around."

"Your Britt? What happened to your Jennie?"

"Not *my* Britt," Rafe snapped. "Her name is pronounced My-Britt, and she's trying to sink her talons in me."

The Coolidge crew had been separated the day after leaving Malmö. The enlisted men were quartered in Falun, while the officers continued nearly thirty miles further north to Rättvik. The small resort town perched on the eastern edge of Lake Siljan would allow Rafe to could get in some sailing.

The officers had moved into a large two-story lodge. They were told to double up and choose rooms. He and Alan barely took time to drop their belongings in a room with its own balcony before they set out to explore. A nearby hill begged to be hiked, and the

Americans didn't hesitate to oblige. From its summit, a vast panorama delighted their eyes. The quiet blue lake extended for miles, far beyond their view. The region also offered plenty of opportunities for bicycling.

Birds twittered overhead in the pine trees, and a light wind sighed in the boughs. The fragrance of evergreen perfumed the air. A weight Rafe hadn't been consciously aware of slipped from his shoulders. The war was over for him. Here in this restful community, he could forget about bombing Germany into oblivion. Here he was safe from possible capture by the Germans. Here he could ponder his feelings toward his father.

Jennie had promised to visit at her first opportunity. They would have no trouble filling their days as they became better acquainted.

Rättvik was paradise. But paradise had a serpent. Maj-Britt.

When the men had hiked back down into town, they were greeted by a group of young ladies. One took Rafe's arm. Her demeanor shouted her desperation for a man. Wherever he went now, she popped up. He treated her with disinterest, but she failed to take the hint. Her attitude was mystifying. Where was her self-respect?

Other internees had watched in amusement. An airman who'd been there since February offered insight. "She wants a husband. Word is she got dumped by a Swede. With all the Americans coming to town, she's aiming to snag a man who will take her to America where the streets are paved with gold and everyone has a maid."

The men quartered at the guesthouse had chuckled. "She checks out each new arrival and goes to work. The last guy got desperate."

Rafe leaned forward. "How'd he get rid of her?"

"He got transferred to another camp. Just wait until the next group comes. She'll latch on to someone more willing."

Today, the men planned to go sailing. Rafe had selected a boat barely big enough for the four of them. No possibility existed for Maj-Britt to finagle her way onboard. With a last furtive look around, Rafe and his friends headed for the water's edge.

"Annika's a nice girl." Cal put on his American Optical sunglasses. Rafe's sunglasses must have been left aboard *Sweet Patootie*. "She's not proprietary with me. It'd be fun to take her along."

"Rent a canoe with her." There was another possibility for when Jennie came. "If she goes sailing with us, Maj-Britt will insist on going. I refuse to be trapped on a boat with her."

"And if Rafe bails out at the last second, we'll be up a creek, because Rafe's the sailor." Alan stuffed his hands in his back pockets, his cardigan sleeves tied loosely around his neck. "Boy, I sure do wish Ruby was here. This would be like a long honeymoon for us."

They rounded the corner to the pier, and Rafe stopped dead. "Somebody told."

"Oh, there you are." Maj-Britt's shrill call grated on Rafe like fingernails on a blackboard. He didn't blame the Swede who dumped her.

Cal cleared his throat. "I guess I did tell Annika we were going sailing. I didn't know she'd tell everyone else."

Rafe clenched his fists as Maj-Britt bore down on him. "I am not spending the day with her. I refuse."

Steve pushed Cal forward with one hand and prodded Rafe to move with the other. "Cal, you're on point. Alan and I have Rafe's flanks. If being polite doesn't work, we'll be rude."

Maj-Britt's chatter oozed with hyperbole. "I can't wait to go sailing. We haven't been out on the lake at all this year. I'm so glad you thought of this." She tried to weasel her way between Alan and Rafe, but Alan held his position. She looked at him askance. "Excuse me, please."

"You're excused."

Rafe nearly cracked a smile at Alan's rejoinder, but kept his lips firmly pressed. His mother often admonished, "If you had nothing nice to say, keep your mouth shut." Did that ever apply now.

After a slight hesitation, Maj-Britt circled behind and grabbed at his right arm. Steve edged closer so she couldn't squeeze in. Soon they'd be tangling feet and sprawling on the ground.

The yellow sailboat waited at the end of the pier. Everything was in place and ready to go. Except for getting rid of unwanted company.

"We'll certainly be cozy." Maj-Britt remained oblivious.

Ahead of them, Cal and Annika whispered with their heads together. Annika stepped away, looking back at Maj-Britt with wrinkled brow. She squared her shoulders, marched over, and linked an arm with her friend. "We'll see you men for lunch."

Maj-Britt whipped her head around. "What do you mean? We're going sailing with them. You said so."

"I said the men were going sailing."

"Rafe, tell them we're sailing together."

Busy hoisting the sail and directing his crewmates in loosing lines and lowering the centerboard, Rafe barely looked up. "It was nice of you to see us off."

"Rafe."

Rafe let out the line on the sail. It caught the breeze and filled with a snap. The sailboat scooted away from the pier.

"Rafe!"

Three minutes passed before Alan ventured a comment. "Are we in a race with somebody, or just in a rush to gain a little distance?"

Rafe's shoulders slumped. For a few hours, anyway, he was free of Maj-Britt. He adjusted the sail for a slower pace, and offered Alan the tiller. "I do everything to discourage her. What else can I do? Seeing as how we're uninvited guests of Sweden, I don't feel free to flat out tell her to get lost."

His crewmates stared at him. "You kept your cool during a dozen missions flying over hostile territory and now you're coming undone by an obnoxious female." Cal tilted his face into the sun and the breeze. "When you need to be devious, ask a woman for help. In your case, ask Jennie."

It would have been too much to hope that Maj-Britt wouldn't be waiting for him to return to the pier, along with her friends Annika and Karin. "Doesn't she have a job she should be attending to?"

"Here's how we'll handle it." Steve rubbed his hands together. "Cal and I will lead the ladies away while you and Alan load your arms with sailing gear to stow. She'll think you'll be joining us, but you disappear."

Steve's plan might have worked flawlessly, but Rafe and Alan were hungry. As they hurried for their guesthouse, they stopped in at Klingberg's Konditori. The coffee shop and bakery had become a home away from home for the internees. Rafe had just sunk his teeth into his applesauce muffin when Alan hissed, "Here they come. Hide!"

Rafe jumped up from their table, headed for the counter, backtracked to grab his muffin, then ducked under the counter extension and pressed up against the counter, surprising the proprietress.

"Shh. I'm not here."

Mrs. Klingberg sized up the situation in a thrice when Maj-Britt waltzed inside and stopped short. With a lowered hand, Mrs. Klingberg made a flicking motion. Scoot further down. He was visible through the display case glass.

"Where's Rafe?" Maj-Britt's voice advanced into the room.

Alan sounded muffled as though patting his lips with his napkin. "Didn't you see him?"

"We decided to stop in here." Uncertainty colored Cal's voice.

Did anyone notice Alan had two cups of coffee?

Footsteps approached the counter. Rafe scrambled further to the right, and dislodged a mop. The handle clattered against the cash register. Not commenting, Mrs. Klingberg removed the mop to the back door leading into the family's private quarters. The family's miniature poodle took advantage of the open door to slip inside and pounce on Rafe. He shoved the rest of his muffin into its mouth to prevent it from barking. His mouth twisted as he watched the dog enjoy his treat. That did it. He'd contact Jennie and ask about a transfer.

Chapter Thirty-Six

Rättvik, Sweden
Tuesday, June 6, 1944

Jennie stepped down from the train. Three long weeks had passed since Rafe and his crewmates had arrived in Sweden. Plenty of time to settle in and establish some sort of routine. Her plans to visit earlier had been sidetracked with a high volume of messages to encrypt and cable to London.

Blue flags with yellow crosses fluttered from poles and window sills in every direction. Today was Sweden's Flag Day. Jennie looked around. She blended in with her blue dress trimmed in jumbo gold ric-rac. The festive air was reminiscent of Fourth of July celebrations back home.

The beachfront appeared to be a likely spot for a gathering and she headed toward it. Lots of young men milled around speaking English, evidence of an internment town. Rafe should be among them. One man tipped his hat to her.

"Hello. Do you know Rafe Martell?"

His eyes widened. "You're an American."

Not the answer she had asked for. Ordinarily the observation might be amusing, but not today. "Yes, I know." She modified her tart response with raised brows and a hopeful smile. "Do you know Rafe?"

"Sure, the sailor with the millstone around his neck. He's usually with his crewmates and, of course, that girl."

Sailor? Millstone? That girl? What girl? Jennie nodded her thanks and moved on.

Merchants had set up booths like a sidewalk sale. Blue buntings striped in yellow hung from the booths. Stockholm hadn't been decked out like this for Flag Day. Maybe things were different in small towns or maybe this was for the internees' benefit.

Looping her tote bag handles over her arm, she unboxed her camera. Flags would frame her shots on either side. She'd aim for a nice Norman Rockwell-like scene. She focused on a central booth. Ooh, Dala Horses.

Like the Swedish tall case clocks, the Dala Horse originated near Mora, on the other end of Lake Siljan. The village men carved the horses in the long winter evenings. Most were painted with a red paint-pigment from the Falun copper mine, but blue, white, black and natural horses were also produced. Flower-patterned saddles were then added. She should buy a red horse. Maybe a black one too, or a natural, in a different size. As authentic Swedish handicrafts, they would be great for her exhibit.

She photographed a variety of sights, minding the sun angle and people's expressions. One last close-up of the Dala Horse booth to go with her horses and...

311

Rafe! That man now at the booth was Rafe. A woman hugged his arm like her life depended on it. He stepped closer to the display and she moved with him, the two as one. So that's what the internee meant by "that girl." She adjusted her focus. A frown marred Rafe's brow, directed at the femme fatale. He jerked his arm free. The woman didn't back off. Brazen little vamp. Jennie lowered her camera, ready to make her presence known.

"Miss Lindquist?" The ranking airman in Rättvik appeared at her side.

"Hi, Captain." She glanced back at Rafe. He'd have to wait. "My father sent a batch of the forms you requested." They were in her tote bag somewhere. She pressed her camera into his hands. "Hold this, please? Ah, here they are. And this is a new schedule for test flights by the pilots here."

Seated on a bench, they went over Dad's list of housekeeping details. About to rise, the captain paused. "The piano lessons are a big hit. The retired teacher here is working full time and loving it. One of the men acquired a guitar and is teaching several others."

"That's great." Her idea worked! Rafe must have musical ability. Something else to ask him about.

"Well, yes and no." The captain grimaced. "Some fellas have natural talent, but others send us running with our hands over our ears." With a wave, he disappeared into the crowd.

Laughing, she shoved her notes into her tote bag. What was this? A letter addressed to her, from Rättvik. From Rafe. Oh, goodness. Last night, Mom hadn't asked her to post the mail. She must have said she'd put Jennie's mail with her papers.

Jennie fingered the envelope. Rafe had neat penmanship. She glanced over at the Dala Horse booth before sliding her finger under the flap and withdrew a single sheet of paper.

Dear Jennie,

Could your father use some help in Stockholm, or at least transfer us to another internment center? Rättvik's a great town, but this girl just will not leave me alone. I'll consider any job — peel potatoes, scrub toilets. Just get me out of here. Please.

Yours sincerely,

Rafe

A stick figure drawing decorated the note. A woman with, she peered closer, yep, two little devil horns spouting from her hair clutched an outraged man.

Rafe spotted the Dala Horses. He ought to get a horse for Jennie. She'd enjoy having one for her exhibit. He examined the selection. A red one, of course. That seemed to be symbolic of Sweden. He should get one for his mother, too, and maybe one for Rita. And Oma. Who else? Certainly not the parasite clamped to his arm. He tried to break free.

"Let go of me, Maj-Britt." No more asking politely. "I need my hand." He shook her off and picked up a large red horse, the better to be seen in Jennie's exhibit.

Maj-Britt picked up a blue horse. "I like this one."

Mother would like that smaller natural horse. Maybe a white one in the same size for Oma. Rita was into miniatures. He'd get her the tiny black horse.

"I like this one."

"So you said." He was definitely not buying a blue horse.

"Going into the equestrian business?" Alan materialized at his side.

Rafe held up the black. "For my sister." He indicated the others. "And for my mother and grandmother. And Jennie."

"Who's Jennie?" Maj-Britt looked like she'd bitten into a sour grape.

Cal and Annika came up behind her. Cal nudged Annika.

"Jennie's his American girlfriend. Didn't I tell you about her? I wondered why you were going after someone else's man."

Rafe kept his back to Maj-Britt as she sputtered. Annika laid it on a bit thick—he couldn't really claim Jennie as his girlfriend. Not that he wouldn't like to.

Steve and Karin joined them.

"Say, Rafe, look who's here."

He turned to gaze into dancing blue eyes. "Jennie!"

He dumped his horses in Alan's arms and reached for her.

He bought her a Dala Horse. Jennie caressed the carving as they walked along the lakeshore, away from the crowd. "Thank you, Rafe. I've wanted to get one. This is perfect."

"I thought you might already have one, but it could always use a friend."

She tucked the horse into her tote. "Your tormentor likely won't bother you anymore." Not after the way she'd stomped off when Rafe embraced Jennie at the sales booth. "Do you still want to leave Rättvik?"

He stopped and looked at her. "Is there a job for me in Stockholm?"

"I think there might be." A smile lit her face. "I've been thinking about that. Maybe you can read newspapers."

"Read newspapers?" She must be joking. "With my feet up by a fire, and coffee and cake at my side?"

"No, no, no." Jennie's laugh rang out. "I'm quite serious. So is the job. The British have quite an extensive reading bureau, and we've followed their lead. Newspapers in all the European languages are read for anything of general intelligence or propaganda value. You look for anything of military interest, or political or economic conditions in both Germany and the occupied countries. You, of course, could read German papers."

Her last comment came out more as a question. "Yes." He bobbed his head. "Rafe. Can. Read."

She swatted his arm. "It should be more interesting than scrubbing toilets. In the meantime, I'm headed for Falun. Care to join me? Getting permission shouldn't be a problem. Dad told me Dan's joined the rest of your enlisted crewmembers quartered there."

They hopped aboard the bus just as the driver was ready to pull out. Before long, they chugged into another small resort town. No sooner did they step from the bus then they were hailed. "Jennie? Lieutenant?"

Behind them stood a young man with an arm in a sling and an everlasting smile. Neatly dressed with a vest, tie, and fedora, he looked like he'd raided his father's wardrobe.

"Dan." Rafe laid a light hand on his uninjured shoulder. "How are you doing?"

He shifted his arm. "Hurts like the dickens." His smile never dimmed. "What brings you here?"

"I'm taking care of routine military business for my dad as an excuse to socialize." Jennie grinned at her favorite gunner. "How do you like Falun?"

Dan's eyes gleamed. "Too bad we weren't here two hundred years ago. We could have visited Fet-Mats. You've heard of the copper mine here, right? They make red paint from the copper and that's why all the houses are red."

Dan would make a fine tour guide. "Two hundred years ago, after a mine had collapsed fifty years earlier, they found a dead miner, Fet-Mats, still looking like he did the day he died. His fiancée recognized him and passed out. Course, by that time, she's a real old lady. They put him on display for thirty years until he started decomposing. Wanna see his tombstone?"

Jennie stopped and stared at him. "Dan, that's positively gruesome."

With his smile stretching across his face, he shrugged his right shoulder.

"There's a museum at the mine. It's kind of interesting if you have nothing else to do."

Rafe looked at him sidelong. "And have you nothing else to do?"

Dan nodded at his sling. "I can't go biking or boating with the others."

They were heading for the mine when a bicyclist raced pell mell toward them. "Dan! Dan!" The cyclist raised a hand to wave and nearly upset his balance. George, the waist gunner who always wore overalls. He skidded to a stop in front of them. "Oh, Lieutenant. Good thing you're here. Mickey's dead."

Dan's smile disappeared. "What are you talking about? He took a girl canoeing."

George's head bobbed as he panted. "Yeah, but the canoe went belly up. The girl swam to shore, but Mickey's nowhere to be found."

Rafe waved down a passing wagon and asked for a ride. He dropped the back gate, lifted Jennie up, boosted Dan, and vaulted himself up. George handed up his bike and joined them.

Thoughts swirled in and out of focus. Today was a holiday. Lots of folks ought to be at the lake. Jennie twisted a lock of hair around her finger. Why didn't anyone see what happened? Help them? Couldn't Mickey swim?

Rafe and Dan had questions of their own. While the wagon lumbered north, they quizzed George. "Where's Rusty? Didn't he try to help Mickey? Is there a search party?"

"The guys weren't together. I guess they wanted privacy with their girls. Rusty and his girl heard screaming. Mickey's girl had made it to shore and went crazy. Rusty sent his girl for help and he went out where he thought they'd been, but he couldn't tell where the canoe had turned over." George never stopped shaking his head. "Trying to do a search pattern in a canoe ain't easy."

Lake Varpan was two miles north of town. This was the road they'd traveled when they arrived in Falun. Jennie had idly noticed canoes on the cozy lake she estimated to be a mile across. Maybe she'd seen Mickey, right before he died.

When they finally arrived, Mickey was still missing. Several boats wove back and forth. A policeman appeared to be in charge.

Arms crossed, Rusty stood on the shoreline, two canoes pulled up at his feet. Water filled the bottom of one. He did a double-take at the sight of Jennie and Rafe, and brightened. "Lieutenant Martell, can you believe this? Mickey flies over a dozen combat missions and then drowns in a peaceful lake. Can you beat that?"

A shout rang out across the lake. From one of the boats, a pole was slowly extracted from the water. One man reached down and pulled up a foot. Jennie caught her breath. The pole was shaken free and stowed. A hook glistened on its end.

"Snared like a fish," George muttered.

A man joined the crewmembers, introducing himself as Captain Bryson, assigned as the camp commander of the internees. "Someone will need to identify the body. I'll contact the legation in Stockholm. We'll see what they want done."

Jennie backed up a step, having no desire for an up-close look at the body. His name was Mickey. Didn't the captain know him, or did he no longer want to think of him as a person?

"He'll be buried in Malmö. That's where those who arrived dead or were found washed ashore are buried. They're being kept together and, after the war, their families may want them brought home."

Rusty and George followed the captain, but Dan turned away. He glanced back at Rafe. "Mickey was ordered to return to Malmö to work on planes. He wasn't happy about that. But he would've preferred to go back alive."

Rafe nodded, his gaze on the lake. "Like Rusty said, more than a dozen missions, and he dies because he fell out of a canoe. When you're least expecting it, life can take a terrible swipe at you."

He must be thinking of the day he was kicked out of the Hitler Youth. Or, more likely, the day his father rejected him. Jennie slipped her hand around his, and he gripped hard.

While they rode back to Falun with Captain Bryson, the captain questioned Jennie on the protocol for handling the tragedy, and together they went over routine housekeeping details. He then sent a cable to Stockholm.

Afterwards, she, Rafe, and Dan strolled down a tree-lined lane. Home gardens featured a dazzling early riot of summer's gayest colors. This is what they missed by living in an apartment.

"He's in hell now, where he wanted to go."

Dan's abrupt words brought her to a stop. "You can't be serious."

Rafe slowly nodded. "He thought heaven would be boring, sitting on a cloud, playing a harp all day. The people in hell would be more interesting."

The young man she met on the *Queen Mary* had been a swaggerer, interested in the 'dames.' The parable of the rich man in torment and Lazarus being comforted by Abraham fit this situation. "He's got to be regretting that choice now. Like the dickens."

Shivers convulsed her. Rafe wrapped an arm around her, and she leaned against him. A single tear slipped down her cheek and plopped on his new suit.

Chapter Thirty-Seven

Stockholm, Sweden
Friday, June 9, 1944

Jennie bounced on her toes as the train pulled into the station. Dad had arranged Rafe's transfer and he should be on this train. She scanned the windows. There, the man in the brown suit coat. He disembarked, yawning. His face brightened when he spotted her, and he came forward with a smile and a wave.

"I don't see how people at this latitude can stand it. Sunrise at two thirty in the morning." With a shrug, he dropped a bulging duffle bag at his feet, gave her a hug, and scrubbed his face. "I should be grateful we're not here during the dark days of winter."

"Just remember. The first day of summer is two weeks away and after that, the days will start getting shorter."

"Yeah. Minute by incremental minute." He offered a sleepy grin and picked up his bag. "Where to?"

She looked at his bag. "Is that all you have?"

"All my worldly possessions in Sweden."

Jennie turned to the exit. "Uh, oh. We're under surveillance. I think that man at your ten o'clock position is Swedish police. They tend to be stiffer than Nazi spies."

Rafe took a panoramic look around before settling his gaze directly at the man. The watcher walked ten paces away, stopped, and pivoted back their way.

"Should we go over and say hello?" Rafe smoothed a hand down his suit and finger combed his hair. "Might as well make his job easier."

Jennie linked her arm with his and tugged him toward the exit. She stopped short when a toddler scurried in front of them, eager to investigate a spittoon. Rafe placed a hand on the child's head and steered him away. "You don't want to play with that, little man."

His accented Swedish drew the boy's wide-eyed interest.

The hassled mother caught up with the tot. She nodded to Rafe. "*Tack.*"

As they continued on their way, Jennie grinned at Rafe. "She said thank you."

He narrowed his eyes even as a smile teased his lips. "I actually figured that out myself."

"We'll stop first at the apartment you'll be sharing with other internees assigned to the legation. Then we're free to explore for the rest of the day. You're not expected at the legation until tomorrow."

They centered their explorations on the island of Staden, the Old Town. The Royal Palace stood alongside the canal. "A tour in the royal family's absence costs one krona. That's about twenty-five cents."

Rafe pulled out his billfold. "Why not? We're rich Americans."

"Speak for yourself." Jennie poked a finger in his ribs. "I don't get an airman's paycheck."

"This will be my treat."

Even in the light of day, many of the palace rooms seemed dark. Part of the old castle had burned down centuries before. One surviving wing was incorporated into the new palace. With the different rooms designed in different centuries, the royal home offered a history in decorative styles under one roof.

"My favorite royal story is that of Gustav III." Jennie tucked her hand around Rafe's arm. "Before he was assassinated at a masked ball in 1792, he would invite noblemen to watch him wake up in the morning."

"Now that's disgusting. What if he were drooling, or snoring? His hair messed up, if he had any. He must not have been vain, to present himself at his less-than-best."

She laughed. "Those invitations were greatly valued. What's really disgusting is the jar containing the stomach contents of one of his assassins. That's supposed to be somewhere around here."

The tour guide overheard her. "You will find that in the armory, along with the costume Gustav wore when he was killed."

Rafe wrinkled his nose. "We can skip that exhibit. I've seen enough blood and gore to last a lifetime."

Jennie bit her lip. *Remember where he's been until recently.*

After leaving the palace grounds, they wandered the narrow cobble-stoned streets. Rafe held her arm on the downward slopes. The gesture was so courtly. The pavement wasn't slick, but rushed steps could be dangerous.

"These buildings are so close together, folks could almost reach out their windows and shake hands with their neighbors across the lane." She craned her neck. "Not much sunlight falls in here unless its high noon."

"And remember, the people in olden days had to watch out for anyone tossing out a bucket of slop from an overhead window."

Her gaze swung upward again, and she elbowed him as he snickered. "Thank you, Rafe, for that lovely thought." A light breeze rustled her hair. She repositioned her straw hat and tucked a lock behind her ear. "Everything's neat and tidy now."

Rafe pulled her to a stop in front of a bakery. "Look at that. Mohrenkopf. My favorite sweet." He pushed open the door and marched up to the counter. "*Hej*," he greeted the clerk. "I'll take all your *mohrenkopf*."

Jennie counted the balls in the display case. Eight. He was asking for a belly ache. "What are they?"

"Little round sponge cakes with a bit of custard in the center, and covered with chocolate glaze. Haven't you had any yet? They're delicious."

In the middle of a meandering intersection, a statue on a large pedestal rose up from a planter of greenery. Rafe guided Jennie to a bench beneath the statue where they sat quietly to enjoy the ambience and their treat. Tiny birds pecked and chirped amid the foliage. Footsteps clattered softly on the cobblestones and, in the distance, a bicycle bell rang a warning. Closer by, a conversation in a foreign language filtered through the vegetation behind them.

Beside her, Rafe stiffened. Before she could question him, he put a finger to his lips. He leaned back, his head turned. He was listening to that conversation on the other side of the pedestal. When he pantomimed writing, she fished in her purse for paper and pencil.

Two male voices spoke in hushed tones that required concentration to hear. Too bad Jennie didn't understand their language. Rafe scribbled notes, keeping an ear turned to their words. His writing was legible, but indecipherable. He wrote in German.

The conversation concluded and footsteps paced around the planter. They would be noticed. Rafe dropped the notepad behind them and placed his hands on either side of her face. He lowered his lips to hers. She forgot to breathe. He wove his fingers through her hair on her right side and pulled it forward. Shielding her face. Good thing she'd worn her hair loose today instead of pulling it back in a clip.

The footsteps came around and faltered. They'd been spotted.

Rafe swiveled, moving her with him. He finally broke the kiss but didn't release her. His lips moved toward her right ear. "He's watching us."

She struggled to breathe. "Really?" Someone was watching them? "That's nice."

A rumble of laughter vibrated his chest under her hand. His lips returned to hers. They tasted like chocolate.

After a long hesitation, the footsteps continued on.

Rafe moved his mouth back to her ear and whispered. "Can you see him?"

She peered through her lashes. "Yes, he's paused at a doorway and is looking back at us."

He wrapped his right arm around her while keeping his left hand cradling her head. This time she slipped her right hand around his back while her left hand clutched his shoulder.

"Where is he now?"

Who? Oh. She searched through her messed-up hair. "He's gone inside. I'm not sure if he's at the window or not."

Rafe eased back. He watched her with an expression like a cat lolling in cream. Her hands clenched his jacket. She released him and tried to move away, but his arms were around her. He pulled her back and kissed her again.

A bird fluttered to the ground at their feet with a loud chirp, startling them apart. Laughter released their built-up tension. Rafe grabbed the notepad.

"I think we can stroll on our way now without looking like we're trying to avoid him." He kept his arm around her waist and his head close to hers. "I hope you don't think I'm taking advantage of you."

Concern darkened his eyes. Jennie grinned. "No, just the situation."

Rafe smiled. "We'll have to find more of these situations."

Once they were away from the area, Rafe dropped his hand from her waist. "Would you be able to identify that man if you saw him again?"

"Maybe." She took back her notepad and, turning to a clean page, sketched a quick rendering. "Pretty vague. I had such a brief glimpse. This isn't likely to help."

Rafe studied her artwork. "This is good." He looked at her. "You'll have to show me what you've been doing here."

Tingles shimmied up her spine. Dare she show him the portrait she'd sketched of him? She glanced backward.

"What just happened? What were they talking about?"

"The Germans are bringing pilfered stocks and bonds and gems into Sweden in their diplomatic pouches."

Jennie grabbed his hand. "We need to get to the legation and report this." She got her bearings. "This way."

No "Hello" or "I'd like you to meet someone." Jennie had stuck her head in an office and asked, "Ed, do you have a minute? Rafe heard something that might be of interest."

Now they sat in the office of an OSS spy. A secretary joined them to take dictation of everything they said. Ed directed the questioning.

"You distinctly heard the name Wallenberg?"

"Yes. Somebody named Oppenheim brokered deals with a Wallenberg in the past. The Swedish bank was interested in buying portfolios of stock stolen from Holland. But this man Oppenheim isn't available now." He glanced at his scrawled notes. Too bad he hadn't been able to write down more completely what he'd overheard. "Now a count from Schwerin is bringing diamonds in the diplomatic pouch to sell. I got the impression the diamonds are also Dutch."

Despite the secretary, Ed took his own notes. He looked up. "A count from Schwerin? Could you mean Count Von Schwerin?"

Rafe replayed the conversation in his mind. Had he heard *Count aus Schwerin* or *Count von Schwerin*?

Ed rolled his pencil between his hands. "Von Schwerin is a member of the German Foreign Ministry, and he's been frequently seen in Stockholm."

"They're also bringing in bars of gold."

That raised Ed's eyebrows. "Bars of gold?"

"I don't know where that's coming from."

"Interesting. Very interesting. Anything else?"

"The man who was being told this said something about seeing Hilda tonight."

"Hilda?"

"I don't know if she has anything to do with the diamonds or his social life."

Ed leaned forward. "Did they see you?"

"They left in different directions. One of them saw us, but not our faces. He shouldn't be able to recognize us."

"How did he not see your faces?"

"We pretended to be lovers."

Jennie's color rose along with her grin, and Ed chuckled. He leaned back and studied them.

"Are you willing to go into known German meeting places and listen to their talk?"

"Sure." Rafe shrugged. "I can't really see myself sitting around reading newspapers all day long."

"When you come in tomorrow, I'll brief you on procedures." Ed rose, and everyone rose with him. "That's good work, Martell."

Knowing about stolen diamonds and gold didn't seem likely to help the Allies win the war. Unless the Dutch were informed about their wealth's whereabouts. A lot of Dutch citizens courageously hid and helped downed Allied fliers. Maybe this was a way they could show their appreciation.

He said so to Jennie as they headed for the door. A red-headed whirlwind blew in before they reached it.

"Hello, Jennie and…" The whirlwind came to an abrupt stop and blinked at him.

"Phyllis?" Jennie waved a hand in front of her face.

The redhead blinked at Jennie before returning her attention to him. "Don't I know you?"

According to his crewmates, that was a pick-up line men used. "No, ma'am, we've never met."

She snapped her fingers. "You're in the sketch." She turned to Jennie. "That serviceman on the *Queen Mary* you sketched. It was him."

Jennie's color flared. "This is Rafe. Remember I told you a plane crashed while I was in Malmö? It was Rafe's plane."

"And yet you forgot to mention he was on it." Phyllis rocked back on her heels with an ear-to-ear grin.

Jennie gripped Rafe's arm hard enough to cut off his circulation as she angled toward the door. "We need to run. See you later, Phyllis."

Rafe waited until they were outside. "You drew me?"

"Hmm." Her color heightened. She shoved her hands into her pockets and refused to look his way.

"I'd like to see it sometime." He cleared his throat. "What will Ed do with the information we gave him?"

Jennie's shoulders sagged, even as she finally met his gaze. She hesitated. "Do you understand what the goal of the Office of Strategic Services is?"

"Spying."

She smiled. Slipping her hand around his arm, she spoke quietly as they walked close together. "That *spying* nets us all kinds of information, sometimes just a clue here or there, but matched up with others, it can paint a broader picture."

Rafe paused. A mental jigsaw puzzle that had been missing a few pieces suddenly started forming up. "You're involved. You knew who to go to. You know what they do. Are..." he glanced around, "Are you a spy?"

"No." Jennie didn't hesitate in her answer. "I've received training from OSS and I work for them, but I'm behind the scenes. At least I'm supposed to be. I don't have the courage to be a front line agent. Especially one behind enemy lines. If captured, at the first hint of torture, I'd spill any secrets I have, right down to my kindergarten teacher's name and address."

Her shoulders hunched as she spoke. "However, eavesdropping is a form of spying, so I guess I'll be a spy after all." She grinned, but immediately sobered. "We will not, however, go looking for danger."

"Fine with me. I've wondered sometimes if I could be better serving the army as a translator. This will give me an idea if I'd like that." If he was released from internment before the war ended, maybe he'd ask for a transfer to military intelligence.

"How would you feel about doing black propaganda?" Jennie's eyes sparkled.

"Uh oh. You are up to mischief."

Her laughter rang out. Too bad he couldn't promise her the moon.

"Black propaganda includes demoralizing the enemy with rumors, sowing discord among them. An instructor discussed methods used by agents around the world. I have an idea I'll run past Ed. Maybe we can have a little fun with the Germans." Her eyes hardened. "One German in particular."

Chapter Thirty-Eight

Lake Mälaren, Sweden
Sunday, June 11, 1944

Jennie eased back in the bow of the tiny sailboat. She sat on a cushion that doubled as a floatation device, if needed, but none was available for her back. A little discomfort failed to dampen her spirits. Rafe had spent the previous day familiarizing himself with Stockholm, and found a sail shop. Before dipping into the world of nefarious activities, he'd insisted on taking her sailing.

A breeze filled their sail and sent them skipping across Lake Mälaren. Rafe surveyed the other boats. His eyes narrowed on a fisherman in a rowboat. He leaned toward her. "We should speak Swedish to blend in. Remember, sound carries across water very clearly."

Laughter rolled toward them from another boat, underscoring his words.

Jennie's inexperience in sailing showed when Rafe's "Coming about!" failed to rouse her. Only when he hollered "Duck!" did her peril become apparent. The boom was about to conk her on the head. She hit the deck as it swept over her. Easing back onto the cushion, she offered a sheepish grin. "Maybe I should wear a construction worker's hardhat."

He laughed. "I'll have to remember to use more practical terms instead of being nautical."

His posture suggested not a care in the world as he lounged, one hand on the tiller, the other holding a rope on the sail. He propped his feet up on the opposite bench seat. So at ease was he, she likened his eyes to be at half-mast. He might soon doze off. A gust of wind could catch the sail, capsizing them. Not a pretty picture.

He let go of the tiller to wave at a beat-up boat chugging by with a rough sound. Freed of control, the sailboat lurched. Jennie grabbed hold of the rail while he calmly pulled the tiller back in line and adjusted their course. After scrutinizing the activity around them on the lake, he slid off his perch and indicated the tiller.

"It's all yours. Why don't you try heading for that inlet?"

The boat wallowed with no one at the helm. She stared at him.

"Are you kidding? I don't know anything about sailing," she wailed even as she slid around the starboard side to delicately grasp the tiller.

"Just remember, when you move the tiller to the left, the boat turns to the right, and vice versa." Rafe took her place at the bow, stretching out with his hands clasped behind his head.

If he could look so nonchalant about this, the little boat must not be too hard to master. She wiggled the tiller, not unlike a little kid playing driver by jerking the steering wheel back and forth. When Rafe opened his mouth, she cut him off. "I know, I know, hold it steady." He smiled and closed his eyes. They wobbled into the inlet.

The fisherman drifted directly ahead. Concentrating fiercely, Jennie maneuvered the sailboat to pass on his right. Before she could counter their movement, the sailboat proceeded to circle completely around the fisherman's rowboat.

Rafe shook with laughter. "Where's a traffic policeman when you need one?" He grabbed his camera and stood up. "Accident photos. Insurance adjusters will love them."

He snapped a photo and advanced the film before composing another shot.

Jennie opened her mouth, and clamped it shut. She'd nearly called him Rafe. Good thing she'd remembered in the nick of time to avoid English, but they hadn't discussed using Swedish names. "Sven, will you sit down before we really have an accident? Help me out here."

The fisherman glared at them, gripping his oars with rigid hands. Any effort to maneuver away from them was thwarted as their boat wobbled within inches of scrapping against his.

Rafe collapsed onto the bench, tears of mirth streaming down his cheeks. "I believe you've got the hang of the left-hand turn. Now try a turn to the right. Move the tiller to the left."

"R—Sven!"

"Move the… tiller in the… opposite direction." One hand clutched his middle as his gaiety convulsed him.

Could it be that simple? She jerked the tiller to the left. The sailboat shuddered and rocked as the sail slackened. The fisherman seized the opportunity to dig an oar in the water and inch away from them.

"Not so fast. Smooth and easy does it best." Rafe aimed the camera at her before twisting and snapping another photo of her fleeing victim. He lowered his voice. "Good idea to use a different name."

The gap between the two boats widened. The man didn't look their way.

Jennie dropped her voice to a whisper. "Despite the fishing pole, he had no tackle box or pail for fish. Just a Swedish newspaper. His unfriendly attitude seems unwarranted for our little mishap." She followed his slow progress. "He could be a Swedish policeman assigned to keep an eye on suspicious characters, but he can't follow anyone in a poky rowboat."

Rafe relieved her of the tiller and set the sailboat on a jaunty pace west, away from the city. "He had something with him. Maybe a listening device that amplifies sound. Folks think they can come out here and be alone to talk, but it's still best to keep mum. They're not so dumb."

Jennie had seen the poster he referred to, urging caution to servicemen around strange women. Resenting the insinuation that women didn't know how to use their brains, Phyllis had urged her to create a poster showing smart women avoiding a listening man. She was about to share that tidbit with Rafe when a wave splattered her with cold spray.

"Oh!" The iciness took her breath away. "Suddenly I feel like we're back on *Queen Mary*."

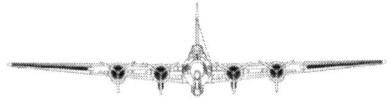

Rafe held her painting of Strandvägen and the legation up to the light streaming through the window. "This is incredible, Jennie. So detailed." He put it back on its stand and picked up her latest painting, the shoreline of Varpan Lake with cottages painted in Falu Red paint. "I like the little girl playing in the sand."

He replaced the painting and joined her on the settee. "You really don't think you'll have a job at the museum when the war's over?"

Jennie sighed. "I have to face facts. My work was little more than secretarial in nature. I've never been in charge of a show." Her voice faltered. "I'm barely out of school."

"Yours wasn't the sort of job a returning serviceman would look for, was it?"

She shrugged. "My boss would question why I should be rehired when I'll probably marry soon. He believes women work only until they can catch a man." Her fingernails dug into her palms. Why did men have to be so patronizing? Not returning to work for him might be a good thing.

"This exhibit you're planning will attract good attention for you." He picked up her notes. "I think you're on the right track here. Your paintings of general Swedish scenes, photos highlighting internee life and activities, and a few objects are all you need." He turned to a fresh page and began writing. "Your idea of getting newsmen to contribute their photos is first rate. Maybe your dad can assist us in making the rounds of the major towns where internees are quartered, like Malmö, Rättvik, Falun, Västerås, and Loka Brunn. I'll be your liaison if you like, if the newsmen don't take you seriously as a woman."

Jennie sat up straighter as she watched his list take shape. Rafe might not be schooled in art, but his interest was contagious.

"How about this? Pick four or five fellows and interview them for a few personal stories."

"Like a mechanic at Malmö. One of the camp commanders. Someone who's benefited from taking a class. A married man. A wounded airman." She ticked off possibilities on her fingers. People would come to see how their boys had fared in a distant land.

"Use Dan. On the slim chance he doesn't want to cooperate, I'll order him to."

Jennie laughed and shook a finger at him. "Play nice with your friends." She laid her hand on his arm. "Thank you, Rafe."

He took her hand in his. "You're good, Jennie. I grew up drawing pretty decent renditions of sailboats, but these paintings are exquisite. You may end up with an unusual exhibition, but variety is good. Folks get bored with the same old thing. Maybe we can book your exhibit at other locations, like the Milwaukee museum. Your old boss will regret the day he let you go."

Jennie could have sat there, staring into his eyes, believing wonders of herself, but her mom stuck her head in the room.

"How about some supper? The soup's hot and the salads are crisp. It'll be just the three of us since your dad's in Loka Brunn."

Mom didn't care about impressing people. Jennie no longer bothered suggesting she remove her apron before sitting down with guests. Today's apron displayed Mom's efforts in the kitchen for the last several days. She'd wiped at the mess created by a squirting tomato, but a seed remained imbedded in the reddened cloth. A brown smear showed where she wiped her hands after making gravy. The streak of crusty white batter must have come when she brushed against a mixing bowl. Mom believed in letting her apron get good and dirty before washing it. Rafe didn't raise a brow at her "art canvas."

Jennie glanced around the kitchen, trying to see it through Rafe's eyes. Like the living room, white was the predominant color. Cheery red-striped curtains at the window and red cushions on the pine chairs brightened the room. They ate at a small table in the center of the kitchen. The table doubled as a work surface, due to scant counter space.

Mom didn't waste time getting Rafe to talk. "Do you think you'll enjoy having a job here rather than staying in the country?"

"Yes, ma'am. Over three weeks to decompress from combat was great, but an endless vacation can start to drag."

Jennie stirred her spoon through her soup to cool it. Potato fragrance rose with the steam. She hid her smile when Mom continued her interrogation. "Will you be doing more than reading papers?"

"Yes. I wouldn't care to sit around reading all day." Rafe sent her a pained look. How much should he say? Did her mother know what she did?

Jennie nodded. Mom knew she had a minor role with OSS. "Ed was pleased with what we overheard yesterday. He's in favor of us eavesdropping on a regular basis."

Ed included her in Rafe's work because she had the training. She may have heard yesterday's conversation, but she'd understood not a word. A couple, however, was less likely to gain attention than a lone man. Being a foil for Rafe couldn't be considered a hardship.

"At places like restaurants the Germans are known to frequent? I hope Ed gave you an expense account." Mom turned a stern eye on Jennie. "I hope you won't try to provoke the Germans the way your friends Phyllis and Emma do."

Rafe nodded at her question. "We'll be eating out a lot." He turned to Jenny. "He suggested we go to Zum Franziskaner on Friday. It's on the old town island, by the waterfront."

"What if you were to engage a German in conversation?" Mom never let Rafe's bowl get empty. He didn't seem to mind as he continued spooning it up. "You couldn't be overt, of course, but she doesn't know you're an American, so you may learn something."

She? "Do you have someone in mind, Mom?"

"A German lady walks her little dachshund in Kungsträdgården. We're nodding acquaintances. If we weren't enemies, we'd probably be good friends. She seems lonely, and might be glad for someone to talk to."

Jennie's shoulders sagged. The only possible scenario didn't include her. Her lack of German proved to be the biggest obstacle. "You'd have to try to approach her on your own, Rafe, and have a story ready about who you are and why you're in Sweden."

Rafe pushed away his bowl and leaned back with a satisfied sigh. "Ed's already concocted that. My grandparents lived on Sweden's west coast near Gothenburg, and that's where I'm supposedly from. It's too far away to facilitate easy checking up on me. Ed suggested I plan on visiting Opa's brother and his family. That way they'll know about me, should I need an alibi, plus it'll be a place I can go if I need to lay low."

That didn't sound good. She frowned. Ed wasn't above taking advantage of Rafe. "Whatever happened to the nice, safe reading room?"

Rafe grinned. "Oh, I'll read the papers, but not in a stuffy room. I'll read in cafes or parks where I can discuss the news with Germans and get their opinions."

He would have been safer being reassigned to Falun. The gleam in his eyes, however, told her he relished a bit of skullduggery. She wouldn't be able to accompany him on a lot of these trysts with her lack of German and her Swedish not quite fluent enough to pass as a native. Oh dear, what had she gotten him into? Some day he might fail to show up and no one would ever know what happened to him.

Chapter Thirty-Nine

Stockholm, Sweden
Tuesday, June 13, 1944

The Kungsträdgården had originally been a kitchen garden for the Royal Palace, but was now a popular park. The palace rose directly across the Norrström strait on Staden. Rafe strolled at a leisurely pace along the waterfront, passed the Royal Opera House, and entered the park at nine o'clock. Mrs. Lindquist said she saw the dachshund lady at midmorning. He paused by the statue of Karl XII. No sign of any dachshunds. The benches by a fountain offered a broad view of the park. He sat down and opened his magazine.

The *Signal* was a slick German propaganda photo magazine that enjoyed great success. Rafe skimmed articles on military prowess and anti-Semitism, and restrained himself from tossing the thing into the trash. Did the Germans still believe the atrocious claims? Still, it was better than the virulent *Der Stürmer*. He couldn't trust himself to maintain a friendly guise after perusing that rag, even if the German was a lonely woman.

"Mitzi, *kommst hier*." The feminine voice intruded into his sun-induced lethargy. His eyes rose from the page he'd been staring at. Heading down the path with jaunty steps and swinging tail was a bright-eyed, black and tan dachshund.

"Mitzi." Rafe lowered his magazine. Barely moving his mouth, he spoke again. "Mitzi." The little dog's ears perked up. "Hier, Mitzi."

With an excited bark, Mitzi made a beeline for him and jumped up on his leg. Her lady scolded as she hurried to catch up, but Rafe laughed. He leaned down and ruffled the dog's ears. *"Wie geht es Ihnen, kleines Mädchen?"* The pendulum swing of her tail never stopped as she licked at his fingers. "I'll take that to mean you're doing very well, indeed."

He laughed again and scooped the dog up onto his lap.

A petite woman stopped in front of him and he beamed a smile at her. "What a delightful dog you have."

Tension faded from the woman's eyes. "Mitzi loves attention."

Mitzi stretched up to lick his face.

"But she does have a penchant for licking." The lady reached for Mitzi.

Rafe kept his grip on the dog. "Puppy dog kisses. We couldn't have a dog in the apartment where I grew up." He should stand, to be polite, but Mitzi was a handful. "I'm Rolf Schilling."

After seven years in America, his birth name sounded strange on his tongue. Stranger still was speaking his native language in public.

"I'm Frau Pasch."

Pasch. Rafe's mind raced. He heard that name just the other day. Ed had flipped through a stack of photos with him. Prominent Germans he was likely to see or hear about in Sweden. Pasch. He mentally snapped his fingers as a face materialized. Salt and pepper hair, a huge nose, deep ear lobes a woman would have camouflaged with large earrings. The German Minister of their legation in Stockholm.

So this was his wife. Braided hair coiled about her head. The hat perched atop the braid looked like Mitzi might have played with it. A button has been sewn back on her coat with white thread instead of navy like the others. She didn't appear as sophisticated as he thought a top diplomat's wife would be. Maybe that explained her loneliness.

He nodded toward the bench and she sat beside him. He began his questions before she could start her own. "Where are you from?"

"Flensburg. I do miss it."

"On the border of Denmark. So you had some familiarity with Scandinavian life before coming here." Best to avoid asking about air raids on the submarine facilities in Flensburg, or the naval academy nearby. "Have you been to Gothenburg?"

"Only once. Oh, that was many, many years ago. We attended a wedding at Masthuggskyrkan."

"Really? I believe that was the church my grandparents were married in." Actually, he had no idea where they were married. "However, I didn't attend the wedding."

Frau Pasch laughed gaily, now quite relaxed. "Of course you didn't attend your grandparents' wedding, my dear boy."

Rafe stroked Mitzi's silky fur. Time to start probing. "I've spent considerable time in Cologne. That's a beautiful city."

"It was," her gaiety dimmed, "until the Englanders bombed it. How they could destroy a city full of women and children is beyond me."

Rafe raised one shoulder. "I've heard the Luftwaffe had been busy bombing British cities."

Puzzlement flashed across her face, followed by resignation. "*Ja*, the *Führer* did say something about wiping English cities off the map." She heaved a great sigh. "And now the Luftwaffe is toothless, *nicht wahr?*"

Apparently German propaganda bragged about their intentions, but neglected to inform the citizenry of their own unrestricted aerial warfare against civilians. Time to redirect the conversation. "Have you been to Berlin lately?"

"We were there last autumn. My husband met with the *Führer*." She didn't say the title with pride.

"We went to the Wolf's Lair for the meeting. What a trip that was. We took a train to Gerdauen, and a ministry car took us through the countryside of Masuria and the forest of Rastenburg. Goodness, I never saw so many birch trees. And mosquitoes! We had to slather our hands and necks with Dr. Zinsser's lotion."

The eastern German localities she threw out weren't familiar to Rafe. Hopefully they weren't important. "Did you see many well-known people there?"

"I didn't see many, but there were two camouflaged trains. One for Ribbentrop, and one was Goering's. Oh, that one is a veritable palace on wheels with every necessity. Private salons, dining car, toilets and showers, radio room, anti-aircraft batteries. All the top Nazi officials want a train of their own."

Rafe's brows shot up. Only opponents of the regime used the "Nazi" epithet. Adherents insisted on the more dignified National Socialist. Before he could tactfully broach her affiliation, she spared him the trouble.

"Many underlings were there. They have such dull minds. I've noticed a decline in good German manners since the Nazis came to power. Minor officials have assumed such authoritarian airs, or they act excessively familiar. They are uncouth." She spat out the word like a curse. Tension radiated off her, and tears glistened in her eyes. Rafe marked her as a proud German helplessly watching her country self-destruct. "I fail to understand why so many rich, elderly ladies support Hitler so enthusiastically. They do nothing but attend teas and socialize."

Mitzi reared up, her paws on Rafe's chest, and tried to lick his face. He wrestled her down and tickled her belly. Her tail never stopped swishing.

"Has your husband always been a career diplomat?" Her chattiness was worrisome. Either she was a clever actress trying to dupe a gullible foreigner or she was so against the Nazis she didn't care if she revealed secrets.

"He's been in the foreign service for over twenty years, always at the heart of German social life. Oh, he has panache. Speaks several languages, knows many big industrialists." Wistfulness colored her tone. She must not feel his equal. "But serious health issues caused us to reconsider life. Stockholm is out of the frenzy."

The Swedes might not appreciate that last sentiment. Not the way the belligerent nations tried to pull their strings like a puppeteer.

"Did you see the *Führer* when you were at the Wolf's Lair?"

"Oh, yes. The war has aged him. And the palsy. His left hand shakes continuously. He was much more vibrant when I saw him in 1941. Things were going his way at that time."

That was interesting. How much did the Allies know about Hitler's health?

"Has Berlin changed much?" The way they'd been bombing Berlin, the city better have lost its vibrancy as well.

"Most Berliners have only one wish: to get some sleep. Air raids occur at all hours of the day and night. They are more in favor of the Russians now than the Allies, because the Russians aren't bombing them."

That attitude would change when the Russians advanced into Germany. He seized the opportunity to end their chat when Mitzi needed to visit the shrubbery. Best not to overstay his welcome.

"I enjoyed our visit, young man." Frau Pasch rose with him.

She'd be willing to chat with him again. He'd have to take flowers to Mrs. Lindquist.

He reviewed what he'd learned as he hurried to the legation. Nothing Earth shattering. Nothing that would help win the war. If only he could be sure she was a disgruntled German and not practicing her own subterfuge.

Jennie spread out seven penetration reports. The subject of all seven reports was certainly a busy boy, making the rounds of internees in three different camps. Foolish of him to use his own name all the time. Unless...

"Phyllis, are there any photos of Hans Schmidt?"

"Not likely. Most people don't have cameras." Her friend rose, stretched, and joined her at the table. "Why do you ask?"

"Hans Schmidt is all over the place. What if the Germans instruct their spies to all use the same name? This would be like our people all saying they're John Smith." She drummed her pencil on the table. "The Germans must have their own reporting system. Would they have files on us?"

"I'm sure they do. There's always someone spying on the legation to see who comes in or out. They learned about you the day you arrived."

"Yeah, Lars made sure of that." He would have reported she visited museums and liked to draw. If anyone followed her, they knew where she lived. Cold shivers prickled down her spine.

What about Rafe? If they opened a file on Rafe, they might realize he frequented German haunts. A smile curled her lips. She'd use her artistic ability to alter his appearance. He might fuss, but her effort could save his bacon.

The door burst open. Her thoughts conjured his appearance.

"May I borrow a typewriter?" Without waiting for an answer, he plopped down at Phyllis' desk and cranked a sheet of paper into her machine. His index fingers pounded away at the keys with more gusto than ability. A firm return of the carriage nearly sent the typewriter flying. Jennie and Phyllis exchanged grins.

"Did you have a good morning?"

"Hmm."

Jennie took that as a yes. She pulled out more penetration reports and attempted to concentrate on them, but her attention kept straying back to Rafe.

"There." Rafe sat back and read through his work. He ripped the page out of the typewriter and joined Jennie at her table. "I met the dachshund lady. She's the wife of the top Kraut."

Hearing Rafe refer to his former countrymen by the disparaging term raised her brows, but she refrained from comment and pulled his report closer. "Rudolph Pasch? The German Minister? And she talked about all this?"

"Your mom's right. She's lonely. She's not comfortable with the Nazi breed of civil servants. And Mitzi's a lot of fun."

Jennie looked up. "Mitzi? Her dog? How cute." She pointed at the report. "She met Hitler."

Rafe turned to Phyllis. "Are the Allies aware of his health problems?"

Phyllis shrugged. "I'm only a small cog in an out-of-the-way legation. You didn't have to type that yourself, you know. You could have dictated everything to Ida, Ed's secretary. That's what she's here for."

"No, thank you." Rafe's sudden scowl brought Jennie's head up. "I came here to avoid Maj-Britt. I don't need another one."

"Why?" Jennie laid a hand on Rafe's arm. "What did Ida do?"

"She smiled at me."

Jennie removed her hand and made her face emotionless. "Really?"

She tried to sound serious, but couldn't hold back her laughter.

Rafe's shoulders sagged. "It wasn't just a smile. It was an inviting smile." He gave her a brilliant smile with widened eyes and a flirty bounce to his brows. "She wants something."

Palms pressed together, Jennie raised her hands to her lips, trying to stifle her laugh.

Phyllis didn't hold back. "Goodness, Rafe, haven't you looked in a mirror lately?" She fanned a hand in front of her face. "You do set a girl's heart to fluttering.

And there aren't that many eligible American men here in Stockholm, you may have noticed."

Rafe pursed his lips, sat up straight, and glared at her. "I'm not eligible for her. I don't like aggressive women." He stabbed a finger at the phone. "Now, would you please call Ed's office and see if he's available? I don't want to get stuck talking to her."

Barely containing her mirth, Phyllis picked up the phone. "Hello, Ida. I'm Rafe Martell's assistant. Is Ed free for a debriefing?"

Chapter Forty

Stockholm, Sweden
Friday, June 16, 1944

What made Ed think Rafe could help the OSS by taking Jennie to dinner at Zum Franziskaner? Ed's zeal for a coup overrode his common sense. Rafe had taken a quick scouting trip to the harbor establishment earlier in the day. Nothing sinister had turned up. He breathed deeply. This was his first foray into the lion's den, not a chance encounter in a park. Highly unlikely they'd come to harm. They would keep to themselves, seeming to ignore everyone else. Maybe it was Jennie's insistence on disguising him that had him on edge.

He eyed her in the mirror. The hood covering her hair suggested she had her hair in rollers on the top of her head. Having her hair stacked up would be a different look for her, but poufy hairdos were stylish for women. His sister called them victory rolls.

"They're sure to note everyone who comes in, suspecting strangers as possible spies." Jennie rubbed pomade into his hair. "You've probably been spotted at the legation, so they know you're on the American side. It makes sense to keep them from realizing where they've seen you before."

She made a valid point, but he cringed as she parted his hair down the middle and combed it to the sides. He looked like a village idiot. The wire-rimmed glasses she insisted on pinched behind his ears, their round frames making him look like a bookkeeper. The eyebrow pencil she brought out was the last straw. He tried to move away.

"Adding glasses and recombing hair is so conventional. You need to look different, Rafe. A few beauty marks will go a long way in making you look like a different man."

Beauty marks, ha! His face looked dirty now. He raised his hand and she slapped it down.

"Don't touch them. They'll be obvious fakes if you smear them."

He grabbed her hand. "Why the red-painted fingernails? You've never painted your nails."

Jennie tsked. "Hello? Rafe, you answered your own question. I polished my nails because it's different. Now behave yourself while I get ready."

She left to attend to her own makeover and he sat on his hands to avoid the intense urge to wash his face. His rearranged hair gave him a headache. Crossing his legs, he bounced his foot in a nervous cadence. He glanced at his watch, and shook it. Time must be standing still.

A woman with deep red hair looked in on him. Her hair was parted in the center with the sides flipped up in big curls crowning her head. The rest of her hair curled under at the back of her neck, displaying her ears, to which pearl earrings were clipped. Her bright red lipstick matched her bright red fingernails in the same shade as Jennie's.

He ignored her. Chatting with a stranger held no appeal while he was decked out like a fuddy duddy.

"Oh, good reaction." Her voice was familiar.

His head jerked up. "Jennie?"

What happened to her reddish blonde curls? Besides the lipstick, she'd used rouge on her cheeks. Her eyebrows looked like someone else's. And her hair…

"What have you done to yourself?"

"Rafe! I'm in disguise."

"What did you do to your hair? It was so pretty."

Her look said he was acting like a sulky four-year-old. She reached back and touched her hair. "This is a color rinse. We better hope it doesn't rain or it'll wash out and make a mess of my clothes."

"Right. Well, let's get this over with." He jumped to his feet and grabbed the unfamiliar tan coat out of her hands. After she slipped into it, he offered his arm. "Shall we go, Brigitte?"

"Brigitte?"

"I can't call you Jennie, and Brigitte's easy to remember since it used to be my sister's name. Remember to call me Sven."

They snuck out the legation's back door.

As they approached the restaurant, more doubts assailed him. But what could go wrong? There was nothing unusual about a man and a woman dining out. Pushing aside his trepidation along with the door, he ushered Jennie inside.

A cloud of cigarette smoke hovered under the rounded ceiling. A shelf atop the dark wood walls held a vast collection of beer steins. His gaze dropped to the tables, and his heart sank. A long row of small tables for two lined one wall. One long bench seat abutted the wall, with chairs opposite at each table. No possibility of confidential conversations with diners so close on either side. More private tables filled the rest of the room, but they couldn't expect to be seated at a table for four. Of course, listening to others would be easier.

A hostess directed them to a table. He nodded to the man dining at the neighboring table as he pulled out the chair for Jennie. He'd take the bench seat so he could keep an eye on the room. A man seated on a stool at the gleaming mahogany bar watched them settle in. Either Swedish police or German agent, he would bear monitoring. After a first curious glance, no one else seemed to pay them undue interest.

Jennie laid a hand on his to claim his attention. She leaned forward and spoke in a low tone. "From the rationing coupons required, I'd say they serve beef."

His knot of tension began to unravel. He turned his hand over to capture hers, and smiled. "Don't care for badger or crow? Ed said this place was supposed to have been founded by German monks and still serves classic German fare. I'm going to try the sausages and schnitzel."

He sat across from a stranger. Her eyes resembled Jennie's, but with the heavy makeup, she wasn't the girl he'd met on the *Queen Mary*. And that fussy hairdo…

Jennie jiggled his hand. She leaned close and whispered, "You're staring at me."

"I can't help it. You look like you should be right at home seated at that bar, a drink in one hand and a cigarette in a long holder in the other. In that get-up, you remind me of someone who's bossy and hard and not very nice."

Her penciled eyebrows rose. What had she done with her real brows?

"Are you talking about someone you know? Or just a characterization?"

Rafe huffed. "Someone real. Haven't thought of her in years. My friend Ludwig's sister. The way she was always trying to get us in trouble, I wouldn't be surprised if she works for the Gestapo."

Jennie raised a manicured finger to lightly touch an eyebrow. Maybe they felt as lousy as his dirty face.

"Promise you'll go back to being your real self when we're done here?"

She grinned. "I promise, at least until we play dress-up again."

He leaned back while placing their order, and spotted the curious gaze of the diner on his left in his periphery. Ignoring him, he took Jennie's hand in both of his. "What is your favorite grandmother memory?"

Jennie's eyes widened but she readily fell into the role of getting-to-know-you.

"Dressing up on Easter Sunday. My mom, grandma, and I wore new matching dresses and Easter bonnets." She frowned slightly and her eyes darted to the right.

He guessed at her hesitation. Did the Swedes have a tradition of Easter bonnets? Every topic could be a landmine.

Jennie rushed on. "And we'd all go together to Christmas Eve services. Actually, the song I most remember Grandma singing was 'The Old Rugged Cross.' Oh, and all my grandparents would come to watch our school plays."

She toyed with her tableware. "My grandfather died after he was hit by a car in 1929. He'd been bringing home some ice cream. I remember Grandma leaning over him in the coffin. She was crying and saying, 'So cold. So cold.' I didn't understand why he'd be cold. When she stepped back, she stepped on my foot."

He brushed his thumb back and forth across the hand he still held. "I remember Oma telling Opa what flowers the bulb company should concentrate on. He'd say, 'Let me run my business, woman.' He acted henpecked, but we all knew it was for show."

Their meals were delivered and they ate in silence for several minutes while he tuned in to surrounding conversations. The man on his left was Swedish, home on leave from the military. Nothing of interest there. A voice on his right offered tantalizing snippets. A clerk at the German National Tourist Office complained of the difficulty of getting supplies from Berlin.

Rafe held back a snort. Their bombing missions to Berlin had better be making life more difficult for the Germans. His grim delight vanished with the man's next comment.

"I received more names and addresses of German refugees living in the Gothenburg area. Several are Jews. A copy will be forwarded to Berlin on the next Lufthansa flight."

A list of German refugees! He could end up on it if he wasn't careful. He'd given his German name to Frau Pasch, and mentioned Cologne. She may have reported her contact with him. Someone with nothing better to do might ascertain a Rolf Schilling his age used to live in Cologne before disappearing in 1937. He gulped down a bite of sausage without tasting it.

Rafe fished out of his pocket the tiny Minox Ed had given him. He inclined his head to the right as he slid the matchbox-sized camera to Jennie. She'd have to photograph his suspect. As a trained employee, she knew how to use it. He watched as she hid it in her palm and, using both hands, fiddled with an earring. A quiet click and the deed was done.

"This schnitzel is very good." Jennie slid her hand across the table. "Astrid gave me a recipe for herring balls. I thought I'd try it for our next meeting with Lars."

Rafe covered her hand with his own. When she withdrew, the camera was in his hand.

"That's a good idea. Add pickled beets and a crab salad, and he'll be a happy man."

Their comments made no sense, but they didn't need to. They spoke for the benefit of surrounding diners. Rafe's concentration wasn't required, and he began surveying the room. Three men sat in a booth behind Jennie. Their conversation looked intent, but he couldn't make out more than the occasional word. German words they were, too. Something about the eastern front. Someone died. Nothing of interest.

"I think it was the same bird again this morning. I couldn't see it with all the leaves on the tree, but it sang the same tune. I think it's a red-flanked bluetail, or maybe a yellow hammer. Have you seen the bearded tit? That's my favorite bird around here."

He looked back at Jennie and grinned. Hopefully she knew what birds were indigenous to the area, and was not making up names.

After leaving the restaurant, they strolled south on Skeppsbron. The Zum wasn't terribly far from the Lindquists' apartment on Södermalm and with sunset after nine o'clock, they planned on a leisurely walk. They hadn't gotten as far as the bridge to the next island when Jennie grabbed Rafe's arm and turned down a narrow lane.

"Detour," she hissed. "We're being followed."

They maintained their unhurried pace. Everything Jennie had learned about losing tails had sounded so easy in theory, but this was real.

"Where to now?" Rafe's voice whispered in her ear. "The scenic route?"

"I'll show you my favorite place."

She indicated another street and they turned. His strategy on his first day in Stockholm should work here. Jennie stopped and slid her arms around him. His eyes widened, but he enfolded her in his embrace. She put her mouth near his ear and sneaked a look back. "That man was at the bar."

"Right. Hopefully just trying to get a feel for who we are, instead of knowing who we are."

She hugged his arm as they resumed walking. "How do you like your roommates?"

"They're okay. Lance is a typist for your dad in the internee section. He must have been bored to take the job because his typing isn't worth beans. I'm much better than him. All I know about Sandy is that he snorts a lot in his sleep. Fortunately, I sleep in a closet off the kitchen that I believe was meant for a maid." He paused and pointed at a window display as though they were shopping.

They stood in front of a music store. A violin rested on a velveteen cloth. Jennie tapped the window before they moved on. "I wish I had learned to play a musical instrument. Too bad I don't have time for lessons like the internees."

"My mom plays piano. She wanted me to learn, but I hated to practice, and she gave up on me." Rafe's voice dropped to a whisper. "He's edging closer to hear us."

"You speak Swedish so well. Did you learn it from your grandparents?" She stopped beside a gate.

"Not really. Swedish isn't difficult for someone who knows German." He looked up at the gate. "'Fear God and honor the king.' Is this a German church?"

"It is. The outside doesn't look like much but the interior is gorgeous. I've never seen its equal in America."

They stepped inside. The low-hanging sun beamed light through the stained glass windows, spotlighting the golden altar. Jennie resisted the urge to drink in the beauty and instead watched Rafe for his reaction.

His gaze wandered from the shining king's gallery to the brilliantly colored window scenes to a row of paintings lining the balcony from the front of the church all the way to the back. "Those paintings depict scenes from the life of Christ."

"Aren't they fabulous? Imagine continually being surrounded by these visual reminders of who Jesus is."

In the balcony above them, the organ pipes rose, sheathed in gold like the sacristy. Rafe followed the pipes up to the vaulted ceiling. She allowed him a moment to absorb it all. "No one's around. Why don't you go to the washroom and wash your face. We'll leave our watcher at the front door and duck out the back door."

While he washed up, Jennie removed her earrings and touched her hair. Only sticking her head under a faucet would change her appearance, too big a job to attempt at the church.

Rafe returned, combing his hair, the glasses stuck in his pocket. She smirked at his relief to have a clean face.

"If someone at the legation had fixed you up, you wouldn't have recognized yourself." She pointed to the back door.

"Something to look forward to." He peered outside and waved Jennie through. "Time now to make our escape."

Walking at a brisk pace, they headed for the bridge to Södermalm. "Did you hear anything interesting?" Their stride made Jennie breathless and brought a stitch to her side. "Can we slow down now?"

Rafe smiled. "I think we've lost our shadow. How would you like to visit the airport tomorrow?"

"What's there?"

"Maybe something. Maybe nothing. The man you photographed mentioned the Lufthansa flights. The Germans fly openly into Stockholm, but the Allies have to sneak in."

Jennie nodded. "A Lufthansa plane was parked near us when my flight arrived."

"I'm sure someone's always there keeping an eye on who comes or goes, but I'd like to see it for myself."

"We'll do that. Then on Monday, we'll play games with the Germans."

He eyed her when she didn't elaborate. "That's a devious smile. Should I be concerned?"

She chuckled. "The Swedes have phone lines tapped. Were you told that?" At his nod, she continued. "We'll select German phone numbers from the phone directory and call with suspicious sounding messages. That'll stir up the police to investigate them. We can use public phone boxes in neutral locations so the calls aren't traced to us."

A burst of laughter slipped out of Rafe. "Aren't you the mean little kid? But that's a good idea for stirring up discord."

Chapter Forty-One

Stockholm, Sweden
Saturday, June 17, 1944

Rafe's eyes lit up when they met at the legation. "You're you again."

Jennie laughed. "I liked being someone else last night."

They started for the train station at a brisk pace. A frown puckered Rafe's brow. "Don't you like you as you are?"

Jennie pulled her lips between her teeth. She looked away from Rafe's probing gaze. "I wish I was clever."

Rafe grasped her arm, bringing her to a halt. "Clever? What are you talking about? You're intelligent. You wouldn't be working for the OSS if you weren't."

He wouldn't be satisfied until she explained herself. Jennie stepped up against a building to avoid blocking other pedestrians.

"Ed wants me to do more than I expected. Pretending to be Brigitte, I don't have to worry about stupid Jennie Lindquist. I can be bold and…"

Rafe still held her arm and he shook it now. "Why do you think you're stupid?" When she didn't answer promptly, he shook her again. "Did someone say something to make you think that?"

Jennie looked around. This was hardly the place for such a discussion. She'd just always known she wasn't clever. Hadn't she?

Rafe propelled her to the end of the block and across the street to a little park. He led her to a bench. "Who told you you're stupid?"

"What about the airport, Rafe?"

"Forget the airport. It's not going anywhere. Neither are we until I know who hurt you." Rafe would make a good prosecuting attorney.

Why assume someone had hurt her? Why couldn't he let it go? "I've just always known I'm not as smart as everyone else."

"When was the first time you thought you weren't smart?" Now Rafe held her hand, his thumb swishing back and forth across her palm.

Jennie sighed. Was there a first time? Yes. Yes, there was.

"I didn't understand double digit multiplication."

Rafe's eyes popped, but he stayed silent.

"It was fourth grade. Everyone else understood. We had to solve a page full of problems, and then exchange papers to grade. Joey Lardnois got mine. I had them all wrong. I'd multiplied like we do addition. He started laughing, loud, and said, 'Boy, are you stupid.' The teacher, Miss Ratner, called me up to her desk and had to give me extra instruction."

Her voice cracked and tears filled her eyes. Once again she was that mortified little girl.

Rafe scooted close and wrapped his arm around her. "Joey was the stupid one, not you. I'll bet you never did a wrong multiplication problem again. Even if you did, what does it prove? Only that you're human. You don't need to hide behind hair dye or a painted face to act brave or smart or anything. How many people get accepted by the OSS, or speak more than one language, or paint beautiful pictures? Who cares about arithmetic?"

Jennie managed a laugh. She dug through her reticule and fished out a handkerchief. After blotting her eyes and tending to her nose, she took a deep breath. "I suppose you whizzed through all your arithmetic classes."

"Oh, well, I liked working with numbers. That's how I came to be a navigator. Keeping track of history dates is what bedeviled me. I kept trying to put the Franco-Prussian War at the beginning of the nineteenth century, seventy years before its time." He jumped up and pulled her with him. "I never again want to hear you say you're stupid. Understand?"

She saluted. "Aye, aye."

He frowned and smiled at the same time. "Come on. Let's go see if anything exciting is happening at the airport."

The normal bustle of an airport hung over the field, but it looked like more than the air traffic warranted. Rafe stared at the American Liberator parked alongside a German Lufthansa DC-3.

"Do the Swedes seriously expect to avoid problems by putting enemies in such close proximity? I wouldn't be surprised if someone drew a gun and they started shooting each other."

"Rafe, dear, this isn't a gangster film or the wild west. The Swedes are neutral. They want to pretend there isn't a war going on and expect everyone else to do likewise." Jennie patted his arm like he was three years old.

"Very funny, missy. The Swedes keep the internees separated. They even separate the Americans from the British. And all we could do is give each other fat lips and bloody noses. Here they could do a bit of serious sabotage."

He studied the layout. The Germans watched the Allied planes and the Allies watched the Germans. The man lounging against the shed over there, fiddling with a clipboard, must be a watcher, but for whom? The fellow unloading the Liberator spent more time watching the German plane than what he was doing. He looked too nervous to be a spy. Must be a first-timer in awe of his proximity to the enemy.

Jennie fidgeted beside him. She hadn't insisted on disguises, but had tucked her hair up in a net and wore a wide-brimmed hat. Her large dark glasses weren't fashionable, but hid her face.

Her caution gave him an inspiration. "Why don't you head for the chairs by the terminal entrance? I'll reconnoiter by the mechanics' shed, see if anyone will tell me who's who."

Inside the shed, he found a cleanish pair of overalls and slipped into them. He grabbed a toolbox and headed for the Liberator like he knew what he was doing. At the front wheel crouched a mechanic, likely an internee.

"How's it going?"

The mechanic looked up with narrowed eyes. "Got any grease in there?"

"I don't know what's in here. I didn't look." Rafe set down the toolbox. The guy looked trustworthy, but he might think Rafe was a spy. He looked up at the plane. "I flew on B-17s myself. Did you fly on these pregnant cows?"

The mechanic laughed. "Sure did. They've got better speed than your Forts."

Rafe dropped to a knee and pulled out his rank insignia. "I'm assigned to the legation now and am trying to get a feel for the layout here. Do you know who's watching us, German or Swedish?"

The mechanic stared at him for a long moment before glancing around. "Goons are more likely to hang around when a plane comes in so they can see who gets off or on." He inclined his head toward the man with the clipboard. "Don't know who the goldbricker is, but he's not a Yank or a Limey."

Goldbricker. That stumped Rafe for a moment. Someone who excels at goofing off and lets everyone else do the work. He nodded.

"That fellow over there by the Kraut plane we like to think is Gestapo," the mechanic continued. "He never seems to work either. The other Krauts avoid him."

Too well dressed to be a mechanic, and he did seem to have his nose in the air.

"Never saw that light chassis by the door before, but she's not doing a good job of reading her book."

Rafe stifled a laugh. "She's okay. She's with me."

And, he didn't add, she wouldn't appreciate the moniker even if it was complimentary.

"Some guys have all the luck," the mechanic muttered as he gave his wheel a crank.

Rafe smiled. "Are any of the Krauts friendly?"

"We don't speak the lingo and if they know English, they're not saying. We do exchange civilized nods with some of them."

Another mechanic hurried out from the supply shack. "A cylinder head cracked on the flight from Scotland and we don't have a spare. There's no way we'll have it ready to go back tonight."

The mechanic at the wheel stood. "Did you tell McGuire?"

"No way. He'll flip his wig."

While the two mechanics argued about who should tell, Rafe eyed the Lufthansa plane. The DC-3 used the same engines as the Liberators. "Why don't you ask the Krauts if you can borrow one?"

The men stared at him like he'd spoken Japanese. "Don't be a yuck."

The wheel mechanic looked alarmed and hit his friend's arm. He'd seen Rafe's insignia and knew he was an officer.

Yuck translated to fool, like the way Jennie disguised him yesterday. Rafe smiled and tried a bit of slang himself. "They'll be so impressed with my *cajones,* they just might give me one."

He headed for the enemy's plane. A mechanic stood over a rolling tool cart.

"*Entschüldigen.*" The man turned around. All thoughts fled Rafe's mind. He could only stare. The man stared back, reflecting his disbelief.

"Bertil?"

He hadn't seen his best friend in eight years. Christoph hadn't known what became of him.

"Bertil?" He cleared his throat. "You are Bertil?"

"Rolf." Bertil wasn't in any better shape, and he swallowed hard. "Ever since you disappeared, I've wondered if I'd ever see you again."

Heedless of any Americans, Germans, and Swedes who may be watching, two long-lost friends, torn apart by a war that still separated them, embraced. Tears stung Rafe's eyes. He pushed away and held Bertil at arm's length. Lines fanned out from his eyes. Eyes that looked old, set in a face much leaner than in their teen years.

"I don't want the Gestapo questioning you about me." Rafe led the way behind a truck and bins of aircraft paraphernalia. "Christoph told me you'd switched to a motorized unit, but I never considered you'd be here."

"Christoph knew where you were? He always said he had no idea."

"No, no, he didn't. I saw him a couple months ago in an English prisoner of war camp." Rafe pulled off the stained mechanic's cap he wore and raked a hand through his hair. "We bombed his boat."

Bertil leaned forward. "You bombed his boat? You did? Or the Allies?"

"I was a B-17 navigator in the American air force, and we… my crew… we bombed his boat."

Bertil rocked back on his heels. "You bombed your cousin." A slow grin crossed his face. "And I always thought you two were such good friends."

"I didn't know Christoph was on that S-boat, not that I could have changed anything. They were going to pick up one of our crews that had ditched. We knew Air-Sea Rescue was on the way. We had to stop them from grabbing our men. Only later, when I saw pictures, did I realize…" The thought of how close they'd come to harming Christoph still sent shivers up his spine.

Bertil's smile kept growing. "Does he know you were involved in his demise?"

"No." The word exploded out of him. "I'll tell him. Eventually. Maybe in fifty years, when he'll be ready to laugh."

Bertil was already laughing. A snicker worked its way passed Rafe's lips.

"I'd do it again, just for the chance to see him. He filled me in on what he knew. There was a lot he didn't know, like what happened to you."

Suddenly serious, Bertil glanced around. "I'm lucky to be here. If Germany wins the war, life won't be worth living. I won't pick up a gun."

Jennie sauntered past. Looking around rather than at them, she paused beside Rafe. "Your mechanics' jaws are scraping the tarmac."

"Forgot all about them." He peered around the truck. Yep. Standing there scratching their heads.

"I came over to ask if you have a spare cylinder we could borrow."

Bertil's eyes bulged and he inclined his head. "You want to borrow a cylinder from the Germans?"

"Sure, why not?" Rafe nodded at the Lufthansa plane. "That DC-3 has the same equipment."

"Never mind that we're on opposing sides." Bertil laughed. "As a matter of fact, we did receive a cylinder from Berlin just yesterday. It came off a B-24 that crashed in Germany." After turning in a complete circle, satisfied no one watched, he opened a bin, grabbed the cylinder, and reached out as though to shake Rafe's hand, passing on the cylinder.

Rafe stared at the part. A plane had gone down for them to get this. What happened to the crew? Shaking his head, he handed the cylinder to Jennie and switched to English.

"Bertil, meet Jennie." He turned to her. "Bertil and I go all the way back. We know each other's worst secrets. Would you give this to those guys and ask them to close their mouths?"

She took the cylinder gingerly even though it wasn't greasy.

"Bertil, I'm glad to meet you. I hope we have a chance to talk and you can share some of his secrets." With a nod and a smile, she turned away.

Bertil stared after her.

Rafe cleared his throat.

His friend snapped his head around, but then his eyes widened and he turned away. Over his shoulder, he said, "See that Swedish mechanic in the green shirt coming around the water tank? He's a German stooge. We don't want to be seen together. Where can we meet?"

Rafe moved over to the terminal and casually leaned against it while Bertil rummaged in the bin. "I've got freedom of movement in Stockholm." Talking like a ventriloquist wasn't among his skills. "Where can you go?"

"Do you know Tyska Kyrkan, the church?" At Rafe's nod, Bertil continued. "Come tomorrow." Without acknowledging Rafe's presence, Bertil carried some equipment back to his plane, nodding to the passing Swede on his way.

Chapter Forty-Two

Stockholm, Sweden
Sunday, June 18, 1944

Rafe surveyed the church. There, on the far right, toward the front. Bertil was alone. Good. He hadn't thought to ask if Bertil had married and brought a wife along. No one else in the congregation looked familiar, but that didn't mean he could let down his guard. Taking a deep breath, he relaxed his shoulders. Attracting attention wouldn't do. He strode forward and entered the pew behind his friend.

He accidentally on purpose bumped his hand against Bertil's shoulder, dropping a note onto the pew before sitting down. Bertil reached for a songbook. His arm moved back against the pew and it was a sure bet Rafe's note would disappear into the pages.

His message was short. *Can we meet after services in the garden in back of the church?*

In a moment Bertil's head raised and gave a barely discernible nod. Rafe blew out his breath. That policeman who followed him and Jennie on Friday night did them a favor. The garden they'd escaped through was the only safe place he could think of suggesting where they might meet.

The minister's sermon probably was interesting, but Rafe heard none of it. God surely understood. Like his meeting with Christoph, Rafe's reunion with Bertil was an epical moment in restoring some of the best aspects of the life he'd been forced to give up.

Bertil. His best friend. Here. Unbelievable.

Time passed quickly after they rendezvoused in the garden. Bertil's family's misfortunes were worse than Christoph's. "My father's a prisoner of the Russians. Mother doesn't believe he'll ever come home. She lives outside of Cologne now, with three other women whose husbands are dead or missing. My brother's dead. And all for what?"

Rafe jumped up from the bench where they sat in the shade. He paced four steps and back. Bertil would make a good contact. Too bad Jennie wasn't here. She'd have a better grasp of how to recruit operatives. He didn't want to involve Ed or deliver Bertil into his clutches. The best way to keep his friend safe was to keep him off the OSS radar. He stopped in front of Bertil. "Would you consider informing me of German intentions here in Sweden?"

"You want me to spy on my own countrymen?" He looked intrigued.

"You'd be helping to liberate Germany. The Nazis have to go." At least, the bad ones had to be eradicated. Those bent on destroying the country and as much of the world as they could get their hands on. Not all party members were bad though. Not those who, like his father, had to join the party to keep their jobs.

The pastor came out to invite them to lunch. Rafe nearly swallowed his tongue when Bertil asked the man's opinion on being an informer. The pastor didn't need to think about it. "It's a worthy proposition, Bertil. Think of the Germans actively involved in the underground to thwart the evil that has our countrymen in its grip."

Bertil shifted uneasily. "That's true, and they're risking their lives, losing their lives. What's the worst that could happen to me? I'd lose my job."

"How is it you haven't been transferred back to a fighting unit, or at least maintaining the warplanes?" Why hadn't Rafe thought to ask before?

"My boss protects me." Bertil adjusted his glasses. "And these help keep me from active duty. What would I have to do?"

Rafe leaned forward. "You told me about the Swedish mechanic who's on the German payroll. Anything like that, no matter how insignificant you think it is. Jennie says all these little bits of information are put together like a puzzle to get a big picture."

"The mechanic isn't the only one. A freight manager monitors shipment of materials arriving here or going to England. He provides daily copies of the lading bills. They also report passengers who arrive or depart. Somehow they find out the passenger lists of every plane. They're paid seventy-five hundred kroner each."

Rafe scribbled notes on his pew sheet.

"The local representative of Lufthansa is actually an *Abwehr* agent."

Rafe frowned. "Do the Swedes know that? They arrest people for unlawfully gathering information."

He began formulating the incriminating phone call he'd make in the morning. The Swedish listeners would be sure to investigate.

Chapter Forty-Three

Stockholm, Sweden
Sunday, June 18, 1944

A knock came at the Lindquists's door late in the evening. After hiking on the islands of the archipelago that afternoon with Phyllis, Emma, and others from the British legation, Jennie concentrated on painting the scenery she'd enjoyed. Artistic license allowed her to move the deer from the trail they'd hiked to a rocky shore. She smudged the foliage at the animal's feet with a rag. Perfect.

"Very nice," a voice agreed with her.

She looked up into Rafe's dancing eyes. He looked at her, not at the painting, his gaze drifting down and back up. Sudden heat caused her face to flame. "Rafe!" she squeaked. She thrust her brush and palette into his grasp. "Dad, how could you let him in?"

Fleeing to her room, she shut the door and collapsed on her bed, her chest heaving. Quiet laughter came from the living room. Rafe? Dad? Mom? All three? She rose, twisting her ratty blue robe in her hands.

Her reflection stared at her from the mirror. Wisps of hair escaped in all directions from the ugly pink rollers circling her head. Her robe hid her pajamas well enough, but it should have been retired years ago. She jerked it off, throwing it on the bed along with the pajamas, and donned the red Swiss dot dress she planned to wear when she met him at the legation in the morning. Digging in a bureau drawer, she found her hooded cape. A bizarre outfit to wear indoors, but what did it matter? Rafe should have known better than to show up without calling first. She hurried back to the living room.

Rafe gestured to her easel. "Your mother tells me you went into the archipelago where you were inspired to paint your new masterpiece." His praise diminished her pique with him. He pulled his tiny camera out of his pocket. "This little toy is proving to be a lot of fun. I took lots of pictures, mostly for practice, but maybe someone will match a rogues' board photo. Hopefully they'll turn out well, although no one's likely to be centered. I hold the camera like this."

He palmed the camera and brushed his hair from his forehead, clicking a shot of the major as he did so. Then he repositioned it and, adjusting his coat, photographed Mrs. Lindquist.

"Oh, goodness, Rafe. Why did you do that?" Mrs. Lindquist blustered. "You turn that in for the rogues' board and they'll pin me up with their suspicious persons."

"Now, Agatha, don't you worry." Major Lindquist patted her shoulder. "If it turns out well, I'll remove it and put it up in my office."

"And if it's a poor likeness?" Her brows arched over glowering eyes.

"Then I'll leave it on the board."

They all laughed, but a melancholy air seemed to settle on Rafe as he watched their interplay. Did his father used to tease his mother like that? Jennie's heart ached for him. He shook his head, as though to dismiss the thought, and turned to her.

"Ready for a day of telephone calls tomorrow?"

"Should be fun." She rubbed her hands together. These cloak-and-dagger shenanigans would be so much more enjoyable with a partner.

"I ran into Ed at a diner and he says your scheme has a good possibility of causing friction among the Germans. If something goes wrong and we get in trouble, however, he'll deny any knowledge of our plans." He pulled out his copy of the *Stockholm Illustrated Guide*. "Let's meet here, just west of the legation, and go up to the Stureplan. Enough people should be around that we'll blend into the crowd, and have no trouble finding a phone box."

Chapter Forty-Four

Stockholm, Sweden
Monday, June 19, 1944

Several streets converged in a wide open space that formed the Stureplan. Buildings formed acute angles, topped with turrets, to match the street corners. The Hotel Excelsior looked like a gingerbread house with its towers, balconies, and dormers. Overhead, tram cables stretched out like a giant spider web. A shower of sparks scattered at their feet as they waited at a corner. Jennie covered her nose as a car accelerated around the tram in a cloud of coal smoke.

She studied the center of the intersection. "Let's head to the newspaper stand under that sheltering roof. Just beyond it, I think I see phone boxes. We'll make our first call there. As first on our agenda, do you want to call Lufthansa?"

"I can do that."

She pulled a notebook from her reticule. "I'll record time, place, phone number, and message. We need to keep track of our mischief. What's your plan for the airline?"

"Bertil said the Lufthansa representative is really an *Abwehr* agent. I want the Swedish eavesdroppers to know he's part of German Intelligence. Ed suggested we drop the name Admiral Canaris, who's in charge of

Abwehr. Our message will be that Canaris wants more precise details on the quantities of machine parts from Bolinders and Atlas Diesel, and the steel drills manufactured by Sandviken, being shipped to Britain. That ought to make a listener sit up and take notice."

They arrived at the phone box. Rafe lifted the receiver. "Say, look at this. A rotary dial. We don't have to go through the operator."

Jennie's hands shook as she held the phone directory. True, the call couldn't be traced to an American phone, but if anyone had tailed them, their time at the phone box could be matched to the call. This was it, her debut as an active OSS operative. Her stint as courier to Uppsala didn't count.

"What's the Lufthansa number?" Rafe waited with a finger poised over the phone's rotary.

Jennie laughed at the devilish glint in his eyes. She traced her finger across the line. "Two six, zero six, zero four."

Rafe grinned at her and her face heated. No need to whisper. She copied the number and time on her pad.

Rafe began talking loudly even as he dialed the last two numbers. "Ludwig, *wie gehts*? Can you join us for lunch at the Gondolen?... Noon?... Great. See you there." He released the rotary on the final number and it spun back to its starting place. He took a deep breath and blew it out.

"What was that all about?"

"Just in case anyone's listening." He winked at her.

Oh, dear. He was a natural at this. Jennie lowered her head over the phone directory as though she had no cares, and peered around. No one seemed to be loitering near them. Next time, if there was a next time, she'd wear a hat with a veil to hide her eyes instead of the lacy crocheted head scarf she'd chosen this morning.

Beside her, Rafe straightened. "*Guten morgen. Ich bin Werner Kratz.*"

Jennie's eyes widened. He was Werner? As in Lars the pest? Lars could be accused of meddling where he didn't belong. Rafe's memory was phenomenal.

He repeated the message he'd given her.

Jennie frantically scribbled the names she recognized. How had he learned all this? From reading newspapers? He could get the *Abwehr* agent into some seriously hot water.

His message concluded, Rafe casually twisted around, leaned his right arm against the phone box, and disconnected the call. With the receiver still held to his ear, he said, "Right. See you there." Hanging up the phone, he chuckled. "That was fun. Too bad we'll never know if we succeed in causing mayhem among the Germans."

Jennie could only shake her head. She considered herself adventurous, but this activity could have serious ramifications of the international legal variety. Her ideas of adventure included white water rafting or horseback riding on the shore of Lake Michigan. Tame stuff, like creating posters for Morale Operations.

Rafe looked around the Stureplan. "Hitler would have used this spot for one of his rallies. Swastika banners would have hung from all the buildings. All the people would have been jammed into the intersection. Cameras would have been rolling." He sighed. "Lots of speeches that didn't make much sense to me."

Jennie leaned forward to peer at his face. He talked like he'd actually been to a rally. "Did he visit Cologne while you were still there?"

"Probably. I don't know. I'm thinking of the rally while I was in Berlin."

"You were in Berlin? You saw Hitler?"

He looked at her and laughed. "Sure, why not? Berlin's only about three hundred fifty miles from Cologne. And my dad works for the railroad. That made travel easy for us. My folks liked to travel, and they considered it a valuable part of our education."

"But you actually saw Hitler?" Jennie couldn't suppress a shiver. To be in the presence of such evil.

Rafe shrugged. "Had we known a rally would take place then, I'm sure we would have been elsewhere that day. My mother would have seen to that. But it was interesting."

"Interesting? Hitler was interesting?"

Rafe laughed again. "We didn't know at the time what he would do to Germany. The rally was interesting, not Hitler. He was a lousy speaker. The rally, though. It was carefully staged. If you saw it in newsreels, you'd think it was a spontaneously outpouring of support. But they closed all the factories and shops and herded everyone into place along the motorcade route and especially the speakers' platform." He punched out his right arm. "We were told to salute and 'Sieg Heil.' The music was loud, the drums. You felt it vibrate in your gut. It was hypnotic."

"I've never seen President Roosevelt."

Rafe draped his arm around her shoulders. "Well, the United States is a little bit bigger than Germany. He's not quite as accessible."

Rafe had been in the presence of Hitler. Jennie couldn't fathom it. "How close to him were you?"

He grinned. "Very close. We'd been in a shop right where he would stop and were herded along with everyone else to stand near the platform. We were in front. He walked around a bit, coming right to us. He touched Rita."

"He did?"

"Don't sound so scandalized." Rafe's grin stretched across his face as he briskly rubbed her arm. "He patted her on her head." Rafe patted Jennie's head. "Or maybe her shoulder. Rita was a trouper. She waited until he'd gone by before screwing up her face. She said he had bad breath."

Jennie's breath escaped her as she laughed at Rita's summation. To have stood so close to that madman. Incredible.

Rafe directed her across the street. "I also told them at Lufthansa about the ball bearings from SKF, and that we're concerned about all this essential war material going to the British war effort, if you want to write that down."

He consulted his city guide. "Let's go a block down Lästmakargatan to Norrlandsgatan. That'll take us south all the way to the bridge at the old town island, and we can watch for telephones along the way. Then we'll follow the eastern side of the island, past Zum Franziskaner, and across to Södermalm. That's where the Gondolen is." He tapped the spot on the map. "It's a bit of a hike, but we'll work up an appetite by the time we get there for lunch."

"We're really going there? Is someone meeting us? Who's Ludwig?"

"Yes and yes and nobody. Phyllis will join us there. What could be more natural than meeting your friend for lunch? And she'll exchange my film for a fresh one. Ed doesn't want us going to the legation today. What's next on your phone list?"

Jennie grinned as she tucked her hand around his arm. "The German National Tourist Office. Say something like we've received a shipment of lewd Swedish-language magazines from Berlin. Can they distribute them? Or maybe ask how many Swedish newspapers are still under their thumb."

"Got it. A business might be a good place to call from. We could pretend to be shopping, maybe find an office area with no one around. We could slip in and use the phone."

Oh dear. Her step must have faltered, for he grinned at her. "You're looking very nice today." His smile broadened as he studied her hair. "Do you sleep in hair curlers? Don't they hurt?"

Her elbow connected with his ribs. "Watch it, buster. I'll share Bertil's secrets with your crew."

"Remind me to keep you two apart. Ah, here we go." Rafe tugged her to a doorway.

The stenciled word on the door read *Leksaker*. Toys. How fitting, since Rafe considered their outing a game. He led her through the store with a purposeful stride, and whisked her through a door marked 'Private.' Without slowing to give anyone a chance to question them, he found a darkened room and entered.

"Just what we were looking for. Watch the door. What's the number for the Tourist Office?"

Watch the door and read numbers at the same time? Please. Jennie pulled out the phone directory and scanned the listings. "One one, six two, five two." She reeled them off in under a second, but Rafe never stopped grinning and dialed.

She rolled up the directory and twisted it. A page ripped. What was she doing? She smoothed it out but, peering into the hallway, her hands again rolled the pages tight. Behind her, Rafe spoke in imperious tones. Something about Gothenburg.

Jennie caught her breath. "Someone's coming."

Rafe waved his fingers. Run interference. Oh dear, dear, dear. Safely making posters sounded better all the time.

She stepped out. *"Ursäkta mig."* Horrors. Her voice sounded squeaky. She cleared her throat, and noted the name on the door. "Isn't Miss Ericssen in today?"

The secretary cocked a brow. "No, she's on vacation this week."

"This week? I thought her vacation was next week." Jennie crossed to the far side of the hall, hoping to turn the woman away from the office. "Oh, no, that's right. Midsummer is this week, isn't it?"

"Ursäkta." Rafe excused himself as he brushed by.

The secretary frowned after him before turning back to Jennie.

Jennie smiled. *"Tack."* She hurried after Rafe.

Not until they were a block away did Rafe slow their pace. "That went well, I think. Here." He handed her the notebook. "I questioned the list of refugees from Gothenburg and got the name of their primary spy there. Jorgen Banner. Hopefully he'll come under surveillance if he's not already."

Jennie tried to write but her hand shook so badly, she couldn't read her scribbles. If they did many more calls, her stomach would be twisted so tightly she wouldn't be able to eat a bite at the fancy restaurant. Rafe watched her with a quizzical look. "What?"

"How did you get involved with OSS?"

A fair question, given the state of her nerves. "A friend of Dad's recommended me for my artistic ability. Being surrounded by the enemy, Sweden's a hotbed of intrigue. But I thought I'd be tucked away in an office, not involved in cloak and dagger stuff."

"Exhilarating, isn't it? Sure beats bombing cities into oblivion. And you're doing fine, even without a disguise."

After their fourth call, Jennie tucked the notebook away in her tote bag. An elevator sped them over one hundred feet into the air to an observation deck linking two buildings. The spectacular view left her breathless. "We can see for miles. I missed all this when I flew into Stockholm after dark." The city lay before them on one side. From the other, the archipelago stretched out to infinity. "But where's the restaurant?"

"Right below us. We're standing on the roof."

Jennie looked down, and regretted it. "But this is a foot bridge. The restaurant must be awfully narrow."

"Long and narrow. Let's go find Phyllis."

No Neutral Ground

Chapter Forty-Five

Late that afternoon, Rafe wandered the streets of the old town. He spotted a strangely-shaped sign hanging outside a shop. Krukmakeri. A glance in the window cleared up the mystery. Pottery. The sign was shaped like a pot. He sighed and walked on.

Too bad his crewmates weren't here. They'd been inseparable for months and, all of a sudden, they were apart. The internees were allowed to visit Stockholm for three days every month. He'd have to contact Alan, Cal, and Steve, and get them down here.

He paused beneath another sign. Lindbergs Antik. That bureau on the side there looked just like the one they had in their Cologne apartment. Probably it had been destroyed in one of the many bombings Cologne suffered. That, and the paintings of Rhine River scenes that graced the walls of their living room, and Mother's china that she'd hated to leave. All the little things that made up a cozy life. Another sigh heaved his chest.

Things could be replaced, but not people. Father had told him that when he was four or five years old. The day replayed before his eyes like a movie film.

They waited at a street corner for traffic to clear. Rolf's cap blew off and fell in the street. He stepped down from the curb, reaching for it.

Father grabbed him back. An automobile turned the corner, right where he'd just stood. He looked up into the wide, startled eyes of a woman. The car disappeared down the street.

"Never step off the curb without looking for traffic." Father's voice had sounded shaky.

"But my cap..."

"I can replace your cap, Rolf, but I can't replace you."

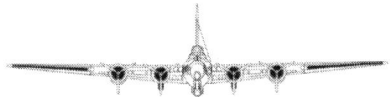

A film of tears watered Rafe's eyes, obscuring his vision. A dozen years later, Father threw him away. Him, Mother, Rita, and Albert. The ache filling his chest made it hard to breathe.

Times like this weren't meant to be handled alone. Someone to talk to would be ideal, but who? Jennie had to work at the office. Bertil may or may not be at the airport at this time of day. His crewmates were too far away. He reached an intersection and looked around. Overhead, a spire loomed. Tyska Kyrkan. He aimed for the church.

Inside, a sacred hush swathed the sanctuary. As before, the stained glass windows glowed in the sunlight. He walked forward and sat down, staring at the scene of the crucifixion. Memories of the choir singing in Cologne Cathedral echoed through the years. *Me thought the voice of angels from heaven in answer rang, Jerusalem, Jerusalem, Lift up your gates and sing, Hosanna in the highest, Hosanna to your king.*

The tears he'd held back on the street streaked down his cheeks, but why? Here, peace surrounded him. It made no sense. The world remained at war, with thousands being slaughtered on both sides, military and civilian. He remained estranged from his father, but God Almighty Himself must have reached down and touched his heart, uplifting him.

How long he sat in quiet communion, he couldn't guess. The sound of footsteps reached him. Good thing they provided warning, or he might have jumped out of his shoes when a hand touched his shoulder.

"Guten abend, Rolf. Wie gehts?"

His mother tongue offered another layer of peace. Spoken gently, infused with caring, German was a beautiful language, quite unlike the strident, belligerent tones on the radio during Hitler's speeches. He turned to greet the pastor.

"Good evening, Jurgen. I'm enjoying the peace I find here."

The pastor studied him for a moment, and sat down. "Tell me why you do not find this peace elsewhere."

Rafe shifted in the pew. "After eight years, I think I should be used to my father's rejection, but I'm not. Sometimes it slaps me upside the head and I wonder all over again. 'Why, Father? Why?' And the hurt continues to churn."

"May I tell you a story?"

Rafe's answering grin wobbled a bit. How often as a little boy had he climbed up on Father's lap, asking for a story? He nodded.

"A soldier came home on leave to find his wife and children dead. Their shelter had taken a direct hit. Our soldier was despondent and wandered the ruins of the city for days. One morning he saw a bedraggled woman marching through the rubble, dragging along an equally bedraggled little boy. He had a hard time keeping pace, for his short legs had difficulty maneuvering the chunks of debris. He stumbled on one large piece and scraped his leg, causing it to bleed. His mother jerked on his arm, but he fell to the ground. As he cried there, she yelled at him most unpleasantly. Our soldier picked up the small boy, pressed his handkerchief to the wound, and said, 'Frau, you don't realize the treasure you have here. I'll be glad to take him if you don't want him.' That's a wonderful picture of our Father in heaven."

Pastor Jurgen paused momentarily. "King David said in Psalm twenty-seven, 'When my father and my mother forsake me, then the Lord will take me up.'

Being here in His house may make you more aware of His presence, but Rolf, never forget, He's with you wherever you are."

Again, Rafe's tears slipped out. The night before his first mission, he had imagined God, the Father of the fatherless, reaching down to lay His hand on his shoulder. Peace had filled him then. Was it wrong to long for his earthly father's care, too?

Chapter Forty-Six

Stockholm, Sweden
Tuesday, June 20, 1944

Jennie rushed into the legation's reading room. Yes, there was Rafe, his nose buried in a Berlin newspaper. She ran to his side and pulled away the paper. He looked up in surprise, but she was too breathless to speak.

He smiled. "Good morning, Jennie. It's nice to know you're so eager to see me."

"Pwsh." She pressed a hand to her chest and breathed deeply. "We just got the news. We're going to Malmö. Right now. You, too. The Eighth Air Force had a horrendous mission to the far eastern side of Germany. Scores of Liberators have landed in Malmö. Dad's contact said it's busier than Piccadilly Circus. The Swedes are overwhelmed and we don't have enough staff to process them all quickly. We'll help out where we can."

Rafe was already on his feet. "If scores arrived in Sweden, that means scores more didn't make it to a friendly roost. Will we take the train?"

"No, we're flying. Hopefully Malmö isn't too congested at the moment." She paused at the door. "You don't need to go back to your apartment first, do you?"

He patted his pocket and grinned. "Just picked up a month's pay. If I need anything, I'll get it at Malmö."

A small plane awaited them at Bromma Airport. Jennie and Rafe climbed into the back seats while her dad sat next to the pilot. After her night flight from Scotland, Jennie pressed her face to the window. Here was her chance to see Sweden from the air. The plane was noisy, however, the flight bumpy, and the temperature soared in the bright sun. They should have taken a train. She pressed a hand to her roiling stomach. If they didn't land soon, she would disgrace herself.

Rafe leaned close and yelled in her ear. "I kind of miss being at twenty-five thousand feet where the temperature's minus forty."

She tried to smile, but must have failed. Rafe frowned. He directed her attention out the window. "They've got lots of forests down there. After the war, the Swedes could do a booming lumber business to help rebuild Europe."

He was trying to distract her from her malaise. So sweet of him. Focusing on a distant object helped some. Still, this flight couldn't end soon enough. She tried breathing deeply. Rafe picked up her hand, his thumb massaging her palm. Her eyes fluttered shut. She could get used to this.

The plane banked and Rafe leaned into the window. She couldn't hear him above the engine noise, but read his lips. "Wow."

She craned her neck for a look and gasped. Bombers, lots of them, were parked wingtip to wingtip. All of them appeared to be Liberators with their twin tail fins, high wings, and blunt noses. Smoke still rose from the wreckage of one bomber. Oh dear. That didn't look survivable.

Their plane had barely bounced to a stop before Dad was out and striding to a waiting jeep. She and Rafe hurried after him and scrambled into the back seat. The driver gave Dad a report. Over three hundred B-24 Liberators had been sent to Pölitz to bomb oil targets. Opposition was anticipated to be light, but intelligence had been dead wrong. Waves of enemy fighters had mauled the formations, sending many bombers down in flames. In one hour's time, fifteen bombers landed at Bulltofta Airfield, leading to chaos.

"They were queued up, waiting to land. Almost like a squadron got lost, but they're from several different bases. Quite a few men have been sent to the hospital. We've got some fatalities too, although half of the crew from that one," he pointed to the smoking wreckage, "is still alive. Both starboard engines were out, the right wing hit a rise in the field, and the plane cartwheeled. Horrible thing to see." The driver paused a moment. "Another half dozen more planes landed or crashed elsewhere, as well. Most of the crews are in that hangar, waiting to learn their fate."

After Dad left to meet with Swedish officials, Jennie pointed to the hangar. "Let's go see the crews."

She and Rafe slipped inside. The few guards present appeared to cause apprehension among some of the men. They milled around, some talking quietly, some looking exhausted, some appearing to be in shock. Rafe nodded to one young man who couldn't have been out of his teens. He was busy chewing his fingernails down to the quick.

"Should we tell them they can relax?"

Jennie smiled. Why not? Already some were eyeing her curiously. She stepped forward. "Hello, boys."

Her greeting caused an instant reaction. The men perked up and moved closer. Their comments swirled.

"You're an American."

"Are you interned here?"

"How long do we have to stay here?"

Rafe stepped up beside her.

She held up her hands. "Since you fellows didn't make reservations," she paused as some chuckled, "your accommodations for tonight may not be the best. The Swedes weren't prepared for this American invasion, but as quickly as possible, you'll be processed and moved to an internment camp."

She glanced at Rafe. He smiled and nodded, encouraging her to continue.

"I can tell you the first thing you will need to do is buy civilian clothes. You may not wear your uniforms here, so you'll dress like Lieutenant Martell."

Rafe raised one arm, his hand bent at the wrist and, with his other hand on his hip, pirouetted. Several men laughed. Jennie smiled. They were relaxing.

"While here you may take part in all kinds of sports. American magazines are available. Some internees are learning to play the piano. You can buy art supplies." She should have thought of that before. The internees themselves could provide paintings for the Svithiod exhibit. "And the best thing of all, no one will shoot at you."

A rousing cheer filled the hangar, followed by "Atten—hut!"

The men snapped to attention. At the door stood a group of officers, her father among them. He quirked a brow at her.

"Hi, Dad."

"I see my daughter is bucking for a commission." Dad claimed their attention and got a laugh from the men before introducing a Swedish colonel who informed them of the rules and regulations.

At his conclusion, many of the officers approached Rafe with questions, the enlisted men lurking nearby to hear his answers. One of the men ogled Jennie. "How'd you get the girl?"

Rafe's eyes narrowed. "The girl and I knew each other before we arrived in Europe."

The man backed off.

Chapter Forty-Seven

Some men had been shipped to camps the previous day in an effort to relieve the congestion. Jennie and Rafe helped in the processing to get more of them on their way, and by midmorning, the transfers were moving smoothly. Then a cry rang out.

"B-17 coming in!"

Rafe dashed outside, and Jennie followed on his heels. The Flying Fortress, with two engines smoking, landed safely, and kept going.

"Stop, stop, *stop*." Jennie clenched her hands so tightly, her nails dug into her palms.

The bomber struck a small building, tearing off part of a wing, and didn't stop until it ran into an embankment at the edge of the field, a row of houses just beyond.

Jennie sagged. Her heart pounded like she'd run a mile. Vehicles raced to the plane. A wounded man was lowered down to a waiting jeep. She turned away, only to hear another cry.

"Here comes another one!"

This Fort didn't have its wheels down. It belly-landed and slid into a ditch.

Jennie puffed out her breath. Another day of chaos for Malmö's Bulltofta Airfield was underway.

The train chugged north through the same forests they'd looked down on while flying to Malmö. Jennie paid no attention as she stared out the window. If she lived to be eighty, she would never be able to wipe out the image of a heavy bomber with brake failure crashing into a ditch. No wonder, since that had happened three times this morning. Minor crashes, but enough to injure the men inside. They were the lucky ones. More men died today. Some were dead on arrival. Others died when they bailed out too low for their parachutes to open.

By the time the last plane landed at twelve thirty, three hours had elapsed since the first arrival. She shoved a hand through her hair and her fingers snagged on tangles. Her hair must look like a bird's nest after the way she'd toyed with it all morning.

The war had taken its toll for years. She'd seen the newsreels, read the papers, even attended a few funerals in Chicago. But today the war happened right in front of her on a large scale. There was nothing hypothetical about the damaged planes, the grimaces of pain, the covered bodies.

In two weeks, the Swedes planned to hold a military funeral for the ten dead American airmen. Her tears spilled down her cheeks.

Rafe touched her arm. "Jen? What's wrong?"

She whirled around. "What's wrong? What's wrong? You were there, Rafe. You know what's wrong. Ten men died in these two days, and," she glanced around at the boisterous airmen heading for Falun, "how can everyone be so happy about it?"

Rafe studied her in silence for a long moment. Then he wrapped an arm around her and pulled her close to his side. "No one from the three crews that lost men is on this train. None of us knew them. I may sound callous, but we've become," his thumb stroked her hand as he searched for a word, "hardened to death. So often a plane takes off on a mission and doesn't come back. Nine or ten guys are gone. Maybe they're dead, maybe captured. Who knows? We didn't try to get acquainted with fellows not in our crew because they might not last long enough to be friends."

He'd had to live with that, day after day after day. Never knowing who would be next. If he would be next. More tears spilled over. "It shouldn't be like that."

He wiped away her tears. "No, but we can't live under Nazi tyranny either. It's just our rotten luck that our generation is called on to do the fighting. Of course, our fathers would tell us to quit complaining. They had to fight a war too."

She tried to smile. "My little exhibit I'm fussing over seems so trivial."

"No." His voice was stern and he gripped her shoulder. "Your father's right. Folks need to understand Sweden's role in the war. The Swedes will enjoy the freedom we're paying for with our blood, but we have to be grateful for the haven they're providing us. Thirty-four planes came here in a span of, what, twenty-seven hours? They all carried nine or ten men. That's over three hundred men still alive who will now enjoy the relative freedom of internment. As well as all the rest of us, and those still to come. That's why it's important for you to celebrate Sweden."

Behind them, a voice loudly exulted, "No more two A.M. wake-up calls. Hallelujah."

Rafe turned around. "No, but you'll have a curfew of ten P.M."

"What?!"

"And you'll have to answer roll call every morning."

"What?!"

"And fend off Swedish girls eager to help you spend your money."

"Really?"

The young airman's outrage turned to intrigue, and Jennie smiled. Rafe was right. These young men were right to be exhilarated that they still lived.

The day brightened even more when the first words they heard when they stepped off the train in Falun were an ecstatic, "Lieutenant Martell!"

Chapter Forty-Eight

Stockholm, Sweden
Friday, June 23, 1944

Rafe fought the desire to take off his hat and scratch his scalp. Of all the times for Jennie to experiment with a new disguise, this wasn't it. Doubts circled like vultures as they approached the train station. Why must he look ridiculous when meeting her look-alike cousin Astrid for the first time?

She had made a good point as she slicked back his hair with a wet comb. "Remember, Rafe, how the airport is always under surveillance. The train station may be as well."

The effect of her handiwork was appalling. His dampened hair blurred with his skin.

"Great. Now I know how I'll look bald."

She had penciled a scar onto his cheek. "Stop fussing, and try on these glasses."

The lenses resembled the bottoms of soda bottles.

"I can't see straight."

"I'll guide you."

"We'll attract attention that way. Especially if I walk into walls and trip over things."

"I won't let you do that. Besides, what spy would behave in such a way as to attract attention? Watchers won't give you a second look."

Something was wrong with that logic. The known factor was that he was about to meet her newfound cousin looking like an ugly yuck. Again. Why couldn't spies look handsome? He looked at Jennie from the corner of his eye, avoiding the soda bottle lens. She'd tightly braided her hair and wound it around her head like a little girl's princess crown before hiding it under a wide-brimmed hat. Large sunglasses further hid her face. Women had such an easy time altering their looks.

He should have stayed in Falun and visited with Dan for a few days. Without their uniforms, it was easier to blur the distinction between officers and enlisted men. Dan had carved out quite a life for himself as an informal scout master. Young Swedish boys were enthralled with the influx of these swaggering heroes. Dan had befriended the group that sidled up to him, and organized activities for them. With many Swedish men away in their military, the town fathers approved.

Rafe shook his head. Dan, the den mother. He couldn't see himself in that role, even if Jennie said he'd acted like that with his enlisted crewmembers.

They reached the stairs to the station. A large black Mercedes idled at the curb. It lacked the customary stove strapped to the rear. A German car with gasoline. Must be someone from the Nazi community. The rear door opened and a blond man stepped out. Jennie froze and clutched Rafe's arm tight, then pivoted away.

415

"That's Lars," she hissed. "He can't see me here."

"So, that's your goon." Rafe lowered his glasses and studied the man. He had an arrogant lift to his head and a smirk on his mouth. This man symbolized everything that was wrong in Germany. He and his ilk had forced Rafe's family to flee the country, along with thousands of other folks with the wrong ancestry. Millions of lives ruined because of the insane desire to be a master race and rule over everyone. He'd cheerfully rub Lars' face in the dirt. "Must be meeting someone coming in on the train. Any way we can bring him down a notch?"

"If you want to tangle with him, you're on your own." Jennie hadn't released her grip, and his fingers were going numb. "I don't want any contact with him."

They followed Lars into the station and out to the platform. The whistle of an incoming train wailed, and the floor beneath their feet vibrated. Rafe pointed to a column supporting the overhang and Jennie scurried behind it. He leaned against the column in a bored manner, arms crossed, hat tilted down. The train rushed in, stopping with a screech of brakes and a gust of hot air.

Lars walked along its length, looking in the windows. As passengers disembarked, he forced them to step around him. He straightened suddenly like he'd put his finger in a socket. But who had he zeroed in on?

"There's Astrid." Jennie bounced on her toes, her voice filled with frustration. If not for Lars, she would have run to meet her cousin.

Rafe stiffened as he spotted Jennie's look-alike. Astrid was Lars' target. The man edged alongside her as she searched the crowd. He slipped something into Astrid's coat pocket.

"Did you see that? He plans on framing her somehow." Rafe scanned the crowd, spotting his quest. "Stay out of sight for now. When I give you a nod, come greet your cousin."

"But, what..."

Rafe plunged into the milling crowd and hurried to a policeman. "That man there," he pointed at Lars who was moving away from Astrid but keeping track of her, "is a German agent and he just put something in our friend's coat pocket without her knowledge."

A shorter policeman stepped around his partner. "I'll check the girl, Anders, while you watch the agent."

Rafe trailed after the policeman.

"Excuse me, miss. Would you empty your pockets and show your identification?"

Astrid looked at the policeman in surprise. She really did look just like Jennie. In fact, maybe Lars thought she was Jennie. Just as they tried to raise strife among the Germans, he was trying to get her in trouble with the Swedes. But why would he think she'd be arriving on the train from Uppsala? Unless the

Germans had circulated photos of Jennie, and someone had spotted Astrid and reported her whereabouts.

Astrid took a quick look around before reaching into her pocket. She pulled out a folded paper. "This isn't mine."

"May I?" The policeman took the paper from her grasp and unfolded it.

Rafe peered over his shoulder. A typed list enumerated Swedish utilities, some of them noted as "soft." Sabotage targets?

Voices approached. "…under surveillance. She's an American spy." Lars brushed forward and stabbed a finger at Astrid.

She gaped at him. "I am not a spy. I've never even been to America."

The policeman continued to finger the list. "This paper is crisp. If it had been in her pocket for any length of time, it would have become wrinkled." His eyes bore into Lars. "A witness saw you plant this in Mrs. Marklund's pocket."

Lars looked down his nose. "Don't be ridiculous."

Rafe nodded to Jennie. She rushed forward and threw her arms around her cousin.

"Oh, how good to see you, Astrid. How are Uncle Bjorn and Aunt Margaretha?" Her eyes pleaded with Astrid to play along.

"They're wonderful and send you their love." Message received. Astrid returned the hug. "But here, everything is confusion."

The tall policeman led a sputtering Lars away. "This is outrageous. The German Legation will hear about this."

A door closed behind him, bringing peace.

"I apologize for this unfortunate incident," the remaining policeman said. He finished copying information from Astrid's identification and returned it to her, along with a card. "Will you please appear at this address tomorrow and sign the official report?" At her nod, he turned to Rafe. "You will also need to come. May I have your name?"

Rafe silently thanked Ed for providing him with an alias. "Rolf Svenson."

Rafe flicked his fingers at Jennie and mouthed what she took to mean, "Your place."

She linked arms with Astrid and led her through the station.

Astrid looked back. "What was that all about?"

"You had your first and, hopefully, last encounter with my tormentor. He lit on me the week I arrived in Sweden and seemed to be stalking me, although lately I haven't noticed him. Maybe now he'll be sent back to Germany." What a relief that would be. Imagine not having to watch every person who came into a restaurant, search the sidewalks before exiting a building, looking over her shoulder.

Of course, someone else might fixate on her.

Beside her, Astrid's eyes widened.

"I should come to Stockholm more often." She laughed as she claimed her suitcase.

Jennie laughed, too. "You should get along fine with my friends Phyllis and Emma. They enjoy bedeviling the Germans. Some of my adventures with Rafe have been nerve wracking, but he tends to exercise caution."

To a point anyway. That escapade at the toy store still gave her shivers.

"I thought he would be here with you. I must say, I've been looking forward to meeting him."

"He was here. Rafe was Rolf. He spotted Lars planting that list on you, and immediately set about turning the tables on him before he could have you arrested."

Astrid stopped short. "That man with the coke bottle glasses? He's your Rafe? I thought you said he was gravy. Isn't that supposed to mean he's good looking?"

Jennie burst out laughing as she tugged her cousin outside. Heads turned in her direction, including

Rafe's. He'd removed those awful glasses. Astrid hadn't seen him, so she angled their way to pass close by him.

"Yes, that's how Phyllis describes him. Today, though, he was in his 'disreputable' disguise. Good thing, too. Now he'll have to admit I was right to insist on it."

She passed too close to Rafe. He poked her ribs and she could have sworn she heard a soft, "Hmpf."

Chapter Forty-Nine

"So we'll spend much of the day on the water?" Astrid and Jennie relaxed in the Lindquists' living room and discussed their plans for Midsummer Day.

Jennie glanced at the clock and tried not to fidget. Rafe should have joined them by now. Her big surprise was due any minute. "Yes, none of us has spent much time out on the archipelago. We thought we'd find an island where we can go ashore and have a picnic lunch."

"Excellent idea. Even if it's a private island, we can still go ashore because of Allemänsträtten. Enjoying the countryside or the islands is every man's right, as long as we do no damage." Astrid leaned back and stifled a yawn. "Just think. The days will now start getting shorter."

Jennie chuckled. "Yes. Sunrise today came at 2:30. That's been very difficult to adjust to."

Just before her eyes strayed to the clock again, a knock sounded on the door and she jumped to her feet. "Rafe took his time. I hope the policeman didn't keep him this long."

But Rafe wasn't at the door. His crewmates Steve, Cal, Alan, and Dan spilled into the room. Dan grabbed her hand and kissed it.

"You don't know how hard it was not to say anything about this little trip when you and Lieutenant Martell left Falun yesterday."

His eternal smile stretched across his face. Jennie hugged the young man she thought of as Rafe's younger brother. The absence of the other enlisted men didn't bother her. Rusty and Harold had already used their monthly passes, and George anticipated a big holiday weekend with a Swedish girl. Since the military expected non-fraternization between officers and enlisted men, the three missing men would have created an awkward situation. Dan was a special case. He transcended rank and could make himself at home anywhere. Jennie had impulsively invited him the previous day during a moment when Rafe was out of earshot.

A throat cleared noisily, and Dan jumped back. Rafe stood in the still-open doorway.

"Lieutenant Martell!" Dan pumped Rafe's hand like yesterday hadn't happened. "It's sure good to see you again."

Rafe spotted his fellow officers, and shook their hands with as much enthusiasm as Dan, amid a lot of back slapping.

"I rounded the corner in time to see a bunch of men disappear into the Lindquists' apartment and couldn't imagine what was going on." He turned to Jennie. "Did you know they were coming?" His crewmates' presence had to be at her instigation. How had she known he longed to see them?

"I invited them to join us for the holiday." Her last word came out in a squeak as he hugged the stuffing out of her.

Finally, he turned to the last person in the room. "Astrid."

Jennie's cousin stood. "I am so pleased to meet you, Rolf Svenson. Thank you for rescuing me."

His crewmates looked perplexed.

Cal pointed from Jennie to Astrid. "Are you two sisters?"

Steve looked from Astrid to Rafe. "You two haven't met before?"

Alan peered behind Rafe. "Who is Rolf Svenson?"

Dan smiled. "You're long-lost relatives who didn't know you're related."

"We are indeed." Jennie introduced them. "Astrid arrived on the train today from Uppsala. No sooner had she stepped off the train than a German agent planted a sabotage list in her pocket." Palms pressed together, she clapped her fingers. "And it was Rafe to the rescue."

The men insisted on hearing the whole tale.

"That's what you do here in Stockholm?" Steve couldn't seem to comprehend Rafe's status. "Tangle with German spies? What happened to reading newspapers?"

"Boring." His smile never faded, but Dan's brows drew together. "That's way too sedentary for the lieutenant."

Beside him on the sofa, Alan nudged his foot. "Sedentary. That's a mighty big word for you, Mr. Quigley."

"I've been doing lots of reading myself. I think I've read every English book in Falun, and they've enriched my vocabulary." His nose angled upward and his smile didn't falter.

From his other side, Cal gave him a stingless head slap. "Good for you, little man." He shifted and crossed an ankle over his knee. "I hate to say this, but after we've hiked every trail and biked every route..."

Alan took over. "...canoed around the lake a half dozen times..."

"...played baseball and basketball and football until we've worn out three pairs of shoes each." Steve hesitated. "Paradise has become monotonous."

Alan scrunched his shoulders. "Sounds like a rotten thing to say when we could so easily have ended up rotting in a German prison camp."

Rafe's thumb absently massaged the palm of Jennie's hand as he studied the bombardier. Alan looked far from rested after a month of internment. Frown lines dug into his forehead between his eyes. Something was wrong. "Have you heard from Ruby?"

"No, and I don't expect to for a long time to come. Hopefully she's received my first letter by now." The frown lines deepened. "I'm told our letters can take weeks to arrive at their destination. They're even placed in new envelopes so our families won't know where we are. What's the big secret? And then Ruby's letters have to take the same slow route in reverse. More weeks. We've only been here thirty-five days. In another week, though, maybe…" His voice trailed off.

"We'll have a memorable weekend that should help make the time go faster, right?" Cal directed his question to Rafe and Jennie.

Steve cut in. "We had a look at the archipelago yesterday. Looks like a great place to explore."

"They got to go flying." Alan still looked glum. "They were taken to the air force's parking lot in Västerås to exercise their skills."

Rafe smiled in sympathy. A bombardier had no need to exercise his skills to keep current. Between missing his wife and his forced inactivity, Alan was sinking into depression. "Well, tonight we can all take part in the spy business." His words brought anticipation to his crewmates' faces. "We'll go to the restaurant at the Grand Hotel. There'll be Germans there. We've heard of American airmen who've discussed military strategy, bogus of course, and sketched plans on the back of menus. Then when they leave, they watch the Germans scramble for the menus. We'll have our own animated conversation and see if we can't fool some eavesdroppers."

Dan rubbed his hands together, his smile nearly stretching off his face.

Chapter Fifty

They walked across the old town island to reach the Grand Hotel. Rafe studied his crewmates. Their boredom was a revelation. He had it good with his role in Stockholm, even though his minor acts of harassment toward Germans and the scraps of information he gleaned could hardly help the war effort.

"We need to decide what sort of tale we'll spin. Anything we say has to sound legitimate but be as phony as a three dollar bill." Rafe looked to Steve. "Any ideas?"

"D-Day is the big news. We could make up strategy for breaking out of the beachhead areas. Problem is, we don't know what's really being planned. If we say the army's marching for Paris, and they are, we could end up court-martialed."

Cal snapped his fingers. "How about this? The 307th Bomb Group will take over the Kraut airfield at Lille."

"Is there any chance of that happening?"

"The remotest. The 307th is part of the Seventh Air Force in the Pacific. My cousin's with that outfit."

Steve rubbed his chin. "I can see where we'd base our fighter squadrons in France, but not the heavy bombers."

"Why Lille?" Unease skittered down Rafe's neck like a horde of ants. If a German took note of their conversation and reported it, might the Luftwaffe be dispatched to Lille to raise havoc? If the Allies did have anyone there, their little game could cause trouble. The German air force might be suffering from attrition, but it was far from dead. "Maybe we'd better stick with what we know and, ah, *explain* how we got there."

"All we know is what's been in the news and the Germans here would have access to the same news. I'll bet they listen to Radio London and read our papers." Alan's shoulders slumped.

Jennie and Astrid trailed behind the men. Jennie's voice drifted forward. "They look like a bunch of salesmen on their way to a convention."

Dan spun around. "We are salesmen, on our way to sell a load of baloney to the Krauts."

They stepped inside the hotel restaurant and stopped. Jennie watched Rafe's mouth drop open. The exquisite chandeliers were dazzling.

"You're gawking." She spoke for his ears only.

He snapped his mouth shut and smiled at her. "Aren't you glad you don't have to clean all those crystals?"

She eyed them. "No big deal. Just lower 'em down into a big bucket of water, raise 'em back up, and let 'em air dry."

He tucked her hand on his arm. "How uncouth."

Their party sat at a table covered with a white cloth. Jennie pulled off her white gloves. She wore her most elegant outfit, a two-piece rose-colored dress with a white print and slim lines. A small-brimmed white hat and white sandals completed her ensemble. It seemed fitting for the Grand.

Dan ran a finger around the rim of the plate in front of him. "This is real china, isn't it?" He looked up at the high rounded ceiling with its moldings and painted scenes before turning to Steve. "Why can't Ridgewell have a mess hall like this?"

Cal knocked his hat forward. "As I understand it, some bomb groups are stationed in the lap of luxury on estates of rich Brits." He rose. "Food's over there. Come on, we don't have to wait. Let's load up on the chow."

Jennie hesitated when Rafe hung back. "Coming?"

He nodded, but his eyes continued to scan the room, the decorated ceiling, the arched windows. A sigh escaped him that sounded like it came from the depths of his soul. "This restaurant reminds me of someplace else, maybe in Potsdam, that I saw when I was young. That place is probably destroyed now." His gaze met hers, sorrow in his eyes. "Not only is this war killing people, its destroying our heritage. Architecture like this isn't being built anymore."

He'd been excited to see his friends and anticipated their spoof of any German listeners, but now melancholy had stolen his joy. To be more exact, Alan had stolen his joy. Jennie had watched it happen.

They'd just crossed the bridge from Staden Island when Alan, frustrated by his separation from Ruby, vented his wrath when Astrid suggested the allied bombing was indiscriminate of military or civilian targets. "Those stupid, mindless Krauts deserve every bit of destruction our bombs are causing. I wouldn't mind being back in combat just so I could drop more bombs myself."

Rafe had flinched as though Alan had slapped him.

Rafe's eyes had shone with amazement and delight when he told her of seeing his cousin, Christoph, in England. She witnessed his pleasure in reuniting with Bertil. He hadn't admitted it, but he missed his father. Not all Germans favored the war or deserved destruction. Not Rafe's loved ones. Alan's thoughtlessness was apt to throw a damper on their whole holiday.

She bumped her arm against his as they arrived at the buffet. "It's kind of like when I complained about my brother's disassembled car parts strewn in the yard. It was okay for me to whine because he was my brother. But let the neighbor rant, and I got mad. You're welcome to criticize your own country, but foreigners should not join in. Alan thinks of you only as an American."

A smile tilted one side of Rafe's mouth. "And that's how I want to be thought of, isn't it? I'm fully accepted." He plopped a spoonful of... something... on her plate. "Kippered herring. Yum."

Her laughter bubbled up. Fish dishes filled the table. "We'll sprout fins before we leave Sweden."

"After the landings at Normandy, the Krauts decided the feint at Calais was a ruse to keep them away from the real landing." Steve would make a good lecturer. His earnest expression and subdued hand gestures lent him an air of authority. "But it wasn't a feint. The Brits landed just south of Calais."

Dan nodded. "At Baloney-sur-Mer."

How Rafe managed to keep a straight face, he didn't know. "That's Boulogne-sur-Mer. Nice place. I visited there before the war."

Now he fought laughter at his friends' surprise. Keeping his hand at table level, he rolled his fingers. Keep the game moving.

Dan responded without delay. "The Krauts were so shocked, thinking they were off the hook, they skedaddled lickety-split quick."

Rafe took pride in his facility with languages. He'd been fluent in English when he first arrived in America. Since joining the army, however, he'd discovered a whole new version of English. Half the time it made no sense and the other half would have made his mother cringe. Astrid stared at Dan in bafflement. Rafe enlightened her. "The Germans ran away very fast."

Her mouth formed a silent O.

Cal caught Rafe's eye, picked up his glass and, with his left hand, pointed into his right hand. *Look to my right.*

Rafe raised his own glass for a sip and looked past Jennie. The man at the next table made no attempt to disguise his interest in their conversation. Rafe should have been keeping a closer eye on their surroundings. He palmed his little spy camera and brushed at his hair. Click.

"Landing near Calais had to be expected, since it's only twenty-five miles from England." Steve kept the conversation going even though he looked fascinated by Rafe's picture taking. "How could the Brits resist?"

With a look of distaste, Alan pushed aside his serving of what appeared to be poached eel. "I can't imagine slogging ashore at Normandy after riding through ninety-five miles of rough water. The fact our boys prevailed proves the superiority of the Allies over the Krauts' vaunted super-race."

A thump on Rafe's back brought his head around. Ed was stalking toward the buffet tables.

Beside him, Jennie leaned close. Her eyes alight with humor, she whispered, "Naughty, naughty."

Reluctance dogged his steps as he followed the OSS man. Despite the leeway he enjoyed as a Stockholm-based internee, he'd been cautioned to avoid revealing military information to anyone. And they hadn't. Doubtless, Ed would disagree.

They crossed paths in front of the cold cuts.

"What do you think you're doing?" Whispering a demand lessened its impact.

Rafe slapped a thin slice of pork on his plate. "Just trying to give a German indigestion with a made-up story."

Ed wasn't listening. "You know not to give out information."

Rafe wandered down the line and picked up a strawberry. "This is pink. It's too early for berries." He dropped it on his plate with a half shrug. "We're not giving information. We're dishing up fairy tales." He looked Ed in the eye. "The Brits haven't landed at Calais, have they?"

That stopped Ed in his tracks. "Of course not."

Rafe speared a cut of cheese and popped it into his mouth. "Mmm, this is a good one." He speared another and added it to Ed's plate. "If our eavesdropper goes back and reports our Calais landing, he'll be a laughing post."

Ed's brows bunched up. Must have gotten the expression wrong. "Did you hear the one about a base being readied for the 307th Bomb Group near Bayeux to protect De Gaulle's provisional French government?"

Ed merely shook his head.

"Never going to happen with the 307th in the Pacific, but that's the fun of misinformation. Got any tidbits you'd like us to drop?"

Heaving a sigh, Ed turned back to his table, his head still shaking.

Rafe didn't wait to sit down before announcing to his friends. "Guess what I just heard. Our victorious army has liberated Cherbourg."

They raised their glasses in a toast to the army. Their diner at the next table turned flaming red.

Chapter Fifty-One

Stockholm, Sweden
Saturday, June 24, 1944

"Today was glorious." Jennie collapsed on the sofa and hugged the pillow her mother had embroidered with daises in tones of white, cream, and pale yellow to match the living room. "What do you think of Rafe?"

Astrid leaned back and shook out her hair. "Gorgeous. He likes to smile. That is an excellent character trait. It indicates a happy disposition." With one arm across her waist, she propped up on the other elbow and raised a finger. "Although I am not certain he was happy with one of his friends."

"Alan, the bombardier. He's bored out of his skull and desperately missing his gem of a wife, Ruby." That didn't explain his barbed remarks that upset Rafe. Too bad he didn't speak Swedish. Then he could attend a university. Classwork was a worthy activity to fill the hours. Maybe Dad could come up with a retired professor for their mental stimulation.

"Steve is a nice man. He reminds me of my husband."

Jennie set aside the pillow and straightened up. Astrid's voice had acquired a dreamy tone. "Steve's mellowed since I met him on the *Queen Mary*. The enlisted men complained that he was stiff. Either he adjusted to his role as plane commander or the stress of combat is off."

"Hmm. You might think Gustav is formal. Americans tend to be more informal than we are. Steve was interested in what our air force is like. He had so many questions when we walked around the island together." She traced a finger along the embroidery of another pillow. "Then Dan tried to convince Phyllis of the benefits of a cold water swim. I noticed he got her to wade with him."

Jennie sank back against the sofa. "I'll miss Dan when we go back to America. I know Rafe will. The crew members are from all over the States. I suspect they'll lose touch."

Astrid turned in her seat and tucked a foot under her opposite knee. "I notice you came back holding a bouquet. I thought you had collected seven different flowers to place under your pillow. But you put them in water." She grinned. "Don't you want to dream of Rafe?"

Jennie laughed. "Sorry. I don't believe the legend that doing so will make me dream of my future husband. It's a cute custom, but it ranks with the Easter Bunny. And I don't need a mess under my pillow to dream of Rafe."

Astrid's smile faded. "Are you serious about him? Do you see a future together?"

"I hope so. Oh, Astrid, I hope so." Jennie's voice dropped to a whisper. She'd already visualized their wedding. The ceremony would take place in Tyska Kyrkan. She'd never seen a more beautiful church, and Rafe liked it too. Bertil would stand with Rafe. How fantastic that would be for the two old friends. And maybe one or two of his crewmates, if they were still here. For herself, she would ask Phyllis and Astrid. Emma too, if they had three couples attending them.

"Last night was the first time we danced together. I got the uncanny sensation that we were dancing at our wedding reception. Which made no sense. Whoever heard of 'There'll be bluebirds over the White Cliffs of Dover' as a bridal song?"

"Hmm." Astrid pressed her lips together and gave appropriate consideration to the question. "As an instrumental number, it's quite lovely. I would leave out a singer. The words don't strike the desired romantic mood."

"I wish I'd seen those white cliffs. Rafe's told me what a beautiful sight they are for the fliers, coming back from a mission, almost home. I hope to see them before returning to Chicago." The possibility existed if they stopped in London. If they didn't leave before war's end. With the war over, the need to fly in secret to Scotland would be eliminated. She'd love to see London, the cliffs, Rafe's air base. Of course, if the war was over, the base might already be closed down. She wrenched her mind out of the hazy future.

"Rafe's favorite song is 'Coming in on a Wing and a Prayer.' Can you imagine trying to dance to that?"

She hopped up and improvised a few steps, did a fast twirl, and changed direction. "Da da da, da da da, da da da."

"That's where he flips you across his back." Astrid nodded to the beat. "I could see someone dance to that, but not wearing wedding attire."

"Oh, that would be scandalous." Jennie segued into their dance to 'The White Cliffs of Dover.' She hummed the melody as she glided around the living room. A turn to her left, and she gasped.

The door stood open. Dad and Mom had watched her sashay about with open mouths. And beside them stood Rafe.

He grinned. "I remember this from last night."

Stepping forward, he slipped one arm around her waist and grasped the other. He led her around the room, dancing, in front of her parents.

"If they had music, we might join them," Dad told Mom.

Rafe chuckled softly. He twirled her one last time, stepped back, and bowed to her. Holding her skirt with her thumbs and index fingers, other fingers gracefully extended, she curtsied. Astrid applauded.

Suddenly, the playful moment ended. Dad and Rafe pulled up chairs to the kitchen table and continued a conversation that had started before they came in.

"You're sure he was Swedish police?" Dad poised his pen over a notepad.

"Definitely. He was the phony fisherman Jennie sailed circles around when we were out on Mälaren Lake. He wore the same frock coat and starched collar, and his hair sticks out over his ears, maybe from having his hat pulled down too low."

"And he stayed in his boat?"

"Yes, and used binoculars. That's why we took notice. Cal spotted him and said we were being watched. After he pointed him out, I recognized him. At least today he was in a sailboat. Previously, we saw him in a rowboat. A rowboat can't keep up with a sailboat, so I think we just had the bad luck to muddle into him before and draw his attention."

"And the other observer who followed you onto the island?"

Jennie and Astrid exchanged astonished glances. Their lovely holiday outing took on a sinister air.

"I'd peg him as a German. He was too suave, too arrogant for the policemen I've seen. He tried too hard to eavesdrop on Jennie and me though. His outdoor skills betrayed him. Dan described him as an easy target for Indians in the Old West. He and Alan sneaked up behind him with no effort."

"Did he know he was observed?"

"Oh, yeah. Dan asked, 'Did you lose something, mister?' Alan said the guy was so mad he spit. Dan described his eyes as creepy. Almost colorless. Gray, maybe."

Jennie hugged herself as Dad's dark frown prompted shivers to race through her. "He was following us? You and me?"

She hadn't noticed the intruder, but Dan had been talking nearby while she and Rafe explored a hidden glen. Rafe had immediately led her back into the open. Had the spy been stealthy, might he have dared to snap their necks? She shook her head. Her imagination was running away. Wasn't it?

"Have them stop by the legation Monday." Dad sat back. "They can check the rogue gallery for his picture. And ask if Ed knows of a colorless-eyed man."

Rafe nodded and stood. "Will do. Then we plan on doing some serious shopping at the NK Department Store before the fellows catch their train."

Chapter Fifty-Two

"This is great."

That had to be the dozenth time Cal declared something to be great. Rafe scrutinized the Crosley record player. "Soon there won't be enough space left in your room for you and Steve to sleep."

"This will make the time go faster." He pawed through a stack of records. "Look at all the American music available here. I thought Sweden was blockaded. They've got Jimmy Dorsey, Glenn Miller, Benny Goodman, Kay Kyser."

As each new selection joined his pile, the saleslady's eyes grew larger. Rafe grinned. She probably hadn't rung up a sale this big all month, maybe all year.

The department store was the fanciest he'd ever seen. Several stories high, the center atrium allowed shoppers to view the floors above and below them. The building's exterior had prompted Dan to question whether it was a store or a museum.

Dan looked through the records as well. "Here's one, Lieutenant. Vera Mills. She sings the White Cliffs song. Get this one."

Rafe shook his head. "You know, Dan, no matter how loud Cal plays that in Rättvik, you won't be able to hear it in Falun."

"Yeah, I know, but maybe he'll get tired of it and pass it on to me. Someone in Falun with a record player might let me use it."

Cal tossed it on his stack with two more as Steve and Alan joined them.

"Yikes." Steve's eyes popped. "I hope the store will ship all this for you."

Rafe chuckled at the image of his crewmates attempting to board the train, peering around towering armloads of packages which would promptly spill into the aisle. By staying in Stockholm, he might miss out on a first-rate comedy act.

Alan picked up one of the records. "Do you know this guy is a Jew?"

Rafe stepped back. Alan may as well have delivered a blow to his solar plexus. First he had lambasted the Germans and now he espoused anti-Semitism? What was going on in Rättvik?

Alan sized up the mounds of Cal's purchases, showing no awareness of the affect his comment had on Rafe. "Have you tallied your final bill? And have you considered that you're unlikely to be able to bring all this back to England or to the States?"

Cal shrugged. "So I'll leave it behind. Our Swedish friends will be pleased to take it off my hands. As far as the cost," he shrugged again, "easy come, easy go. I'm using the winnings I made on the *Queen Mary* blackjack games, not my service pay. Two thousand dollars of mad money."

"Two thousand dollars?" Dan nearly dropped the records he held. If his eyes got any bigger, they'd pop out of his head.

Cal's nonchalance with his money was amazing. If Rafe had such easy-come money, he'd save it for the future, when he got out of the military. He calculated Cal's total expenditure. A couple hundred dollars, tops. A small dent in two thousand.

What would he do if he had two thousand dollars of mad money? Nothing in a quick survey of the store's departments tempted him. Nope, he'd save it. A nice car cost one thousand dollars, like his Milwaukee neighbor's new green Oldsmobile with automatic transmission. Yes, sir. He was saving his money.

He accompanied them to the train station and shook hands with Steve and Cal, promising to see them again during their next month's pass. Dan surprised him with a fierce hug, a big smile, and a "See ya, Lieutenant." A chuckle broke free. Jennie had said he was good for her. Dan was good for him.

Bertil was good for him, too. Now might be a good time to snoop around Bromma Airfield.

Chapter Fifty-Three

"With Rafe's crewmates and Astrid's departures, shopping is the perfect cure for the post-holiday letdown." Phyllis' comment drew Jennie from the window they were passing. "What kind of reception do you need this dress for?"

"The naval attaché is hosting a get-together for our attachés plus several from the Allied nations' legations. It'll be a hoity-toity affair, so I want something elegant."

"And Rafe will escort you. Are you two getting serious?"

"No. Yes. Maybe. I don't know." First Astrid, now Phyllis. Jennie pressed her lips together. Maybe Phyllis could help her figure this out. "I've never had a serious relationship that got beyond a casual level. I'd get the feeling I was being evaluated and found wanting. With Rafe, it's been different. From our first meeting, I've been comfortable with him. Maybe because we met on the ship and didn't expect to see each other again after the crossing. But we haven't spoken of life beyond the war."

"You wait. He's not going to let you go. If you think he needs prodding, remember that American women are in short supply here. Let him think someone else has caught your eye." Phyllis caught her hand. "Just promise me you won't use Stanley."

Jennie wouldn't have been surprised if her cheeks ignited. "I couldn't do that. Pretend an interest." She spun around, getting her bearings. "We better get to the store. Which way did you say it is?"

With a smile saying she would allow the subject to be changed for now, Phyllis indicated their direction. "What kind of elegant dress do you hope to find?"

"A touch of sophistication but simple. Something that can be worn to either church or museum exhibit openings."

"Here we are." Phyllis opened the dress shop's door.

The first dress Jennie spotted was one Mom might suggest. What better to wear to a naval base reception than a sailor dress? With a shudder, she moved on.

"May I help you?"

Jennie turned to a saleslady clad in a long, tight-fitting dress with contrasting bolero. Respectable, but definitely not her style.

"I need a dress for a naval reception." She nodded toward the sailor dress. "Nothing like that."

The saleslady smiled. "No, that might be overdoing it for an evening affair. How about something over here?"

She led Jennie to another section.

The dress shouted "Pick me" the moment Jennie laid eyes on it. She caught her breath as she held the dress to herself in front of a mirror. "Oooh, this is it."

A fitted bodice swept down into a full skirt. Ruffles extended from the shoulders to the waist, bracketing four heart-shaped buttons below the V neckline. The solid, muted blue focused attention on the ruffles and the same-fabric sash tied at the waist.

What would Rafe think of it? Still holding up the dress, she pivoted to the saleslady. "This is it."

Phyllis seemed mystified as they left the shop. "You go in, you try on one dress, and you buy it. We were in and out in less than a quarter hour. Don't you like to shop?"

Jennie laughed. "I know what I want and go for it. Spending hours trying on dress after dress isn't my idea of fun." She glanced across the street. "Oh, there's Rafe."

His posture as he stared in a shop window suggested dejection. His crewmates must have already left on the train. Jennie shoved her dress box into Phyllis' hands.

"Would you mind taking this back to the legation? I shouldn't be too far behind." She hurried across the street, leaving Phyllis sputtering in her wake.

Rafe stared at the window display. Someone stopped beside him, but he didn't look up until Jennie spoke.

"Mmm. Mohrenkopf. Going to get some?" Apparently his mouth didn't smile as he intended, for her smile faded. "What's wrong? Did your crewmates leave as scheduled?"

"Yes, they've gone." His words sighed out of him. He shook his head to dislodge his gloom. "I intended to go visit Bertil at the airport, but I couldn't. Remember Alan's angry words regarding the Germans when we walked to the Grand Hotel?" At Jennie's nod, he continued. "While shopping, Alan said something about a man being Jewish. He never talked like that in England. It's unreasonable, but I feel like he was attacking me. After seeing the guys off on the train, I went to Tyska Kyrkan for a chat with Jurgen instead of going to see Bertil."

The pastor's counsel was dead-on. He'd shared Bible verses that left no wiggle room. *If thou bring thy gift to the altar, and there rememberest that thy brother hath ought against thee; Leave there thy gift before the altar, and go thy way; first be reconciled to thy brother, and then come and offer thy gift.* He needed to talk Alan, for both their sakes.

Rafe crossed his arms across his chest. "I hate confrontation, but I'm going to have to find out what's going on with Alan, even if it means the end of our friendship. I don't know when." He briskly rubbed his arms before pulling open the shop door. "But now, let's get some *mohrenkopf.*"

"I know when you can talk to him. Next week we go back to Malmö for the funerals. You can go up to Rättvik for a visit before returning to Stockholm."

"That's an idea." He paid for the bag of sweets, and they left the store. "Do you suppose *mohrenkopfs* will be among the treats served at tomorrow's reception? That'll be something to look forward to."

They arrived back at the legation to find Jennie's dad waiting for Rafe.

"Several evaders have arrived from Denmark, Rafe. Ready to go solo on questioning some of them?"

"Absolutely. Do you suspect any of them are Germans?"

Major Lindquist chuckled. "We do want to be sure they're Americans. We also want to know everything that's happened to them from the time their planes sustained enough damage to keep them from returning to England." He handed Rafe a clipboard. "Here's the interrogation report with the list of standard questions to ask. If anything comes up that prompts another question, ask it. We'll start you with a B-24 navigator."

Rafe took a seat across from a very young looking, rigid airman. He smiled. "Welcome to Stockholm. We'll start with the easy stuff. Name, rank, and serial number."

The rigid posture didn't relax. "Flight Officer Wendell Harrick." He pulled his dog tags out from beneath his shirt to read his serial number.

Rafe wrote down the information. "I'm Lieutenant Martell. I'm not in uniform because I'm an internee in Sweden since our plane landed here. You, as an evader, on the other hand, will be sent back to England as soon as possible."

The rigid posture relaxed momentarily before stiffening again. "Really? We have to go back to combat?"

"No more combat, at least not in Europe. If you were shot down again, you could be considered a spy. Now, tell me everything that happened in your plane before ditching in Denmark."

"We'd just released the bombs on the secondary target when flak exploded underneath us. We'd already lost an engine and then the bomb bay doors were damaged and wouldn't close completely. Then a bunch of Kraut fighters showed up."

Rafe had stopped writing. His own last mission was still too recent. "You're lucky to have survived."

"Yeah. Lieutenant McDonnell did an amazing job. And it helped that those lousy Krauts took off." Harrick added a colorful commentary on the Germans.

Rafe eyed him over his clipboard. He took a deep breath and counted to ten. "What happened when you landed?"

"A bunch of people showed up out of nowhere. We couldn't understand a word they said, but figured they were Danish. Then a Canadian shows up. He said he works with the underground."

"His name?"

Harrick blinked. "I don't know. He just told us what to do."

"Which was?"

"We ran to this really dense little woods and hid in the undergrowth. One of the Danes raked away our footprints. The Krauts came looking for us. They're searching all around the woods, but didn't come in. I couldn't believe how stupid they were." This time he commented on their parentage.

Rafe slapped his clipboard down, causing Harrick to jump. He'd suffered Alan's snide comments in silence. This guy wasn't getting away with it. Rafe stood and leaned over the table. *"Ich komme aus Deutschland. Verstehen Sie?"*

Harrick turned pale. His mouth opened and closed twice, and he slumped in his seat.

Rafe sat down. "Now, if you will kindly keep a civil tongue in your head, when did you leave the woods?"

By the time the interrogations were concluded, Rafe was ready to go back to reading newspapers. He found Major Lindquist. "I'm not sure I'm the right man for this job. After getting an earful of cussing about the Germans from the first young kid, I gave him an earful of German."

The major's brows quirked. "And what do you say?"

"I said I was from Germany. He got the message. After that, he stuck with simple answers. A little sullen, maybe." Rafe clenched his fist. "What I wanted to do was knock his teeth down his throat. It's okay for me to insult Germans, but not him. Not like that."

"Mind your own house, hmm?" Jennie's dad laid a hand on his shoulder. "They've all been cleared to return to England. We'll have him out of here in a day or so."

Rafe nodded. "Good. I'd rather not see the inside of a jail."

Chapter Fifty-Four

The reception glittered with all the decorations pinned to the uniforms of the military officers. "Too bad you don't have a dress uniform that you could wear tonight." Jennie counted the rows of ribbons worn by a colonel. "How many medals do you have?"

"Couple Air Medals, couple of oak leaf clusters signifying how many missions I flew. I would just as soon be incognito among all this brass." Rafe straightened his lapels. "I'd definitely look like the junior officer here. I don't see any other lieutenants among these career military men."

They circled the room. Few faces were familiar. Being included in her parents' invitation was nice, but without Rafe accompanying her, she would have felt awkward, out of her depth. She stopped and backtracked. Rafe no longer walked with her. Someone had captured his interest.

"Do you know if Germans were invited?"

She frowned at his odd question. "Of course not." She scanned the people he must be watching. Who interested him? "Do you see a German?"

Rafe barely nodded. "Where's your father?"

Dad was talking with their host. Jennie sidled up to them. She kept her voice low. "Rafe spotted a possible German."

The naval attaché whipped his gaze from her to Rafe. "Who?"

Rafe nodded toward a cluster of people. "The man wearing dark green pants. He has a deep scratch healing on his left temple. That's what caught my eye. I saw him at the German church one Sunday. He spoke in perfect German to a ministry official. He should appear in one of my clandestine photos."

Their host sucked in a deep breath. "He's here with the British. He was introduced as a Spitfire pilot who crashed in southern Sweden." After drumming his fingers on his thigh for a moment, he added, "Of course, the real pilot could have landed in German territory and been captured. The Krauts could be trying to slip in a ringer."

Rafe watched the suspicious man. "Or he could be a former German citizen like me, fighting for his new country."

"But not likely. Come with me. We'll mention your sighting to the British naval attaché."

Squaring his shoulders, Rafe smiled at Jennie with raised brows, and left her with her father. She tracked their progress through the room before looking again to the man he'd fingered. "What will happen if he is a spy?"

Dad sipped his drink before answering. "The British can't execute him here in Sweden. They can't smuggle him to England. Can't even arrest him. They may try to turn him into a double agent against Germany. Any punitive action would have to come from the Swedes."

Visions of Rafe being suspected by the Germans of spying sent shivers through Jennie. They could complain to the Swedes and appeal for his arrest. Or Gestapo agents might grab him. Probably the Germans were outside watching everyone who arrived for the reception. Would they recognize Rafe from attending church? Had he worn a disguise? Their trip to Malmö next week and his side trip to Rättvik would serve nicely to keep him off German radar for a while.

Chapter Fifty-Five

Malmö, Sweden
July 3, 1944

"Have you been to many military funerals?"

Jennie's question jarred Rafe. While at Ridgewell, he'd been surrounded by death. "I sometimes went along to the American cemetery in Cambridge for a burial. Guys from my squadron, guys I'd seen at chow the day they died. But there are so many deaths, we didn't have elaborate funerals like we'll probably see today."

"You think it'll be elaborate?"

"Why else would it take place nearly two weeks after the men died? And there are ten men to bury. That's a lot in one day." A lot for Sweden. Not for the air bases in England. When a plane crashed on take-off, nine men died. There was no need to emphasize that to Jennie.

Legation personnel met their train in Malmö and escorted them to Östra Kyrkogärden, Eastern Cemetery. Entire squadrons from Sweden's army and air force appeared to be present. The lineup of ten flag-draped coffins twisted his gut. How many times had his crew come perilously close to not making it back from a mission? He could easily have ended up in a coffin like these men. Or vaporized in an exploding Fortress. He turned away.

"These ten men were torn from their homeland to die on foreign soil. They died at their posts. They died as heroes." Reverend Thorell had never met the young men at whose funeral he officiated, but he excelled at tugging on heartstrings.

Jennie hadn't attended many funerals in her lifetime, but when she had, she'd known the deceased. She certainly hadn't been as weepy as today, and she didn't even know these men. Touching a hankie to her eyes, she needed to look away from those ten flag-draped coffins, but her eyes refused. Ten young American men lay silent in those boxes. They wouldn't be going home. Well, yes, they probably would, but only in their coffins for reburial near their families. Not the way their families wanted to receive them back.

Swedish honor guards bracketed each coffin. They effortlessly raised the coffins to shoulder height and bore them to the ten gaping graves.

A bugler played "Taps" and tears streamed down Jennie's face. Her handkerchief was already sodden. She wiped a finger under her nose, and Mom pressed another handkerchief in her hand. Just in time. The military snapped off a salute, prompting more tears.

She located Rafe, standing among the American airmen present. They wore civilian clothes. Rafe had complained about that. They didn't have dress uniforms, but they should have been allowed to wear their flying clothes. They all looked a little pale, hands jammed in their pockets, eyes down. There but for the grace of God...

She returned her gaze to the coffins, now being lowered on straps into the earth. They wouldn't have gotten anything like this pageantry at home. The Swedes accorded them great dignity and respect, but their loved ones had no idea what was taking place.

She squared her shoulders. That was her job. Two or three photographers were busy snapping pictures. She'd get some of those for her exhibit. She'd show any naysayers back home that these American airmen hadn't run away from the war. These men didn't even get to enjoy their enforced vacations.

The service ended, and Dad and Mom joined other legation staff in conversation. Jennie slipped away. Rafe and a few other airmen busied themselves folding the flags that had draped the coffins. They worked quickly, silently. Rafe's jaw flexed, his lips pressed tight. She turned away to give him privacy.

Placards stood at each grave. She wandered down the line, reading them. Shaw. Heskamp. Traut. Rudisill.

Coats. Lohmeyer. Spencer. Puckett. Deck. Kellerman. Ten lives cut short. Tears pressed her eyes again. She took a deep breath and blew it out.

"Miss Lindquist?"

She turned to a Swedish officer beside her. He wore pilot's wings and his name tag read Marklund. "You're Astrid's husband."

"Yes." He bowed with Old World courtliness. "Gustav Marklund. Astrid enjoyed spending the weekend with you." He glanced around. "May I assist you in any way?"

"Actually, yes." Astrid had said he was formal. She possessed such spontaneity compared with his military stiffness. Maybe out of uniform he'd be more relaxed. "I'd like to talk to the photographers about getting pictures."

"For your exhibit." Gustav smiled and offered his arm. "Right this way."

"I'd rather face another combat mission than face Alan." Rafe shuffled his feet. It wasn't too late to board the Stockholm train with the Lindquists. The thought was tempting.

Jennie's brow knit. "Alan won't bite."

"No, he'd more likely take a swing at me." He raised his fists and demonstrated some light footwork.

Jennie pushed his hands down. "He's your friend, and he's unhappy."

Rafe paced back and forth. He wasn't going back to Rättvik entirely for Alan's sake. Pastor Jurgen insisted it was as much for his own well-being. The desire to avoid confrontation resulted in an agitated spirit and loss of peace. That was true. He'd lost sleep over Alan.

The call for travelers to Stockholm brought Jennie to his side. She cupped his face with her hands. "You'll do fine with Alan. He's a good man who's lost his way. You'll be a big help to him." She stretched up on her toes and kissed his cheek. "I'll be praying for you."

Rafe wrapped his arms around her and hugged her tight. The lure of Stockholm tugged hard at him. He stepped back and watched Jennie board the train. A last wave from the window and she was gone.

Filling his lungs with air and his heart with determination, he strode for his own train. Why did he have such a hard time confronting people? He didn't used to. When he was fifteen, he'd challenged Ludwig when his friend wanted to pillage old Herr Lerner's garden. The miser deserved it for running over Ludwig's bicycle with his car and blaming Ludwig, but his poor wife had always been kind. And he'd stood up to Fraulein Jung when she wanted to keep the class after school because the vase on her desk was broken.

When had he become such a doormat, letting people stomp on him? He'd let Maj-Britt hound him. In basic training, he'd voiced no objection when the sergeant ordered him to scrub the latrine for someone else's infraction, but of course, drill sergeants were naturally nasty folk and he hadn't wanted to jeopardize his training.

The worst incident came when his father... Rafe's steps faltered. His father's betrayal. He hadn't stood up to his father. He sucked in his breath to stem a wave of dizziness. The wounds of his father's betrayal had crippled his will to stand up to conflict.

Chapter Fifty-Six

"Happy Birthday America" covered the center of the cake, while starbursts in red and blue icing decorated the edges. Everyone applauded when Mr. Johnson, the legation minister, cut the cake, and his secretary brought out tubs of ice cream.

Jennie and Phyllis carried their sweets outside to eat by the waterfront. Phyllis forked up a mouthful and closed her eyes in bliss. "Someone's been hoarding sugar for this treat."

Jennie dragged her fork through the icing before lifting a star intact and setting it aside on her plate. She added a taste of ice cream to a bite of cake. "Not bad."

"Not bad?" Phyllis lowered her plate to her lap and stared into Jennie's eyes. "Are you feeling all right?"

Jennie huffed a laugh. "Sure, I'm fine." She scooped up a larger bite and savored it. "Mmm, so delightful."

"Your sarcasm is unbecoming." Phyllis' tart expression renewed Jennie's laughter.

"Sorry. It's just that I expected today to be so different. Rafe and I planned to go sailing. Or maybe go to the amusement park, Gröna Lund Tivoli. Or maybe even Skansen, although probably not. An open-air museum isn't Rafe's first choice for holiday fun."

"I know. Let's go shopping. Shopping's the perfect cure for the blues, and I do need a few things." Phyllis jumped up and would have headed back into the legation if Jennie hadn't grabbed her arm.

"Finish your treat. Then we'll go." Shopping didn't hold the same appeal to her, but a little mindless diversion was more appealing than, oh, a doctor's appointment.

Within an hour, they were wandering the ladies section of a big department store. Jennie browsed among the dresses while Phyllis sought the assistance of a sales clerk. Jennie held a dress up to herself in front a mirror before shaking her head and returning it to the rack.

"Excuse me, miss." A man her father's age stood before her, hat in one hand and two garments in the other. "I'm looking for a gift for my wife. Which would you prefer if you were buying a sweater? This one..." He held up a blue cardigan. "Or this one?" He flipped the cardigan aside to reveal a pullover, also solid blue.

Jenny fingered the soft wool of the cardigan. "This is lovely. But tell me, what's your wife's hair style like?"

The man pulled a photograph from his wallet with a quizzical expression. Jennie tried to hold back a smile. Ask an artist a fashion question, and he'd get an artistic answer. She studied the woman's image. "Not a fussy hairdo, so a pullover wouldn't be a problem. Her face is oval shaped." She held up the pullover. "This has a V-neck. You might want to look for a rounded neckline. That would help an oval face look less long."

She handed back the photo and stepped over to the sweaters. She located a crewneck pullover with a design in blues and greens. "This has a cheerful look."

Not for the world would she admit his wife possessed a careworn look and could use some cheer.

With profuse thanks and much bowing, the man took the suggested sweater and hurried to a sales register. Jennie grinned at the woman's imagined delight over the pretty gift as she turned to find Phyllis.

A policeman stood in her way. "You'll come with me, miss."

"Excuse me?"

Jennie sat beside her friend in the store manager's office. She tingled with cold and felt sweaty at the same time. The policeman accused her of being a spy. Someone had observed her slip something to a Swedish citizen. She thought they'd gotten rid of Lars.

"Of course I gave something to a citizen. A man was shopping for his wife, which I thought was very nice of him, and he asked for my opinion. He showed me her picture and then I gave it back. If we appeared to be secretive, it was only because whoever was spying on us was too far away to see what we were doing." If only she could press her hands together between her knees to keep them from shaking, but that would hardly be ladylike. She grabbed her reticule and yanked out her notepad, flipping to her sketch of Lars. "Is this your spy?"

The policeman took the pad and eyed the sketch before raising his gaze to Jennie. "Did you do this?"

"Naturally she drew that." Phyllis swelled up like a rooster. "Jennie's an artist and that's why the man was wise to ask her help in selecting his gift."

A smile teased Jennie's lips. The shopper hadn't known of her artistic ability.

"Who is this?" The policeman tapped the sketch.

"A German who's been the bane of my existence in Stockholm. We thought he'd been sent back to Germany."

A salesclerk slipped into the office. "I can confirm that a Claes Ericsson purchased a sweater on the advice of this young lady."

The policeman nodded to Jennie. "You may go."

They were barely outside the office door when Phyllis exclaimed, "Just like that. No apology, nothing."

The saleslady twisted her hands together. "Is there anything else you need to find today?"

Home, that's all. Before Jennie could decline her help, Phyllis answered. "Yeah, do you have any recipes for fried kraut?"

Chapter Fifty-Seven

Rättvik, Sweden
Tuesday, July 4, 1944

Rafe hiked up the trail. What a stroke of luck that Alan had gone off on his own and headed for the bluff that offered a panoramic view of the area. Rafe's favorite place to escape Maj-Britt. Maybe now it was the place where Alan sought to escape his demons. Steve had filled Rafe in on what had happened after he'd left Rättvik. A new internee had moved in with Alan, a man who identified with Nazi ideas of racial supremacy. His bigoted ranting had rubbed off on Alan.

Rafe spotted his crewmate slumped with his back against a fallen log. His hands dangled from his upraised knees and his chin rested on his chest. He was the picture of gloominess.

Rafe hesitated. Now that he was here, what did he say?

"Happy 4th."

After a moment, Alan's head rose, surprise etched on his face. "What are you doing here?"

Promising. No hint of revulsion. No annoyance. Jennie's prayers were working. Pastor Jurgen hadn't told him what to say. He said God would bring the words to mind. *Okay, God, fill me in on those words.*

"I stopped by on my way back from the funerals in Malmö yesterday. Bunked with Cal and Steve last night."

"The funerals?"

"The ten men who didn't survive the big American invasion of Sweden two weeks ago."

"Oh, right. You mentioned that." Alan straightened, moving his elbows to his knees. "How was it?"

"Depressing." Rafe took a deep breath. This was it. "Are we still friends?"

That got Alan's attention. His elbows came off his knees and he leaned back against the log. The focus in his eyes told Rafe he didn't know what he was talking about.

"Is my ancestry a problem?" His voice remained calm despite the thundering of his heart.

Alan exhaled a gusty breath and stretched out his legs. "Yeah, friends." A smile tipped one side of his mouth. "I guess I owe you an apology. That weekend in Stockholm wasn't the break I thought it would be."

Rafe held his tongue to allow Alan to set his own pace. Alan startled him by jumping to his feet.

"It's just that I'd really like to knock heads together." He held up his hands like he was clutching two heads.

Rafe stepped back.

Alan laughed and relaxed his hands. His laugh sounded like the old Alan. "Come on. I want to show you something."

They didn't go far before Alan eased aside the branches of a shrub. A bird chirped from its nest. "She's used to me," he whispered. Returning the branches, he turned back to the trail and looked out over the lake. "A bird built a nest in one of Ruby's flower pots back home. I can still hear her when I got too close. 'Gently, gently. Don't frighten her.'" His fists clenched before he waved a hand back toward the nest. "I thought about that when I first realized how I've been changing. Only this time, Ruby was saying 'You're frightening me.' She wouldn't like what's happening here. And that scares the stuffing out of me."

He shoved his hands into his back pockets and stared out across the lake.

Steve had scored a bull's eye on what was ailing Alan.

"Are you still rooming with the bigot?"

A moment passed before Alan turned to face Rafe. A wry smile pushed up the left side of his mouth. "Did Steve or Cal tell you about him?" He barely waited for Rafe's nod. "Did they also mention whether they requested he be transferred? Because he abruptly left and I heard he's now at Korsnäs, which has a disciplinary section. Can't say I miss him."

The two stood side by side, surveying Rättvik and Lake Siljan. A cool breeze swept across the lake and up the hill to ruffle Rafe's hair. He watched fluffy little clouds play tag and smiled at the game. A heavy load fell from his shoulders. He'd worried for nothing.

"Have you, ah, seen Maj-Britt lately?"

Alan snickered. "Oh, yeah. She sank her claws in a technical sergeant from the 389th Bomb Group. Then she found out he's enlisted rather than an officer, and dumped him. So now she's fishing again. Wanna go another round with her?"

"*Himmel hilf mir.*" Rafe shuddered.

They headed down the hill and approached the first house on the road leading into town. Two children, probably brother and sister, stood in the yard with a flimsy cardboard box. A calico cat wound around their legs.

"Say, would you like a kitten for Jennie? They've got a batch and are looking for good homes."

"Just what she doesn't need in the city." First Brenda Jane Prescott in England, now these kids in Sweden. Children were the same the world over.

The children's hopeful expressions tugged on his heartstrings. The boy opened his mouth and Rafe half expected him to say, "Have any gum, chum?"

Instead he asked, "Want a kitten, mister?"

"Do you still have them all?" Alan leaned forward to look in the box.

"No, just five," the girl answered.

Just five?

The box twisted and the children lowered it. One side broke free and five kittens tumbled out. They scampered around the yard, looking like wind-up toys that wouldn't last long in the hands of a three-year-old. Rafe and Alan knelt to help the children corral them. Two bounded to Rafe and climbed on his legs, digging through his trousers with their tiny needle claws. "Mew, mew, mew."

He pried loose one furball. It sure was cute. Jennie would love it, but Stockholm was no place for it.

Alan and the children each held a kitten. "These are boys." Missing a front tooth, the girl spoke with a lisp. "Those two are girls. They like you, mister."

Of course they did. He was a magnet for females.

Chapter Fifty-Eight

Stockholm, Sweden
Wednesday, July 12, 1944

Ed had requested a meeting, something about a special assignment. Rafe arrived early, and found Jennie in Phyllis' office. "Any idea why Ed wants to see me?"

"None at all. I've got something to show you." Jennie rifled through a file and pulled out a mimeographed copy. "I wrote this based on your conversation with Mrs. Pasch. Remember her comment that wealthy elderly women do nothing but attend teas? The British and Americans are starting a radio program aimed at German troops. It'll feature music and slanted news aimed at eroding morale. I submitted this little news item."

Rafe scanned the copy. *Wehrmacht* soldiers complain that the home folk engage in frivolous activities instead of contributing to the war effort. One private stated his grandmother's letters are filled with gossip from tea parties, and never accompanied by packages. Couldn't the ladies at least knit gloves and socks while they chitchat? "They probably don't have any yarn to knit with."

"Are you trying to excuse them?"

He laughed at Jennie's outrage, belied by the sparkle in her eyes. "Far be it from me."

In Ed's office, another man attended the meeting. Rafe wasn't given his name, although he had noticed him at the legation before. They pored over a map of what appeared to be Staden, the island of the old town. That was fine with Rafe. He'd become quite familiar with all the twists and corners of the ancient labyrinth.

Ed spun the map in front of him. "Here's your destination, Den Gyldene Freden, on Österlånggatan. It's an old restaurant with a cellar meeting room that's actually a cave. That's where we anticipate the meeting between these characters."

He nodded to his cohort.

The man offered two photographs that had clearly been taken on the sly. One man raised his face to the sun, offering easy identification. Rafe shook his head. The man was unfamiliar. The other subject's hat shadowed his features to the extent he could walk up and slap Rafe in the face without Rafe suspecting a problem.

Ed's cohort set the photos aside and tapped the map. "This place is a rock's throw from Zum Franziskaner."

And not far from Tyska Kyrkan, Rafe's favorite escape valve. He looked up to find Ed and the other man watching him intently. Something wasn't right. "What do you know about these two?"

"Not much. We have no idea who the shadowy figure is. The other one is connected with the German National Tourist Office."

A pseudonym for Nazi sabotage, or espionage, or some kind of mischief. It would sure be nice to know if Rafe had caused trouble for anyone with his prank phone call a couple weeks ago. Only a couple weeks ago? Boy, it seemed longer than that.

"We received a tip from a Swede who's given us worthwhile intel before. Mystery Man likely just arrived from Deutschland. We want to know why. Get close to them. Chat with them if possible. If you notice they're about to depart, leave before them and try to tail them."

Rafe listened with butterflies hatching in his gut. This sounded like an assignment for a trained agent, not a casual just-happened-to-be-in-the-same-place-at-the-same-time occurrence. "Why me?"

Ed shifted, causing the butterflies to flutter up and down Rafe's spine.

"Think of this as a probing mission. If anything's there, we'll bring in the experienced guns, but for this, we believe you're our man."

By the time Rafe left the office, one thing was clear. He'd let Jennie make him over with one of her disguises. What Ed hadn't said but Rafe understood was that he was expendable if anything went wrong. He'd take his own precautions.

Jennie drummed her fingernails on the desk. Had they left anything to chance? She'd parted Rafe's hair down the middle and done a slapdash job of rubbing in a dark rinse with a rag. As long as he didn't get rained on, he didn't look blond. Round glasses gave him a bookish air. The jacket with its pleats and half belt shouted Swede.

"That was a stroke of genius, Phyllis, suggesting he meet Bertil there. Two friends having a quiet meal together are much less apt to attract attention than a lone man."

Phyllis toyed with a stack of reports on her desk. About to shuffle them, she caught herself and set them aside. "I just hope Rafe made contact with him. Good thing he remembered to phone from somewhere else. I actually forgot the Swedes tap our calls."

Jennie groaned and jumped up to pace. "It's a long shot that he would catch Bertil at the airport. Or that Bertil could drop everything and join him." She wrung her hands. "I've got a bad feeling about this."

The Germans weren't likely to cause problems, unless they kidnapped Rafe and smuggled him to Germany. She shook her head. Highly unlikely scenario. But they could jump him on a dark street and

475

beat him up, toss him in one of Stockholm's many waterways. No one would know what happened until a bloated body was discovered.

The Swedes wouldn't have cause to arrest him. They couldn't prove he was eavesdropping, and Rafe wouldn't write anything down until he was safely back in his apartment or at the legation. They could search him to their hearts content and not find incriminating evidence.

Jennie snapped her fingers. "Why didn't I think of this before?" She swiveled to face Phyllis. "What's stopping us from going to dinner?"

Her friend's eyes brightened, and her smile bloomed. "You mean at Den Gyldene Freden?"

"Yes, the Golden Peace place."

"Lovely idea." Phyllis yanked open a bottom drawer and pulled out a rich brown shawl. "Here, throw this over your shoulders. That's a lovely dress, but bright colors attract attention. We want to blend into the woodwork. How about this hat?"

With a sigh, Jennie draped the shawl around her neck. Her dress was a solid jewel blue except for the bodice. A floral inset featured tiny red and yellow blooms with a thin blue bowtie at the neckline. Hiding the flowers made sense, but she drew the line at Phyllis' beret. Her pompadoured hair nicely framed her own hat with its sloping brim and blue ribbon around the crown. Looking ridiculous in a mish-mash of styles would attract attention as surely as eye-catching colors.

They decided to walk. A taxi appealed to Phyllis, but Jennie insisted they didn't want a taxi driver knowing their destination. Who he might report them to or why he would report on where two ladies dined, she couldn't say. They had time, however. Maybe the exercise would use up her nervous energy.

When they arrived at the restaurant, Phyllis spoiled her goal of blending in when she flirted with the maitre d'. Who knew they needed reservations? Jennie's bowtie tightened around her neck as she listened to Phyllis' blatant fuss over the elderly, balding man wearing a too-tight collar of his own.

"I've been telling my friend what a great place this is. And we walked all the way here. Surely you can find one little out-of-the-way table for two."

Out-of-the-way. Great. They wouldn't know if Rafe needed help or not.

A table alongside the old man's podium was set up for dining. Jennie suspected the maître d' sat there whenever he had a chance to get off his feet. Now he could keep an eye on them. At least they could see everyone who came in or out. She maneuvered Phyllis into the chair with her back to the door.

"Keep your hat on. That wide brim will hide us from curious eyes."

The menu selections swam on the page. Nothing appealed to her. Her appetite had evaporated. When Phyllis placed her order for *får i kål*, Jennie smiled weakly. "I'll have the same."

Not until their meals were served did she ask what they were having.

"Lamb and cabbage. Delicious, don't you think?"

Jennie didn't care for lamb. She should have asked for meatballs. Their meal progressed uneventfully until she managed her last bite.

Newcomers arrived. Two men approached the maitre d'.

"We're looking for a spy who's supposed to be here." The speaker's eyes roved the dining room instead of looking at the maitre d'. He held up a photograph. Jenny glimpsed it, and stars danced before her eyes.

Rafe!

The maitre d' didn't recognize the photo. The men moved off, slowly canvassing the dining room.

"I have to warn him." Jennie gripped the table and fought a wave of dizziness. How had the Swedish police learned Rafe would be here? Were the Germans extracting revenge for his pointing out Lars?

"Breathe. Take slow, deep breaths before you faint." Phyllis patted her hand. "You don't know where he is. Besides, he's in disguise."

Jennie shook her head. Phyllis was too used to toying with the enemy to take a threat seriously. "I know he's in the cellar. I saw the seating chart on the podium. The stairs are over there. I have to warn him."

She stood up before Phyllis could delay her. For the maitre d's benefit, she said, "I'm going to the ladies' room before we leave. Be right back."

She headed for the water closet, waiting until the last moment to glance back. The maitre d' was occupied with new arrivals. The policemen were working their way around. Ducking her head, she dashed to the cellar stairs.

Chapter Fifty-Nine

"Remember the time Ludwig ran out of the darkroom and ruined Herr Baesler's film? That tiny room had been too crowded for him. But Christoph said Ludwig was on a submarine. I can't comprehend that."

The men Ed wanted Rafe to watch sat on the other side of the room. Ed clearly had never been here. The cellar was long, narrow, and dimly lit. One long table ran down the center, with seating on both sides. Side tables snuggled up against the walls. Diners sat on one side only, facing the wall, their backs to the room. Eavesdropping was impossible.

With the unlikelihood of learning anything, Rafe settled down to enjoy the time with Bertil. "Submarines are cramped, foul. Even if they're on the surface, you can't step out for a breath of air unless you have business on the deck. They're no place for a claustrophobe."

"I heard he requested a capital ship but was too far down the list to get his choice. He told his skipper he couldn't stand confined spaces, but the guy scorned him. Said he'd make a man of him." Bertil sipped his coffee and grimaced at the bitter taste. "The U-boat disappeared on his first tour of duty. I hope he didn't cause its demise, opening the hatch to get out while submerged, or screaming in panic and alerting an enemy ship to their presence."

Rafe shook his head. "I want to deny that prospect, but such a scenario is all too possible."

He tuned in to surrounding conversations. The lady seated to his left urged her boyfriend to marry her before joining his military unit. Rafe dismissed them.

Behind him, four men discussed the difficulties facing their export business. Rafe had to set down his glass before it shattered in his clenched hand. If the Swedes hadn't continued to sell their iron ore to Germany, thereby prolonging the war, maybe it'd be over now and they could have been back to business as usual.

He pushed back his plate. Ed's ambiguity with this assignment had sabotaged his appetite. And if he didn't get out of here soon, he just might start throwing things. Playing cat-and-mouse games while men were fighting and dying was ridiculous.

Here he was with Bertil, and he was tied up inside tighter than a knot. The war tainted everything. "Christoph said Johan got on the *Bismarck*."

"The *Bismarck*? Or the *Tirpitz*? Doesn't matter, I guess. Neither one proved healthy. *Ja*, he would have gotten his first choice of assignments, smart as he was. Johan might have scorned the S-boats, but at least Christoph got to be the boss officer."

Sadness tinged their laughter. So many friends had lost their lives.

A hand gripped Rafe's shoulder. Before he could turn, Jennie's urgent whisper filled his ear. "Two policemen are upstairs searching for you. They'll be down in a moment."

And she was gone, disappearing back up the stairs on silent feet.

Bertil's brow furrowed.

"Did she say police are looking for you?" His voice was barely audible.

Rafe set his hands against the table to rise. Finally, an excuse to leave. But why was Jennie here? "We need to go."

"Wait." Bertil caught his arm. "You do not look like yourself. We do not want to pass them on the stairs." He caught the eye of their waitress and beckoned her.

Even as his friend spoke, they heard descending footsteps. They rose and stood in the passageway between tables, blocking the path of the policemen. The officers moved to the other side of the room. Keeping his back to them, Rafe allowed Bertil to speak with the waitress.

Bertil's voice rose unnecessarily. "We enjoyed our meal. Thank you for your hospitality."

Rafe climbed the stairs with the same sense of wondering whether the next piece of flak to pierce through the bomber had his name on it. Any second he might hear, "There he is."

They made it upstairs. No hand clamped down on his shoulder. No one in the main dining room turned to stare at him. Jennie stood by a table near the door. The woman seated there rose, tilting her head back far enough that he could see her face behind the wide brim. Phyllis. They'd come here to eat. And watch out for him. He would have hugged Jennie, and Phyllis too, but he and Bertil had been speaking German. To maintain their ruse, he had to walk on by.

As they passed her, Jennie directed her words to Phyllis, but they were meant for him. "Shall we see if the church is open?"

Rafe set a brisk pace for Tyska Kyrkan. Bertil jogged to keep up.

"Who was under the big hat with your lady?"

"Someone from the legation. A good friend. Phyllis is trustworthy." His words came out in bursts before a stitch in his side slowed him down. They slipped into the church's back yard. The setting sun cast long deceptive shadows. Rafe spun around at a sudden clatter.

"Easy. A cat knocked over a watering can." Bertil prodded him over to a bench. "What's the worst that might happen?"

Rafe exhaled hard, drumming his fingers on his knees. "I'll have to go back to the internment camp in

Rättvik. Bertil, I don't want to leave Jennie now." His hands stilled. "I love her."

"Does she know that?"

"I didn't know myself. Not really. I mean I did, but…" He jumped up. "She's the one, Bertil. She's the one for me."

Bertil chuckled. "I knew that the day I saw you two at Bromma. You should have seen the sappy look in your eyes when she joined us."

Rafe glared at his friend, but couldn't stop a smile that quickly faded. "Where are they? They should be here by now."

Before Bertil could comment, they heard quick, light steps, and the girls entered the yard. Jennie nodded to Bertil, but went straight to Rafe. "You need to come see my father. Now."

"You can't go back to your apartment," Phyllis continued. "They may know your address, and try to find you there."

"Before they contact anyone at the legation, you need to report what happened."

"Grab the initiative."

Rafe's gaze bounced back and forth between the two. "I'll have to go back to Rättvik, won't I?"

Jennie's mouth tightened and she blinked rapidly.

"Maybe not, if you stick to reading the newspapers." Phyllis sounded hopeful and dubious at the same time.

Bertil laid a hand on Rafe's shoulder. "I'll head out first. If I spot them, I'll try to interfere." He hesitated. "I hope to see you again soon." He nodded to the ladies, saying, "City hall has a nice view of the water. I like to go there on Sunday afternoons."

Rafe watched him go. They'd spent little time together during the weeks he'd been in Stockholm. Such meetings were risky for Bertil. Saying good-bye turned his dinner into rocks in his stomach. Or maybe the uncertainty deserved the blame. He'd gotten too comfortable in his new life. Now it was over.

They burst into the Lindquists' apartment, startling Jennie's parents.

"Goodness, now I've dropped a stitch." Mom fussed with her knitting before arching a brow at them. "One would think you were being chased by a herd of wild elephants."

"Worse, Mom." Jennie pressed a hand to her chest. Now that they ceased their hurried pace, all the heat she'd generated had no release. Snapping at Mom wouldn't help though.

Dad frowned. He stared at Rafe, who pulled off the glasses and attempted to finger comb his hair back to his usual style. "What happened?"

Not *did* something happen. *What* happened.

"The police went to the restaurant to arrest Rafe as a spy."

Dad's gaze swung to Rafe, now fiddling with the glasses. "They didn't recognize you?"

"No, sir. Jennie warned me, so I was able to leave before they could take a close look at me."

They explained their evening, interrupting each other as they sought to include every little detail. Dad's frown deepened. When they fell silent, he studied them a moment longer before turning his attention to Jennie's easel and her latest painting, the ten flag-draped caskets in Malmö. His forefinger tapped his lips.

Dad turned back. "Someone has you under surveillance, Rafe. I think now would be a good time to visit Gothenburg. Isn't that where you have relatives?"

Rafe stiffened beside Jennie. "Koster, actually. Maybe eighty miles north of Gothenburg. Although some distant cousins may be in Gothenburg."

Dad nodded. "Now would also be a good time to reclaim your German name." He nodded again. "As for any explanation which the Swedes may demand, what happened tonight is quite straightforward. You, an American citizen who fled Nazi Germany, met up with a German friend while interned here, and enjoyed an evening with him, catching up on old times. Naturally, we knew nothing about the meeting, so as not to endanger your friend's status."

"How…" Jennie had to clear her throat. "How long does he have to stay in Gothenburg?"

For the first time, Dad smiled. "No longer than a couple weeks, I should think. Time enough for the Swedes to forget about this little clash."

A couple weeks. That wasn't so long. These days most families were separated for months, years. The time would pass quickly. Just think of all the paintings she could work on. She'd outlined in exquisite detail her idea for her exhibit. With no distractions, she'd have plenty of time to plan the layout, write placards, find and fill in any blanks.

Her hand sought Rafe's. She'd rather have the distraction.

"You'll stay here tonight, Rafe," Dad was saying, "out of sight until we get you on that train. We'll contact our office in Gothenburg and have someone meet you at the station.

Jennie had no chance for a private moment with Rafe before she and Dad left for the legation early the next morning. She'd twisted up her hair and stuffed it into a snood. Mom insisted on fussing with the big bow

487

tying it up. Almost like she knew Jennie wanted a good-bye kiss from Rafe. She had images of him being spirited away as soon as she departed.

Phyllis joined her at the legation and they immediately began typing their official report. Phyllis' fingers hovered over the typewriter keys. "What time did they come into the restaurant?"

"I don't know. About seven? Sunset's at nine fifty-three, when we got to the apartment. Put down seven." The finished report in hand, Jennie went in search of her dad. He was briefing Mr. Johnson.

"We've received Swedish permission for him to travel to the west coast. His cover story is true. He's a naturalized American with Swedish roots who fled Germany and is now visiting relatives."

Jennie's hand went slack, and she dropped the report. A short visit with his relatives and he'd be back. Maybe. She decided not to ask if he'd return to Stockholm or Rättvik. And while he was away, she'd limit her OSS activities to encrypting messages and other behind the scenes work.

Chapter Sixty

Stockholm, Sweden
Thursday, July 13, 1944

The train chugged through long stretches of forest, spotted here and there with small towns. It looked a lot like the route to Malmö. If nothing else, Rafe was acquiring a thorough acquaintance with Sweden.

"Next stop, *Yoo-te-bor.*" Rafe stirred at the conductor's call. That was Swedish for Gothenburg. He reached for his bag. He hadn't been allowed to return to his apartment. One of his roommates brought his gear to the legation. At least he'd been able to stop there and say a proper good-bye to Jennie.

The ancient conductor watched passengers disembark at the station. The waddle hanging below his chin would have been the envy of a Thanksgiving turkey back in Milwaukee. Rafe jerked his gaze to the man's eyes and nodded farewell. He needed to quit sulking.

"Rolf Schilling?"

His old name no longer seemed to fit. He wasn't the same person he'd been when he left Germany. Memories of Cologne rose like specters. Not even time spent with Bertil had this effect. The name belonged to someone else.

The American accent and the military bearing identified the man offering his hand as his contact. "I'm Giles Lafferty. Stockholm didn't tell us much. Just that you're looking for your grandfather. We need to know where you are in case anyone asks, although that's not likely. Here's a card with the phone number of the consulate. Do you know where you're headed first?"

Hello to you, too. The guy said all that on one breath of air. The way he jiggled his keys in his pocket, he must be in perpetual motion, body and mouth. If Rafe had to spend much time in his company, he'd turn into a nervous wreck.

"I'll need to check a city directory. My grandfather's brother lives north of here. He's supposed to have a grandson living here."

"Fine. Fine. There should be a directory inside the station here." Giles Lafferty spun on his heel and headed for the door, leaving Rafe to hasten after him.

Several Svensons were listed. Rafe tapped a finger on the page. "Michael. He's likely my distant cousin."

A vague memory of playing with a slightly older boy on a beach in Sweden failed to provide a face. Question was, would Michael remember him?

Giles Lafferty stood waiting. Rafe placed the call.

"*Hej.*" The deep voice might be Michael's.

"Uh, hello. This is Rolf Schilling, grandson of Gunnar Svenson's brother Göran."

"Rolf? *Rolf?* I don't believe this. Rolf! We have been wondering about you. Praying for you. Uncle Göran's last letter to arrive was full of concern. Where are you?"

The yoke of uncertainty he'd carried across Sweden had been an unnecessary burden. He was coming home to a family that cared. He snatched a pen from Giles Lafferty's pocket and scribbled the trams and connections and directions Michael rattled off. Rapid-fire speech must be a Gothenburg trait.

"I'll call my sister and Uncle Leif. They're also in Gothenburg. We'll have a grand time tonight."

Chapter Sixty-One

Stockholm, Sweden
Sunday, July 16, 1944

When Bertil remarked that city hall had a lovely view of the water, he must have meant to meet him there. On Sunday afternoon, to be exact. The Germans might not try to keep the day holy, but Bromma was a Swedish airport. He must have the day off.

Jennie strolled along the walkway bordering the South Terrace. Across the sparkling waters of Riddarfjärden lay Södermalm Island. The roof of their apartment building was all she could see of it.

Stairs leading down to the water interrupted the balustrade. When a sweep of the grounds showed no sign of Bertil, Jennie descended a few steps and sat down. A breeze ruffled her hair. Unlike a sultry summer day in Chicago, Stockholm's temperature hovered at seventy degrees Fahrenheit. She watched clouds skid across the brilliant blue sky. If only Rafe sat beside her.

"*Guten Tag*, Jennie." Bertil eased down on the step, keeping a respectable three feet between them. He nudged his hat further back on his head. "Where is Rolf?"

"Gothenburg, to visit his grandfather's relatives. I have no idea how long he'll be gone. Dad thought a couple weeks, but the minister plenipotentiary has made it sound like he won't be able to return until autumn, and only then to be sent back to England."

The internees didn't have to stay in Sweden for the duration, like they did in Switzerland. Rafe's crewmates would be thrilled to leave, especially Alan. And if Rafe's job at the legation were truly compromised, he'd leave too. Her heart faltered at the thought.

Bertil had been leaning forward on his knees, watching her sidelong, but now he sat up and punched his fists down on his thighs. "What is it about Rolf that females find so appealing? Even as a boy, he got more than his share of valentines. I think every girl in our class gave him one. Why is he so special?"

Jennie smiled. Bertil looked so perplexed, but what could she say? "I noticed him on the *Queen Mary* because he was standing all alone, looking a little seasick."

Bertil's jaw dropped. "Rolf, seasick?" He threw back his head and laughed. "Ach, I wish I could have seen that. Rolf Schilling, sailor extraordinaire, seasick." He slapped his leg. "That's rich."

He listened avidly as she described their voyage. "He decided a combination of things ailed him. The late, unappetizing meal they had. The crowded, stuffy cabin he slept in. He'd been on rougher water than that."

"Sure, he can make excuses if they make him feel better."

Oh dear. If Rafe and Bertil stayed in each other's lives, Bertil would never let him forget this. "Tell me about Rafe as a boy. Did he appreciate all those valentines?"

"I think he was sweet on Marianne Ockstadt. He gave her a valentine. And they danced together in a school production. My mother says they did a quite respectable waltz. We must have been seven. They were still good friends before he... before he left. He'd walk her home from catechism class." His head wagged slowly as he spoke of Rafe's abrupt departure from Germany.

"Did you know his father well?"

Bertil studied the sky. "Herr Schilling was the man every boy wished was his father. He'd take us sailing, he'd kick a soccer ball with us at the park, and he taught Rolf how to play tennis. He was there for him. No father I knew was so involved with his *kinder*."

He glanced at Jennie. "When Christoph told us Herr Schilling had divorced his wife and left his family's safety to his wife's parents, we could not believe it. He had to join the Nazi Party, you know, to keep his job. He doesn't believe in it, but party membership is required for civil service jobs."

Bertil threw up his hands, fingers splayed. "He works for the railroad, though. It may be an important position, but it's nothing special. Not at the expense of his family. I would have jumped at the chance to go to America, even if it meant being dependent on a father-in-law." He heaved a sigh and stilled for a moment. "It didn't take him long to wish he had gone with them. I last saw him in 1941. He'd aged twenty years. He's an old man now, living with nothing but regrets."

Jennie stared down at her hands folded in her lap. Her heart ached for Rafe. Not just any father, but the best father possible had turned against him. No wonder he had a hard time forgiving his dad. She needed to go home and hug Dad.

A swan glided toward them. Bertil reached into a small sack and tossed a bread crust onto the water. The swan gobbled it up and watched for more. Bertil offered the sack to Jennie.

"Uh oh, a Nazi stooge is looking our way." He tossed another crust. "He's walking by. Maybe he isn't watching me."

Jennie cautiously peered over her shoulder. The man didn't look sinister, but she shivered nevertheless. "How do you manage to stay here rather than join the fighting?"

Bertil's shoulders shook as he chuckled. "According to my records, I am color blind. That makes it difficult for me to distinguish between friend and foe. I expected to be sent to a Luftwaffe base to service warplanes, but have decided I am forgotten here. Fine with me. I do not believe in their war." He eyed her for a long moment. "Should they discover I am not color blind, I would be sent to the eastern front on a punishment squad."

Jennie resisted the inclination to gape at Bertil. It took courage to stand against the Nazi regime, even if he did so from a neutral country. Neutral didn't necessarily mean safe. She wouldn't have the nerve to withstand the pressure to conform. Making prank phone calls had been hard enough.

Did Rafe realize how much she was like his father?

Bertil brushed crumbs off his pants. When he stood, a folded paper remained on the step. "I made that for Rolf. It lists the main people in the German espionage network in Sweden. Copy it in your own writing before you do anything with it."

He sauntered off.

Jennie stared at the list as though it might burst into flame. The swan glided close. "Shoo." She flapped her hand at it before sliding over enough to pick up the paper. She unclasped her purse and shoved the list inside. She stood, brushed off her skirt, took a deep breath, and walked away. A bull's-eye had likely materialized on her back. American spy.

Chapter Sixty-Two

The bracing ocean breeze contained a fishy scent that shouldn't have been so strong. Leaning back on his elbows, Rafe looked around for a dead fish floating among the rocks, but didn't spot one. He should move to another rock, but couldn't summon the ambition.

A beautifully desolate view spread out before him. Centuries of wave action had smoothed the rocky islets. The slab he perched on boasted a crack from which sprouted determined purple wildflowers.

The roar of the surf filled his ears. Gulls soared overhead, adding their cries. Somewhere nearby, a seal barked. He squinted open one eye in time to see a flipper splash. He sat up and stifled a yawn.

Red, white, and yellow cottages clung to the rocky coastline of the mainland, their gables all pointed in the same direction. Probably the red ones got their paint from Falun. Most folks around here fished for their living. Theirs was a hard life.

Uncle Gunnar approached, hopping from rock to rock, still spry for an old man. His looks, voice, and mannerisms matched those of Opa. More than once, Rafe mistook him for his grandfather while talking with him. Since arriving at Uncle Gunnar's home in

Strömstad near the Norwegian border, he'd battled homesickness for his family in Milwaukee.

"Pretty cove, isn't this?" Uncle Gunnar lowered himself on Rafe's rock. "I don't suppose you remember being here before."

"I've been here? When?" Scenery like this was impossible to forget. The remote outpost was so sparse and isolated, they could be alone in the world. Only wresting a living from the sea concerned the inhabitants. Not war or spies or betrayal.

Jennie would love this view. She'd paint a picture that did it justice. Since he was the only internee likely to be here, however, sharing Koster's barren beauty in her exhibit made no sense.

"You were a little tyke. You wanted to splash in the water, and your father kept pulling you back up on the rock."

His father. Rafe wrapped his arms around his knees. "How well did you know my father?"

"I saw him only three or four times. We always thought he was a fine husband and father."

"Until he threw us out. I'll never understand that."

Uncle Gunnar stared out to sea. Apparently, he had no answer. Rafe's sigh came from his heart, where the ache continued to fester.

"I can't imagine living under the Nazi regime."

Rafe looked up at Uncle Gunnar's sudden words. "Father didn't have to. He could have left with us."

Uncle Gunnar continued to search the horizon. He filled his lungs with the sea air. "What do you know of your Uncle Helmut?"

Father's uncle, actually, on his mother's side. "Only that he died young of a heart attack, before I was born."

"Mm, hmm. He was in England."

"England?" Rafe did the math in his head. Uncle Helmut had died mere months after the armistice ending the Great War. "Why was he in England?"

"He went to see an old friend who was interested in some sort of joint venture. His friend saw it as a means to help Helmut financially and to promote good will. Unfortunately, Helmut wandered into a rough neighborhood. Hooligans attacked him, screaming 'Death to the filthy Hun.'" Uncle Gunnar shook a fist in the air. "Helmut wasn't seriously injured, but come morning, he was dead."

Rafe sagged over, elbows on his knees. Why had he never heard this? Thoughts ricocheted in his head. Grossmutter's brother. Grossmutter, a kindly, dignified lady, now living in a bombed-out cellar with Father. Photos of Father fishing with Uncle Helmut, laughing. Father, intent on staying in Germany.

"Why wasn't I told?" He swallowed hard. "It wasn't like that in America. We were welcomed."

"Would your father have been able to slip into a new life as well as you did? Remember, Rolf, he doesn't have your talent with languages." Uncle Gunnar laid a hand on Rafe's shoulder. "You loved your father deeply, my boy. You raised him up on a pedestal, allowing him no room for error. But he's a mere mortal with the same fears and insecurities as the rest of us."

His hand dropped away. "I'm sure he didn't foresee the extent of the Nazi evil. Who could have? Had he known the cataclysm to come, I'm sure he would have left with you. Göran believed he anticipated a brief parting until the Nazis were swept away, then you would have returned, your parents would remarry, and your comfortable life resume intact."

The conversation Rafe had overheard all those years ago hadn't hinted of a happy ending. Of course, Opa was an eternal optimist. If he were in Father's place, what would he have done?

One voice in his head insisted he wouldn't have abandoned his family. Another voice urged caution. Hindsight made the matter too simple. Rafe hung his head between his knees.

The breeze caressed the nape of his neck, cooling his heated emotions. A memory teased him. He and Father had been outside late one evening. A similar breeze swooshed off his cap. He grumbled as he snatched it up. Father had laughed. "Listen to the breeze, Rafe. It carries the music of the stars." Mother and Father often laughed about the music of the stars. They shared a joke he wasn't privy to.

That snippy young evader Rafe had interrogated had demonized the whole German nation. But not everyone was in favor of the Nazis. Lots of good Germans had been intimidated into silence. And Father was one of them. He must have been far more aware of what was going on in Germany than Rafe had been. That knowledge, and knowing what happed to his uncle, had paralyzed him into inaction. And Rafe had condemned him as a coward.

Tears stung his eyes and he brushed at them. Another minute and he'd be bawling. *Think of something else. Anything.* "I thought you lived on Koster. Good thing I found Michael as soon as I got to Gothenburg."

Uncle Gunnar eyed him silently for a moment. "This is a wonderful spot in summer, but I wouldn't care to live here year round."

Rafe nodded, picturing Uncle Gunnar's cozy house. White, not red, with throngs of hollyhocks and poppies.

A long-buried memory sprang to the surface. "Did I pick your hollyhocks?"

A chuckle rumbled before bursting out of Uncle Gunnar. "You sure did, my boy. You yanked them up and presented them with such pride to your mother. Your poor parents were mortified." He continued to chuckle. "Some still had their roots and we managed to salvage a few. Your father had a hard time getting you to understand the pretties would be better appreciated where they grew."

A distant cry of "Tomas" drifted on the air. They turned to see several people combing the shoreline.

"Tomas. Isn't that the little boy whose father was scolding him when we moored your sailboat?"

"Yes, I believe so. His father told him to stop pestering him and he ran off." Uncle Gunnar clucked his tongue. He rose slowly to his feet. "I need more padding on my bones if I'm going to sit on rocks."

They began making their way back to shore. Rafe's blood raced when he slipped on a wave-washed rock. With one hand down, he recovered his balance. A flash of green caught his eye.

"Oh, no." He closed his eyes and dragged in a breath. His eyes opened. Still a bit of green. "Uncle Gunnar, wasn't that little boy wearing a green shirt?"

Uncle Gunnar followed Rafe's gaze. They hurried to the edge of the rock. There, bumping in the current between three large slabs of stone, floated the missing Tomas.

Rafe closed his eyes and sank down to his knees. Even after two months of combat, he wasn't used to death. Especially not the death of a child.

Uncle Gunnar hailed the islanders and they bore the tragic burden to shore. The parents were summoned. The father's wails of anguish drifted over the island and pierced Rafe's soul.

Is that how his own father felt after shoving them away? Wishing like the dickens to call back that rash moment when he'd turned them out?

He straightened. He would not live with regrets. Two things needed to be done. One would take time. When the war ended, he would find his father. But the other he could do right away. As soon as he got back to Stockholm.

Chapter Sixty-Three

Stockholm, Sweden
Monday, July 31, 1944

The train chugged into the Stockholm station. Rafe scanned the people waiting. There she was. Jennie clasped her hands together as she searched the train's windows. She spotted him. One hand came up in an enthusiastic wave, startling a nearby woman. He grabbed his gear and headed for the exit.

She made it to the door before him. No sooner did he step down than she flung her arms around him. He'd come home.

"Honey," he gasped, "I need to breathe."

Jennie loosened her grip and stepped back, running her hands across his shoulders. Stretching up on tiptoe, she kissed him. If he wasn't blocking other disembarking passengers, he'd drop his belongings, wrap her in a hug of his own, and kiss the daylights out of her. "We have to get out of traffic."

She tugged him to the side of the platform. "You've been gone less than three weeks, but it seems more like three months."

He dropped his bag and talking ceased as he greeted her properly. When they broke apart for air, her eyes looked dazed, but she smiled. "You missed me, too."

His gaze roved over her. "I didn't have a photo of you, and my memory didn't do you justice."

A blush tinged her cheeks. She looked good in pink.

"Did you enjoy getting to know your family?"

"They're great, especially Uncle Gunnar. You'll get to meet them when they come for the wedding."

"Wedding?" Puzzlement furrowed her brow. "Whose wedding?"

This wasn't the right place. His sister would roll her eyes and say, "That's not romantic."

Phyllis would tsk. He didn't care.

He sidestepped a moment of doubt. They hadn't discussed postwar plans, but now they would. He took her hands in his.

"Jennie, will you marry me?"

Epilogue

Coolness embraced them when Rafe and Jennie stepped inside the Cologne Cathedral. Grit on the floor crunched underfoot. Patches of sunlight filtered in through hastily repaired holes. Groups of people slumped in chairs or on the floor. Their eyes sought out the newcomers, then skittered away at the sight of Rafe's American Army Air Force uniform. No one approached them, but sullen stares bore into Rafe's back. Hopefully, Bertil would quickly locate Father.

A badly scratched upright piano leaned against a wall. He ran his fingers across the keys. The discordant sound caused Jennie to wince. "In need of a tune-up, I believe."

Rafe tried to smile. The whole city needed a tune-up. What he had seen from five miles high the year before had been bad, but not nearly as appalling as at ground level. To think, the people had been living in the rubble for years.

He continued fingering the keys, unaware of a specific tune until Jennie softly sang, "O sacred head, now wounded, with grief and shame weighed down."

Grief and shame. That described the Germans they'd encountered since arriving in Germany.

His fingers stilled. A tingling sensation bloomed at the back of his neck, like his hair stood on end. Jennie looked beyond him. He turned, slowly.

The man approaching him didn't blink. Wonder filled his face. And regret. And hope.

Father.

He stood tall, but Bertil was right. He had aged far more than natural in the nine years since Rafe had seen him. He stopped three feet away. His mouth worked, but he made no sound.

Rafe covered the distance and flung his arms around him. His father's arms closed around him. He hadn't lost any strength. He clung to him like he would never let go again. Nine years lost.

Father.

Even with his eyes squeezed shut, tears escaped. Father rubbed his shoulder. How well he remembered that touch. When he was devastated by a mediocre school grade or a wrecked kite, his father's touch could right his world. When they sailed the Rhine or worked on models, his father's touch affirmed him.

"I love you, Father." His throat was clogged, his voice barely audible, but Father's arms tightened.

"I love you, Rolf. I love you."

How many minutes passed? It didn't matter. A presence beside him touched his elbow. They were not alone. "Father, may I introduce my wife, Jennie."

Jennie inched forward. "I'm very pleased to meet you."

Father showed no surprise. Bertil must have warned him. He may not understand all of Jennie's English words, but he recognized her meaning. She found herself enveloped in a hug of her own, and grinned at Rafe over Father's shoulder.

Grossmutter had come, too. For the first time in his life, she didn't smell of lilac soap. She reached up to hold his face between her gnarled hands. When had she become so small?

Their time together slipped away. Jennie opened the photo album she'd brought along. She pointed out various pictures. Rafe and his fellow officers enjoying a late summer sail on Lake Siljan after Rafe's return from Gothenburg. Their wedding pictures taken at Tyska Kyrkan, attended by Bertil, Steve, Phyllis, and Astrid, the wedding she had dreamed of, just before the men returned to England. Jennie had left soon after on a civilian flight, taking her entire exhibit collection. Another page showed more pictures of the whole Martell family with her at her triumphant "Sweden, Shelter from the Storm" exhibit. Among the photos, she'd included flattering *Chicago Tribune* reviews.

Rafe presented Father with photographs to keep —
his and Jennie's wedding picture, and recent portraits
of Rita and Albert. "Our addresses are on the back.
We'll stay in touch."

He meant it as a statement, but it came out as a
question.

"We'll stay in touch," Father agreed, mesmerized
by the images of his far-away children.

When they returned to the military jeep waiting for
them, Jennie retrieved her camera for a father and son
photograph. Then they waved good-bye until their
driver turned a corner.

Jennie wrapped her hands around his. Her eyes
shone. "That went well, don't you think? How is your
heart now?"

Rafe twisted his hands so he held hers. "My heart
is at peace. My private war has ended."

Author's Note

Squadron and medical diaries of the 381st Bombardment Group are readily available, including the mission log. Using these, I was able to maintain accuracy with the dates and destinations of all missions included in this story, except one. I needed Rafe to go on a mission to Cologne, but the 381st did not fly there during Rafe's tour of duty. On a day of bad weather, I swept the skies clear and sent the planes on their way.

While researching my first book, *Friends & Enemies*, I came across a B-17 navigator who came from Germany and had been a member of the Hitler Youth. When his plane was badly damaged and the pilot told the crew to bail out, the navigator hurried to the cockpit and urged the pilot to try for Sweden. He was the inspiration for Rafe Martell.

A grateful "Thank you" goes to Pat DiGeorge. Her research for her book, *Liberty Lady*, shared on her website, provided me with inspiration to make the scenes in Sweden come alive.

If you're on Pinterest, visit my board for No Neutral Ground and discover Rafe's and Jennie's worlds:

http://www.pinterest.com/terriwangard/

I hope you enjoyed *No Neutral Ground*! I need to ask you a favor. Would you help others enjoy this book too?

Recommend it. Please help other readers find this book by recommending it to friends in person and on social media. Tell other readers what you thought about this book by reviewing it at Amazon, Barnes and Noble, or Goodreads.

Discussion Questions

1. Rafe's grandfather foresaw the danger for Jews and prepared for their escape from Germany. Rafe's father did nothing. How well do you prepare for the future?

2. Jennie is pushed outside her comfort zone by doing field work for the OSS. How do you handle uncomfortable situations?

3. Rafe helps Jennie identify the reason she feels inadequate. Does an incident in your past still affect you today?

4. Jennie experiences unease when her friends Phyllis and Emma bait Germans in Sweden. What do you do when you don't agree with your friends' actions?

5. Rafe needed to confront Alan about his perceived anti-Semitism. How do you handle confrontations?

6. Christoph tells Rafe his father regrets sending his family away. Have you taken a

divergent path and can't return? How do you handle it?

7. Jennie's father believes in an Augustine quote, "The world is a book and those who do not travel read only one page." Do you agree?

8. Are you willing to stand against injustice? What are some ways you could today?

9. Why does Rafe think Dan is good for him? Do you have a Dan in your life?

10. Uncle Gunnar pointed out that Rafe had his father on a pedestal. How did that hurt their relationship? Do you have someone on a pedestal? Why?

11. Mickey thought Heaven would be boring and Hell would have more interesting people. How would you respond to him?

About the Author

Terri Wangard grew up in Green Bay, Wisconsin, during the Lombardi Glory Years. Her first Girl Scout badge was the Writer. These days she writes historical fiction, and won the American Christian Fiction Writers' (ACFW) Woodland's Chapter 2013 Writers on the Storm (WOTS) contest and the ACFW 2013 First Impressions contest, as well as being an ACFW 2012 Genesis finalist. Holder of a bachelor's degree in history and a master's degree in library science, her research included going for a ride in a WWII B-17 Flying Fortress bomber. *Classic Boating Magazine*, a family business since 1984, keeps her busy as an associate editor.

Connect with Terri:
www.terriwangard.com
Facebook:
www.facebook.com/AuthorTerriWangard
Pinterest: www.pinterest.com/terriwangard/

'Promise for Tomorrow' series:

Friends & Enemies (Book 1) – 2013 ACFW Woodland's Chapter WOTS winner

No Neutral Ground (Book 2) - 2012 ACFW Genesis finalist

Soar Like Eagles (Book 3) - 2013 ACFW First Impressions winner

Printed in Great Britain
by Amazon